A FAN'S NOTES

Frederick Exley

A
Fan's
Notes

THE MODERN LIBRARY

NEW YORK

LIBRARY OF CONGRESS CATALOGING-IN-PUBLICATION DATA
Exley, Frederick.
A fan's notes/Frederick Exley.—Modern Library ed.
p.   cm.
ISBN 0-679-60271-2 (acid-free paper)
I. Title.
PS3555.X58F3   1997
813'.54—dc21   97-7047

Modern Library website address:
http://www.randomhouse.com/modernlibrary/

Printed in the United States of America on acid-free paper

2 4 6 8 9 7 5 3

FREDERICK EXLEY

Frederick Exley and his twin sister, Frances, were born on March 28, 1929, in Watertown, New York. Their father was Earl Exley, a telephone lineman who had been a high school football star and continued to play, as a young man, for the Watertown semipro team. Like his father, Fred attended local schools and participated in sports, though he was not a standout. His shortcomings as an athlete and his sense of rivalry with his father haunted him, and eventually became major themes in his writing. He attended college at the University of Southern California, where he discovered the pleasures of literature and observed from afar the popularity enjoyed by his schoolmate and contemporary Frank Gifford, the great running back, another prominent influence on his work.

Exley never held a job for longer than a few months. He worked briefly in advertising and public relations, and had various schoolteaching positions, but he believed that the world owed him a living and usually was content to let fortune be his guide. He was funny and ingratiating, so people were willing to pick up his tabs, mostly incurred at the bars he frequented. In the late 1950s and early 1960s he was hospitalized several times at mental institutions, but no certain diagnosis was ever reached. The chief benefit he gained from these periods was that he was forced to dry out and encouraged to try his hand at writing.

In 1968, when *A Fan's Notes* was published by Harper & Row, all who knew Fred were astonished. But the book was well reviewed, received a couple of prestigious if minor literary awards and established him as a significant writer of his generation. For the rest of his life he strived, honorably if unsuccessfully, to repeat this triumph. In each of his other books, *Pages from a Cold Island* (1975) and *Last Notes from Home* (1988), he employed the device that had worked so well in his first: contrasting his own failures with the successes of another man through whom he lived vicariously. In *A Fan's Notes* this was Frank Gifford; in *Pages* it was Edmund Wilson, the literary critic; and in *Last Notes* it was Exley's older brother, Bill. But Exley's only subject was himself, and he had exhausted it for the first time around. Though his subsequent books were respectfully reviewed, his reputation rests solely on *A Fan's Notes.*

Exley's private life was messy. He moved from pillar to post, sponging off family or friends; he never owned a dwelling and only irregularly rented. He was married twice, briefly and unhappily; he had a daughter by each of his wives, but did not show interest in either until late in his life. By then he had settled in Alexandria Bay, twenty-five miles north of Watertown on the St. Lawrence River. He became a local character in this resort town, as well as a habitué of most of its bars. His health began to fail in the late 1980s, primarily because of alcoholism. He died in Alexandria Bay on June 17, 1992, at the age of sixty-three.

INTRODUCTION

What a great pity it is that Fred Exley did not live to see this day. *A Fan's Notes* in the Modern Library! The news couldn't have blown his mind, since that had already been accomplished by infusions of alcohol too copious to measure. But in his fashion he would have been thrilled, and he wouldn't have been shy about letting everyone else in on the news. I know just how he would have told his many friends and acquaintances: through his long-distance telephone system, which went into operation around 2:00 A.M. and stayed busy for the next three or four hours.

It is, say, 3:45 A.M. and I am dead to the world. The bedside phone rings and rings and rings until, finally stirred awake, I mumble a sleepy "Hello?" into the mouthpiece.

"Jon," the slurred, blurred voice at the other end says. "It's Ex."

"Good God, Fred. Do you know what *time* it is?"

"Jon. *Fan's Notes* just made it into the Modern Library. The Modern Fuckin' Library. Can you believe that, Jon? The Modern Fuckin' Library."

You see, for a bookish person of Fred's generation—mine too, though he was a decade older than I—the Modern Library was the literary equivalent of the Baseball Hall of Fame: Selection thereto was conclusive confirmation of a literary work's immortality, and thus its author's. The Modern Library still enjoys much the same distinction, but now there are many other "libraries" that choose what they represent as the classics of world literature and publish them in hardcover or paperback. In Fred's day, there was the Modern Library and little else, certainly nothing else to rival its prestige. Mostly it published long-dead certifiable giants whose work was conveniently in the public domain, but it also acquired rights to the stories, poems and novels of modern writers whom its editors regarded as fit company for Horace and Homer, Shakespeare and Milton, Tolstoy and Dickens.

I well remember how excited and impressed I was, as a young reader madly in love with books, to see the likes of Hemingway and cummings, O'Hara and Welty, granted admission to the Modern Library. I had visions of a sacred rite in which these still-living writers—men and women whose subject was the world in which I myself lived—were ushered into the presence of the gods of literature and granted eternal life.

Whether Fred Exley had any such fantasies I do not know, but he had been brought to many of the world's greatest books through inexpensive, durable Modern Library editions, and quite surely he venerated the Modern Library much as many others did. He also had a powerful desire for acceptance in the highest literary circles. Though he was uncomfortable at the ceremony where he received the Rosenthal Award of the National Academy and Institute of Arts and Letters for *A Fan's Notes*, and though he was contemptuous of the writers who gathered at Elaine's and other self-consciously lit'ry watering holes, he craved approval by these people even as he scorned them. The telephone lineman's son from Watertown, New York, wanted to be one among equals in the big city of literature, and there can be no question that he would have regarded admission to the Modern Library as the most conclusive evidence that he had arrived. Even the Pulitzer Prize that he longed for but never won would have paled by comparison to the Modern Library, which with this edition of *A Fan's Notes* places him not among mere journalists but in Faulkner & Company.

As it happens, this Modern Library reprint of *A Fan's Notes* appears at the same time as *Misfit*, my biography of Fred. While I have no illusions that everyone who reads *A Fan's Notes* in this edition will also read *Misfit*, it remains that the central part of my book is concerned with the writing, publication, critical reception and literary quality of Fred's "fictional memoir." I have no desire simply to rewrite or condense what I have already written, so I have chosen to make a few points about the book—some covered in my biography, some not—that may prove of use to the reader approaching it for the first time.

It is certain that you will have read only a few pages of *A Fan's Notes* before you begin wondering where autobiographical "truth" ends and fiction begins. The question is unanswerable, but this much is indisputable: the disclaimer with which Fred prefaces the book is not to be taken seriously. All the evidence indicates that *A Fan's Notes*—early on it seems to have been called *Footnotes of North Country*—was first written as a memoir, and turned into a "novel" only after lawyers for Harper & Row, its original publisher, insisted that this be done in order to forestall libel actions. It is not hard to track down the real people who served as Fred's models—hundreds of people in Watertown know exactly who they are, or were—or to find documentary evidence of events in his own life that are central to this narrative. The only important missing link is the "real" Bunny Sue Allorgee, who probably is a composite drawn from several women with whom Fred had been—or wished he had been—involved.

If this relationship between the actual and the fictional is one of the most beguiling mysteries about *A Fan's Notes*, an even greater one is, simply: where did this book come from? There was nothing in Fred's family background or in the first four decades of his life to suggest that this tormented, self-destructive man had it within him to write a book of such harsh honesty and brutal beauty. Apart from a handful of public relations pieces written for a couple of railroads for which he worked as a young man, Fred had published nothing before this book appeared. He liked to talk occasionally about his "writing," but his family and friends mostly assumed that this was just Fred blowing smoke about the dream world in which everyone thought he lived, as in great measure he really did. No one expected him to be anything more than an irregular schoolteacher at best, Watertown's pet drunk at worst.

Art is often mysterious, but it is rarely more so than in the case of this book. Not merely can no one speak authoritatively about the inner resources upon which Fred drew to write it, no one knows for certain when and where he wrote it. The mystery is so impenetrable that it is tempting to adopt Peter Shaffer's simplistic and condescending view of Mozart, as expressed in *Amadeus,* and dismiss Fred as an idiot savant through whose typewriter some higher power chose to pass this minor masterpiece. The trouble is that for all his childish misbehavior and irresponsibility, Fred was no idiot savant. He wrote this book with no significant help, tore it from the innermost core of himself with determination, persistence and courage. No questions we raise about this book's origins can be permitted to belittle its enduring accomplishment.

Today, nearly three decades after its publication, *A Fan's Notes* has become both a cult novel and a staple of university courses in modern fiction. It even seems to have acquired a life of sorts in the recovery movement, or so a search for "Frederick Exley" on the Internet leads one to believe, leading one to ponder as well the raucous laughter with which Fred would have greeted *that* news. But at this moment in our literary history, perhaps it will achieve its greatest significance and influence as a model of the confessional memoir against which all others must be measured.

For better and for worse, the memoir is crowding the novel out of the American literary center. Writers who in previous times would have disguised their stories in fiction—inspired, as Fred probably was, by *The Catcher in the Rye*—now feel liberated to tell them as autobiographies. Because too many of these writers are products of university writing programs, there is a self-indulgent sameness about too much of their work that soon becomes wearying and offensive, even to one who loves memoirs as much as I do. The memoir is becoming a publishing genre rather than a literary form, with calamitous consequences for its future.

We must turn back to *A Fan's Notes* to understand just what the memoir at its best can do. There is not a contrived or coyly self-conscious word in it. What is true of it is true as well of all great literature: it *had* to be written. Unlike so many of today's memoirists, who seem to be doing little more than fulfilling classroom assignments or publishing contracts, Fred had no choice in the matter. He had to write *A Fan's Notes* because it is what he was put on earth to do. Thus there is an urgency about this book that can be diminished neither by the years nor by repeated rereadings. I have now lost count of the number of times I have read it, yet each time I reenter it I find something new, something surprising, something that moves and changes me. It is one of the most important books of my life, and I consider it an honor beyond my powers of description to be permitted to escort its author up the long stairway—watch your step, Freddie!—to Olympus.

Baltimore, Maryland, 1997

A NOTE TO THE READER

Though the events in this book bear similarity to those of that long malaise, my life, many of the characters and happenings are creations solely of the imagination. In such cases, I of course disclaim any responsibility for their resemblance to real people or events, which would be coincidental. The character "Patience," for example, who is herein depicted as my "wife," is a fictionalized character bearing no similarity to anyone living or dead. In creating such characters, I have drawn freely from the imagination and adhered only loosely to the pattern of my past life. To this extent, and for this reason, I ask to be judged as a writer of fantasy.

For Nancy
And for C. and H.W.R.

If his inmost heart could have been laid open, there would have been discovered that dream of undying fame; which, dream as it is, is more powerful than a thousand realities.

—NATHANIEL HAWTHORNE, *Fanshawe*

All Wales is like this. I have a friend who writes long and entirely unprintable verses beginning, "What are you, Wales, but a tired old bitch?" and, "Wales my country, Wales my sow."

—DYLAN THOMAS
TO PAMELA HANSFORD JOHNSON

Contents

A FAN'S NOTES

THE NERVOUS LIGHT
OF SUNDAY

On Sunday, the eleventh of November, 196–, while sitting at the bar of the New Parrot Restaurant in my home town, Watertown, New York, awaiting the telecast of the New York Giants–Dallas Cowboys football game, I had what, at the time, I took to be a heart attack.

It wasn't. It—the "seizure" or whatever one chooses to call it—was brought on by the high and delicious anxiety I always experienced just prior to a Giants game, and by a weekend of foodless, nearly heroic drinking. For me it was a common enough drinking; but the amounts consumed had been intensified by the news, received by mail from Scarsdale two days before, that my wife intended to divorce me and to have custody of my two-year-old twin sons. It gives me feeble comfort to report it was not a heart attack. The pain was excruciatingly vivid, and for many moments I was terrified by the fear of death. Illogically, this was one terror I believed I had long since cast off—having cast it off, I thought, with the effortless lunacy of a man putting a shotgun into his mouth and ridding himself of the back of his skull. That the fear of death still owns me is, in its way, a beginning.

Each weekend I traveled the fifty-odd miles from Glacial Falls to Watertown, where I spent Friday night and all day Saturday in some sustained whisky drinking, tapering off Sundays with a few bottles of beer at The Parrot, eyes fixed on the television screen, cheering for my team. *Cheering* is a paltry description. The Giants were my delight, my folly, my anodyne, my intellectual stimulation. With Huff I "stunted" up and down the room among the bar stools, preparing to "shoot the gap"; with Shofner I faked two defenders "out of their cleats," took high, swimming passes over my right shoulder and trotted, dipsy-doodle-like, into the end zone; with Robustelli I swept into backfields and with cruel disdain flung flat-footed, helpless quarterbacks to the turf. All this I did amidst an unceasing, pedantic commentary I issued on the character of the game, a commentary issued with the patronizing air of one who assumed those other patrons incapable of assessing what was taking place before their eyes. Never did I stop moving or talking. Certainly I drove a good many customers away. Most of those who remained had seen the show before and had come back for more, bringing with them the morbid fascination which compels one to stare at a madman.

For the Giants they were exhilarating and lovely afternoons. With Y. A. Tittle passing to Shofner, Webster, Gifford, and Walton, the team was displaying its most adroit and exciting offense in memory; I was giddy with admiration. Despite those few felicitous hours, the weekends were tedious and could as well have taken place at Glacial Falls had I not been earning my drinking money at what my colleagues, with disarming somberness, referred to as "teaching school." It wasn't that teachers weren't permitted to drink in Glacial Falls, or that anyone would have frowned on a teacher's cheering in a local saloon. My case was somewhat different. Prior to his offering me a contract, Mr. A., the superintendent, had told me, half apologetically, half menacingly, that he understood I drank heavily. I should have said, "Well, friend, if you *understand* that, you'd best not expose me to and run the risk of my polluting the kids"; but I badly needed the job and so found myself in the humiliating position of having to assure the man I'd refrain from "excessiveness" around Glacial Falls, a rural community of ten thousand, buried half the year under leaden skies and heavy snows, and all the year under the weight of its large and intransigent ignorance.

"The children come first," Mr. A. said to me at the time. "You understand that. We have to protect the children at all costs."

He said this sincerely, and I had no reason to doubt him. I wanted to believe him. For me it was another autumn, a time of new beginnings, and I was thirty-two; but I had only to teach a few days to realize the children came anything but first. The curriculum was, as it had been in the two schools where I had substituted, as bland as hominy grits; and there was a faculty that might most kindly be referred to as not altogether cretinous. A freshman had nuns cloistered in a "Beanery," a sophomore thought the characters in *Julius Caesar* talked "pretty damn uppity for a bunch of Wops," a junior defined "in mufti" as the attire worn by "some kind of sexual freak (like a certain ape who sits a few seats from me!)," and a senior considered "Hamlet a fag if I ever saw one. I mean, yak, yak, yak, instead of sticking that

Claude in the gizzard, that Claude who's doing all those smelly things to his Mom."

Compounding the touching bewilderment of these students was an English department chairman who clung to such syntactical myths as that either *different from* or *different than* are permissible as the former is used in America and the latter in England. Though I had done some substitute work, this was my first contractual obligation, I was bringing to it a typically asinine and enthusiastic aplomb, and at this point I sought the floor. "I've heard this for years," I said, "have always looked for it, and have found that most English writers use *different from*. Without a Fowler handy I haven't the foggiest how this argument got started, but I suspect that some prose writer of Dean Swiftian eminence got smashed one day, inadvertently substituted *than* for *from*, and for the past two hundred years the dons at Oxford and Cambridge have been scratching their heads and picking their noses over it. But this professorial bickering has nothing to do with us. Between getting smashed and cracking up their hot rods, initiating each other into their sex clubs, and having their rumbles, these little dears are looking to us for direction"—a loud laugh here from the back of the room, issuing from a Dartmouth man who taught English and Latin—"and we ought to give it to them. Oughtn't we to take a hard and arbitrary line and say it's *different from*, period? Certainly they'll come to us and show us how Hemingway strings together ten compound sentences without employing a single comma, but we'll just have to tell them they *ain't* Hemingway. I doubt there's anything stifling to creativity here. If any of these kids are going to write, they'll write in spite of us, and at least they'll know what rules they're violating."

This tastelessly long-winded monologue occurred at the

first department meeting in September. Thinking that the laughter of the Dartmouth man had reflected the sentiments of my colleagues, when I finished, feeling rather proud, I looked round to see how the rest of the English teachers were reacting to the witty and brilliant new addition to their staff. To a man they were glum, somewhat wretched. Immediately after the meeting I discovered why. Approached by a broad-assed, martini-swilling, brazen, and theatrical old termagant, I was informed as a teacher new to the system that one did not enter discussions at department meetings, that "talking took time," and that there were all sorts of places one would rather be. "I'm sorry," I said. "I thought these meetings were for a purpose."

As the year progressed I learned that due to this conspiracy of silence the department chairman was forced to carry single-handedly what were supposed to be give-and-take discussions. Knowing he was no more ignorant than those boobs seated around me patronizing him, I felt sorry for him. At the beginning of each meeting he handed to his English teachers mimeographed sheets containing lettered items, *A, B, C, D, E,* reflecting the wisdom of thirty years spent in combat with the language. Unsure of our ability to read (our ability to talk hadn't encouraged him), he read each and every item to us. Beginning with a lovingly theatrical enunciation of *A,* he thereupon was off. Matchlessly vapid, the items were such that I remember only one of them, and that only because to this day I have no notion of what he meant by it: *The best place to make out your lesson plans is at your desk.* In fairness to the man, he did not feel dutybound to the continuity of his mimeographed sheets and often interrupted his readings to impart to us some newly acquired gem. One day he told us he had come across the word *apostasy* but hadn't bothered to look it up as he had no fear of encountering it again. He was implying that if an English teacher looked up every unknown word he came across, he'd spend half his waking hours poring myopically over the dictionary. Smiling, he then permitted us to nod our heads in acquiescence to his canniness. He beamed. Then he did something unforgivable. Having admitted to not comprehending a word known to most high school seniors, he suddenly chose to group his teachers within the limits of his own scant vision. "Do any of you know the meaning of the word?" he challenged. The silence was awesome. Everyone stared at the floor. I don't know why I chose to speak. It would be the last time I ever did so at a meeting. I defined the word, trying to speak in a matter-of-fact, self-disparaging way, as though I were admitting that nobody but a fool or a freak would know the meaning of such an esoteric word. "Apostasy," I said, "is the disavowal of previously avowed principles." And, oh lord, my impatient, querulous, pompous voice too clearly reflected the long weeks of my anguish at these sessions. Led by the theatrical *grande dame*, all heads cranked round to peer in utter astonishment and loathing at me, loathing not only for having committed the gaffe of entering a discussion but for suggesting that the world wasn't, after all, bordered by the town signs proclaiming Glacial Falls.

Though distressing, these problems seemed not invincible; and I had hopes that by going my own way I could do a good job despite my surroundings. I was wrong. In the Glacial Falls teacher's manual, a booklet I had been assured was Biblical in its authority (chiseled in stone), I one day came across a high-toned and vague clause (very much like a paragraph in any education textbook) calling on teachers to pass with the grade of *C* any student who was "working to capacity"—a capacity one could, I guessed immediately, determine from the IQ records in the guidance office. With a number of seasoned teachers in the system I tried to discuss this clause, but they seemed reluctant to talk about it—more than reluctant, tired, very tired, as though the clause had been discussed all too many times. There were some obvious questions needing answers. What about the superior student who doesn't make any effort but still manages to get a *B?* Reversing the principle, do I give him a *C,* and if I do, does that *C,* in the eyes of the administration, represent the same as the *C* of a student capable of doing only 40, 30, 20, percent of the work?

"What the clause means," one young and spirited teacher said finally, winking outrageously, "is that *everybody, but everybody, daddy,* passes."

That outrageous wink answered everything. Through some impossible-to-administer policy, the faculty had been rendered moral monsters. Asked to keep one eye open, cool and detached, in appraising half the students, we were to keep the other eye winking as the rest of the students were passed from grade to grade and eventually into a world that would be all too happy to teach them, as they drifted churlishly from disappointment to disaster, what the school should have been teaching them all along: that even in America *failure is a part of life.* (At Glacial Falls the *F* had been eliminated altogether on the genteel assumption that the *D,* the—in *Newspeak*—"unpassing" grade, somehow represented a less equivocal failure.) In the end, of course, the policy didn't hurt the student nearly so much as the teacher: a wink eventually becomes a twitch, a twitch the sign of some inner disturbance. Still, everything had now been solved for me. I would go through the motions of teaching and try to prevent my students' believing my contempt was leveled at them. Not succeeding, I found that by the Thanksgiving holiday the majority of my students despised me, I loathed them, and we moved warily about each other snarling like antic cats. So I went each weekend to Watertown to drink and come alive those Sunday afternoon hours before the television screen. At game's end I returned to Glacial Falls, where during the day I continued to snarl and be snarled at, and where during the evening, in the isolation of my bleak, eight-dollar room, I fell with incredible ease into profound and lengthy sleep. Occasionally sleeping as much as four-teen hours, I rose as though great lead weights were tied to me and returned to the agitation of the classroom.

But the weeks passed with paradoxical swiftness. It was as if they were no more than prolonged slumbers burdened by nightmares populated with pimple-picking, gum-chewing, pea-brained, sex-overwhelmed adolescents. When I awoke, perspiring, I was in Watertown standing at the bar of the Crystal Restaurant, drinking a beer and look-ing across the bar at Leo, who was one of the owners and whom I had known since childhood. Occasionally I drank two or three before the perspiration dried and I could speak to him. Then I would say, "How the Giants going to make out Sunday, Leo?" Having known the question would come, Leo would smile. With that question life would begin again. The nightmare of the week was over.

Why did football bring me so to life? I can't say precisely. Part of it was my feeling that football was an island of di-rectness in a world of circumspection. In football a man was asked to do a difficult and brutal job, and he either did it or got out. There was nothing rhetorical or vague about it; I chose to believe that it was not unlike the jobs which all men, in some sunnier past, had been called upon to do. It smacked of something old, something traditional, something unclouded by legerdemain and subterfuge. It had that kind of power over me, drawing me back with the force of something known, scarcely remembered, elusive as integrity—perhaps it was no more than the force of a forgotten childhood. Whatever it was, I gave myself up to the Giants utterly. The recompense I gained was the feeling of being alive.

—

The choice of The Parrot as a place to view the games was not an arbitrary one. There had been a time, some two or three seasons before, when I had been able to bounce up and down—shouting, "Oh, God, he did it! Gifford did it! He caught the goddam thing!"—in any place, in any company, and feel neither timidity nor embarrassment. But as one year had engulfed another, and still another, each bringing with it its myriad defeats, as I had come to find myself relying on the Giants as a life-giving, an exalting force, I found myself unable to relax in the company of "unbelievers," in the company of those who did not take their football earnestly or who thought my team something less than the One God. At those times, in those alien places, I felt like a holy man attempting to genuflect amidst a gang of drunken, babbling, mocking heretics. I tried a number of places in Watertown before settling on The Parrot; though it was not exactly the cathedral I would have wished for, it was—like certain old limestone churches scattered throughout the north country—not without its quaint charms. It was ideally isolated on a hill above the city; sitting at the bar I was seldom aware of the city's presence, and when I was, I could think of it as a nostalgic place beneath me, a place with elm trees and church towers and bone-clean streets; sitting at the bar, the city could be thought of as a place remembered, and remembered as if from a great distance.

This distance was important to me. For a long time I had been unable to engage my home town with any degree of openness. What friends I had had were married, raising families, and had locked themselves, ever so tightly, behind their neat-trimmed lawns and white clapboard houses, their children cute, their wives sexless and anxious, my friends plotting their next moves to achieve the Black River Valley Club, never asking themselves what, if they achieved that—the town's most venerable institution—could possibly be left for them. My friends and I had long proved an embarrassment to one another; I embarrassing them because I drank too much, was unreliable in my debts and working habits, and had been "hospitalized" a number of times; I embarrassed because they were. We never stopped each other on the streets without, eyes avoiding mine, their patronizing me with queries about my health. It was distressing because there was a kind of gloating—undoubtedly a good deal imagined on my part—in these encounters, as though they were telling me that getting myself proclaimed mad and dragged away a number of times was only a childish and petulant refusal to accept their way of life as the right way, that in seeking some other way I had been assuming a courage and superiority I hadn't possessed. After a time these encounters had proved so painful that whenever I found myself compelled to move about the streets in daylight hours, I dropped my eyes to the sidewalk and charged through the streets as though in a hot-brained hurry. A dim-lighted haven for inarticulate young men and women who arrived in the late hours of the evening and, throwing themselves together in mock couplings, struggled energetically about the dance floor to the plaintive, standard tunes rendered by a local trio, a piano, a drum, a first-rate horn, The Parrot was not a place where I feared encountering any of my "friends." Most of these young people I knew by name or by sight, and I felt comfortable with them. They took me for what I was, a youngish-old teacher from Glacial Falls, one who drank too much and who was a little tetched on the subject of the Giants; but they seemed to like me and didn't appear to begrudge me that I was without the desire to achieve the Black River Valley Club. Sunday afternoons were different. Then, with the music stilled and the blinds thrown open allowing the golden autumn sunlight to diffuse and warm the room, I would stand at the bar and sip my Budweiser, my "tapering-off" device; munch popcorn from wooden bowls; and in league with the bartender Freddy, whose allegiance to the Giants was only somewhat less feverish than mine, cheer my team home. Invariably and desperately I wished that the afternoon, the game, the light would never end.

On the night of the tenth—the night before the "seizure"—I stayed late at the bar, drinking heavily and talking with B., a grieving young man of twenty. Having recently been rejected by a girl he loved, he was in a state near hyperesthesia. I don't know why he chose to burden me with his lament. I did not know him well. In high school his brother and I had played football and basketball together; we had at the same time, or I would guess that we had, taken long aching looks at the same girls who were, in some celestial way, blossoming right before our eyes, so that we must once have been "almost friends." But a few years before, when I was without a job, drinking and drifting, I had borrowed twenty dollars from that brother; and many months later, when I had attempted to repay him, he had steadfastly refused the money, saying, "If the tables had been reversed, buddy, I know you'd have helped me." He had said this with a certain "style," as though he were not trying to prove how well he was doing in business (and he was doing well); but *still*—we could, of course, never again be "almost friends." Perhaps B. had heard his brother speak of me, and this coupled with my teacher image and the flecks of gray at my temples, led him to assume that I had answers, a conclusion that was not without its irony. In the inner pocket of my jacket was the letter from my wife—"until we are much more firmly settled on our separate roads"—and only moments before B. slithered up to me and said, "Jesus, Ex, I can't eat or nothin'," in an alcoholic fury I had telephoned long-distance to my wife and got my sister-in-law, who, refusing to call my wife to the phone, had prompted me to shout "Fuck you!" into the wire. All I wanted to do was conform to the role—that of the drama's villain—my sister-in-law had assigned to me; and after I had hung up the receiver, and until B. approached me, I had stood at the bar chuckling pensively at the thought of my sister-in-law's hysterically indignant *I-told-you-so's*. Because I was unhappy I offered B. no easy consolation. While he kept saying, "Oh, Jesus, Ex, *Jesus H. Keeriiisst, don't tell me that,*" I told him the ordeal of my own first love, how it had taken me two years to alleviate the pain, how I had risen with it, gone to bed with it, and lived with it all my waking hours until, accepting its naturalness, it had begun to recede. Doubtless B. thought I was being cruel; and I really knew no way of convincing him otherwise. I told him I wished that when I was his age I had sought out some dismal creature for advice. Having gone to fat-assed, "successful" souls (making the American mistake of equating success with wisdom), I was glibly assured that "you'll get over it"; and when I did not, I despised myself for what I deemed a flimsiness of heart. Seeing a younger version of myself in B.'s wild eyes, I offered him all I could. "Look, B., accept your pain as a part of life. There is, really, absolutely no consolation in telling you that I or any man has undergone the same thing. And then, how would I know I've suffered anywhere near what you're going through? And not knowing that, isn't any advice I give you presumptuous?"

We drank together until closing time, one whisky after another, our heads bent close together. We talked through the velvety blue smoke, whispering about isolation and loss; with our sibilant voices we were trying to protect the privacy of our hearts from the ears all about us. Presently the lurid white lights, with almost a violent snap, caught us cheek-to-cheek and Freddy was shouting, "You don't have to go home, gang—*but you can't stay here!*" Reluctantly I rose, finished my drink, put on my raincoat, and walked to the door to wait. B. had moved quickly down the bar and was attempting to pick up a young, snub-nosed, and attractive girl who frequented the place. He picked her up, too; and I had to admire the ease with which he did it, speaking only a few words to her. He was a handsome, sensitive boy, and watching him so facilely "move" the girl I wondered what that other girl was searching for, the one who had tossed him over. The three of us left together. We drove around town for an hour or so nipping on B.'s bottle, then went to an all-night diner, The Red Moon. We had been looking for a girl friend of snub-nose's, one who was, without my being consulted in the matter, supposed to be my date. We found her at The Red Moon. Before getting back into the car, I drew myself up, unzipped my fly, and stood in the middle of the street taking an enormous piss. A car tooted at me, swerved erratically, and just missed me. Speaking out of the corner of her mouth, my new date said, "Jeez, I ain't going with that crazy bastard!" As she was going back into the diner to her leather-jacketed friends, she added, "Some schoolteacher!"

B., the snub-nosed girl, and I ended at my motel room, where, getting me alone in the bathroom, B. offered me what he called "first shot" at the girl. I declined, thanking him rather too profusely. I fell asleep that night listening to their mating noises from the adjoining bed. My initiation into sex had taken place on the ground behind a billboard sign advertising beer within walking distance from where I was now lying. The girl had received, with neither complaint nor enthusiasm, a good part of Watertown High School's 1945 football team. Afterward I had had to help her up and walk her, while she clung unsteadily to my arm and wept, to her house some distance down the highway. Listening now, it occurred to me that I hadn't come very far over the years—no farther really than from one "gang bang" to another, save that I had learned, as B. had yet to learn, that tomorrow the pain would be even greater.

———

When I awoke, B. and the girl had gone, leaving in the wake of their coupling a great mountain of disheveled bedding, a brilliant stain of orange lipstick smack in the middle of the pillow, and on the exposed sheet the untidy evidence of their urgency. It was only eight o'clock, and though I had hoped to sleep longer, and had the night before drunk one whisky after another for that reason, as much as any other, I was not surprised at the earliness of the hour. For a couple years past, on these autumn Sundays, I had wakened, started up really, with the terrifying notion that *the game* was already under way, that I had missed—God knows what—some unsurpassably executed play. Leaping from bed, I would be confronted by the clock and from that moment on my morning would be hell; for I would begin undergoing the nervousness to which only the players should be subjected: the giddiness, the thirst, time's protracted passage.

On this morning my tension was intensified by my inability to keep my eyes from the awful ruin of the adjoining bed. I closed my eyes and opened them; I rolled over and rolled back, always with my eyes returning to that bed. It was as though I expected to see there some frightful clue to my destiny, some forbidding look into the darker recesses of my being. When I could stand looking no longer, I rose and, with the swift and mechanical propriety of an outraged landlady, made up the bed. Then I made up my own, took a scalding shower, shakily shaved, dressed except for my shoes, and lay back on the bed to watch television. It was a "religious" show, a drama about the redemption of an alcoholic woman through the discovery of Jesus Christ. There was a time when these shows had provided me with unending amusement; but understanding the slightness of that which provided my own sustenance, I was no longer able to find amusement where others took comfort, no matter how asininely presented. In this show, though, the woman looked incredibly like my sister-in-law, so that it was impossible for me to believe in either her degeneracy—for my sister-in-law, in her way, was a decent woman—or the resultant redemption. The resemblance awoke in me, moreover, the memory of my ill-advised telephone call of the night before; and I now, in the nervous light of Sunday, became ruddy with shame, then literally sick, dropping to my hands and knees to throw up in the toilet bowl. By nine-thirty, when I decided to go downtown for the Sunday papers, I was pacing the carpeted floor, smoking one Salem after another, and cursing myself for not having bought a six-pack—an abstinence imposed upon myself under the idiotic pretense that I was not a drunk.

At the newsstand in the lobby of the Hotel Woodruff I bought the New York and Syracuse papers, the *Times*, the *Tribune*, the *Post-Standard*, and the *Herald-Journal*; and with that great weight under my arm I walked east on Public Square to The Crystal, where, sliding into a booth, I ordered tomato juice and black coffee and began my weekly ritual. Removing the sports sections from the various newspapers, I stacked them in a neat pile to one side of the table. Now I removed the various magazine, entertainment, and book sections and piled these on top of that pile. Finally I gathered up the bulkier parts of the papers, the sections containing the world news—that record of yesterday's monstrous deceptions, betrayals, and obscenities—and flung them into the seat opposite mine, where, for all of me, they could remain forever unread.

It was my habit to read the magazine and entertainment sections first, and read them in the most cursory of ways. I read, or glanced at, only those articles about cinema starlets nobody has ever heard of. These pieces fascinated me for their subjects were well on their way to becoming insane. Their world was bordered by skin-diving; by Cary Grant, "the most luscious man I've ever seen"; by Tolstoi (their favorite author); and by their own astoundingly juicy selves (aping Elizabeth Taylor, they all had "the mind of a child and the body of a woman"). I never finished one of these articles without staring, lengthily and gloomily, at the accompanying pictures. Invariably the girls were scantily clad, posed in such a way as to show to advantage the highlights of preposterously lovely bodies, and always one photo showed a close-up of their luscious mouths puckered suggestively, round and hot and soft and ready for erotic oral business. I used to imagine flogging them to death with a truncheon. Like Orwell's Winston Smith I would imagine raping them and, at the moment of orgasm, slashing their throats or bashing in their lovely faces with a spiked club. Imagining these things, I felt neither guilt nor horror but a kind of gleeful detachment; like Orwell's Outer Party members who were well on their way to the Inner Party, it would be no time at all before these girls believed the "realities" their press agents were molding for them, believed that their minds were attuned to Count Tolstoi, no time before they were in a state of whimsical dementia. For more than any other reason I wanted to truncheon them to death because I would never have them, knowing that they were rewards—like a Rolls-Royce—for those obedient men who accepted society's standards of success, standards that seemed to me not only wrongheaded but grotesque. The girls were part of America's plenty and, once used, one disposed of them the way one got rid of a Cadillac and moved on to an Aston-Martin.

Next I read the book reviews. I read them with nostalgia and remorse. There was a period when I had lived on book reviews, when I had basked and drawn sustenance from what I deemed the light of their intelligence, the beneficence of their charm. But something had gone sour. Over the years I had read too much, in dim-lighted railway stations, lying on the davenports of strangers' houses, in the bleak and dismal wards of insane asylums. That reading had forced the charm to relinquish itself. Now I found that reviews were not only bland but scarcely, if ever, relevant; and that all books, whether works of imagination or the blatant frauds of literary whores, were approached by the reviewer with the same crushing sobriety. I wanted the reviewer to be fair, kind, and funny. I wanted to be made to laugh. I had no better luck that Sunday than on any other.

Finally I turned to the sports sections. Even then I did not begin reading about the Giants. I was like a child who, having been given a box of chocolates, eats the jellies and nuts first and saves the creamy caramels till last. I read about golf in Scotland, surf-boarding in Oahu, football as Harvard imagines it played, and deep-sea fishing in Mexico. Only then did I turn to the Giants, having by then already torn from the *Times* and stuffed into my pocket Arthur Daley's column, which I always saved to read but a couple minutes before kickoff, the biggest caramel of them all. I read every word of these articles over and over again. Knowing precisely what I was looking for, I sought assurance that by five that afternoon the Giants would have another victory, some statement that would allay my mounting anxiety. I wanted the Giants' coach, Allie Sherman, to be quoted from some unequivocal position of superiority: "We've got the best team in football; and we're going to beat them just as we're going to beat everybody." Because coaches are notoriously pessimistic, one rarely came across any such statement. The outer reaches of Sherman's optimism ran to statements like, "We're in good shape; if we lose, we won't have anyone to blame." But on this Sunday I found nothing even this adventuresome. Occasionally the opposing coach would jeer. He would say the Giants were lucky, or that they were a bunch of weary old men, the latter a comment that circulated rather freely that year. I searched now for a statement to this effect. Certain that the statement would be pinned to the bulletin board of the Giants' locker room in an attempt to infuriate the team to unbelievable feats, I could attach the insult to my heart and, with it, sneer and gloat as Robustelli, Grier, Huff, and Katcavage pitilessly stomped their opponents into the hard, dry turf of Dallas. But on this Sunday the opposing coach proved equally genteel; and by noon I was back at The Parrot helping Freddy move some tables to get the bar ready for the afternoon and knowing no more about the outcome of the game than I had at the same time the Sunday before. As we worked, though, Freddy and I reassured each other over and over again that there was nothing whatever to worry about. Freddy said, "Dallas? Are you kidding me?" I said, *"Dallas? Are you kidding me?"* We laughed disparagingly.

Freddy said, "You'll miss the Counselor, though, huh?"

" 'Deed I will," I said. " 'Deed I will."

—

The Counselor was my best friend, and until a few Sundays earlier had always been my game-watching companion. We had known each other since high school and had, from the moment we met in a Plane Geometry class, recognized each other for what we were—hedonistic. To the Counselor's credit, he still believed in one thing I no longer did. Aside from Liquor and the Giants (and I had brought him round to that team), he still believed in the consoling power of Fornication. On his last Sunday in Watertown, he, his most recent girl (a lithe, lovely university coed), and I had stood at the bar while the Counselor, his blond head towering above us, had sipped his scotch on the rocks, patted his girl affectionately on her backside, and, eyes glued to the television, had kept repeating with the composure of a British barrister, "All right, Giants, *all right.*" Unlike mine, the Counselor's enthusiasm was restrained, as though he never for a moment doubted the Giants' ability to overcome all obstacles. In this case his restraint was admirable. Freddy was holding a hundred dollars of his, a bet he had made with a transplanted Detroiter who had believed, to the Counselor's vast and studied amusement, that the Detroit Lions were fourteen points better than our club. The Counselor could not afford to be overly amused. The money was all he had, and it was his "getting-away" booty. Having recently been disbarred, the Counselor, unhappily, was a counselor no more. To make a living, he had had on Mondays to leave that Sunday idyl of football, scotch, and fornication and go down the hill and into the city where the play gets a good deal rougher than ever it gets in Yankee Stadium; at one awful moment his colleagues had looked behind his white-toothed and patronizing smile and had made the discovery, which must have been horrible to them, not only that the Counselor didn't believe in them, their little white houses, or the Black River Valley Club but that, unlike those peers who were to sit in such harsh judgment of him, he did not imagine himself Justice Holmes. It wasn't that the Counselor had no pride of law (he was, in fact, a good lawyer) but that, knowing his limitations and his financial obligations, he saw the law as a way to make a living like any other, selling false teeth or writing bestsellers.

After the game the Counselor collected the two hundred dollars, his own hundred plus that of the Detroiter's, slid it into his pocket, and we made our curt good-byes, promising to get together someplace out of town in late December when the Giants, who had beaten a great Lion team that day, would undoubtedly be meeting the Green Bay

Packers for the championship of the National Football League. Then the Counselor walked down the half-dozen steps that led out of the bar, a surprisingly proud figure, I thought, his nymph clinging tightly to his arm, and out through the door into the cool October evening. I had wanted to call to him then, to offer him something, affection or gratitude. In my own bad time, when I had been shuttling back and forth between asylums, when even my family had despaired of my recovery, he had given me a davenport to lie down upon, and books to read, and money with which to buy liquor. Never once had he inquired about my health. He hadn't because he had understood that what I needed was time to get used to being an outsider, a condition he had long ago accepted about himself and which had become an article of the faith by which he moved. I wished I had money or a haven to offer him, but I had neither; and I never loathed my home as I did at that moment. It wasn't as if the Counselor had been some shyster from Brooklyn come to take over the tank town. He had been born in Watertown, educated in its schools, and had been young together with its sons and daughters— quite some time before; and I couldn't help thinking that a few in the bar association might have stood up for him, might have sensed that his destruction and his betrayal and his failure were their destruction and their betrayal and their failure. At that moment, watching him descend the stairs, I had this unnerving vision of my friend drifting from bar to bar, from girl to girl, with no kind place whatever to look back upon. I tried to call to him then, but all I could think to say was, "I'd like to cut their fucking hearts out," and that hysterical imprecation would have given him little consolation.

———

By one o'clock, after helping Freddy move the tables and get the bar ready, I was sitting on a stool sipping my second or third brandy and coffee and recalling the Counselor's melancholy departure some weeks before, when Freddy suddenly pointed at my wallet, which lay open before me on the bar, and said, "Who're the little guys?"

I told him they were my sons.

"Your sons?" he said. He was surprised, very surprised. His dark eyes widened exposing the whites, and his mouth went lax, forming a cavern of disbelief. "I didn't know you were married."

I told him my problem was that I hadn't known it either.

He thought this witty and began to laugh. He was engaged in washing a great mass of dirty glasses from the night before. As his hand pumped up and down in the soapy water, he kept looking at me and smiling idiotically, waiting for me to tell him that it wasn't true. I smiled, too. He had only known me as a drinker—practically a solitary one—with no life apart from booze and football. He was trying to get used to that part of me which existed away from The Parrot. Drying his hands, he walked down the bar to me and picked up the wallet again. He stared at the picture, then at me, then at the picture again, shaking his head in good-natured disbelief. Laying it down, he said, "Healthy little bastards, aren't they?" I proudly agreed. He looked at me as though to say, "C'mon, who are they? Your nephews or who?" He seemed incredulous about this discovery. I just kept smiling. Then he began doing an imitation of me, one with which he often got laughs from the regulars in the place. I didn't recognize it as resembling me. Dropping his eyelids to half-mast, and weaving slightly but steadily, he began talking in a dull monotone, slurring his words terribly and demanding from some imaginary bartender what time the Giants game went on. Then he began improvising. "I can see you ten years from now," he said, "in some saloon waiting for the game to go on." Now he picked up the wallet and went on with the imitation. Staggering down the bar, he pretended to be showing the picture to imaginary customers. "Dese here's my sons," he kept saying with pathetic insistence, pretending that the customers were intractable and finding this aspect of my life as hard to believe as he did. "Dey are," he repeated to these phantom skeptics. "Dey are! Dey are! I ain't lyin' to yuh!" Abruptly Freddy fell to one side. Apparently one of those phantoms had brushed him rudely away, not really caring whether he had sons or not. We were alone in the bar, Freddy and I, and we laughed like hell, laughed and laughed and laughed.

But then, quite suddenly, quite frightfully, my laughter went cold in my stomach, and my joy and my exhilaration curdled to the point where I thought I might vomit. With a kind of omniscient clarity I suddenly recognized the truth of this vision. I saw myself some years hence, drunk, waiting "for the game," without self-denial, without perseverance, without hope. In this vision there was nothing but dark rooms from which love and grace and charm were fled, and indeed—how very acute Freddy was!—all I had to cling to, yellowing now with age, was this fading photo of my twin sons, my only and final link with humanity, and one, at that, which people neither believed in nor really cared about. With this vision came alarming chills, then hot flashes. When my left arm went limp as pudding and the pain began shooting up and down it, when the symptoms became unmistakable, I struggled to my feet and without saying a word to Freddy walked down the half-dozen steps and went out into the sunshine. It was silly—but I did not want to die there in the barroom.

Outside it was a lovely, thrilling autumn day. The sky was an unvarying, heady blue; as far as the eye could see—which from up on that hill was a long way—the fields were mottled with gold, the trees dripping with wine. I don't know how long I just stood there, looking, waiting. My left leg had by now gone equally limp, followed by intermittent and excruciating pains in both arm and leg. I waited for one sharp explosion in my breast. If it had hit me then, I'd have died the way I had for a long time believed I could die, impenitent, chill of heart, unloving, unloved. But nothing happened except that the pain became even more unbearable, and I began, suddenly, to weep. Lifting my head, I stared, with my eyes wide-open, at the sun, hoping that its brilliant rays would not only obscure the lovely view but the pain and the memory. Still I lived, still I felt pain, and still time passed, so that each moment I lived only increased—in violent, mad proportions—my thirst for life. Suddenly I began to walk. I walked first tentatively, putting one foot slowly out before the other and dragging my left leg up to make its agonizing step, then faster, then furiously, round and round The Parrot's macadam drive in a lunatic parody of life. Believing motion life, I felt as long as I moved I would have that life. As I moved I was still weeping profusely; scalding tears streamed down my cheeks, and all the time I called, if not to God, to the insidious and arbitrary forces of the universe—*Oh, don't let it be like this! Not like this!*—even attempting, in my fear, to bargain with that force, asking time for one more beer, time for one more game, time to get used to the notion of an eternity of darkness. "You son of a bitch!" I said. "I want to live!" With those words, spoken out of my mouth and into the brilliant November air, I struggled back up the stairs and into the bar, where I told Freddy I was sick and ought to go to the hospital. Freddy only looked at me and, seeing the large fear in my heart, threw on his coat and helped me back down the stairs and into his car. Together we started down the hill toward town.

Washington Street was as lovely as I had ever seen it. The houses looked formidably neat and snug, the immaculate lawns had their first tinges of lemon, the trees were shedding their multicolored leaves. Even up close it looked like some dream of place, and because I hated that place, I hated myself for having to seek its aid. Indeed, so much did it seem to me some place I had no right to be that it would not have surprised me had the city refused its aid. We were just turning into the House of the Good Samaritan's drive when I said to Freddy, "I'm scared, Freddy—*really scared.*" Because he saw how afraid I was and it embarrassed him, Freddy didn't say anything except, "Easy, boy—*easy.*"

———

Mrs. C., the on-duty nurse in the receiving room, was right out of Dickens, one of those eternal mothers, broad, sympathetic without being maudlin, and appallingly efficient, a woman whose very presence seems to heal. Listening to my choked, fearful complaints, she helped me off with my jacket and shirt and onto the hard, white-sheeted leather table, where she quickly and expertly took my blood pressure while the entire left side of my body went cold. Save for the terrifying palpitations of my heart, I might, I thought, have already been dead. I stared at her. She had a face made handsome by virtue of its very amiableness. But it told me nothing. I searched and searched that face, but it revealed nothing of what that awesome gadget was telling her. Finishing, she took a rather forbidding look at me and asked if I had a personal physician. When I said that I hadn't, she told me a Dr. D. was on call and asked me if he would do. "Fine," I said quickly. "Just fine." How long it was before the doctor came, I can't say. But I had never felt more alone, or more terrified, thinking still that the apocalyptic explosion in my breast was imminent. Both my arm and my leg were now all but immovable. My heart was beating violently, my head was throbbing. Propping myself up on my right elbow, I kept looking over my tensed feet at Mrs. C., who was sitting at a desk engaged in some paper work. I had to reassure myself that she was still there; over and over again I had to reassure myself. Though not once did she look in my direction, I had the feeling she knew I was watching her and that she expected me to speak. So I repeated my words to Freddy: "I'm afraid, Mrs. C.—*really afraid.*"

"Just lie still."

"Look here," I demanded, by now half crazy with fear and upset with what I interpreted as her dour indifference, "have I had—I mean, am I having some kind of attack?"

There was an agonizing pause while Mrs. C. obviously sought the tactful words. I wanted the answer because there were loose ends yearning for connections. One can imagine the kind of thing I wanted to say: "Look, if anything should happen, tell my mother I loved her—and my wife— well, tell her that in my way I loved—no, she won't believe that. Tell her—well, tell her I'm sorry." Had Mrs. C.'s reply been the expected one, how feeble, how hopelessly groping, these words would have come out! But Mrs. C., who had by now found her own words, saved me the embarrassment of mine; her reply made me feel foolish.

"Your blood pressure doesn't indicate anything like an attack." Once again she paused, as if trying to find the right words. At the last moment she apparently decided against tact, no doubt thinking it would be wasted on me. "You've been drinking too much."

"Drinking too much?" I said. "For Christ's sake, you don't mean to tell me that booze can do this?"

Mrs. C.'s reply came swiftly, and in its authority it was fierce. It was the reply of a woman who has seen all things, birth and death and pain unbearable, children maimed beyond recognition, the ravages of cancer; it was the voice of a woman who had seen, even where I now lay, God only knows what things that once had laughed and loved and danced the jig of life.

"And a lot worse, as you'll damn well find out if you ever come in here with—" Here she mentioned the medical term for the massive stomach hemorrhages she had seen drinkers undergo.

For a moment I hated her for putting me down so peremptorily, and my first incredible thought was that she was trying to offer some stupid or misdirected comfort to the dying. I was perfectly aware that I was a paranoiac—which, of course, had caused the entire "seizure" to begin with—though instead of imagining people poisoning me, I suffered the suspicion that people were always trying to make me see things in a less complexly morbid light than I was wont to see them. No philosophy aroused shudders in me as quickly as "Oh, nothing's *that* bad." But *this?* Of course she wasn't trying to console me. There had been no heart attack. Absolutely none.

"I feel foolish," I said.

"None of that," she said. "No reason for that. You're sick. Just as sick as you can be."

Before the doctor arrived, Mrs. C. and I had a few moments to talk. She asked me if I had ever thought of joining Alcoholics Anonymous. I told her that I had thought of it. I could have told her that for a time, when I was incarcerated in the nuthouse, I had gone at the "request" of the authorities to the meetings of the hospital branch of that organization but that the "confessions" had embarrassed me; that, though AA professed to the contrary, it was evangelical in character; and that I could not bring myself to call daily upon God for help in abstaining, feeling that if there were a God I'd like to hold Him in reserve for more lovely mercies than my own sobriety. Quite frankly, it was more than this: I wasn't sure I *wanted* to live without an occasional binge. But I couldn't go into this with Mrs. C., knowing her argument would be that there was no such thing for me any more as an occasional binge. Though I respected the validity of this argument, it didn't assuage my need for drink. After a month's sobriety my faculties became unbearably acute and I found myself unhealthily clairvoyant, having insights into places I'd as soon not journey to. Unlike some men, I had never drunk for boldness or charm or wit; I had used alcohol for precisely what it was, a depressant to check the mental exhilaration produced by extended sobriety. "You join it," Mrs. C. said. As her tone signaled the end of the conversation, I fell to thinking about the "messages" I had wanted to leave behind. Had I loved my mother? My wife? At the existential moment I had wanted to believe that I had; but I could understand now, listening to my ever-quietening heart, that I had probably deceived myself into believing that I was still capable of love. More than anything I mourned the loss of this capacity. The realization of this loss suddenly made me want

to weep again. I didn't, though. I only bit my lip, very severely, and waited.

Dr. D. was a fine-looking man. In his middle or late forties, he was over six feet, graying, and he had an extremely
handsome, open, and masculine-looking face. He seemed
the kind of man to whom one would readily entrust one's
diseased and weary body. Dressed in a sport shirt, he
looked anxious to get back to the easy comfort of his Sunday afternoon. He confirmed Mrs. C.'s diagnosis and came
directly to the point. I was, he said, suffering from malnu-
trition aggravated by the alcohol which I had consumed the
past two days. Did I, he wanted to know, have relatives in
Watertown? I could not imagine why he wanted to know
and said that I hadn't. "That's too bad," he said, explaining
that the alternatives were being released in the custody of
a relative or his admitting me to the hospital for acute alcoholism. I said something to the effect that I doubted his
authority to do this. His tone was firm, his manner unwavering, a kind of "try-me" posture. I gave Mrs. C. my sister's telephone number. "That's more like it," he said, and
smiled. Telling Mrs. C. that he wanted me to have sweet orange juice and to remain on the table until the arrival of my
sister, he started for the door, stopped as though he meant
to say something else, started again, stopped, and turned
back to me.

"Earl Exley your father?" he said.

In Watertown it was a question that came to me frequently. Though my father had been dead for eighteen
years, he had in his day been a superb athlete, as good,
some say, as any who ever came out of northern New
York—certainly no great distinction but not without its effect on a son who had never been permitted to forget it.

Still, the question put in that place, at that time, struck me as funny, damned near hilarious, and I thought I was going to laugh aloud. I thought I was going to laugh from anticipation. Invariably the question was followed by the disclosure that the inquirer and my father, "Old Ex," had played ball "together." Certain that Dr. D.'s query was leading to this revelation, and trying not to smile, I said that Earl Exley had most certainly been my father. The doctor fooled me, though. All he said was, "He was a good fellow—a hell of a good fellow." And, just before he went out the door, *"And tough too!"*

It was this latter that got to me, said as it was in such a way as to indicate that my father's son *might not be* so tough. That got me thinking about having to face my sister, my kid sister at that. I tried to feel embarrassment. But it was no good. My life had been one long series of things imposed upon those closest to me; having faced the reproachful and pained eyes of relatives so many times before, I couldn't really summon up the shame I thought I ought to feel at such a confrontation with her.

My brother-in-law came for me. He was a good guy and tried to make it easy. Laughing uncertainly, he said, "What the hell's going on? You don't look stinko to me." I said, "I'm not." Rising, I put on my shirt and jacket and turned to Mrs. C. She looked directly at me. "You think over what I told you," she said. I promised I would, and then I apologized again, mumbling the words. She said, "Oh, *posh,*" and waved me off. I wanted to say something else, something definite, but it eluded me. In the embarrassing lapse my brother-in-law said, "C'mon, c'mon, we're missing the Giants game!" To which I laughed and exclaimed, *"Jesus, yes,"* though for the first time in years I didn't at all care.

2

Cheers for Stout
Steve Owen

When Steve Owen, who coached the New York Giants from 1931 through 1953, died of a cerebral hemorrhage at his home in Oneida, New York, I debated for a day whether to make the trip south for the funeral. For a long time I had felt that I owed Owen such homage, and I'd never again be able to pay it. Envisioning the scene, I saw myself a kind of Owl-Eyes come to Gatsby's wake, a little aloof, sequestered from the one or two mourners, a curiosity weeping great, excited tears in the blue shade of funereal elms. The vision was as close as I came to such demonstrativeness.

In the hours after his death the newspapers began to name the many sports dignitaries who were to make their own pilgrimages to Oneida, the funeral began to assume the hues of an obligatorily festive occasion, and I sensed that genuine grief would be distasteful in such surroundings. I did write a note to Owen's widow. Quoting Brutus on Cassius (I have said that I teach English— pedagogically, I might add), I wrote with a tense, forced hand, *I owe more tears to this dead man than you shall see me pay.*

Appearing over a signature she wouldn't recognize, the message, it occurred to me, was not only pretentious but might bewilder and embarrass Mrs. Owen. In the end I did nothing to help put the ghost on its way. I had wanted to make the pilgrimage because it was Owen, as much as any other, who had brought me round to the Giants and made me a fan. Unable to conceive what my life would have been without football to cushion the knocks, I was sure I owed him sorrow. It occurs to me now that my enthusiasms might better have been placed with God or Literature or Humanity; but in the penumbra of such upper-case pieties I have always experienced an excessive timidity rendering me tongue-tied or forcing me to emit the brutal cynicisms with which the illiterate confront things they do not understand.

—

In the hot summer of 1953, after spending three unrewarding years (popping benzedrine tablets into my mouth, I recall the shiver-inducing snap and crack of new texts opened for the first time on the eve of final examinations) at the University of Southern California, I returned east to New York, an A.B. in English my portfolio, a longing in the heart the clue to my countenance. What did I long for? At twenty-three, I of course longed for fame. Not only did I long for it, I suffered myself the singular notion that fame was an heirloom passed on from my father. Dead at forty, which never obviates the stuff of myths, my father acquired over the years a nostalgic eminence in Watertown; and, like him, I wanted to have my name one day called back and bantered about in consecrated whispers. Perhaps unfairly to him (I have his scrapbooks and know what admirable feats are inventoried there), I'm not sure my father's legend was as attributable to his athletic prowess as to his personality. The tales men selected to pass on about him were never so much about a ninety-yard run as about an authentically colorful man having a ball and in an amiable way thumbing his nose at life.

In 1938, the day before President Roosevelt snipped the ceremonial ribbon opening the International Bridge spanning the Thousand Islands and uniting the U.S. with Canada, it is told, apocryphally or otherwise, that my father beat that exemplary poseur to the punch, with wire cutters severed the cable which had been strung across the bridge's entrance to bar *hoi polloi*, climbed into the back seat of a convertible roadster, and had himself driven over the arcing, sky-rising span, while in imitation of F.D.R. he sat magnificently in the back seat, his jaw thrust grandly out, and, hand aflutter, bestowed his benedictions on the lovely and (one somehow imagines) startled islands.

In the way of timorous women everywhere, my mother's life with my father was one of trepidation that some such shenanigan would eventually get him arrested, land his name on the back page of the Watertown *Daily Times*, and disgrace the family. The back page of our newspaper is the one Methodist ministers, old maids, and city councilmen turn to for forbidden transports; my mother viewed it as a source of eternal ruination for our local sinners; it never occurred to her that to an adult or jaded mentality such items might be viewed with tolerant or jolly sympathy; and for many years, whenever one of my acquaintances made that page, she had a distressing habit of reading the articles aloud to me, by way of object lessons. One man was arrested for drunken driving, challenged the arresting officer, and it eventually took three state policemen, using their billies, to get him into custody. "Good," I said. "I hope he busted all three of those fascist pigs in the nose." Another man I knew was indicted for the statutory rape of a fourteen-year-old girl. "Lovely age, fourteen," I remarked. "Same as Romeo's Juliet." In a Thousand Islands restaurant, still another acquaintance expectorated into a locally prominent attorney's spaghetti dinner. "Marvelous!" I exclaimed gleefully. "Remind me to buy that guy a drink!" That was the last object lesson my mother ever tried on me. In fairness to her, two years before my father's death there were sibilant and awful rumors of an intemperate fist fight in a barroom involving broken noses, bits of marrow, rich red blood, and many troopers; but if the newspaper's editors ever heard of it, in deference to my father they never printed it.

Once, when I was very small, I actually saw my father play football; but like the propagators of his legend I remember nothing about the game save that at one point in it an opposing player, whose cleats had been removed to expose the sharp steel screws that held them (a customary bit of nastiness among the old-timers), stepped on my father's hand, tearing it rather badly. The field where the game was being played was without bleachers, and what crowd there was stood huddled behind the players' benches, the Watertown fans behind ours and those of the opposing team across the field behind theirs. For the first time that day I was to discover that it was a crowd to which my father was very precisely attuned. My father had left the playing field and was standing bent over before our bench, holding the wrist of his right hand with his left, exposing the wound. It was a nasty, jagged tear; it bled profusely, a heavy, brilliant, crimson blood; and the trainer no sooner began pouring iodine into it than my father let out a high, fierce, almost girl-

ish howl, one that—representing, as he did to me, the epitome of strength and courage—immediately induced in me
the urge to scream in terror. But then, almost as suddenly,
the substitutes on the bench, the crowd behind them, and
even the trainer who was ministering to the wound were
uproarious with glee, were bellowing and guffawing, slapping their thighs and pounding each other's backs, and I
saw that my father was parodying how a lesser man might
react to iodine. Suspended between tears and laughter, I
stood there listening to the gleeful homage of the crowd;
then I, too, began to laugh, hysterically, wildly, until my father looked up at me, surprised and not a little upset, recognizing what had transpired. It was the first time the
crowd had come between my father and me, and I became
aware that other people understood in him qualities I did
not—a knowledge that gave them certain claims on him. It
is a terrifying thing to have a wedge driven into one's narrow circle of love.

In later years I was, of course, to become very aware of
this wedge, and to learn to despise it, particularly on brilliant autumn Saturdays. Hand in hand, on those fall mornings, we strolled about the Public Square, ostensibly "on
errands"; but the nature of these errands was vague (I don't
ever remember bearing home for lunch so much as a lettuce head) and more of a leisurely ceremonial, the supernumerary method through which my father assured
himself of his continuing fable. We could not go a hundred
feet without being accosted by all manner of men. My father talked with the town elders and the town dregs, with
pompous counselors and their least estimable clients, and
as likely as not these men revealed to him things of the
most distressingly intimate nature. My father was, surpris-

ingly, *a listener.* He had a way of tilting his head plaintively to one side and pursing his lips in a solemn, commiserating way; he always looked directly at his confessors. A baroque fountain commanded the grassy, tree-shaded island at the center of the square; confronted with the contemplative, strong, open, and sympathetic face of my father, men seemed to hurl their fastidiousness, as the fountain did its spray, into the air; and with no furtiveness whatever made public exposure of deluded passions, heartfelt betrayals, and timid sins. Though not an educated man, my father was a man of mercurial intelligence. If he believed the grief to be of a passing nature, he took the man's story and reworded it in a droll way that often left the mourner in helpless and profoundly grateful laughter. On the other hand, he had a singular, unnerving habit with those men past articulating their petulance, their rage, their sorrow. Grotesque, crooked, repulsive, wasted, pitiably drunk, they looked through watery-red eyes and jabbered away in what, to me, might just as well have been Zulu. With his free hand, my father always touched these men. Listening as deferentially as ever he listened to the Mayor, my father gripped them tightly on the upper arm, patted them affectionately on the back, occasionally even put his muscular arm about their bent, emaciated shoulders. Whenever he talked to these men, I always squeezed his free hand fiercely and looked over my shoulder to see if anyone was watching us. One day my father asked me if I was ashamed to have him talk with these men. The question came unexpectedly, and I stammered, "No! No!" But when I looked up at my father, I saw that he knew otherwise, and that he was sad.

It was in the afternoon at the Fair Grounds, where the high school played their games, that my father's autumn

Saturdays reached a kind of culmination. He never—or so it seems to me now—paid to go anyplace. Doors opened before his growing legend, and through the one into the high school games he took not only himself and me but every scrawny-kneed, matty-haired, nose-running, jug-eared, obscenity-prone kid in town, boys orphaned by a depression that had left them without the price of their dignity. We never stepped onto the grounds without being surrounded by a multitude of these boys, and there always ensued a scene my father loved, though in its way it was a small-town and grotesque parody of the public figure. "Hey, Ex!" they bellowed in beseechment. "Hey, Ex! Hey! How 'bout gettin' us in? Hey! Would cha?" My father teased. He wasn't certain. He would have to think about it. Folding his arms on his chest and tilting his head in the way he had, he surveyed them. On tiptoes, mouths agape, they were a strikingly comical picture of impatience (comical to me now: they seemed then lamentable). They knew my father was going to take them in. Now was no time for teasing. The game's imminence was in the atmosphere; and from across the way, behind the pale-orange stands, one could hear the gradually rising roar of the crowd signaling the kickoff. Now they jiggled about in something like anger—as they had a right to do; they were subjected to this chafing every week. Always at this point my father dropped his arms to his sides, lifted his head, smiled, said, "Okay! Let's go!" and "Don't forget: tell the man at the gate you're my sons!" "We know!" they shouted. "We know all about it!" Then I joined the group, indistinguishable from all the rest. Leading my father who trotted behind us, we broke into a furious run toward the gate. The gateman was both moody and deferential, like a culturally inclined manservant. Moments before he had unquestionably been kicking these boys in the ass for trying to sneak in, and he had now to undergo his weekly humiliation. "These are all my boys!" came my father's voice from behind us. The gateman smiled weakly, grudgingly, and stepped aside as we crushed our way through the narrow entrance. One of the boys, safely inside, invariably shouted back at him: "Yeah! Earl's my ol' man, yuh fucking rat!" I never heard that declaimer without the blood rushing to my face. And not because of the obscenity.

———

Other men might inherit from their fathers a head for figures, a gold pocket watch all encrusted with the oxidized green of age, or an eternally astonished expression; from mine I acquired this need to have my name whispered in reverential tones. There were, that summer in New York, other things I longed for. I wanted the wealth and the power that fame would bring; and finally, I wanted love— or said that I did, though I know now that what I wanted was the adulation of the crowd, and that *love* was just a word that crowded so many other, more appropriate words off the tongue. Having no precise idea how to achieve these things, I told myself I would one day write The Big Book; but I can understand now that I never believed I would. At college I had written only one story—"A Portrait of Constriction"—which possessed any merit whatever, and this but a tentative feeling for the language. Aside from this grievously asinine tale—its first line was: "I am a spider without filament; I extend to no place"—my literary efforts ran from soggy-soda-cracker sentimentality to worse, and those professors who were kind to those efforts would have been kinder to inform me I had neither the talent, ambition, nor syntax to write even a bad book. In Liebling's phrase, I could not "write for free seeds." Knowing nothing about writing, I had no trouble seeing myself famous. If, according to a reviewer, So-and-So had written a "masterpiece," I quite facilely imagined myself as So-and-So. "Frederick Exley," I read over the review, "has written a masterpiece"; then I smiled pleasurably as, in the imperative yet chummy style of so many reviewers, half counseling, half admonishing, the astute critic added, "You'd better read it."

This dubious fame would have to wait until some future time. First I would get a splendid job in public relations or advertising, rent an apartment, and begin lining the walls with the shelves to hold my books. For that apartment I would also get a girl. I once had a very clear picture of her: she was to have a degree from Vassar (I was willing to go as low as a B.A. in Fine Arts from Wellesley); she must have bobbed, blond hair, green eyes, and golden, vibrant legs; to offset my increasing "melancholy," I determined that she must be a gregarious girl, spontaneously witty, and capable of thunderous laughter; still, apart from this delightfully fresh façade, I conceived her adept in the most "enlightened" sexual acts. She was to allay the ache in my heart, and when the ache disappeared and contentment reigned, I would get down to the distressing chore of acquiring Genius. I believed this, too; none of my professors, talking about books in their even, slightly somber tones, had bothered to tell me that literature is born out of the very longing I was so seeking to repress.

———

The ache stayed, the Vassar-bred nymph never materialized, and the bookish apartment turned out to be free room and chow at the house of an aunt (a widowed schoolteacher) in upper Westchester. It was a compromise with my fantasies which still amazes me, for few young men have come to New York better armed to conquer the city than I. It was a compromise which might never have been necessary had I not, one scalding June day, bestowed on New York City a quality it may or may not possess—magnanimity.

My chums at USC were, like me, outcasts: poker and horse players, drunken veterans, petulant instructors, would-be novelists, homosexuals, talentless poets, an occasional Negro, all the patrons of an off-campus bistro on Jefferson Boulevard. There a few weeks before my graduation, in league with some friends of mine, a Negro homosexual and his beloved, a frail, brilliant, and gentle blond boy (a psychology major, naturally), a new Frederick Exley capable of storming the high and indifferent towers of Manhattan was created. Because our preparations were absolute in their abominable cynicism, we must have felt those towers not only indifferent but nigh invincible. Setting a pitcher of beer (one we kept full throughout the long afternoon) on the table with a stack of white-lined paper, sharpened pencils, and a job-hunting tome entitled *Go Get the Job You Want!,* we conspired on a creation that severely indicted either us or that world we were seeking to impress.

I haven't a copy of the résumé or covering letter we fashioned that afternoon, but I remember enough of the résumé so that thinking of it even now forces the blood to my face and arouses a giddiness in me. Most of it was created by my friends, facts assembled, put down, and rewritten in an exhilarating zealousness that swung them, pendulum-like, between violent laughter and spitting bitterness, that even caused between them arguments over what and what not to include. It was a bitterness enhanced by the tacit but real knowledge that, being what they were (and they were very gay), they could never hope to enter the world whose door I was trying to unlatch, an exclusion that only whetted their desire to force themselves, through me, into that world. At the top of the résumé, under "Personal Data," we listed my name, age, and address, and from that point on anything resembling truth, save for "Race: Caucasian" (which, of course, was included on the Negro's squealing insistence: "You'se a white man, Freddy boy!"), was purely fortuitous. We listed as my religion "Episcopalian" ("All the shits are Episcopalian!" the blond said), as my birthplace "London, England," my nationality as "English-American" (whatever in the world that might be). We listed with little regard for truth my "Courses of Study and Grades Received," and following the pattern of résumés as set forth by the job-hunting wizard, we created a heading called "Extracurricular Activities and Academic Distinctions Received." It was under this sweeping banner that the résumé reached its peripheral absurdity: Sigma Chi Fraternity, vice president and social chairman (I was never in the place); Sigma Tau Delta, national English honorary society (I didn't know there was such an organization till the Negro included it and explained to me what it was); football, '51, '52 (at USC? Brother!); literary critic for *The Daily Trojan* (for this newspaper I straight-facedly reported one story about a USC alumnus who, having published a book about his escape from the bondage of booze, was arrested in downtown Los Angeles for disorderly conduct and public intoxication; the editor read it, laughed, said he daren't print it: I quit); editor of *Wampus,* the college humor magazine (there was such a sheet, but its mirth was never in evidence); president of Scribes Creative Writing Club (at USC there was no such presumption); and recording secretary of the USC Young Republican Club (I am not now, sir, nor ever have been a young or an old Republican). Under the final heading, "Hobbies and Outside Interests," we listed everything from Elizabethan Drama to golf to Renaissance Art to sailing to Early American Antiques, trying to convey the image of an indescribably well-rounded and right-thinking young man; we did so by alternating one lower-case piece of Americana with one upper-case intellectual pretension, skin-diving with Linguistics.

Of the covering letter created that day I remember only the first two lines: "How does one get into this business? I have asked myself that question a hundred times." It was, I do remember, composed with great fastidiousness, its tone was numbingly earnest, and its contents were just asinine enough to draw forty-odd replies from the sixty or so I mailed out to public relations and advertising firms. About half of these replies were from men who would "be delighted to chat" with me about the possibilities at ———.

One scalding June morning a month later, I found myself walking up Park Avenue on my way to the first of these chats when suddenly, altogether unexpectedly, I felt a twinge of panic. Stopping, I pulled under the awning of a store front, out of the sun. Even prior to this, I had experienced another kind of panic. A few days before leaving Los Angeles, as part of my program to assault the big town, I had purchased a new suit—the only one I owned. Out there the suit had seemed completely right, but I had only to walk two blocks up Park Avenue and watch the men nod approvingly at each other's snug-shouldered splendor

(New York is the only city in the country where I have noticed this peculiar effeminacy) to see that it was unequivocally wrong, nearly disastrous. It was steel-gray—in the bright sun it had sheen—and California-cut, with those wide, dandified lapels that run all the way down to one's belly before a button can be detected; it had those monstrously padded shoulders, making my neck appear a lily shoot rising from a pile of *papier-mâché* boulders. Its effect was unalterably wrong, and I was walking along smarting somewhat from this sartorial deficiency when, as I say, I suddenly experienced something more provocatively wrong. I stopped because for the first time it occurred to me that certain false information in the résumé might elicit from the interviewer questions I wasn't prepared to answer. Thus I removed a copy of it from my shiny new attaché case and started studying it. That was as close to the interview as I ever got, as close to that or any of the interviews my friends had worked so passionately to get me. For suddenly I saw my father as I had seen him last. Perhaps to the question, "Born in London I see, Fred?" I was suavely responding, "Yes, chap, Pops was with our Embassy there; of course, we left London when I was only two, so I, heh, heh, heh, don't remember too much—" Whatever, it must have concerned my father, for he rose before me as I had seen him last—in his casket.

As Dr. D. was to remind me in the emergency room of the hospital so many years later, my father was "tough." He was not a big man, standing five feet, nine or ten; but over that height was spread a solid one hundred and eighty-five pounds, a weight that he carried on hard, heavy, and lightning-quick legs, walking with the precise, pigeon-toed, and slightly affected steps of so many athletes. He supported his family by climbing telephone poles for the Niagara Mohawk (until he was fired for fighting); and when I think of him now, I think of rough-cotton work shirts open at the collar, a broad masculine face made ruddy by exposure, and a Camel cigarette dangling from the corner of his pensive mouth. There was nothing about him that did not suggest his complete awareness that he got his bread by the sweat of his brow and the power of his back. He seemed almost the prototype of the plebeian. Yet my father had more refined dreams. Like most athletes he lived amidst the large deeds and ephemeral glories of the past, recalling a time when it must have seemed to him he had been more Elevated, and this continual and melancholy look into the past had drawn his brows into a knot, giving him a look of unmistakable hostility. Moreover, in an attempt to more vividly re-create that past, my father drank—I was about to say *too much*, which would not be entirely accurate. My father could not, or so my mother recalls, drink even the most limited amounts of beer without becoming moody, argumentative, and even violent; and on one occasion he beat a man so badly that the man had to have pulled what few teeth my father left him.

The man himself told me the story many years after my father's death. He was drunk and he bore my father no grudge. He implied that it had been his own fault. He said, "I wanna see your ol' man was tough as said"; here he smiled the remorseful, tolerant smile with which one views youth's intemperance. *"He was,"* he said. The man seemed to look on his dentures as a kind of trophy and kept calling them "Earl Exley's teeth." At one point he removed the plates from his mouth and laid them on the bar, beaming a drunken smile through elastic lips. Looking at the teeth, I was struck with the notion that they were not real false teeth at all but one of those vulgar novelty toys, and I expected that at any moment they might begin chattering away in a terrible chopping motion as they started moving down the beer-stained bar. I excused myself, told the man I was happy to have made his acquaintance, and left him staring affectionately at Earl Exley's teeth.

In death, my father was another matter. He was, of course, tough no more. The lung cancer had done its job superbly; where he had once seemed to epitomize the plebeian, he might, in death, have been a patrician, perhaps a great poet who had died young. Outwardly calm, he looked as if he had been consumed by his vision, a wraithlike votary rendered dumb with excess of knowledge. But I was unable to sustain such images. He weighed seventy-nine pounds, and in one of those unforgivable jests we permit that profession to make on our corpses, the undertaker had removed the fixed and melancholy scowl; this, together with the wasted body, the carmine rouge and lipstick, and the heavy, sensual odor of moribund roses, conspired to gravely compromise his manhood. There was nothing here to suggest the interminable, anguishing months of his dying, an anguish that in its later stages reached such a peak that a young doctor, in a fit of impotent pique, had had to strike my father across the face. I don't blame the man. My father had reached the point where maximum amounts of morphine no longer afforded comfort, and I suppose that the novice, terrified by his inability any longer to minister to my father's unearthly pleas for calm, had struck out, not at my father but at his own ignorance. Still, it was quite a while before I understood and forgave. For years I harbored the secret yearning to seek out that surgeon, to knock him down, and to kick his teeth through the back of his skull.

No, now there was nothing to suggest either the kind of man my father had been or the life he had led. In death he carried with him the aristocratic nicety of drawing rooms, the inane chatter of teacups. At St. Paul's church, a stranger in a profound-blue, rigidly cut, and expensive-looking suit wailed for all of us. His eyes were protected by great, green shades, from under which poured rivulets of shiny tears; once or twice there issued from him, amidst his crushing, incessant sobbing, an animal-like, tortured sound so terrible that provincial heads cranked themselves about, bringing every eye in that crowded chapel to him, eyes that made no more impression on him than a soft, beneficent rain. No one knew who he was. But afterward there was much surmise; and it was finally decided, against any evidence to the contrary, that he had been a boyhood friend of my father, one who was said to have "gone away young" and become a Prince of Industry.

That was how I remembered my father that June day on Park Avenue, while I stood in the shade of the awning—stood naked and stony with shame. On my father's death, and even that day on Park Avenue, I had not known whether I loved him or not, whether he was the Earl Exley who "beat up on" people or the man whose strong hands went out to the dregs of this world. I was younger then and wanted to apprehend the world in terms of thrust and parry, of point and counterpoint, and could not see that he was both men and that in order to live successfully I would have to love both. Had such a thing happened today, I know I could have gone through with the interview, fake, suave father and all. My father was not without his subtlety and his humor, and I know he would have got rather a kick out of the whole business. But the denial of one's father, in whatever spirit, requires great sympathy between the denier and the denied, and this my father and I had never had.

How long I stood glued in abasement to the store front I don't know, perhaps an hour, perhaps only moments; but eventually I began to walk, at first tentatively, like an invalid just liberated from the sedentary months of his sickbed, taking one precious step and then another until, by a truly enormous effort of will, there came into my step the spirited scrupulosity of a man knowing exactly what he is about. I spent most of that torpid, shimmering day walking, frequently stopping at corner saloons to sip pensively on draft beer. Very late in the afternoon, for no reason I can think of, I took a ferry to New Jersey, went to a saloon, drank a half-dozen beers, and headed back. It was coming back that I saw the city for the first time. Standing in the tuglike prow, while the cool spray of the Hudson mingled with the sunshine, I looked up through the mist of heat and water and saw, to my astonishment, not many towers but one august pillar of gold. Its golden shadow on the water was like an arm stretched forth in benediction, promising that it would deny me nothing. Hans Christian Andersen came to mind: I saw him come fresh from Odense in his ill-fitting confirmation suit, looking for the first time at the wonder of Copenhagen. Thinking thus of him, I made one of those wild, regrettable vows to which youth are prone: I vowed that those things, literary fame *et al.*, would come to me—and come to me on my own terms. What had I to do with fake fathers, with artifice and legerdemain? The city commanded me to stay, and in obeisance I did in my mind's eye reach out and offer up my hand. It was at that moment I granted the city magnanimity.

—

After that unnerving day my approach to the job market took a new tack. My knowledge of the advertising–public relations world had been culled from lightheaded novels and nonsensical movies, especially *The Hucksters* starring the late and peerless Mr. Gable. Recalling how a nattily pin-striped Clark, after blowing his last fifty dollars on a hand-painted four-in-hand, had walked casually into a superbly appointed advertising agency and complacently announced that for "twenty-five thousand per" he would permit himself to be considered for employment, I derived the grandiloquently absurd notion that the way to fame and fortune in New York lay in playing it cool. I became The Cool Man, though there were of necessity certain differences between Gable's approach and mine. Where in the movie Gable *had been* an advertising man, I was—well, a *Poet,* and, determined to remain glued to this vision of myself, I began a round of interviews in which I attempted to convey to prospective employers that on the far side of their desks Genius resided, that I considered both them and advertising to be monumental frauds, but that, in exchange for certain sums of money (say, ten thousand a year), I would use that genius to sell cornflakes. It was to be a kind of Mephistophelean pact in which they would pay me until that time when the apartment and the Vassar blonde materialized, and I could get down to the business of realizing my talent. Where, in scene after scene of the movie, Gable had been resplendent in pin stripes, charcoal grays, and midnight blues, I had only one shiny suit, which now became perfect for my purposes—just hideous enough to keep me hopelessly removed from the world of my interviewer. Where for character Gable had his famous mustache, I bought a Yello-Bole which, stuck in my teeth, gave me, I thought, a properly ruminative air. Finally, for the *coup de grâce,* I substituted for Gable's striking Homburg a coiffure modeled after an idol of the moment, Truman Capote; though I had then no knowledge of that writer's appreciable talents, I knew that, like me, he was young, and that, as I hoped to be, he was famous. Simply by my neglecting to comb it, my hair now cascaded down my forehead in piquant little bangs. Thus attired, my pipe between my teeth, my hair in a state of wondrous disarray, I was ready to suggest to the communications industry that it was in the presence of Genius.

The interviews themselves? Ah, well, all this happened fifteen years ago, and even now, at the oddest moments, taking a shower or patting a stray dog, I will suddenly remember, hardly knowing whether to thunder with laughter or hide my head under a pillow. If I was kept waiting beyond a carefully scrutinized five minutes, there was no interview! Rising from my chair and ambling over to the man's secretary, I would bow ever so slightly, the very image of genteel breeding; then suddenly, bringing myself up to a dictatorially rigid posture, I would proclaim, my tone controlled but testy: "I'm sorry, young lady, but will you tell your employer that Mr. Exley had other commitments and couldn't wait. If he wishes to set up another appointment and begin it at the—ah—designated time"—I would be looking at my empty wrist as though it contained a hundred-jewel job—"then he knows where to reach me." Clicking my heels slightly and smiling my distant smile, I would depart, saying, *"Adieu,* my dear, *adieu,"* terribly certain I had rendered the girl sexually tractable. To those luckless men more disposed to life's proprieties, those who began the interview on time, I didn't so much walk as drift—I was absolutely wispy—into their carpeted offices where, into their outstretched and eager glad-hands, I would lay a hand as limp and clammy as a dishrag, quite as though I expected them to kiss it! Then, surveying the room with a distastefully arch expression which found the appointments irreparably vulgar, I would fling myself into a chair, stick my Yello-Bole into my jaw, and to their preliminary and "ice-breaking" questions begin issuing a sequence of noises not unlike hog noises.

Their questions ran pretty much to a pattern, and for them I had stock replies. If I was asked if I thought I could sell chocolate bars, I always answered in the most negative of ways, saying, "I haven't the foggiest idea." Then I would smile my smile as though to add, "But, of course, my dear, you can see that I'm a genius; and I'm certain we can work out some satisfactory arrangement wherein I will try to sell your imbecilic peanut brittle." Only once during these interviews did I rise out of my shrieking indifference; it was to a question which, after a number of interviews, I knew would invariably be asked.

"Why do you want to work for HKI & W?"

To this preposterous assumption I would come up icily in my chair, fix the interviewer with a deadly menacing gaze—he might have just swatted me right across the face with his desk lamp—and snap, "I'm not at all sure I want to work for HKI & W. Just suppose you tell me *why I should* want to work for HKI & W."

More often than not, taking the offensive had the desired effect, proving so disarming to the man that he was rendered momentarily dumb. Recovering himself, he would be off on a litany of reasons why HKI & W and I could make a marriage: paid vacations, hospitalization, good working conditions, annual bonuses; while I, in what must have been an infuriating response, shook my head *no*, decidedly *no*, to every inducement save high salary, as though I considered them all totally irrelevant. "We'll call you," they'd say, extending their glad-hands. No doubt remembering our opening handshake, they would then redfacedly withdraw these hands. I would smile knowingly, as though I never for a moment doubted that indeed they'd call.

Did I really believe I'd get a job in this way? It would be easy for me to say that I didn't, that for some perverse reason, masochism or a neurotic need to be rejected—a possibility to which I would later in my life give great weight—I was willfully acting in such a way as to alienate myself. But I doubt the validity of this. I had large faith—the faith of youth—in the city's capacity to absorb me, hair-do and all; and it was only after summer was gone and autumn was casting long shadows that I began to take these rejections as personal affronts. It is very wearing to be honest, no matter how naïve or misreckoned that honesty is, and continue to be spurned for it. After a time it becomes numbing, like heavy, repeated blows to the face. I spent a lot of time that autumn on my aunt's davenport, watching slow-legged, sexless women in soap operas drink coffee and weep into each other's teatless bosoms while I spun the ever-increasingly detailed fantasy I called my future.

After a time I developed another outlet for my mounting fury, and it was this more than anything which prevented me from slipping over into that state the world seems so facilely prepared to pronounce psychotic. Each morning I found in the *Times* the most ludicrous advertisement and answered it. I always answered other advertisements, but it was only after I had answered the former that I could get on to those that might reasonably hold out hope of a job to me. Now these advertisements, the most puerile, were generally display advertisements and could be found anywhere from the classified to the sports to the financial sections:

> This shop is looking for an intelligent, ambitious young man interested in becoming a copywriter—one who won't wilt like a tired flower under a little sound, even harsh criticism, one who isn't afraid of a hard knock or two, one who, in short, can roll with a punch and come out fighting. Write Box ———.

Occasionally I spent an hour, even two, composing my replies, wanting them to be exactly right. It was only after they were completed, placed in an addressed envelope, and sealed that I was able to get on to answering those more reasonable advertisements.

> Hard knocks? I used to have a boss who rapped me on the head just for kicks. He was a stupid bastard, though. From him I didn't learn a thing, save that working for a stupid bastard is without profit—humiliating, loathsome, and utterly demoralizing. With you—and it is obvious from your advertisement that you are a man of high parts—it would be different. When you begin bouncing me off the ropes, just make sure I get the point. Okay? Then, after a time, I'll be as knowledgeable and as flinty as you, and together of course we'll live in your—shop, isn't it?—as miserable sons-of-bitches forever after.

It was due to such an advertisement and the foregoing reply, or one not unlike it, that one day in late autumn I found myself in the presence of a man I will here call Cary Grant. When I received his letter asking me to stop by and see him, I thought my name had come to him from one of the placement agencies I was dealing with: I didn't ordinarily sign my name to these letters, preferring to sign them Billy Earnest or Wilbur Straightshooter, giving my address as the Waldorf Towers or the Plaza. It was only when he handed me the letter and asked, "Did you write this?" that I realized that through some grievous mistake I had signed my own name. Even prior to this I had felt thoroughly intimidated by Mr. Grant. He looked not unlike that movie man, a tall, dark, and suavely graying man with an ocher complexion, the product no doubt of many hours spent in southern suns. He wore a royal-blue suit that didn't so much fit as lie against him, a soft blue button-down shirt, and an expensive-looking and brilliantly shaded maroon-and-gold four-in-hand. On his feet—and he casually kept one foot on his huge, uncluttered mahogany desk throughout the interview—he wore black, grained shoes that appeared to weigh about five pounds apiece; though I had never before been conscious of seeing a pair, I knew they were the goods: *custom-made.* He was, in brief, the kind of man who makes other men feel pale by comparison. It was a discomfort he was aware of arousing. Even before he said anything to me, he spent many moments looking me up and down, over and around, and all the time he smiled, as though I were striking in him some humorous chord and it was all he could do to restrain himself from laughter. It was a smile that had me trying to hide my scuffed-up shoes beneath my chair, brushing my bangs from my forehead, and staring uneasily at the deep, Chianti-colored carpeting. Then he handed me the letter and asked me about it. I read it over and over again, even in a groping and moronic way mouthing the words, as if I were actually having trouble appraising it as my handiwork. I was of course stalling, as I could not imagine—save for the worst: postal inspectors waiting in the wings to spirit me off for conveying obscene material through the mails—why in the world he had written me.

"Know why I sent for you?" he said finally, obviously cognizant of my bewilderment.

I smiled blankly. "No."

"Because you remind me of myself twenty years ago. Arrogant. Snotty. Got a hard-on for the world."

I smiled blankly. "Oh."

He paused, obviously determining the best way to proceed. He smiled that unnerving smile: he had obviously hit on the best way. He told me that if I were Hemingway I should go to Paris, live on fried potatoes and ketchup, write The Great American Novel and have done with it; but that if I wanted to go into advertising—which I think even he conceded to be a rather absurd business—I should meet that world on its own terms. He, of course, didn't care a good damn whether I went into the business or not. The truth of his words was having its effect on me. The blood was hot, constant, and throbbing in my face; the room had begun to drift away beneath me: I was stony with shame. There was an agonizingly lengthy pause now. From the comments that followed, I determined that he must have been judging how much of my appearance was attributable to indigence and how much to affectation, and that he settled the balance on the latter. "For Christ's sake," he said. "Look at those shoes. They haven't been polished since you bought 'em. And that goddam suit. Ever hear of a dry cleaner?" I didn't do or say anything until he got to my hair, which, he said, might go just "swell down in the Village," but would hardly inspire confidence in the Wildroot people. "It's all part of the game, *kid.* Either play it by the rules or forget about it."

I attempted to be master of the situation: "Look—look here—" but my words came out in stammers. "I came up here to—in good faith—"

"Oh, cut the whining!" he said. "You write me a letter like this"—and here he rattled the air violently with my letter—"and you expect me to treat you like a goddam prima donna! Brother!"

I was on my feet then, trembling. When I looked at him, I meant to ask, very evenly, "Just how fucking tough are you?" Bringing my eyes up to his with great and dramatic deliberation, I was right on the verge of speaking when he laughed; and I did, too, laughed easily and without self-consciousness. I laughed because in his laughter there was now neither cold detachment nor condescension, but the sense that we were sharing some grand joke: his laughter seemed as much directed at himself as at me. Together we roared, as people do who have carried a confrontation with each other to its distressingly uncomfortable limits and suddenly have safely passed those limits. For a moment I thought of resuming my seat. He was the first man I had met in New York who seemed neither diffident nor, quite frankly, dishonest. I liked him. But I was in those days much given to self-dramatization and believed that, once on my feet, I should leave lest he take my staying as a kind of submission and invitation to continue his abuse.

Later I was to recall that he asked, with something like concern, where and why I was going, but by then it was already too late. Before leaving I wanted to say something to him. He had so successfully intimidated me up to this point that it occurred to me he did not know the real sound of my voice. In college I had gone about with a brilliant, balding Boston-Irishman, Slattery, who was much given to a certain expression: "You're some sack of potatoes, *you* are." At the moment before turning and leaving, that is what I said to Grant. They were the weirdest words that ever issued from my mouth; the voice was not mine at all but my balding, Irish friend's!

———

The next few days were among the longest and least comfortable of my life. No sooner had I reached the haven of my aunt's couch than it occurred to me that Grant had been the city I had been seeking all along—the magnanimous city. What else, I reasoned, could he have done but hire me after subjecting me to such humiliation? Whether or not this was the case, in my mind I played out that interview over and over again, trying to inject into its slightest nuances the most preposterous import. I might be there yet, the scene having expanded itself into an O'Neill-like drama, had I not read in the newspapers that Steve Owen was being fired.

For months I hadn't been able to read anything except advertisements. Sustaining my literary fantasy had required such fierce concentration that my energies were not in long enough supply for even cursory reading, but now, in boredom, I forced myself to read. Even then I did not at first understand what was happening to Owen. The newspapers kept using the euphemisms "retiring" and "resigning," and it was only after I had gone to the columnists that I began to piece together the truth. When I did so, I was outraged. Owen had always maintained that defenses win football games, professional football was increasingly deferring to the forward pass as the ultimate and only weapon, and apparently Owen was being asked to step aside by men whose vision of the game proclaimed it unalterably given over to offensive techniques. These "men" were of course shadowy, never identified; but one had only to understand the childishly petulant character of the New York sportswriter (he takes every New York defeat as if he had been out there having his own face rubbed in the dirt) to know who the men were. Owen had been losing for a number of years now, and the writers had been on him. Victorious, there was something nauseatingly reprehensible in their doleful, sentimental invitations to the public to come to the Polo Grounds on Sunday to witness Owen's swan song as head coach.

I would never have left the davenport that murderously damp Sunday had I not read that Frank Gifford was starting for the Giants at halfback. When I read that, my mind—as isolated minds are wont to do, offered the least stimulation—began to fabricate for itself a rather provocative little drama. I began to imagine how wonderful it would be if Gifford single-handedly devastated the Detroit Lions as a farewell present for Owen. I had had encounters with both of these men at different times in my life. In a way both had given me something, Gifford a lesson in how to live with one's scars, and Owen no less than perhaps my first identity as a human being. And so that bleak, cold Sunday, I rose—to the astonishment of my aunt, I might add—from the davenport, bundled up as warmly as I could, took the commuting train to Grand Central, sought directions to the Polo Grounds, and got on the subway to the Bronx.

—

I met Steve Owen in the late thirties or early forties, when I was somewhere between the ages of eight and eleven. I suspect it was closer to the time I was eight, for I remember very little of what was said, remembering more the character of the meeting—that it was not an easy one. My father introduced me to him, or rather my father, when the atmosphere was most strained and the conversation had lagged, shoved me in front of Owen and said, "This is my son, Fred."

"Are you tough?" Owen said.

"Pardon, sir?"

"Are you tough?"

"I don't know, sir."

Owen looked at my father. "Is he tough, Mr. Exley?"

Though more than anything I wanted my father to say that I was, I was not surprised at his answer.

"It's too soon to tell."

Owen was surprised, though. He had great blondish-red eyebrows, which above his large rimless glasses gave him an astonished expression. Now he looked baffled. As the meeting had not been a comfortable one to begin with, he said in a tone that signaled the end of the conversation, *"I'm sure he's tough, Mr. Exley."* Turning abruptly on his heels, he walked across the lobby to the elevator of his hotel, where this meeting took place.

This was a few years after my father had quit playing football, when he was managing Watertown's semiprofessional team, the Red and Black. A team which took on all challengers and invariably defeated them, they were so good that—stupefying as it seems—the ostensible reason for our journey to New York had been to discuss with

Owen the possibility of the Red and Black's playing in exhibition against the Giants. I say "stupefying" now; but that is retrospectively fake sophistication: I thought we could beat the Giants then, and I use the "we" with the glibness of one who was committed unalterably to the team's fortunes—the water boy. On the wall in the bar of the Watertown Elks' Club hangs a picture of that team; seated on the ground before the smiling, casual, and disinterested players is an anguishingly solemn boy—the solemnity attesting to the esteem in which I held my station. I can still remember with what pride I trotted, heavy water bucket and dry towels in hand, onto the field to minister to the combatants' needs. Conversely, I recall the shame I experienced one day when, the team's having fallen behind, the captain decided to adopt a spartan posture and deprive his charges of water, and he had ordered me back from the field, waving me off when I was almost upon the huddle. My ministrations denied in full view of the crowd, I had had to turn and trot, red-faced, back to the bench. Yes, I believed we could beat the Giants then. Long before Owen so adroitly put my father down, though, I had come to see that the idea of such a contest was not a good one.

The trip began on a depressing note. The night before we were to leave, my father got loaded and ran into a parked car, smashing in the front fenders of our Model A Ford roadster. It was one time—in retrospect—that my father's drinking seems excusable. Such a journey in those days was one of near-epic proportions, made only at intervals of many years and at alarming sacrifices to the family budget; I have no doubt that that night my father was tremulous with apprehension, caught up in the spirit of *bon voyage,* and that he drank accordingly. Be that as it may, because he was drunk he left the scene of the accident; and the next day, fearing that the police might be searching for a damaged car, my mother wouldn't let him take the Ford from the garage. For many hours it was uncertain whether we should make the trip at all; but at the last moment, more, I think, because I had been promised the trip than for any other reason, it was decided we should go on the train.

We rode the whole night sitting up in the day coach, without speaking. My father was hung over, deeply ashamed, and there was a horrifying air of furtiveness hanging over us, as if we were fleeing some unspeakable crime. As a result, the trip—which might have been a fantastic adventure— never rose above this unhappy note. In New York we shared a room at the YMCA (I can remember believing that only the impossibly rich ever stayed in hotels), and the visit was a series of small, debilitating defeats: bland, soggy food eaten silently in barnlike automats; a room that varied arbitrarily between extreme heat and cold; a hundred and one missed subway connections; the Fordham-Pittsburgh game's having been sold out; the astonishment I underwent at no one's knowing my father; and finally, the fact that our meeting with Owen, which I had been led to believe was prearranged, was nothing more than wishful thinking on my father's part.

I don't know how many times we went to Owen's hotel, but each time we were told that he was "out." Each time we returned to the YMCA a little more tired, a little more defeated, and with each trip the Giant players whose names I knew, Strong and Cuff and Leemans and Hein, began to loom as large and forbidding as the skyscrapers. At one point I knew, though I daren't say so to my father, that the idea of such a game was preposterous. Moreover, for the first time in my life I began to understand the awesome vanity and gnawing need required to take on New York City with a view to imposing one's personality on the place. This was a knowledge that came to haunt me in later years.

It was not until my father, his voice weary, suggested that we make one final trip to the hotel that I saw that he, too, was disheartened. All the way there I prayed that Owen would still be "out." I had come to see that the meeting was undesired by him, and I feared the consequences of our imposition. The moment we walked into the lobby, however, the desk clerk (who had, I'm sure, come to feel sorry for us) began furiously stabbing the air in the direction of a gruff-looking, bespectacled, and stout man rolling, seaman-like, in the direction of the elevator—a fury that could only have signaled that it was he, Owen. My father moved quickly across the lobby, stopped him, and began the conversation that ended with Owen's *I'm sure he's tough, Mr. Exley.* As I say, I don't remember a good deal of the conversation prior to my being introduced; I do remember that Owen, too, thought the idea of such a contest ridiculous. Worse than that, my father had already been told as much by mail, and I think that his having made the trip in the face of such a refusal struck Owen as rather nervy, accounting for the uneasiness of the meeting. On Owen's leaving, I did not dare look at my father. It wasn't so much that I had ever lived in fear of him as that I had never before seen any man put him down, and I was not prepared to test his reaction to a humiliation which I had unwittingly caused. Moreover, my father's shadow was so imposing that I had scarcely ever, until that moment, had any identity of my own. At the same time I had yearned to emulate and become my father, I had also longed for his destruction. Steve Owen not only gave me identity; he proved to me my father was vulnerable.

—

On the subway going up to the Polo Grounds, I was remembering that meeting and contemplating the heavy uneasiness of it all anew when suddenly, feeling myself inordinately cramped, I looked up out of my reverie to discover that the car was jammed and that I had somehow got smack among the members of a single family—an astonishing family, a family so incredible that for the first time in my life I considered the possibility of Norman Rockwell's not being lunatic. They were a father, a mother, a girl about fifteen, and a boy one or two years younger than she. All were dressed in expensive-looking camel's-hair coats; each carried an item that designated him a fan—the father two soft and brilliantly plaid wool blankets, the mother a picnic basket, the girl a half-gallon thermos, and the boy a pair of field glasses, strung casually about his neck—each apparently doing his bit to make the day a grand success. What astonished me, though, was the almost hilarious similarity of their physical appearance: each had brilliant auburn hair; each had even, startlingly white teeth, smilingly exposed beneath attractive snub noses; and each of their faces was liberally sprinkled with great, outsized freckles. The total face they presented was one of overwhelming and wholesome handsomeness. My first impulse was to laugh. Had I not felt an extreme discomfort caused by the relish they took in each other's being—their looks seemed to smother each other in love—and the crowdedness that had caused me to find myself wedged among them, separating them, I might have laughed. I felt not unlike a man who eats too fast, drinks too much, occasionally neglects his teeth and fingernails, is given to a pensive scratching of his vital parts, lets rip with a not infrequent fart, and wakes up one morning to find himself smack in the middle of a *Saturday Evening Post* cover, carving the goddam Thanksgiving turkey for a family he has never seen before. What was worse, they were aware of my discomfort; between basking in each other's loveliness they would smile apologetically at me, as though in crowding about me they were aware of having aroused me from my reverie and were sorry for it. Distressed, I felt I ought to say something—"I'm sorry I'm alive" or something—so I said the first thing that came to my mind. It was a lie occasioned by my reverie, one which must have sounded very stupid indeed.

"I know Steve Owen," I said.

"Really!" they all chimed in high and good-natured unison. For some reason I got the impression that they had not the foggiest notion of what I had said. We all fell immediately to beaming at each other and nodding deferentially— a posture that exasperated me to the point where I thought I must absolutely say something else. Hoping that I could strike some chord in them that would relieve the self-consciousness we all were so evidently feeling, I spoke again.

"I know Frank Gifford, too."

"Really!" came their unabashed reply. Their tone seemed so calculated to humor me that I was almost certain they were larking with me. Staring at them, I couldn't be sure; and we all fell back to smiling idiotically and nodding at each other. We did this all the way to the Bronx where, disembarking, I lost contact with them—for the moment at least—and felt much relieved.

—

It seems amazing to me now that while at USC, where Gifford and I were contemporaries, I never saw him play football; that I had to come three thousand miles from the low, white, smog-enshrouded sun that hung perpetually over the Los Angeles Coliseum to the cold, damp, and dismal Polo Grounds to see him perform for the first time; and that I might never have had the urge that long-ago Sunday had I not once on campus had a strange, unnerving confrontation with him. The confrontation was caused by a girl, though at the time of the encounter I did not understand *what* girl. I had transferred from Hobart College, a small, undistinguished liberal arts college in Geneva, New York, where I was a predental student, to USC, a large, undistinguished university in Los Angeles, where I became an English major. The transition was not unnatural. I went out there because I had been rejected by a girl, my first love, whom I loved beyond the redeeming force of anything save time. Accepting the theory of distance as time, I put as much of it between the girl and myself as I could. Once there, though, the prospect of spending my days gouging at people's teeth and whiffing the intense, acidic odor of decay—a profession I had chosen with no stronger motive than keeping that very girl in swimming suits and tennis shorts: she had (and this, sadly, is the precise extent of my memory of her) the most breath-taking legs I had ever seen—seemed hideous, and I quite naturally became an English major with a view to reading The Books, The Novels and The Poems, those pat reassurances that other men had experienced rejection and pain and loss. Moreover, I accepted the myth of California the Benevolent and believed that beneath her warm skies I would find surcease from my pain in the person of some lithe, fresh-skinned, and incredibly lovely blond coed. Bearing my rejection like a disease, and like a man with a frightfully repugnant and contagious leprosy, I was unable to attract anything as healthy as the girl I had in mind.

Whenever I think of the man I was in those days, cutting across the neat-cropped grass of the campus, burdened down by the weight of the books in which I sought the consolation of other men's grief, and burdened further by the large weight of my own bitterness, the whole vision seems a nightmare. There were girls all about me, so near and yet so out of reach, a pastel nightmare of honey-blond, pink-lipped, golden-legged, lemon-sweatered girls. And always in this horror, this gaggle of femininity, there comes the vision of another girl, now only a little less featureless than all the rest. I saw her first on one stunning spring day when the smog had momentarily lifted, and all the world seemed hard bright blue and green. She came across the campus straight at me, and though I had her in the range of my vision for perhaps a hundred feet, I was only able, for the fury of my heart, to give her five or six frantic glances. She had the kind of comeliness—soft, shoulder-length chestnut hair; a sharp beauty mark right at her sensual mouth; and a figure that was like a swift, unexpected blow to the diaphragm—that to linger on makes the beholder feel obscene. I wanted to look. I couldn't look. I had to look. I could give her only the most gaspingly quick glances. Then she was by me. Waiting as long as I dared, I turned and she was gone.

From that day forward I moved about the campus in a kind of vertigo, with my right eye watching the sidewalk come up to meet my anxious feet, and my left eye clacking in a wild orbit, all over and around its socket, trying to take in the entire campus in frantic split seconds, terrified that I might miss her. On the same day that I found out who she was I saw her again. I was standing in front of Founders' Hall talking with T., a gleaming-toothed, hand-pumping fraternity man with whom I had, my first semester out there, shared a room. We had since gone our separate ways; but whenever we met we always passed the time, being bound together by the contempt with which we viewed each other's world and by the sorrow we felt at really rather liking each other, a condition T. found more difficult to forgive in himself than I did.

"That?" he asked in profound astonishment to my query about the girl. *"That?"* he repeated dumbly, as if this time— for I was much given to teasing T.—I had really gone too far. *"That,"* he proclaimed with menacing impatience, *"just happens to be Frank Gifford's girl!"*

Never will I forget the contempt he showered on me for asking what to him, and I suppose to the rest of fraternity row, was not only a rhetorical but a dazzlingly asinine question. Nor will I forget that he never did give me the girl's name; the information that she was Gifford's girl was, he assumed, quite enough to prevent the likes of me from pursuing the matter further. My first impulse was to laugh and twit his chin with my finger. But the truth was I was getting a little weary of T. His monumental sense of the rightness of things was beginning to grate on me; shrugging, I decided to end it forever. It required the best piece of acting I've ever been called upon to do; but I carried it off, I think, perfectly.

Letting my mouth droop open and fixing on my face a look of serene vacuousness, I said, "Who's Frank Gifford?"

My first thought was that T. was going to strike me. His hands tensed into fists, his face went the color of fire, and he thrust his head defiantly toward me. He didn't strike, though. Either his sense of the propriety of things overcame him, or he guessed, quite accurately, that I would have knocked him on his ass. All he said, between furiously clenched teeth, was: *"Oh, really, Exley, this has gone too far."* Turning hysterically away from me, he thundered off. It had indeed gone too far, and I laughed all the way to the saloon I frequented on Jefferson Boulevard, sadly glad to have seen the last of T.

Frank Gifford was an All-America at USC, and I know of no way of describing this phenomenon short of equating it with being the Pope in the Vatican. Our local *L' Osservatore Romano, The Daily Trojan,* was a moderately well-written college newspaper except on the subject of football, when the tone of the writing rose to an hysterical screech. It reported daily on Gifford's health, one time even imposing upon us the news that he was suffering an upset stomach, leading an irreverent acquaintance of mine to wonder aloud whether the athletic department had heard about "milk of magnesia, for Christ's sake." We were, it seems to me in retrospect, treated daily to such breathless items as the variations in his weight, his method of conditioning, the knowledge that he neither smoked nor drank, the humbleness of his beginnings, and once we were even told the number of fan letters he received daily from pimply high school girls in the Los Angeles area. The USC publicity man, perhaps influenced by the proximity of Hollywood press agents, seemed overly fond of releasing a head-and-shoulder print showing him the apparently proud possessor of long, black, perfectly ambrosial locks that came down to caress an alabaster, colossally beauteous face, one that would have aroused envy in Tony Curtis. Gifford was, in effect, overwhelmingly present in the consciousness of the campus, even though my crowd—the literati—never once to my knowledge mentioned him. We never mentioned him because his being permitted to exist at the very university where we were apprenticing ourselves for Nobel Prizes would have detracted from our environment and been an admission that we might be better off at an academe more sympathetic with our hopes. Still, the act of not mentioning him made him somehow more present than if, like the pathetic nincompoops on fraternity row, we spent all our idle hours singing his praises. Our silence made him, in our family, a kind of retarded child about whom we had tacitly and selfishly agreed not to speak. It seems the only thing of Gifford's we were spared—and it is at this point we leave his equation with the Bishop of Rome—was his opinion of the spiritual state of the USC campus. But I am being unkind now; something occurred between Gifford and me which led me to conclude that he was not an immodest man.

Unlike most athletes out there, who could be seen swaggering about the campus with *Property of USC* (did they never see the ironic, touching servility of this?) stamped indelibly every place but on their foreheads, Gifford made himself extremely scarce, so scarce that I only saw him once for but a few brief moments, so scarce that prior to this encounter I had begun to wonder if he wasn't some myth created by the administration to appease the highly vocal and moronic alumni who were incessantly clamoring for USC's Return to Greatness in, as the sportswriters say, "the football wars." Sitting at the counter of one of the campus hamburger joints, I was having a cup of chicken noodle soup and a cheeseburger when it occurred to me that he was one of a party of three men seated a few stools away from me. I knew without looking because the other two men were directing all their remarks to him: "Hey, Frank, how about that?" "Hey, Frank, cha ever hear the one about . . ." It was the kind of given-name familiarity one likes to have with the biggest man on the block. My eyes on my soup, I listened to this sycophancy, smiling rather bitterly, for what seemed an eternity; when I finally did look up, it was he—ambrosial locks and all. He was dressed in blue denims and a terry-cloth sweater, and though I saw no evidence of *USC* stamped anyplace, still I had an overwhelming desire to insult him in some way. How this would be accomplished with any subtlety I had no idea; I certainly didn't want to fight with him. I did, however, want to shout, "Listen, you son of a bitch, life isn't all a goddam football game! You won't always get the girl! Life is rejection and pain and loss"—all those things I so cherishingly cuddled in my self-pitying bosom. I didn't, of course, say any such thing; almost immediately he was up and standing right next to me, waiting to pay the cashier. Unable to let the moment go by, I snapped my head up to face him. When he looked at me, I smiled—a hard, mocking, so-you're-the-big-shit? smile. What I expected him to do, I can't imagine—say, "What's your trouble, buddy?" or what—but what he did do was the least of my expectations. He only looked quizzically at me for a moment, as though he were having difficulty placing me; then he smiled a most ingratiating smile, gave me a most amiable hello, and walked out the door, followed by his buddies who were saying in unison, "Hey, Frank, what'll we do now?"

My first feeling was one of utter rage. I wanted to jump up and throw my water glass through the plate-glass window. Then almost immediately a kind of sullenness set in, then shame. Unless I had read that smile and that salutation incorrectly, there was a note of genuine apology and modesty in them. Even in the close world of the university Gifford must have come to realize that he was having a fantastic success, and that success somewhat embarrassed him. Perhaps he took me for some student acquaintance he had had long before that success, and took my hateful smile as a reproach for his having failed to speak to me on other occasions, his smile being the apology for that neglect. Perhaps he was only saying he was sorry I was a miserable son of a bitch, but that he was hardly going to fight me for it. These speculations, as I found out drinking beer late into that evening, could have gone on forever. I drank eight, nine, ten, drifting between speculations on the nature of that smile and bitter, sexually colored memories of the girl with the breath-taking legs back East, when it suddenly occurred to me that she and not the girl with the chestnut hair was the cause of all my anger, and that I was for perhaps a very long time going to have to live with that anger. Gifford gave me that. With that smile, whatever he meant by it, a smile that he doubtless wouldn't remember, he impressed upon me, in the rigidity of my embarrassment, that it is unmanly to burden others with one's grief. Even though it is man's particularly unhappy aptitude to see to it that his fate is shared.

———

Leaving the subway and walking toward the Polo Grounds, I was remembering that smile and thinking again how nice it would be if Gifford had a fine day for Owen, when I began to notice that the redheaded family, who were moving with the crowd some paces ahead of me, were laughing and giggling self-consciously, a laughter that evidently was in some way connected with me. Every few paces, having momentarily regained their composure, they would drop their heads together in a covert way, whisper as they walked, then turn again in unison, stare back at me, and begin giggling all anew. It was a laughter that soon had me self-consciously fingering my necktie and looking furtively down at my fly, as though I expected to discover that the overcoat which covered it had somehow miraculously disappeared. We were almost at the entrance to the field when, to my surprise, the father stopped suddenly, turned, walked back to me, and said that he was holding an extra ticket to the game. It was, he said, the result of his maid's having been taken ill, and that he—no, not precisely he, but the children—would deem it an honor if I—"knowing Owen and all"—sat with them. Not in the least interested in doing so, I was so relieved to discover that their laughter had been inspired by something apart from myself—the self-consciousness they felt at inviting me—that I instantaneously and gratefully accepted, thanked him profusely, and was almost immediately sorry. It occurred to me that the children might query me on my relationship with Owen—perhaps even Gifford—and what the hell could I say? My "relationship" with both of these men was so fleeting, so insubstantial, that I would unquestionably have had to invent and thereby not only undergo the strain of having to talk off the top of my head but, by talking, risk exposure as a fraud.

My fears, however, proved groundless. These people, it soon became evident, had no interest in me whatever, they were so bound up in their pride of each other. My discomfort was caused not by any interest they took in me but by their total indifference to me. Directing me by the arm, father seated me not with the children who, he had claimed, desired my presence but on the aisle—obviously, I thought, the maid's seat (accessible to the hot dogs)—and sat himself next to me, separating me from his wife and children who had so harmoniously moved to their respective seats that I was sure that the family held season tickets. Everyone in place, all heads cranked round to me and displayed a perfect miracle of gleaming incisors.

It had only just begun. The game was no sooner under way when father, in an egregiously cultivated, theatrically virile voice, began—to my profound horror—commenting on each and every play. "That is a delayed buck, a play which requires superb blocking and marvelous timing," or, "That, children, is a screen pass, a fantastically perilous play to attempt, and one, I might add, that you won't see *Mr.* Conerly attempt but once or twice a season"—to all of which the mother, the daughter, and the son invariably and in perfect unison exclaimed, "Really!" A tribute to father's brilliance that, to my further and almost numbing horror, I, too, soon discovered I was expected to pay—pay, I would expect, for the unutterable enchantment of sitting with them. Each time that I heard the *Really!* I would become aware of a great shock of auburn hair leaning past father's shoulder, and I would look up to be confronted by a brilliant conglomeration of snub noses, orange freckles, and sparkling teeth, all formed into a face of beseechment, an invitation to join in this tribute to Genius. I delayed accepting the invitation as long as I could; when the looks went from beseechment to mild reproachment, I surrendered and began chiming in with *Really!* At first I came in too quickly or too late, and we seemed to be echoing each other: *Really! Really!* Though this rhythmical ineptness chafed me greatly, it brought from the family only the most understanding and kindly looks. By the end of the first quarter I had my timing down perfectly and settled down to what was the most uncomfortable afternoon of my life.

This was a superb Detroit team. It was the Detroit of a young Bobby Layne and an incomparable Doak Walker, of a monstrously bull-like Leon Harte and a three-hundred-and-thirty-pound Les Bingaman, a team that was expected to move past the Giants with ease and into the championship of the Western Division. Had they done so—which at first they appeared to be doing, picking up two touchdowns before the crowd was scarcely settled—I might have been rather amused at the constraints placed on me by the character of my hosts. But at one thrilling moment, a moment almost palpable in its intensity, and unquestionably motivated by the knowledge of Owen's parting, the Giants recovered, engaged this magnificent football team, and began to play as if they meant to win. Other than the terrible fury of it, I don't remember the details of the game, save that Gifford played superbly; and that at one precise moment, watching him execute one of his plays, I was suddenly and overwhelmingly struck with the urge to cheer, to jump up and down and pummel people on the back.

But then, there was father. What can I say of him? To anything resembling a good play, he would single out the player responsible and say, "Fine show, Gifford!" or "Wonderful stuff there, Price!" and we would chime in with "Good show!" and "Fine stuff!" Then, in a preposterous parody of cultured equanimity, we would be permitted to clap our gloved right hands against our left wrists, like opera-goers, making about as much noise as an argument between mutes. It was very depressing. I hadn't cheered for anything or anybody in three years—since my rejection by the leggy girl—and had even mistakenly come to believe that my new-found restraint was a kind of maturity. Oh, I had had my enthusiasms, but they were dark, the adoration of the griefs and morbidities men commit to paper in the name of literature, the homage I had paid the whole sickly aristocracy of letters. But a man can dwell too long with grief, and now, quite suddenly, quite wonderfully, I wanted to cheer again, to break forth from darkness into light, to stand up in that sparsely filled (it was a typically ungrateful New York that had come to bid Owen farewell), murderously damp, bitingly cold stadium and scream my head off.

But then, here again was father—not only father but the terrible diffidence I felt in the presence of that family, in the overwhelming and shameless pride they took in each other's being and good form. The game moved for me at a snail's pace. Frequently I rose on tiptoe, ready to burst forth, at the last moment restraining myself. As the fury of the game reached an almost audible character, the crowd about me reacted proportionally by going stark raving mad while I stood still, saying *Really!* and filling up two handkerchiefs with a phlegm induced by the afternoon's increasing dampness. What upset me more than anything about father was that he had no loyalty other than to The Game itself, praising players, whether Giants or Lions, indiscriminately. On the more famous players he bestowed a *Mister,* saying, "Oh, fine stuff, *Mr.* Layne!" or, "Wonderful show, *Mr.* Walker!"—coming down hard on the *Mister* the way those creeps affected by The Theater say *Sir* Laurence Olivier or *Miss* Helen Hayes. We continued our *fine show*'s and *good stuff*'s till I thought my heart would break.

Finally I did of course snap. Late in the final period, with the Giants losing by less than a touchdown, Conerly connected with a short pass to Gifford, and I thought the latter was going into the end zone. Unable to help myself, the long afternoon's repressed and joyous tears welling up in my eyes, I went berserk.

Jumping up and down and pummeling father furiously on the back, I screamed, "Oh, Jesus, Frank! Oh, Frank, *baby! Go! For Steve! For Steve! For Steve!*"

Gifford did not go all the way. He went to the one-foot line. Because it was not enough yardage for a first down, it became fourth and inches to go for a touchdown and a victory, the next few seconds proving the most agonizingly apprehensive of my life. It was an agony not allayed by my hosts. When I looked up through tear-bedewed eyes, father was straightening his camel's-hair topcoat, and the face of his loved ones had been transfigured. I had violated their high canons of good taste, their faces had moved from a vision of charming wholesomeness to one of intransigent hostility; it was now eminently clear to them that their invitation to me had been a dreadful mistake.

In an attempt to apologize, I smiled weakly and said, "I'm sorry—I thought *Mr.* Gifford was going all the way," coming down particularly hard on the *Mister.* But this was even more disastrous: Gifford was new to the Giants then, and father had not as yet bestowed that title on him. The total face they presented to me made me want to cut my jugular. Then, I thought, *what the hell;* and because I absolutely refused to let them spoil the moment for me, I said something that had the exact effect I intended: putting them in a state of numbing senselessness.

I said, my voice distinctly irritable, "Aw, c'mon, you *goofies. Cheer. This is for Steve Owen! For Steve Owen!*"

The Giants did not score, and as a result did not win the game. Gifford carried on the last play, as I never doubted that he would. Wasn't this game being played out just as, in my loneliness, I had imagined it would be? Les Bingaman put his three hundred and thirty pounds in Gifford's way, stopping him so close to the goal that the officials were for many moments undetermined; and the Lions, having finally taken over the ball, were a good way up the field, playing ball control and running out the clock, before my mind accepted the evidence of my eyes. When it did so, I began to cough, coughing great globs into my hands. I was coughing only a very few moments before it occurred to me that I was also weeping. It was a fact that occurred to father simultaneously. For the first time since I had spoken so harshly to him, he rallied, my tears being in unsurpassably bad taste, and said, "Look here, it's *only* a game."

Trying to speak softly so the children wouldn't hear, I said, *"Fuck you!"*

But they heard. By now I had turned and started up the steep concrete steps; all the way up them I could hear mother and the children, still in perfect unison, screeching *Father!* and father, in the most preposterously modulated hysteria, screeching *Officer!* I had to laugh then, laugh so hard that I almost doubled up on the concrete steps. My irritation had nothing to do with these dead people, and not really—I know now—anything to do with the outcome of the game. I had begun to be haunted again by that which had haunted me on my first trip to the city—the inability of a man to impose his dreams, his ego, upon the city, and for many long months had been experiencing a rage induced by New York's stony refusal to esteem me. It was foolish and childish of me to impose that rage on these people, though not as foolish, I expect, as father's thinking he could protect his children from life's bitterness by calling for a policeman.

———

Frank Gifford went on to realize a fame in New York that only a visionary would have dared hope for: he became unavoidable, part of the city's hard mentality. I would never envy or begrudge him that fame. I did, in fact, become perhaps his most enthusiastic fan. No doubt he came to represent to me the realization of life's large promises. But that is another part of this story. It was Owen who over the years kept bringing me back to life's hard fact of famelessness. It was for this reason, as much as any other, that I had wanted to make the trip to Oneida to make my remembrances. After that day at the Polo Grounds I heard of Owen from time to time, that he was a line coach for one NFL team or another, that he was coaching somewhere in Canada—perhaps at Winnipeg or Saskatchewan. Wherever, it must have seemed to him the sunless, the glacial side of the moon. Owen unquestionably came to see the irony of his fate. His offensively obsessed detractors had been rendered petulant by his attitude that "football is a game played down in the dirt, and always will be," and within three years after his leaving, his successors, having inherited his ideas (the umbrella pass-defense for one), took the Giants to a world championship with little other than a defense. It was one of the greatest defenses (Robustelli, Patton, Huff, Svare, Livingston, *et al.*) that the game has ever seen, but, for all of that, a championship won by men who played the game where Owen had tenaciously and fatally maintained it was played—*in the dirt.*

After that day at the Polo Grounds, I went the way I must go, a little sluggardly, smiling a smile that mocked myself. If I went wrong, it was because, like Tonio Kröger, there was for me no right way. I lived in many cities— Chicago, Los Angeles, Colorado Springs, Baltimore, Miami—and with each new milieu my jobs grew less remunerative, my dreams more absurdly colored. To sustain them I found that it took increasing and ever-increasing amounts of alcohol. After a time I perceived that I was continually contemplating the world through the bubbling, cerise hue of a wine glass. Awaking one morning in a jail cell in Miami, I was led before a judge on a charge of public intoxication and vagrancy, given a suspended sentence of thirty days on the county farm, told by the judge I was a fatuous lunatic, and ordered to be out of the city of Miami within the hour. I came home then, back to Watertown, and by the autumn of 1958, a brief five years from the autumn I had stood in the Polo Grounds, I was in the Avalon Valley State Hospital for the mentally insane and not particularly interested in the reasons that had brought me there.

3

Straw Hat for
a Madman

The Reception Building of the Avalon Valley State Hospital for the mentally insane lies high up on the eastern slope of the valley. A new patient is placed for orientation on its topmost or third floor. By bringing his face up close to the window—so that the bars begin to blur, then closer till those imposing reminders of lost freedom disappear altogether from view—he can look down the hill and see the entire hospital spread out below him. From that point—though for a time one is conscious of the cold, somber, and unyielding bars on one's cheeks—the place looks not unlike an Eastern university where anxious parents send their apple-cheeked sons and daughters to discover man's heritage.

In the fall—although I was there twice, in all seasons, it is in the autumn that I best remember it, for it was in that fanciful season that first I saw the place—a mist hung silently in the valley. The trees were all shot then with wine-reds, brilliant golds, and breath-taking lemons; even the sidewalks, bordered by the neat-trimmed lawns that swept down from the three-story, red-brick buildings, and crowded with easy-promenading patients, seemed, from that comforting distance, to be conveying chattering, eager students to their "Psych 202" class.

My first few days at Avalon Valley were spent standing at that window, caressing the illusion that I was in the sheltered bosom of a university. There came reminders to the contrary. Once I noticed a man, looking little more than buglike from where I stood, walking with the stiff, stick-legged trot of the cretin; another time a man bent with the ravages of age. Again, from behind me once came the long, plaintive wail of suffering, and I turned to see a man with whom I had struck an acquaintance, and whom I had till then judged quite sane, curled up, fetus-like, in the corner of the barren ward, sound asleep and dreaming some vision of his private hell, emitting the language of the tortured heart. On one particularly stunning day, when the sky was summer-blue and the autumn colors were defined with the richness of some dream of season, and I had finally succeeded in giving myself up totally to the illusion that I was some other place than I was, I felt an anxious nudging at my elbow and turned to find a short, hideously wasted, blue-black Negro. Speaking between brackish, putrescent teeth which emitted a dizzying, nearly eye-watering, odor, he told me there was a man within him, pestering him, allowing him no peace; then, in a very precise and startling way, he tapped with his forefinger at his diaphragm, indicating the exact location of the man, and asked me to listen—to hear for myself! With great solemnity, I bent down, placed my ear to his chest, and listened, hearing nothing, though I really was prepared to hear.

Lifting my head, I said, "What do he say?" adopting his

manner of speech in the hope he would feel comfortable with me.

"He say he the *debbil,* an' he gwoan kill me."

There was terror in the poor man's eyes.

"Dey *gottah* cut 'im out," he said, meaning the doctors would literally have to take their scalpels, make their incisions, and reach in and remove the man. The Negro's anguish was so reasonably modulated that I pictured the whole thing, saw the rubber-gloved hand go in between the spread flesh, feel tentatively around, and suddenly grab the little bugger by his slimy neck. It was here I lost the picture. I wondered if the little man would be blue-black, too, though it suddenly occurred to me—and I had smiled then—that he would be white as alabaster. Detecting my smile, and misinterpreting it, the Negro repeated, "Dey *got* to. Dey *got* to."

"Dey *will,*" I said. "Dey *will.*"

Because I couldn't think of anything else to say, I then put my arm about his shoulder, and together this hideous, unredeemable black paranoiac and I stood at the window for a long time, our eyes in the direction of the stunning autumn valley, though I was conscious now not of any scenery but only of the spasmodic, terrifying pulsations of his furious heart. It was this interruption that forced me finally to accept the knowledge that I was at no university; more importantly, that those apple-cheeked sons and daughters don't really learn much of man's heritage at a university.

In the Reception Building we were moved, according to our condition, or alphabetically, or at the doctor's whom— I never determined which—from the third to the second to the first floors. We were moved until the day came when, our names having been rather too dramatically called from a list by a fatuously inflated attendant, we descended the stairs into a long, concrete room in the basement. There we signed a receipt for what few clothes—all tagged now with white cloths bearing our names—we were permitted to have, gathered the clothes up into our arms, and climbed back up the stairs to await the trucks that would bear us to the main part of the hospital—*down the hill*. As we waited, the doctors, the nurses, the attendants, all approached us with sanguine gaiety. "Isn't it grand?" they seemed to be asking. Indeed, this was to have been a grand day. We had been told ever so many times that it would be a lovely day—a kind of moving-up day; when this day arrived, it was the sign our cases had been diagnosed. We had now only to go *down the hill* to be cured, and in a matter of weeks be back in the bosoms of our loved ones. Waiting and sitting in silence, wolfing cigarettes and basking in cheerful smiles, we knew better. Our faces showed it. We were not glad.

The Reception Building had been crowded with patients who had been at Avalon Valley before, who had gone *down the hill* and back to those bosoms to find them as cold, obdurate, and insensible as granite; having come back now bitter and defeated, they told us terrifying stories of the indignities that would be heaped upon us *down there*. They told us stories covering everything from the hideousness of the food to the gross inhumanity of the attendants, and they warned us to avoid, as long as possible, that trip *downward*. (Most of these stories turned out to be untrue; later I was to wonder why the hospital hadn't segregated these repeaters from us new patients, though I eventually came to see that it had been for the best: if one is led to expect the worst, nothing can really touch him.) I was not in the least worried. I had been in a hospital before—a private one, to be sure—and had come to understand that there was in the treatment of patients (I had come to call them inmates) certain overtones of punishment, some subtle, some not so subtle. We had failed our families by our *inability to function properly in society* (as good a definition of insanity as any); our families, tears compounded by self-pity in their eyes, had pleaded with the doctors to give us the goals that would set our legs in motion again. The goals—a wife and family, a vice-presidency, a Cadillac—varied only with the imperceptibility, the bland vision of the relative.

Moreover, I had also come to understand that most doctors—at least those with whom I had come in contact— were a not particularly competent lot, thoroughly accepting the notions of normality that society had imposed upon them. For the most part they did not consider it their duty to probe the strange, anguished, and perverse realities we had fabricated for ourselves. No doubt to a great extent motivated by lack of time and an unconscious awareness of their own shortcomings, they found it simpler to eliminate our realities and substitute those of society. It had seemed to me, too, that these doctors were quite willing—perhaps unconsciously eager—to punish patients for refusing these realities. About their treatment there was a kind of melancholy brutality; hadn't we, after all, long since put aside society's realities as being incompatible with our abilities to live? On discovering this "truth" about doctors some months before, I had evolved what I had come to call Exley's Law of Institutional Survival. It was simple. It involved leaving the mind as malleable as mush and letting them impose any inanities upon it they wished. It had worked for me once. I was sure it would again.

That is why, waiting for the truck to go *down the hill,* I had no fear at all. I did, in fact, even look forward to the trip with morbid though detached relish, wondering if I weren't about to witness some new essence of man's stupidity or viciousness or cruelty to his fellow man. From the moment these repeaters had started talking, I found I wasn't so much interested in their "horror" stories as in the tellers, some of whom were back at Avalon Valley for the fifth, sixth, seventh time—well on their way to the permanent and endless listlessness of incarceration. These people fascinated me.

There was in their tone as they told their tales more than the pleasure of upsetting us; there was a very real hope that we wouldn't survive the outrages they described. Talk of these outrages brought our eyebrows into scowls, twisted our mouths in pain, rendered us hideous. It was on noticing this transfiguration that I began to understand. For some time I had detected that if these repeaters had anything in common, it was sheer and naked ugliness—often so marked that it required an enormous effort of will to look directly at them when they were talking. These repeaters were the ugly, the broken, the carrion. They had crossed eyes and bug eyes and cavernous eyes. They had club feet or twisted limbs or—sometimes—no limbs. These people were grotesques. On noticing this, I thought I understood: there was in mid-century America no place for them. America was drunk on physical comeliness. America was on a diet. America did its exercises. America, indeed, brought a spirituality to its dedication to pink-cheeked, straight-legged, clear-eyed, health-exuding attractiveness—a fierce, strident dedication. It was the dedicated spirituality of the dancer to the ballet, except that the dancer might come to that experience we call Art.

To what, I asked myself, was America coming? To no more, it seemed to me, than the carmine-hued, ever-sober "young-marrieds" in the Schlitz beer sign. The sin of these repeaters was that they obtruded frightfully in the billboard sign, rather like fortuitously projecting Quasimodo into an advertisement to delineate the Male Ideal (I saw Julie London, her sensual lips blowing the lazy smoke of Marlboros into the sexually smug and outrageously winking visage of Charles Laughton's "Quasi"). I was aware of oversimplifying. One didn't know whether these people had been rendered grotesque by their perverseness or whether their grotesqueness had rendered them perverse. Still, I saw the comfort America could purchase itself by getting rid of them. Meeting payment in kind, they delighted in rendering us hideous. If we did not have common humanity on America's level—the level of the advertising commercial—then they would bring to our countenances the ugliness of despair, and at that unhappy level we would come together and make our marriage. "Oh, God," I thought, "they want nothing more than to be at one with us."

So I sat and waited, without fear, guided only by a vow I had made occasioned by an incident which had taken place the day before. For a number of days I had been putting my head down to the Negro's chest and listening for the devil within him; the other patients, whom he never tired of asking to listen, were apparently too embarrassed to do so. As a result we had become involved. He believed me the only one who accepted his reality. I was standing at the window when I suddenly heard a shrill, indignant, near-hysterical shouting and turned to see an attendant, his body tensed as if with pain, his face livid with rage. He was screaming at the Negro, whose body, in turn, seemed to be bending backward in the onrush of the man's anger. I don't remember the attendant's precise words, but they were enunciated with that chilling clarity that anger sometimes induces and were to the effect that the Negro had no man inside him, that there wasn't going to be any *goddam* operation, and that if he persisted in pestering people, the attendant would *goddam* well see to it that the Negro got an operation he wouldn't forget. There was saliva on the attendant's chin. The Negro began to weep. He wept quite openly, wept as the child he was. I turned away, back to the window. My hands went to the bars, my fingers found a grip on them, and I squeezed and squeezed and squeezed—watching my knuckles go white as hoarfrost and listening to the thunder in my head.

I wanted to kill that attendant, kill him in the same way that I wanted to destroy that America in pursuit of its own loveliness, kill him and it for their utter and unending lack of imagination. Of course the Negro had the devil inside him. Wasn't he the ugliest America of all—the black America? His devil was, like those others, his alienation from his countrymen, and that alienation and that devil were *gwoan* kill him sure, were even now engulfing him in fires more horrible than any of which Beelzebub ever dreamed—the fires of rejection. They might make the devil's voice less audible, they might cool the flames, but to tell him there was no devil was not only lack of imagination, it was a lie. Watching my hands on the bars, a little looser now, the knuckles going from snow-white to crimson, I made a vow. I vowed that never again at Avalon Valley would I get involved with a patient. I knew how to beat the bastards; I had beat them before; and the way was simple—one didn't tell them about one's devils. One didn't give their unimaginative mentalities an opportunity to hear about one's little man. My hands still on the bars and utter murder in my heart, I knew that if I got involved again I was only exposing myself to the risk of suffering another's defeat—a defeat that seemed to me as inevitable as did my victory. As it turned out, that vow was to make my voyage through Avalon Valley swift and painless, or nearly painless, and what pain there would be wouldn't come until the very end. It wouldn't come until I was all but ready to leave the hospital and go back into the America I knew. And though it is indeed best to keep one's devils within, one still has to learn to live with them; and this, when it came time to leave Avalon Valley, I yet hadn't learned to do.

———

My own devils—those which, prior to my commitment to Avalon Valley, had already sent me to a private hospital the preceding spring—were not particularly disturbing, at least not to me, and at least not at that time. During one of my three stays in funny farms, I once saw written on one of my records either "paranoiac-schizophrenic" or "schizophrenic-paranoiac" (I was obviously one type with overtones of the other), and the term had struck me so impressively that I had made a mental note of it, promising myself to reread Freud, with whom I had made only a desultory and uninspired effort at college. I never bothered to reread him. Before getting to him, I read the pre-Freudians, Hawthorne and Dostoevski, and because they seemed to me to grasp the human psyche better than all the post-Freudian writers lumped into one glibly analytical and monstrous bulk, I decided I had best remember the details of my particular illness truly and precisely: I was certain that understanding was contained in the very detail.

But I did not know this then; and without having read

Herr Doktor closely, surmising only from what I could remember of him, I supposed that I was more typically paranoiac: I was much given to fantasy. I was never incapacitated by fantasy. America had gone wrong for me, or me for America; I had held up my hand, said, *"Whoah* there: this has gone far enough!" and had gone home to Mummy, where I lay on the davenport for many months. I had incapacitated myself; the fantasy had followed to consume the endlessly idle hours. There was nothing grossly unusual in the fantasy: it was a projected compendium of all that was most truly vulgar in America: I was rich, famous, and powerful, so incredibly handsome that within moments of my entrance stunning women went spreadeagle before me. But I never for a second "lived" this fantasy. There was always one I, aloof and ironical, watching the other me play out "his" tawdry dream. We were like illicit and Puritan lovers who had given birth to a monstrous fantasy child; as happens in all unions coupled in guilt, we as lovers would come to loathe both each other and the monster child. By the time we did so, I had been on the davenport much too long, my mother's eyes had gone from sympathy to the myopic squint of pain; and when she suggested I enter an expensive private hospital downstate, I quite readily acceded.

Even apart from the "loathsomeness of the lovers," or my mother's pain, I needed little persuasion. Learning that the hospital was going to cost two hundred dollars a week, I naturally assumed something would be done for me (if, indeed, there was anything to be done). I wasn't then so un-American as not to believe that enough money can do anything, restore the soul or whatever. Moreover, my particular fantasy had paled to the extent that even thinking of exploring some new facet of it—the seduction of a half-dozen of those downy blondes simultaneously—tired me to the point of heavy and massive weariness, and I wanted to explore this fantasy with a doctor in the hope that once uttered (like a curse against God that drifts into the wind) it would be gone forever. I wanted to lie hour after hour on a couch, pouring out the dark, secret places of my heart—do this feeling that over my shoulder sat humanity and wisdom and generosity, a munificent heart—do this until that incredibly lovely day when the great man would say to me, his voice grave and dramatic with discovery: "This is you, Exley. Rise and go back into the world a whole man."

That *hospital* (the word is frightfully harsh) was lovely. Its buildings—château-like houses—commanded a high, green hill, and its shrubbed, carpet-like lawns ran sweepingly down between ancient, verdant trees. It was spring then, the spring just preceding my autumn commitment to Avalon Valley; and the azure sky seemed always mottled with sailing, billowing clouds, which, when we turned our eyes heavenward, seemed to caress and cool our faces. Beneath us in the valley, deep blue and turgid and heartstopping, was the Hudson River. A tennis court lay down the hill to our right, a swimming pool to our left. We dined—all save one of us who, past caring, ate with greasy fingers and was therefore consigned to another room, thoughtfully isolated from our genteel views—on white linen, murmuring pleasantries and avoiding all mention of the particular perversities which had brought us there. We were creatures of phrases—"Indeed!" and "On my word!" and "Is it possible!" and "Pray tell me!" Nothing rude or native ever issued from our mouths, and after a time the effect seemed so consummately artificial that I began to wonder if we had enough substance to cast shadows. Our doctors were hoary-maned and sharp-featured. They exuded tweed and pipe tobacco and managed their Camel cigarettes with a most ethereal delicacy, displaying their aristocratic hands. They left us giddy, nearly dizzy, with admiration at the way they somberly enunciated the jargon of the psychiatrist. Indeed, indeed! Everything seemed so perfect that even now it rather surprises me to confess that these doctors proved to be as insubstantial as the patients, not only incapable of understanding but unwilling to listen to the language of the heart.

After the most cursory of examinations, it was determined that I undergo insulin-shock treatment; and, though I must have experienced qualms at the rapidity of this determination, I soon dismissed them, replacing them with the utter and adoring devotion for the doctors and the attendants that the treatment instilled. Each morning I rolled over in bed, turned the cheeks of my ass to the ceiling, and received my injection. While the insulin began to burn the sugar—the very life—from my body, I quite cheerfully lay back to await the disappearance of debilitating dreams, ancient insults, past hurts inflicted—the disappearance, as though they had never existed, of all the things that ravage the soul and age the body, that turn the eyes inward and settle a melancholy on the countenance.

Is it any wonder I expected so much? At first one experienced a kind of bizarre giddiness, one felt slightly drunk. This was followed by heavy perspiration, then something like fever. Now came a feverish chatter, where one lay talking out his soul to the ceiling—at times even going into a hallucinatory state, a state in which I was once virtually

certain that I was in Limbo waiting to be judged by a personal and very vindictive God. Finally, at that moment just
prior to shock, one learned what hunger was—terrible, excruciating hunger. On the California desert I have walked
all the forenoon on Route 66 and have had to beg water—
I got a half-cup—from two vagabonds who had long since
denied their alliance with their fellows; after three days
without food in Miami, I have gone among the wide-
beamed, large-breasted tourists, my palm face upward, and
begged for money. But these were trifling and contemptible
exercises in degradation compared to the majestic loss of
dignity rendered in one by insulin.

I screamed. I babbled. I swooned for food. "Oh, don't do
this to me!" I shouted; for, lying alone in my room, I was
never certain that by some crazy happenstance I had not
been forgotten. But they always came, bringing with them
not a rich, sugary orange juice but an elixir—the very stuff
of life; and I drank it as though, having been taken to the
very pit of death, the indifferent universe had suddenly
and inexplicably assumed a beneficence and decided to
grant me life; drank it with such voraciousness that the
heavy syrup cascaded over my chin and came to settle in
sticky, thick pools at my throat. I drank it wanting to kiss
the hands and feet of the attendant, my savior.

After a number of days, as the amounts of insulin were
increased, I drifted quite mercifully into shock where I lay
in a dreamless death in which I was supposed to rid myself
of my devils, leaving them, when I rose to life again, back
there in the deep and heavy darkness. At the appointed
hour, the doctor gave me an injection of glucose, I rose
from that death into life, and was given another glass of the
elixir. Moments later the insulin patients, still in their pa-

jamas, were seated at breakfast. We piled our cornflakes high with sugar. Shoving great spoonfuls into our mouths, we remarked to each other the pleasantness of the weather, the beauty of the hospital, and how much better we were feeling. We all agreed that insulin shock was a wonderful treatment. We could not believe otherwise. We were all making penance for the grief we had caused others; and we had to believe that a treatment in which one fawned and begged, drooled and prayed, a treatment which cost so much in loss of pride and manhood, in humiliating dependency, would have to bear miraculous results. We had to believe that in the end we would be purified.

Had my consultations with the doctor proved so fruitful, I might have gone back into the world trim and wide-eyed and upright, and all my days caressed the illusion that Life was Ennobling, that God was Beneficent, that the Universe was a Joyous and Profoundly Simple Thing. For a very long time that doctor, working with hardly more than his tweed jacket, his Camel cigarettes, his hoary mane, his chiseled features, and his clear blue eyes, had me convinced that these things were so. To my surprise we sat facing each other, while through the heavy smoke of our cigarettes I talked. I began tentatively, skirting all over and about the real reasons why I believed my life's labor had earned me this: a mental hospital at twenty-seven. I told him of my gold mine in Eldorado, of my vineyards in the south of France, of my merchant ships moored at Cadiz; I told him of my seductions of lazy-legged Jewesses in Tel Aviv, of incredibly aseptic blondes in Copenhagen, of golden, burnished mulattoes at Port Said. Each time I looked up at him to see how I was doing, I saw (and I was glad) that his mouth, a fine, distinguished, knifelike mouth, was twisted into a benevolent, tolerant smile.

That smile gave me the courage to go on. I had, as I say, exhausted my fantasy before even entering the hospital; and because fantasies seemed to me to rise out of some deep inability to live with myself, I thought it best to reveal to the kindly man my self-loathing. I revealed to him my sense of my own putrefaction—my dreams of rape and murder and incest, talked and talked and talked, while on the other side of the smoke he sat like some great god. But as I talked in this new way, something began to go wrong; the smiles became less frequent, more galvanic, until there were no smiles at all, and, to my bewilderment, I began to notice that whenever I spoke of certain things, his countenance went from one of restrained tolerance to one of sobriety—nay, more than that, to one of downright somberness—he might, I thought once or twice, be one of Hawthorne's elders sitting in judgment of Hester Prynne. As the days wore on, this somberness verging on judgment distressed me so much that I began to demand from him some comments on my revelations. His response was extremely disconcerting. Invariably, and to my extreme bewilderment, he met my demands by talking lengthily and unintelligibly—to me at least—about the way insulin works on the human cell, and what the best psychiatric thinking believes—for they don't really know—insulin shock does for one. My first impression was that he was exercising the prerogatives of the analyst and withholding his cogent discoveries about me till his assessment of my character was complete. But he continued to ramble on with this irrelevant monologue until I could stand it no longer. Embarked upon it one day, he was going along very glibly when, suddenly and rudely, I interrupted him. "You want to be irrelevant?" I snapped. "I'll be irrelevant, too!" Then I proceeded to tell him something from my past that I had told to no one before him, nor will ever tell again. My eyes avoiding his, I spoke in the fitful, hesitant monosyllables of grief. When, finally finished and exhausted with relief (as one is with the ultimate confession), I looked up to make sure that he had understood me utterly, the room drifted away beneath me, the dizzying blood rushed to my head, something in me snapped: I broke. On his face was written the unmistakable legend of distaste.

I started to giggle. For the next two weeks I did little other than giggle. I was certainly as mad then as I had ever been. My first thought was to get away. A few days later I left the grounds, intent on I know not what—going to a movie or California, or simply intent on registering a protest. I was almost immediately picked up—as I no doubt intended to be—and the next day, without warning, I was ordered onto a bed to receive my first electroshock treatment. Pleading with the doctor, one of the younger staff members, that this was an unnecessary, even a vindictive, measure did no good. So I tried saber-rattling, telling him that if he wanted those electrodes on my skull, he'd damn well have to put them there. "We can do that, too," he said. Now I turned to the attendants who were standing by to prevent my injuring myself in the convulsions that succeed the electrical charge. They would not look at me. They looked instead at the floor, as though rather ashamed at what they were helpless to prevent. Now I asked the doctor if I mightn't have the treatment explained to me, saying that it was only natural to fear the unfamiliar. When he shook his head *no*, my first impulse was to flee, to scamper as fast and as far as my legs would carry me. Looking from the doctor to the attendants, neither of whom would now return my glance, I suddenly became unbearably thirsty, which was followed immediately by an abrupt, tortured breathing. I don't know how long I stood there, breathing in this terrified way; but at some moment—a moment wonderful in its protectiveness—the listlessness of defeat engulfed me, and I walked, trancelike, to the bed and lay down.

The wide rubber band containing the electrodes was wrapped tightly about my skull, just above the ears; the doctor checked my pulse, told me he was going to give me an injection to relax me (most of the uncomfortable effects of electroshock are back injuries caused by the patient's inordinate tension). I wanted to say something in a very manly though pleasant way—"Whatever you say, Doc"— something to get the man back on my side. I did not know then that these goodly men did not know any more about electroshock than about insulin therapy, and I thought it might be prudent to remind him, despite his apparent hostility, of my humanity in the hope that he would not approach his work too stridently. But my fear was so great that I despaired of saying more than a word, *okay;* even this came out to the tempo of my palpitating heart, *'kay!*—came with a rushing, girlish feebleness. Then I felt the needle go into my arm, my eyelids came over my eyeballs like a deep blue velvet curtain over my mismanaged life, I sensed a quick movement behind me, all was darkness.

Many times after that I lay down for electroshock. Never once did the despair and the fear of the initial treatment diminish, the fear of having one's consciousness so irrevocably laid on the indifferent altar of science. My insulin shock was continued mornings, and I believed that I was getting these new treatments twice a week, in the afternoons. Rising out of the deep slumber of the insulin one morning, and beginning to experience that incredible hunger, I was suddenly aware of that tight rubber band about my skull, conscious that they were giving me both treatments simultaneously. At first I was astonished, then terrified, then angry. About to bellow my protest, I sensed that quick movement behind me, all again was darkness. Because of the temporary loss of memory induced by electroshock, I did not, until some time in the afternoon, piece together this knowledge. I lived that day in an agony of apprehension, conscious throughout it that something disturbing was lurking beneath the conscious level of my mind. When I finally did remember, feeling again that inordinate hunger and that strap about my skull, I was once again surprised, again frightened, finally furious.

Subsequent to the consultation that had ended in my perpetual and uncontrollable giggling, my doctor had discontinued our sessions together; and it suddenly occurred to me that where he—or I—had failed, he was determined that science would succeed. This possibility opened before me fantastic vistas; I could not help wondering how far the man was prepared to go. I had seen my fellow patients reduced to infantilism by a gymnastic treatment called regressive shock, an intermittent series of electrical whacks on the head that go on night and day for ten days. I had seen the results of that ultimately humane treatment, the frontal lobotomy. For this, they remove a chunk of skull in the forehead area, stick an instrument not unlike an ice pick down to the brain where, with a few curt brushes, they scrape away all grief, all rage, all violence, all the things that make us Man, leaving one great hulk of loonily smiling protoplasm. Although I knew that either of these treatments would be out of the question in my case, I had this fear. In a way I suppose I was prepared to believe them guilty of anything.

For days I lived in a cocoon of rage, wanting to strike out, to run, not knowing what to do. For a time I thought of telephoning attorneys and writing passionate, eloquent letters to the Governor and the New York *Post*, letters which would arouse a slumbering world and bring it, indignant and righteous with wrath, descending upon the grounds to free my fellow patients and me. Had I not taken a long, hard look at my fellow patients, I might have done these things, too. "On my word" and "Don't tell me," they were still blabbering away at each other, quite unaware of poor Exley's indignation. I had to laugh. "My God," I thought, "they are insane—and always will be, whether they leave the grounds or not." I laughed and laughed and laughed. This discovery led me to the obvious question: how about me? Was I, too, insane? It was a difficult admission to make, but I am glad that I made it; later I came to believe that this admission about oneself may be the only redemption in America. Yes, I was insane. Still, I did not despise my oddness, my deviations, those things which made me, after all, me. I wanted to preserve those things. To do it, I had to get out of that place. Then—as quickly as the rage had come over me—I suddenly knew how to do it. I would be the kind of man I suspected the world wanted me to be. I played the game with all the loathing the benevolent doctor had put at my command.

I whistled. My gait took on a cheerful, nearly joyous bounce. Each Wednesday evening I went to the dances in the Recreation Room and there waltzed wacky old maids round and round the room. I was of good cheer, exclaiming to all and any who inquired after my health, "Great! How's yourself? Wonderful! Couldn't be better!" I spent my mornings in the Arts and Crafts Room making a briefcase. With it, I never tired of proclaiming, I intended to re-enter the great and wonderful world. That briefcase became symbolic, the conspicuous admission on my part of the efficacy of the doctor's decision to give me electroshock. It was made of grained, extremely expensive black leather. With the intense and cheery disposition of a saint, I wove it together at the seams, whistling. For its interior I fitted it with celluloid containers. In these I put samples of the deathless prose I had written for various corporations (when I had worked, I had worked in public relations) and a sheaf of handsomely printed résumés from which I excluded certain information, such as that they had been printed up at a mental institution. For the case's crowning touch, I had it fitted with a gold-plated zipper and had mounted on its grained surface a gold-plated name-and-address plate. Completed, it was a wonderful creation. It was so wonderful that as work had progressed upon it the doctor put at my disposal a younger head shrinker, one with whom I whiled away the lethargic afternoons, feeding him incredible stories of my ideas of future bliss.

"Look here," I said, with stunning self-assurance, "I'm a relatively intelligent young man," and smiled modestly to await his nodding agreement. "I can, when I'm up to it, put on a rather striking appearance. There's no reason whatever I shouldn't go right down to Madison Avenue, make boodles of money, and start raising a family. Yes," I added gravely, as though the latter had struck me as an unusually vivid idea, *"I think I'd like a family!"*

My relationship with this doctor was strange and not a little unsettling. He was leaving the hospital—to begin his own practice, he said; but I suspected that he had come to be disturbed by some of the practices he had seen around him, suspected that his thoughts about the hospital were not incompatible with mine. He never said as much, but I always suspected that he saw through me. "No, no reason whatever, Exley, if that's what you want," he would reply to such nonsense as the above. And he would smile. That smile seemed to say, "Let's cut the bullshit and talk about baseball." But if he did suspect that I was frolicking, he understood and held his peace. In his defense, I did my job so beautifully that when it came time to leave the hospital I had all but convinced myself that these things were what I thirsted after.

Moving into my aunt's guest house in Westchester, and adhering to a strict diet to lose the weight the insulin treatment had put on me, I bought in Chappaqua a splendid, olive-green, snug-shouldered suit; a half-dozen regimentally striped neckties; a pair of expensive black shoes; and for my head—for it was *that* summer—a wild, preposterous, round-rimmed, plaid-banded, pancake-topped, yellow straw hat. Tilting that marvelous thing to one side of my head, my wondrous briefcase under my arm, I began bouncing all over New York, practically glad-handing strangers on the avenue. Carrying my new-found self-assurance into job interviews, I didn't so much ask for jobs as tell employers they must have me; I didn't beg, I commanded; I wasn't deferential, I was haughty. And no one was more amazed than I to discern the favorable impressions I was making: I left employers quite fearful of their own jobs.

It was at the moment when I was being seriously considered for a half-dozen positions that I went, one afternoon after an interview in which I was practically assured of the job, down to Greenwich Village. I ordered a Budweiser, two, three. Then I switched to whisky. Awaking the next morning in a hotel room, I could not, after dressing, find my straw hat. I found it finally in the bathroom, in the bathtub, immersed in a foot or so of sad, still water. With either my fist or my foot I had knocked the top of it completely through, and I left its unhappy remains, its striking plaid band floating out from it like Ophelia's gown, for the chambermaid.

That afternoon I went back to the guest house behind my aunt's. I lay there the month of August, unshaven, reading, and scratching my joint. On a lovely day in early September, I looked out the window and saw the men in the white jackets moving wide apart from one another up the lawn in the cool shade of the trees toward me, one a white man and the other a Negro as huge and forbidding as the late Pittsburgh tackle, Earl Lipscomb. Sighing, but really rather relieved, I lighted a cigarette, took a drag, got up, opened the door, and stepped out to meet them, saying, "Relax, Big Daddy—I'm okay." A few days later found me standing up close to the bars in Avalon Valley, looking down into the autumnal mists, imagining that I was at a university. A few days later still, I was sitting and waiting for the truck to bear me *down the hill.*

———

The truck driver finally came for us. He was cheerful, too. "All set, kids?" he said. We rose, gathered our clothes, followed him out the door, got into the back of the truck (it was built like a paddy wagon), and started down. No one spoke all the way; neither did we look into each other's eyes. I suppose the others were apprehensive, but I was already beginning to apply Exley's Law of Institutional Survival (be of good cheer, yearn for color-television sets). It had worked for me once; it would again. The main thing was to avoid those attachments, to avoid setting myself up for the possibility of experiencing another's defeat. When the truck finally came to a halt, we heard the cab door open and close, the driver's footsteps on the drive, the sound of him opening the door into the back of the truck. When he stood exposed to us, he was cheerful no more. He said, "The end of the line, sweethearts."

After a few more days of observation, I was placed with seventy others in an open ward—one from which the patient was permitted, during the day, to wander freely about the grounds. On close scrutiny the hospital no longer seemed a university. The foliage was now above one's head, not a sea of autumnal hues beneath one. Between the trees' bare trunks the buildings were a veritable triumph of fact. Each had three stories, each was of red brick, and each was so like the other that a stucco cottage stuck amongst them would have seemed an outrageous piece of shilly-shallying. Even the separate wards consisted of three main rooms. We slept together in a long, partially partitioned hall, with ten or twelve of us grouped together. I did not sleep for many nights—or, rather, I slept the sleep of the aged, a sleep diffused with wakefulness, or a wakefulness diffused with sleep. The only man in my section I recognized from the Reception Building was my Negro friend. He had stopped speaking to me. His medications had started to give him relief, and he was now embarrassed by what he had revealed to me. Perhaps, though, the attendant had just scared the poor bugger to death. For whatever reason, he now avoided my eyes. Each night he pomaded his kinky hair, put some kind of snug tuque fashioned from a woman's nylon on his head, slipped quickly out of his pants, and kneeled down by his bed. His skinny blue-black fanny exposed beneath his shirt, he said his prayers quite loudly. I don't remember them, but I know that Jesus was mentioned a good deal. Later I heard that the tuque business was an attempt to get his hair as straight as mine, and I was sorry to hear it; apparently he figured if he couldn't beat us, he'd join us. He was always the last in bed, it would be silent for a time, then the night noises would start. They began with unobtrusive things like snoring and scratching and belching; later in the night one would hear terrified screams or violent, crushing weeping. The odor was always heavy with male sweat. In the first nights I often rose and went to the john for a cigarette. But this was sometimes more unnerving, for I often discovered one of my bunk-mates kissing another's genitals. Some of them were flaunt-ingly homosexual and did not embarrass easily; one had either to smoke his cigarette and look away, or go back, lie down, and wait for sleep. After a time I said to myself, "Fuck you guys," smoked my cigarette, and looked right at them.

These johns were huge places, too, consisting of three open and cavernous showers and a dozen or so washbowls. In a separate room an entire wall had been fitted with toi-let bowls from which, for sanitary reasons, the wooden seats had been removed. For a number of days the cold porcelain to the cheeks of one's butt constricted the bow-els; but after a time the intestinal tract, suffering under its burden, forced the defecation painfully from the body. The largest room in the ward was the day or sitting room, a vast and monumental tribute to bleakness. The room was big in every way, in length and width and height. It was the kind of room in which one could imagine high and intemperate winds circulating forever. All about its barren, brown-enameled floor, lining the walls, and as close together as stacked plates, were monstrous, thronelike wooden chairs. To look at those chairs broke one's heart. Some right-hearted soul—some B.A. in Psychology, no doubt—had had them painted, in about equal proportions, either a sunny pastel blue or a shocking brilliant orange. It was an attempt to brighten our existence. The effect, in that sad place, was overwhelming, rather like an ugly woman attempting to make herself more amenable by overpainting her hideous features, thereby only bringing to her grossness a disarming attention. Looking at those chairs, one imagined himself looking upon such a woman, trying not to let his face reveal the evidence of his eyes. All over the hospital we confronted these touching and wrongheaded attempts to please us.

Our daily routine was unvarying. Each morning prior to breakfast, we lined up for our "treatment," which in most cases consisted of receiving a tranquilizing pill; then we were marched upstairs to a huge, barnlike cafeteria. There we picked up a partitioned tin tray, allowed it to be covered with something not unlike food, then went to one of the tables and took a seat. In the same way that I could not in the first days sleep or defecate, I could not eat. About the third day I succumbed and ate both voraciously and gratefully. By then I had learned to seek out a seat that did not fall opposite those men past caring, those who ate both toast and oatmeal, potatoes and gravy, with their fingers, licked their fingers, thwap, thwap, thwap, then upturned the tray and, with precise, snakelike motions, licked it clean.

Because we were forced to work—no one said we were forced to, but knowing what I knew I quickly surmised that the Powers considered working (I had wanted to read in the library—a decadent activity) not only properly humbling but a sign that one understood what makes the wheels go round in America—I succeeded, on the promise of getting the same food as the attendants, in getting a job in the employees' kitchen. I worked on the dishwasher. The work was hot and hard; but the food was good, and I had a chance to study at close hand the hospital employees, who seemed to be made up in about equal parts of Negroes and Whites. The Whites looked down on the Blacks as niggers, the Negroes looked down on the Whites because they (the Negroes) were for the most part better educated and still unable to find a more suitable work. Both groups looked down on us patients as little more than animals, loathing us—in their eyes, in their furious little gestures—to such an extent that the only thing that distinguished them from the most paranoiac among us was their not-very-clean white uniforms, their mantles of authority. I could understand and forgive this in the Negro. We reminded him— the sweat streaming down our faces—of his long and menial past. The Whites, or most of them, seemed as unredeemable as any Southern racist. Whenever I got anything like a patronizing look from either group, I always put on my face a blissful smile and winked outrageously. To one such wink I heard one of the Negroes say to his buddies, "Another fucking loony!" They all laughed.

It occurs to me that I have suggested that life at Avalon Valley was unlivable, perhaps unbearable, and I do not mean to do this; I loved Avalon Valley and will all my life remember it the way other men remember the chance seduction of a cinema queen (I know such a man: he was disappointed) or the Thanksgiving Day they blocked the punt to win the game against Big Bad High. It is true that the grounds were bleak, nothing more than a city of imposing red-brick façades, but against those brick walls people threw precise, well-defined shadows. No one here ever felt *grand*; one heard, without even inquiring, about one another's little men and believed in them. The food was pallid, but only to an American palate already undone by cigarettes; when one accepted the fact of food's design to be sustenance, the food became as good as any. Both sleep and bowel movements came with adjustment. There was a consolation in believing that someone had recognized these homosexuals as being ill, even more of a consolation in believing that they had perhaps committed themselves. They were not walking their pink poodles, leeringly clacking their eyeballs all over their made-up sockets, and "slaughtering the innocents" along Third Avenue. Neither were they holding "open meetings" with a view to persuading their legislators that they were just a bunch of jolly-good boys exercising a Hellenistic inclination. The library was as good as that in my home town.

Finally, there was our doctor, Dr. K., who above everything else was a man—a not altogether common phenomenon in America. He was a short, squat man with a heart as big as his girth. He leaked real sweat and was touchingly solicitous of us, perhaps too much so. In a way he hated to come into our ward; he could not go from one end of it to the other without listening to and weighing our minutest complaints. Listening to us, he always dabbed at his perspiration-streaked forehead with a large white handkerchief. One day when we had all crowded about him, awaiting our separate turns to "jump him" with our outrageously petty complaints, he gave me my most vivid memory of him. A young boy about eighteen was talking with him. Because the boy was speaking in hushed, furtive tones, those of us who waited had judged his complaint was of an intimate nature, had widened the circle about them, and were staring timidly at the floor. When I next looked up, the boy was weeping. His great tears streamed effortlessly down his boyish cheeks, and between terrible sobs, he continued to pour forth his complaint in something like a low, guttural groan. Suddenly Dr. K.'s stubby fingers shot out to the boy's cheeks and with furious anxiety began wiping away his tears. The boy continued to weep; Dr. K. continued to do battle with his awful anguish. He wiped and wiped and wiped, furiously. When I looked at his face, I saw that behind his spectacles, forming there and beclouding them, were tears of his own. We had all moved away then, aware that our griefs were not so very real. We had large love for Dr. K. We sensed his manhood and felt easy with him. I did, in fact, eventually come to such an equanimity that I believed I could live out my life at Avalon Valley, live it there as well as live it in any America I had yet discovered.

Sex—or the lack of it—was a very palpable problem; but not as real as the sense of one's anonymity, the loss of self. This loss was brought vividly home to us one morning on coming down to the ward from breakfast.

A boy had hung himself.

He had hidden in the toilets until we were safely upstairs, shoveling in our oatmeal. Then he had stood astride the edges of a toilet bowl, tied the loose ends of his necktie (I can remember wondering if it had regimental stripes) to a steel rod separating the partitions between the separate bowls, let his feet slide away from the porcelain, and swung himself free from the hot, awful agony of his life. Immediately on our arrival downstairs, he was discovered by a man intent on relieving himself of yesterday's slop to make way for today's. The next few moments proved a panic of running, shouting, and cursing.

We were instantly forced by the attendants into the ward across the hall, where the door, for the first time in weeks, was locked behind us. There, like indigent children pressed to a window of the grandest house in town, we flattened our noses against the glass of the door, our breaths steaming the window, our breathing as labored as defective engines. A number of attendants ran by. Then came Dr. K., trying to speed up his great weight and testing a hypodermic even as he ran, squirting a spray of fluid into the air. It was the hugest hypodermic needle I had ever seen. It was one of those containing adrenalin that they shove into the human heart; but it looked big enough to destroy life, not restore it. After Dr. K. went by, it was very, very still for a long time; and I suppose all of us could visualize him, having made his injection, now bent intently over the boy, giving him mouth-to-mouth resuscitation. A priest came next. He was running, too. At that point we began breathing again, began drifting away from the door, began smiling self-consciously at each other. When we were able to talk, we all agreed the boy had been a good fellow.

It was this latter that preyed on me. I had not known the boy. I could not visualize him, and it was only because a new patient to our ward could not place him either and made inquiries that I learned anything at all. The boy had been young, quiet, handsome, and inordinately neat; and had been much given to a particular orange chair in one corner of the ward where he had sat by the hour staring amiably off into space. I knew why I couldn't remember him. My attempt to stay uninvolved had worked so admirably that I had lived with him without being cognizant of him. Out of embarrassment I never in the ensuing days mentioned that I could not for the life of me recall him. I now sat by the hour myself, staring at the chair he was said to have occupied, trying to call him back. But I never had any luck. And I never mustered the guts to tell the other boys I couldn't remember him. Out of a misplaced shame, and in answer to inquiries about him from one or another incoming patient, I even began to describe him as knowledgeably as I could. I know it was shameful of me, but in my way I felt his death as much as anyone. Where the others looked upon it as the passing of a buddy, or an acquaintance, or simply of a face (but still a face of flesh and blood, one capable of expressing hope and melancholy and tenderness), I looked upon it as the passing of something faceless; where the others had the memory of something that had lived and laughed and known pain, I had only the memory of a thing dead that had never lived; for a number of days I lived benumbed, horrified by the possibilities this fact suggested. My dreams had had nothing really to do with gold in Eldorado, or sensual mulattoes in Port Said. But the dream of fame had been real enough: I had wanted nothing less than to impose myself deep into the mentality of my countrymen, and now quite suddenly it occurred to me that it was possible to live not only without fame but without self, to live and die without ever having had one's fellows conscious of the microscopic space one occupies upon this planet. The thought almost overcame me, and I could not dwell upon it without becoming unutterably depressed.

It was at the moment when things were bleakest that Paddy the Duke began to throw his abundant and alarming shadow all over the hospital. It was he who taught me that a man can have self no matter where he is. Now I needed only sex to come to terms with Avalon Valley. Even in this respect the possibilities were not out of reach. One could always ask for increased amounts of saltpeter or, I suppose, even castration. I asked for neither, of course, because it occurred to me one day, reading a smuggled copy of de Sade, that even on the "outside" one never comes to terms with desire.

———

I had my first encounter with Paddy the Duke in the Reception Building on the day we had our initial consultations with the doctor—those preliminary consultations in which they want to know whether we love Mommy and Daddy, why we won't work, and the frequency of our masturbation. A number of us were lined up in wooden chairs on either side of a long hall, facing each other, and awaiting our separate turns to talk with the doctor. The conversation was animated, those men who had already had their interviews filling in the rest of us on the kind of question to expect. "What did you answer?" someone would say breathlessly. On being told, we would all fall into grave and momentary silence, doubtless brooding on whether that particular answer suited us. Then immediately new questions would be put.

Throughout this only two of us remained silent, Paddy the Duke, who sat directly across from me, and myself. In the interest of self-preservation I wanted to hear the questions and determine how best to answer them, even to the extent of formulating in my mind the proper pauses in speech and voice inflections. More than anything, I knew it was mandatory to convince the doctor that I took him as earnestly as he took himself, dilettantism being a lamentable sin with psychiatrists. I did, in fact, get so carried away that I began silently mouthing answers and, after one particularly long and convoluted reply, I became suddenly aware of what I was doing, looked up to see if anyone had noticed, and immediately the blood rushed to my face. Paddy the Duke was looking directly at me, smiling. It was a strange smile, both patronizing and hostile. It seemed to accuse at the same time it laughed at me. It seemed to indicate that with my methods I was making a grievous tactical error. "That nonsense," it seemed to say with finality, *"will get you nowhere."*

Waiting for the blood to subside from my face, I sat staring gloomily at the floor. When I did finally muster the courage to look up, I was relieved to see that he was no longer looking at me, he had lost interest. With his chair now propped against the wall, leaning back, he was smoking and blowing smoke rings, one after another—smoke rings as symmetrical and full-bodied as doughnuts. He seemed now indifferent not only to me but even to the predicament—that of being hospitalized—in which he found himself; it was almost as if, through the holes in the smoky doughnuts that rushed toward the ceiling, he were looking deep into some sphere beyond other men's apprehension. There was about Paddy a funereal depth, the kind of gravity that made other men turn from him. It was this solemnity that surprised me.

It surprised me because I had noticed Paddy two days

before, on his arrival at Avalon Valley. He had made a definite impression on me then, but it was nothing at all like the impression I got this day. On first seeing him, I had detected a slight suggestion of gravity: he had a big upper body, strong heavy arms and shoulders that he carried on thin, almost sticklike legs, walking with precise, arrogant little steps; holding his torso in a militaristic, yes, regal way, he had a spine as curved as a celery stalk. It was a bearing that had created an illusion of height. I had thought him at least six feet, where now, to my astonishment, I discovered he was a good deal shorter, no more certainly than five nine. His features were broad and pock-marked, his face had been ruddy and swollen with drink, his eyes as misty as heavy dew. My early and very distinct impression was that he was a parody of the drunken Irishman, middle-aged, sentimental, sloppy—and I was even sure that he would, when he sobered up, entertain us with songs about Mother and Sister Kate and Galway Bay. Studying him now, when he was sober, I got a rather different impression. Where I had originally taken him to be in his mid-fifties, it was now alarmingly obvious that he was probably this side of forty; where he had been ruddy-complexioned, the swelling of drink had now gone from his face, and his features, if not handsome, were not unprepossessing. But now that their heavy mist had vanished, it was his eyes that struck one. They were huge and black and almost impossible to look into, to meet, impossible for the astonishing and somber sagacity they intimated—as though he looked "quite through the deeds of men." Continuing to study him, I felt at first astonishment, then distaste, finally a kind of loathing. A moment later I was sure I loathed him.

A young man who had only recently come from the doctor's office suddenly broke into a violent spiel of indignation aroused by the questions the doctor had put to him. This was surprising. Like the rest of us, he must have known a number of these questions before going into the office. Still, he cursed and ranted, demanding to know of us who the doctors thought they were, then rhetorically provided his own answer—*God?* We assumed that the doctor had unwittingly hit very close to the boy's distress. Hence we tried to offer him sympathy. "Everyone's asked the same things," a number of men said, trying to convince him of the universality of his plight. But the more we assured him, the more he seemed to take these assurances as license to bellow about his rights, about the dignity of the human specimen, and about how he was, at the first opportunity, going to call his attorney. He seemed unsatisfied with this solution. Dropping his voice to a secretive whisper, he revealed to us that he had a friend in Albany. *"A big man,"* he said. Waiting for our response, he looked at each of us in turn; he looked in such a meaningful and melodramatic way that none of us could doubt he had the Governor in mind. Not doubting that, we all fell silent. As he rambled on now at a near-fever pitch, it occurred to us all, simultaneously I would guess, that the man was, as we used to say, far, *far gone.* He continued his terrible diatribe against the doctors, revealing as he went along the measures he contemplated for putting them in their places. Then he lost all coherence and began a hysterical giggle, compounded with a slight twitch and very pronounced emission of saliva from his mouth. When he finally fell silent, the stillness was of that horrified kind that follows a fart in a Methodist church.

At that point I looked up again and saw that Paddy the

Duke was looking at me, smiling, amused. In the most audible of voices, a voice that could be heard from one end of
the corridor to the other, at the same time nodding in the
direction of the Governor's friend, he said: "What the
fuck's he think he's here for—*dandruff?*"

Down the hill Paddy the Duke found himself in our ward
and succeeded, in only a matter of days, perhaps hours, in
making himself the most despised man in Avalon Valley.
His sins were many and grievous, oh, so very grievous, and
perhaps best epitomized in his *adamant*—in its way *monstrous*—refusal to accept the camaraderie of his fellow patients—his total inability to recognize that we were
undergoing an ordeal together. Now even I, who had sworn
against involvement of any kind, feigned this togetherness,
though I seldom knew the names of patients I talked with
by the hour. I feigned it because I was certain the doctors
expected it. Paddy would have no part of it. Not only did
he not speak to any of us; should any of us speak to him, he
acted—coming up out of some deep reverie characterized
by staring into smoke rings—as though he thought our impertinence warranted a good thrashing. The look that came
over him when someone approached him familiarly is beyond any art. Once or twice in the first days he was approached in this way. Particularly I remember a young man
trying to enlist him in a card game. Paddy's body had
tensed; he had gazed at the youth, his piercing eyes had
seemed to sink deeper into their sockets; then he had risen,
bolted upright from his chair. For many moments he had
stood staring, his right arm making whipping motions
against his flank as though he were General Fierceheart
whopping it with a riding crop. The boy had turned to us,
smiled weakly, someone had waved him away, and, turning,

he had fled. The doors to the sleeping room were opened immediately subsequent to supper; after a time Paddy, to protect his privacy, took to going directly to his bed where he lay fully clothed, eyes wide open, searching the ceiling for whatever truth it was he hoped to come to.

Paddy's sins were not all of omission. He did not in the least understand that the hospital was a place of endless and fatiguing waiting, a place of queues. One waited to brush his teeth, to get his orange tranquilizer, to be served his rice pudding, sometimes even to relieve his bowels. Paddy waited for none of these things. Though I took only one meal, breakfast, in the patients' cafeteria, it was here that his disregard of us was most striking. Walking by a hundred, two hundred of us at a clip, walking by as though we had no more existence for him than so many bugs, walking in his arrogant, military way, he proceeded to the head of the line. Once there, he blithely forced his way into it, picked up his tin tray, demanded from the help double orders of his favorite dishes, turned and proceeded to his table. And it was *his* table. Such was his forbidding aspect that we daren't intrude; and there he sat alone amidst us— a bunch of chattering, food-slopping, tray-clanking lunatics—like some holy man, delicately nibbling at his food, his black eyes staring off into space with the intensity of a man set on discovering the Gimmick To Move The World. Once or twice his cafeteria etiquette was challenged by one of the braver among us; but he succeeded, by the very regalness of his bearing and the coldness of his eyes, in backing the challenger down. After a time we began to live granting him his privileges, a docility on our part that we justified by permitting ourselves a shameful rumor that Paddy had friends in high places. Before a month elapsed, the rumor had taken such a firm grip on our imaginations that we began to live in the apprehension of Paddy's revealing himself as someone other than a patient, Someone Elevated, someone who would suddenly begin barking commands at us. His running roughshod over us was despicable, but not so much so as our cowardice. It had to end of course. Things might have remained pretty much the way they were, with us remaining servile to his imposing demeanor, had he not finally committed a profound sin of commission.

He beat us all in Ping-pong.

He beat us utterly. He beat us to the point of bringing tears to our eyes, homicide to our hearts. When he did so, he rallied us and made us One. In some wards the favorite game of the patients was whist, in others pool, and in ours it was Ping-pong. Each afternoon, on completing our various jobs, we went to the Recreation Room where the members of our ward monopolized one of the three tables, playing round-robin games of twenty-one. Our rules were simple. The winner of the game retained his paddle until he was defeated, which in the case of some of the better players occasionally took two, even three afternoons. I don't know how Paddy found us. He might have heard some of the endless and good-natured boasting, the threats and counter-threats, the wondrous bets ("Hey, Exley! Betcha million-trillion dollars I beat your ass off tomorrow!") that went on in the ward each evening—all done in the exhilarating anticipation of the next day's contests. But this seems unlikely because of Paddy's habit of going immediately to his bed. All I do know is that one afternoon, while I was playing, a silence descended on the Recreation Room, a kind of melancholy almost, and when I looked up

I saw that Paddy was seated near the table, watching us. In his mouth he had a cigarette, of course, and he was watching us in a half-amused, half-abstracted way, blowing smoke rings. The men presented to me one face of loathing and disgust. Paddy sat there for three afternoons, scarcely watching us; at the same time we knew he wasn't missing the scoring of a single point. Slumped down in his chair, pursing his lips in a rather obscene way, he formed his disgusting doughnuts. The melancholy stayed with us. Nobody played well, tempers became very short. We had just about determined that he was going to sit there forever when a player, having been defeated by me in a close game, threw his paddle angrily on the table. At that point Paddy rose, brushed aside the challenger who was approaching the table, picked up the paddle, and began a volley with me. The unseen ball went floating by me. As one man we went tense. Frightful little hissing noises issued from our throats. The nerve! Paddy the Duke had ignored our lines for the last time! It was incredible! We were just about to jump him—to jump him together as one furious animal—jump him and break his goddam neck!—when, quite suddenly, quite astonishingly, quite marvelously, a superb idea—a stroke of genius—occurred to me. Having detected the way Paddy held the paddle, perpendicular to the table, like a goddam girl, I suddenly realized how to humiliate him utterly—beat his Irish hide in a game! Instantly I started winking insanely at the men, who were even now moving toward Paddy. Coming to a jolting stop, having seen my frantic winks and having interpreted them correctly, they now let their faces beam idiotically in recognition. Presently the room was filled with as many winks and gleeful giggles as the sky with stars. Paddy beat me twenty-one to two. He then went on to hold the paddle for nine days.

How can I describe those nine days? Even after my fiasco, we began them on a note of contemptuous and hopeful hostility. We ended them—we who had already been locked up as being, well, let's be kind and say *rather singular personalities*—as drooling, raving, temple-pounding, hairpulling lunatics, as close probably to real insanity as any of us had ever been. Paddy's Ping-pong game was no game. He had no serve. He had no backhand. He had no slam. He had, in effect, no offense whatever. All Paddy could do was return the ball—and that return became our monomania. It was the fever in our brains. It was the longing in our hearts. It was Ahab enlisting us in a blasphemous bargain toward our own destruction. We went to bed with that return; we dreamed about it. We rose to that return; we lived all our waking hours with it, trying to fathom its perverseness. During the game Paddy never moved. He stood ramrod straight only inches from the middle of the table, and no matter how furiously we slammed the ball at him, or how adroitly we placed it, he invariably—with a girlish movement we could scarcely detect—had his paddle there waiting. The paddle made contact with the ball, met it, and the ball, seeming to float at us so softly, would scarcely clear the net as we went crashing into the table bent on bashing it down his throat. It looked so easy. There was only one trouble. Paddy's return was never where *our* paddle was. It took the most erratic bounces I have ever seen, to one's right when it should have gone left, to one's left when it should have gone right, straight back at Paddy, and, incredibly, sometimes not even bouncing at all but settling down into a horrifying and infuriating little piddle, as if the son-of-a-bitching thing were expiring in The Grand Style. That bounce had us running all over the back of the table, our eyes bulging with the symptoms of apoplexy. We perspired so that our clothes hung leadlike to our backs. We uttered, bellowed really, vilenesses that would make a pornographer blush. We hurtled ourselves into the edge of the table, raising great purple welts on our thighs. We broke a half-dozen paddles in frustration. We ground Ping-pong balls to white dust under the heels of our shoes. We brought the best players—"ringers"—in from other wards. One of our number, the first among us to "crack," showed up one day in tennis shoes and white shorts. Stripping to the waist when his turn came, he ran around the table so furiously the water leaked from him in rivulets bigger than are seen in Arizona. When the game was done, the man was weeping, his nose was bleeding, his white shorts were fouled with dirt, his elbows and knees were scraped raw, and he was sitting in the middle of the concrete floor, his teeth biting deep into his paddle.

It was all for naught. We knew it, and from that day on we did the only thing we could think of to do. We jeered Paddy. We mimicked the girlish way he held the paddle. "Look at *meeeh*—" in a lisp—"I'm Katherine O'Hara O'Sullivan O'Day, and I'm just too *presheeous* for words!" Now the man would proceed around the table, wispily swinging his hips in what he imagined to be a feminine way. Frightful little hissing noises continued to issue from our throats. We decided that Paddy's serve was illegal. He changed it. We even decided that he cheated—how, we didn't articulate. "If we ever catch you," we cautioned him, our voices tense with menace. Throughout all this Paddy continued to stand ramrod straight, playing his game, occasionally smiling at one or another of our more outlandish threats. When the smiles became frequent, when our threats, that is, became more numerous, I began to grow uneasy, sensing something very like hysteria setting in.

In the first days Paddy had held the paddle, we had spent our evenings huddled together in the ward, discussing the best way to beat him. But as the days passed and the futility of our desires became increasingly evident, these meetings had turned from strategy discussions to some more hopeful and concrete ways we could inflict humiliation on Paddy. They began in innocent wickedness. Someone wanted to urinate on his toothbrush. Someone else wanted to duck his head in the toilet bowl. But they began to get increasingly creative. *"I got it!"* one of our number suggested one night. "We'll wait till about two in the morning, see. Then we'll grab one of the fags by his scrawny neck, see. Then we'll set him gently on Paddy's chest. Got the picture?" Here the man's eyes ran quite lewdly wild with the creativity of his vision. We all nodded impatiently, our mouths open. "And then—ho, ho, ho—" and here the man got down on his knees on the floor assuming the fag's position on Paddy's imaginary chest. "And then *what?*" someone squealed in anticipation. "And then—for Christ's sake, what else? We'll make the fag stick his dinker into Paddy's jaw!" One would have thought we had been trapped in a cave for nine days, and the man had just come up with a brilliant idea for breaking us out. "Yeah! Yeah! Yeah!" everyone screamed in unison. "No! No! No!" I bellowed in protest.

My closest acquaintance at Avalon Valley was a brilliant, tobacco-chewing, cynical and acrid Italian man from Staten Island. He was twenty-six, his hair was completely white, and he looked fifty-six. He used the word *fuck* with a frequency I have never heard in a world quite given over to crassness. We called him Snow White. Without removing his hands from his pockets or sliding up in his chair, and prefacing his sour remarks by expectorating a great glob of tobacco juice on the floor (he always maintained, an evil smile on his lips, that it didn't make any difference because the juice and the floor were the same color), he said, "Fuck, no! That fucking bastard would bite the poor fucking bugger's dinker right off at its fucking stump!" Surprisingly, most of these suggestions were made to me. Against my will and for reasons I didn't understand, I had become a kind of leader and had only to nod my head to get Paddy his long-deserved comeuppance. But I remained cautious, trying to think of something a little more subtle, something that would not cost any of us any more time than we were already destined to spend in the hospital. By the time the above suggestion was made, though, the men were tiring of me; and it was really Snow White's protest that saved Paddy that day. I went to bed that night knowing that the men were on the verge of acting on their own.

The next day Paddy, as arbitrarily as he had snatched up the paddle—on the ninth day, after four or five games—permitted me (I was sure of it) to beat him in a close game, laid down the paddle, left the Recreation Room, and we never saw him there again. A loner, he had known exactly how to gauge the hostility of the crowd, precisely the moment to go out the door.

The men were furious. "Did he let you do that?" they screamed at me.

"No, for Christ's sake!" I bellowed back at them.

Whether they believed me or not, they let it go, sank into sullenness, and Paddy's ass had been saved once again.

———

Only once did I have anything resembling a conversation with Paddy the Duke, and this did not take place until some weeks later, on the night before he left the hospital, though at the time I talked with him I didn't know he was leaving the next day. For a number of weeks I lost all interest in Paddy and even succeeded in almost totally obliterating my milieu. My weeks became a long slumber below which I was always conscious that when I awoke it would be to the discomfiting thought of my imminent departure from the hospital. Dr. K. had decided that my illness did not warrant confinement (he expressed distinct alarm, then quickly covered himself to protect his medical brethren, on learning that I had been given shock treatment). It was true that I had violated many of the customs and prejudices of society; but his solution, though I knew it to be precisely to the point, was not so easy to execute: he told me to stop thinking of myself so much, that my disease was the "bosom serpent," egotism. "You'll be going soon," he said to me one day. Because I expressed neither joy nor alarm, he did not mention it again for a number of weeks.

During these weeks the only time I was conscious of Paddy was at the Wednesday evening meetings of the Avalon Valley Chapter of Alcoholics Anonymous, to which all patients whose trouble was compounded by booze, or whose trouble had become booze (there is a difference), were required to go. I always took a table with two skeptics; we called it "Cynics' Circle." Snow White was, of course, one of the men. He wasn't an alcoholic; his problem was that he was tired, and he came to these meetings for laughs. The other man was Bronislaw. He was about forty-five. He had blue eyes, a wonderfully virile face with very pronounced features, a fine crop of thick, graying hair, and he chain-smoked perfectly formed cigarettes that he rolled himself. By his own admission (and without our even inquiring) he was Very Big in Greenwich Village. A number of short stories, he said, had been written about him; and he had also cluttered a good bit of the canvas of a novel called, I think, *Flee the Angry Strangers.* I never understood why. Though I liked him immensely, I never understood a word he said and could not comprehend how anybody could have got him on paper. His reminiscences were completely devoid of transitional thoughts, his sentences dealt only in symbolic essences, hurdling erratically from one to the next. He was as unintelligible to me as Joyce's *Finnegans Wake.* He was not an alcoholic either. He had been both a dope addict (cured in Lexington) and a dope pusher, and he loved people more than any man I had ever met. To him everybody was a "bunny" that he just wanted to "love to death." He came to the meetings for free coffee and doughnuts, and because he was trying to "love Snow White to death," though Snow White always maintained that it was I he was after.

The three of us had a pact, governed by signals—pinching one another, agreeing to step fiercely on each other's toes when we felt riotous laughter welling up within us. It was not that any of us doubted the efficacy of group therapy for alcoholics (it is probably the only treatment), but, oh, dear heart, alcoholics in the loony bin! Their "falls" had been from dizzying, nearly invisible heights. "And so I said to Churchill, 'Winston,' I said—" "My daddy lose twenty-six million in The Crash, so I never get a *etchookashun*—" Paddy had his own table even at these meetings. He had by then drawn his isolation about him like a mantle, and nobody, but nobody, violated it. He had a wooden clipboard, thick with lined paper, on which he furiously took down apparently every word of every confession. This used to infuriate Snow White; he sensed this note-taking was rendering the confessors shy, that they weren't opening up the way they ordinarily would, and that he was being deprived of some of his laughless laughs. "What the fuck's he doin' with that pencil?" he would ask petulantly, hate in his eyes. "He's a bunny, ain't he?" Bronislaw would say. "Ignore duh fucking guy!" Snow White would snap, as though we had brought him up. But I couldn't really ignore him, and often I found my eyes drifting to his table to watch him write right off the page, then crazily flap it over, like a timid stenographer working for a brutish, tyrannical employer. There was a definite fear of not getting it all down. Once or twice he met my gaze, and when he did so, I smiled at him, condescendingly. His blunt Irish features hardened fiercely, his black eyes protruded, but this nonsense no longer worked with me. Once I laughed aloud at him and with the fingernail of my thumb scraped against my upper teeth. Later I heard that it was the Mafiosa sign signaling to the recipient that vengeance was imminent. At the time I only meant to say, "You're a goofy fuck—you know that?"

November came in cold and went; and as it went I began to grow more perceptibly uneasy; I knew—or suspected— that I would be released any day, and in truth, though I daren't say so to the authorities for fear of never getting out, there was in all the world no place whatever I cared to go. I spent a lot of time brooding on this phenomenon, which Paddy the Duke must have sensed. Where I had not been conscious of him for weeks except at the AA meetings, I seemed now always to be looking up out of my apprehension of the future to find him looking at me, his black eyes studying me intently, as if he understood it all implicitly and in a way that not even I did.

Sitting in the ward one night, staring at the floor, and

caught up, as I say, in what had become for me a perpetual anguish of the future, I suddenly became conscious of him sitting right next to me, staring at me. In a way I was surprised: it was Paddy's custom, as I have said, immediately after supper to go lie on his bed and study the ceiling. Knowing this habit, I now had no doubt he intended to speak to me and the longer he held his peace, the more uneasy I became. I was on the verge of moving when he spoke.

"You'll be leavin' soon, huh?"

"Maybe so," I said indifferently. I meant to suggest that I didn't care a bit whether the conversation continued or not.

"You won't make it." Though he did not say this arrogantly, there was in his voice an alarming finality.

"That's hardly for you to determine," I snapped.

"Oh, you *won't*," he persisted. "Take my word for it. I've watched you and your big-shot buddies up at the meetings. You're even worse than they are. You think you're better'n everybody. You think your duty is to fox everybody, instead of what it should be: to find out what you're doin' here. It's only the last couple of days you thought about that," he assured me. "Ain't that right?"

It was, but I couldn't grant it to him (perhaps I didn't understand it then). Desiring to humiliate him in some way, to jeer at him, I said, "And you? I suppose *you will* make it!"

"Yes, I will," he said. Then he smiled that pain-in-the-ass smile. "You know why?"

"God knows! Tell me why!" I almost shrieked.

At this point he did a ludicrously dramatic, profoundly unsettling thing. Looking slowly over his right shoulder, then over his left—and in either case there was nothing there but blank wall—he brought his head down close to mine and whispered, in the most chillingly solemn tones, and almost choking on the words:

"I've discovered what alcoholism is."

My first desire was to shriek with laughter, to dismiss him as a madman. But I found that I couldn't. There was something in his demeanor so totally forbidding that such laughter would have seemed sacrilegious. I considered getting rid of him in a friendly way, of saying with an air of facetiousness, "If you've done that, pal, you've succeeded where a thousand—no, a thousand times a thousand quacks have failed!" But I could not even say that, could not say anything finally. I knew, suddenly, that I wanted to hear his solution, to hear what alcoholism was. All Paddy's stay in Avalon Valley had been characterized by that apartness, that singleness of purpose that might indeed reveal him as a man somehow more gifted than other men, a man who might come to truths not given to other men. Paddy knew then, by my silence, that I wanted to hear. Typically, he made me wait—wait for what seemed an infinitely long time. When he finally did speak, I felt like an intelligent *fin de siècle* priest who, having been given a copy of Darwin, sits now staring at the unopened book, not so much fearing that he won't be able to accept the book's truths, as that the great world, which for so long in his mind has looked one way, will, by his simply turning a book cover, begin to look a new and totally different way.

"It's sadness."

Sadness?

"Sadness?" I exclaimed gleefully. "Why, Paddy! You're a goddam drunken Irish poet!"

I laughed and laughed and laughed.

Paddy did not care. He had told me what he had found on the ceiling, in the smoke rings, and in the furious notes he had taken at the AA meetings. He was off and running now; had I risen and walked away from him, he would have told his story to my empty chair. It was hardly different from any of those we had heard at the meetings, one long grievous history of lying, cheating, and stealing for booze, and in the wake of that story an aggrieved mother and father, a heart-broken wife, neglected children. The thing that impressed me most was that Paddy, in the end, turned out to be barely literate, having no gift for words, and it was this groping search for words that touched me most.

"I'll never drink again!" he said, perfectly exultant. "Don't yuh get it? And in that way I'll never cause another's sadness!" Then he rose and looked directly at me. "And tell me, wise guy—ain't that enough?"

I rose, too, and looked at him. "Whatever you say, Duke," I said glibly. Then I smiled. Then I walked away.

I will live my life a lesser man for having done that, for having walked away from him. Despite his arrogant ignorance, Paddy *was* a poet. It was when he was leaving the next day that I discovered this and understood that Paddy had come to a kind of truth, the truth for himself, a truth that to this day will not let me divorce the term *alcoholism* from *sadness.* I had been in the library, and, having exhausted my cigarettes, had walked back for some to the ward, to notice that it was unusually crowded for that time of day, with men occupying most of the chairs, smoking and shifting uneasily. When I asked what was up, the answer was swiftly curt, even a little fierce—*"Big Shit's leavin' "*—and I knew that Paddy the Duke's departure from Avalon Valley was going to be like no other departure before or since.

When other men left, we crowded round and shouted, "Good luck, Buddy!" and "Don't let us see yuh back here— *yuh hear?"* and "Don't let the shits"—for that is how the insiders view the outsiders—"get yuh down!" Those of us who believed, prayed; those of us who wept, wept; and those of us who had begun to wonder if we were ever getting out, died a little. But I could see in the men's faces, in the cold, silent sneers, that this was going to be different, even a little terrible, a backbiting, clawing affair—"So long, yuh *prick!*"—that kind of furious, unnecessary thing—something I knew I didn't want to watch. But I couldn't bring myself to leave. I would have said, "Look, he's just a crazy Irish bastard," if I had thought it would have done any good. But I knew that it wouldn't. Seeing Snow White slouched down in a chair, seemingly indifferent to the proceeding, I walked over, took an empty chair next to him, and lit a cigarette. He didn't speak to me. The cigarette was about half-smoked when there was an audible rustling, all heads were being turned to the back of the ward. Having just emerged from the sleeping room, Paddy was standing there facing us.

There are certain appeals that quite startle and benumb the heart: Hamlet the Dane's "Hamlet, remember me" to his son; Hester's "Surely, surely, we have ransomed one another, with all this woe!" to the Reverend Mr. Dimmesdale; Willie Stark's "It might have been all different, Jack. . . . You got to believe that" to Jack Burden; I thought of one such appeal looking at Paddy. I thought of Holden Caulfield's line when his sister Phoebe was riding round and round on the carousel in the rain—"God, I wish you could've been there." The state had given him a neat, black wool topcoat, a cheap though nice-looking brown suit, and a pair of sleek-black, patent-leather shoes. In his right hand he carried a small Gladstone bag, containing, no doubt, the entire viaticum of a life spent badly; still he looked, from that distance where one could not determine the material worth of his outfit, like a man just stepped off a plane at some World Capital, a man bound on a mission of forbidding gravity.

Seeing us, he paused only momentarily—and smiled. Though there was nothing deprecatory in that smile, there was nevertheless a patina of defiance, as though he knew what kind of a farewell we had planned for him and did not care. Now he began the walk by us up the long ward. He walked more slowly than usual, taking those precise, military steps, walking by one, then another, of us, much as he had walked by us in the cafeteria. Never again would he cast his eyes upon us. Our breaths suspended momentarily. He went by another, and still another of us, by the orange and blue chairs, walking by us at the same time that our breaths, in expiration, became as audible as thunder. When he reached the middle of the ward, then passed it, I knew suddenly—knew that no one was going to call after him. I knew because Paddy had the power. Call it *sadness* or whatever, he had used his time among us wisely, he would never inflict pain on another again—and, yes, he was right: he would make it! Paddy was almost at the door now, and we stood behind him, too ashamed of our timidity to look at each other. I suppose there even came a moment (at least there did for me) when we hoped he would look back at us, come back with a tentative wave, the suggestion of a smile, hoped that he would leave us something. But Paddy was indeed a man with a grave mission—that of living without causing pain. Without turning (though he did, I think, pause ever so slightly), he went through the door, out of Avalon Valley and the squalor of our lives. When he was gone, I turned furiously on my heels and fled into the lavatory. I did so, for I, who before going *down the hill* had vowed not to get close to another so as not to experience the hurt of his defeat, ended, ironically, by breaking under another's victory, and I did not want Snow White or those others—lest they misunderstand—to see the tears streaming down my face.

———

Paddy the Duke was right. I had one more "tour of duty" to put in at the funny farm. They turned me loose a few days after he left, sometime in the winter months of 1959, but in a little more than a year's time I would be back at Avalon Valley; and I would be a very sick man. Moreover, I would by then be properly humbled and prepared to go back into the past in search of the reasons, prepared, like Paddy, to stare at the ceiling and remember. My biggest problem was where to begin, for I have no doubt that the obstetrician no sooner swats the infant's buttocks inducing the hysterical scream of life than that a certain milieu is prepared and waiting for him, a milieu in which already the shadows and shades exist which will determine whether he goes to Avalon Valley or the White House. I thought finally that I had best begin by filling up those five years between my journey to the Polo Grounds and my arrival at the private hospital. I thought I had best begin in Chicago.

4

ONHAVA REGAINED
AND LOST AGAIN

In the days when I lived in Chicago, I twice fell in love. I fell in love first with that golden city—my Onhava!—by the blue lake, and then with Bunny Sue Allorgee. It was a splendid arrangement, first the city and then the dream maiden, for love, in its awful intimacy, demands to be played out against familiar backdrops. When, one blustery June morning, Bunny Sue walked into my life, I was so altogether in love with *that* city that I did not quite believe in its essentialness, its palpability, and it was against this inessential, this glittering crepe city that I acted out my dream of bliss. It seems of little consequence to me now that Bunny was to say, "Oh, no!"—was to decide against admitting my love—or that then the loveliness would go out of my city, rendering it as bleak and debauched as ever Gomorrah was. It seems of little consequence because for a few precious moments—as long, perhaps, as it is given to any man—I was buoyed up, in a state of exhilarating and dizzying weightlessness, by love, and had the whole world by the short hair.

—

Bunny Sue was the consummation of many long months of incredible, nearly unspeakable apprehension—months in which I had, like the mad Kinbote, lived my life in exile, waiting to sail back and recover my lost kingdom of Zembla. That kingdom was always a "dim iridescence"—a place above and beyond the next precipice; but I always knew that at any moment, the very next no doubt, the world's colors would fall into place and define themselves. They merely assumed their focus in the taffy, benumbing presence of Bunny Sue. And though I had always expected them to do so, I was, I expect, left quite as speechless by the girl as if I had never anticipated her.

A few days after my journey to the Polo Grounds, I got a job. I would like to believe that my cheering for Owen had rendered my countenance more amenable to prospective employers, but this was not the case. Exhausted by the long months of my defeat, I combed my hair, had my suit cleaned, walked into the personnel department of the New York Central Railroad, and told the man I would take anything he had to offer. He took me at my word—giving me anything: a job as clerk-trainee in the passenger department at a pittance. But my luck was beginning to change, and in a few weeks I had an impossibly splendid job in that company's public relations department. Robert R. Young, the powder-haired, tassel-toed, dapper little financier out of Texas, had just won control of the company in that now-famous proxy war and was, as his first order of business, "clearing the deadwood" (twenty thousand employees) from the Central's payroll. In all the time I was with the railroad, this onslaught on the "featherbedders" seemed to be his only policy. He was more than anything, I think, a phrasemaker—"A hog can cross country without changing trains, but you can't"—and because he seemed to have no clear-cut policy, we gentlemen in public relations, as near as I could determine, were expected to do little more than sit in our cubicles, pick our noses, clean our fingernails, watch Young brush away the scarabs, and wait for reporters to telephone with questions we wouldn't, even if we knew the answers, be permitted to answer. Which is as good a definition of public relations as any.

Working under such conditions, I needed no time at all to decide that one ought to exercise such duties in style. I bought a couple tweed suits, a few delicately patterned bow ties, and a pair of sincere black Oxfords. Putting a lot of impressive-looking and forged documents into my in-box, I closed the door to my glass cage, and for the next few months read cover to cover every issue of *Time, Newsweek, Sports Illustrated, Harper's,* the *Atlantic,* and *The New Yorker,* which still left time for Saul Bellow's *The Adventures of Augie March,* a volume I read till it came unbound and the pages started dropping out and cluttering up the in-box. In public relations there were only three of us who had been retained from the pre-Young days. On Young's enthronement most of the men, including the boss, had been shown the door for having worked too stridently to prevent Young's coronation—for doing their jobs, in other words; and shortly thereafter some of his own people began to seep into the vacated cubicles.

Into the one next to mine moved a raven-haired Radcliffe girl with a superb behind, a pair of legs that must have held their own on the hockey fields of Cambridge, and an authoritative though pleasing voice. It was her job to answer Young's lunatic mail. These letters were from people who believed, quite properly, that eight million dollars was much too much for any one man, and who, as a result, had come up with some rather novel and touching ways of rectifying the situation. Perhaps dear, drunken, and beloved old Uncle Casper was expiring from a minuscule tumor of the brain, and all they wanted was two thousand dollars' *"surtchon's* dues." Others wanted a million or so for a Great Dane hospital, a home for retired pederasts, or backing for an "all-day musical," featuring a thousand sequined chorus girls and songs by an unacclaimed lyricist named August Sugarword (the very same whose soon-to-be-immortalized signature could be seen bringing up the bottom of the letter). The girl was good; she knew her business. For two days I picked my nose and listened to her dictate before introducing myself, and by then I had a case on her.

> Dear Mrs. Curpartial:
>
> Thank you for your letter of October 20 requesting a million dollars to help construct your planned sanatorium for Great Danes.
>
> Let me say at the outset that, though I am unable to give to you the funds for this good cause, there is no one, I think, who is more fond of canines than I, and especially of your particular choice, the noble-hearted Dane.
>
> Without going too deeply into the reasons for my refusal, I hope you can appreciate that I am each year literally inundated with financial requests for one good cause and another. For that reason I have long made it my practice to give to the more general charities, Community Chest, etc., in the hope that what I am able to give will find a more equitable distribution among the needy.
>
> In conclusion, and if it doesn't seem too presumptuous, I

might offer a word of advice. Don't you think you might have better luck by enlarging your plans to envision a sanatorium whose doors would be open to other breeds, the Chow, the Boxer, the Chihuahua, the Red-Bone Hound—perhaps even a mongrel or two? I wonder, really, if there will be enough Great Danes for the ample and lavish space you so obviously have in mind.

Yours sincerely,
Sybil Radcliffe
For Robert R. Young

That letter won me over; and Miss Radcliffe and I had a shy, kissless, and quite unsettling romance for a few weeks subsequent to my introducing myself. We sat in cozy Italian restaurants for three-hour lunches, nibbling delicately on breadsticks and smiling demurely at each other. I talked about Hemingway, she about Young, and that, in a nutshell, was the terrible division of our outlooks. She believed Young to be a Great Man caught up in matters out of the reach of other mortals, where, if I believed him to be anything (and I scarcely looked on him as human), it was as a pipsqueak parvenu out of the Super State gone quite power-loony. Oh, she knew Hemingway—better than I did; but his world was as unreal to her as Young's was palpable. Her alarming backside and luxurious thighs were always virginally enwrapped in black wool and gray tweed, and that was the way she wanted it. I always envisioned that grand thing sheathed in the Tyrolese corduroy of mountain hikers; and I had this vision of following it, so sheathed, up that pale precipice to the iridescent land where, once attained and in a tremble of exhaustion and anticipation, I would decorduroy, depant, and deflower her among the flora, the world's colors coming into focus in the soft raven down of her thingamajig. I wanted to risk great happiness, but I never got the chance. Our "romance" ended one bleak night in Louis' Tavern in the Village. I had taken her there to show her my "dream-tavern," the place to which I fled every night to dream my dreams of fame. She said that she liked neither it nor the people there; I became upset, gave her money for a cab, and watched her walk away from me, wondering if I shouldn't run after her. But I never did. I was hurt and furious that she hadn't taken to Louis'. At that time Louis' was one of the places that made my existence bearable.

In the evening Louis' was always the penultimate stop. There was Louis', then there was bed, though there were always a number of stops before these. Immediately after work I always fled, jogging a little perspiration-inducing trot, to the midtown Young Men's Christian Association I called home. The idea was to get to the communal showers before the fags did. For a time they hadn't bothered me; I had read in a Paul Bowles story about a group of rather playful Arab Moslems who, after strenuously using a young Westerner, had relieved him of his penis, had sewed it into his mouth or belly or someplace (the story was an immense bore), and had left his naked and disfigured body to the African sun: there was some comfort in the knowledge that my sodomites were merely playful Christians. I thought the best way to act in the showers was quite manly, and for a few weeks I had stood among those steam-glistening, wispy young men vigorously lathering my genitalia and buttocks, and yodeling (I am a good yodeler) in a studiously indifferent way. I won't say that I didn't understand I might be making myself as attractive to them as a mustachioed and beribboned Scots Guard, that I was teasing, but I do know that it caught up with me, degenerating into a scene of ludicrously comical possibilities, with a frail, befreckled, and redheaded Christian youth, his manhood all afluster, madly pursuing my scarcely rinsed and virginal body down the long, bleak hall to my room where I just managed to get the chain latched in time. On my way out of the building that night I stopped by at the desk intent on registering a complaint. There I was met by a cross-eyed, sticklike ephebe who, bringing himself gingerly up to the counter in anticipation of my query, smiled demurely at me and said, *"Yeth?"* I laughed like a goddam madman. *"Forgeth abouth* it," I said. After that day I started jogging "home" to get to those showers first.

After showering I lay naked atop my iron cot for a couple hours, drifting between sleep and wakefulness, sometimes staring at the weird patterns made by the peeling lemon walls. Below me in the street, it was the rush hour, and the cabs seemed furious, screeching agonized brakes at each other's behinds, and bellowing violently at each other with their horns. Doors opened and closed in the halls. Giggling, flighty voices drifted by my door. Occasionally I fell asleep to lovers' quarrels that had erupted into clawing, head-banging, tear-laden affairs. On awaking, it would be dusk. The street noises below me now seemed far off—as remote as if they came from some distant city. The silence of evening was encroaching. Rising from the cot, I would dress, take the elevator to the lobby, walk through the door into the autumn night, and go in search of the future.

My search followed a rigid pattern, beginning at P. J. Clarke's saloon at the corner of Third Avenue and Fifty-fifth Street. This bistro was said to have been employed by

Billy Wilder in his filming of *The Lost Weekend,* being that saloon where Ray Milland in his splendid evocation of Don Burnham, the unwriting writer, had drunk his drinks and dreamed his dreams. Because of the notoriety brought on by the film, the place had, for the rich and the near-rich, for the gifted and the near-gifted, taken on a slightly sinister and degenerate aura, a place where these good souls might go and imagine themselves hard by squalor. It was ironical. In the end they only rubbed shoulders with each other. Time after time I stood, as Milland had done in the movie, slightly aglow with drink and tried to imagine myself as Michelangelo sculpting the chin of Moses, or, looking out at the El (which still stood in those days) and seeing not Third Avenue but the Nile.

But I had no luck. The atmosphere was without that bleakness conducive to dreams. The pink-cheeked, tweedy men, the downy-armed, thrilling girls, the antiquated mahogany bar, the murky yellow mirrors, the sawdusted and white-tiled floors, all conspired to remind me of a genteel English pub. It might, one thought, have been sent over by some eccentric Englishman to keep the British Delegation to the UN from becoming homesick; and one could even imagine how, if that august body suddenly dissolved itself, workmen would arrive one day, carefully disassemble the place, pack it, smoky mirrors and all, into vast wooden crates, and send it back across the sea to London where it would be lovingly reassembled on a cobbled lane off Fleet Street. P. J. Clarke's was not the sort of place to imagine oneself mingling with the profligate elements of the earth.

Invariably I arrived there between eight and nine, squeezed my way among the blue blazers at the bar, ordered a fifteen-cent beer, and fixed on my face the smile of a man with implicit faith in the future. That smile was a positive receptacle for life's possibilities. I did not want to miss, as I had with Cary Grant, a second chance to enter the future. When the gentle-voiced, intellectual man from the publishing house told me to get my "notes in shape" so that he could "look them over," I wanted to be ready; when the Vassar blonde, rendered wobbly-kneed in the face of my benign charm, spurned her date and beckoned for me to follow, I wanted to be at her elegant, pump-sheathed insteps, panting. I never doubted that at any moment such a thing would happen, that a mysterious stranger would remark my "good looks" and "high intelligence" and in only a matter of hours I would be winging my way to Bonn or Lisbon or Johannesburg on a mission of grave and singular importance. I never talked with anyone save a young bartender, and no one ever talked with me. Yet for one so guileless I frequently found myself in some unnerving quandaries, having to restrain myself from bursting into anger. My trouble was my sanguine, ingenuous, and lunatic smile. Other men took it to be a piece of foppish coquetry, as if I were proposing to them English public school games; often I heard men in my vicinity make nasty observations about me, speaking with that hateful anxiety that signaled their fear of their own manhood. I had no idea what the Vassar girls thought of me. I expect it was nothing more than that I was a satyr on the make; one of them involved me in a remarkably unnecessary scene one evening.

She was sitting at the street end of the bar with her back to Third Avenue, flapping her shoulder-length blond hair about in a somewhat affected though fetching way and permitting a flanneled, bespectacled undergraduate type to buy her scotch and light her Parliaments. She was extremely attractive, but like all the girls I saw at Clarke's there was something a little aseptically unreal about her. At one time—for no more than a discreet moment or two—I had definitely been giving her the compliment of my stares, but I was now looking through her as through a glassless window frame, looking out at Third Avenue trying to see the Nile. Apparently her vanity wouldn't admit the possibility. Quite suddenly I felt an irritated finger prodding me quite significantly in the elbow and looked up to find the undergraduate in what he assumed to be a posture of indignation. "Stop staring at my date," he snapped.

I did not like his tone. "I wasn't staring at your date," I said. I maintained my smile.

"Don't give me *that!*" he said. "You've been staring at her for the last half-hour!"

He was beginning to raise his voice, and I felt the blood go to the back of my neck, imagining all those sleek necks behind me cranking around in their button-down collars. Now the bartender was involved in it. He whispered to the man something to the effect that I was okay—just a bit "weird." This apologetic tone infuriated me, and it was all Specs needed: he took it as license to become more indignant and began pounding his fleshless hand on the bar and screaming he wouldn't have it! While he was doing this, I suddenly grew bored with him and, spurred on by the bartender's patronizing me, really did start staring lasciviously at his date, ogling her and making tentative but definitely lewd suggestions with my tongue. Miss Vassar went into one of those swoons Victorian women were given to, letting her beautiful blue eyes roll up into her head and, her hands clawing the bar, hurled herself back into an imaginary divan.

My mother has an aging cocker spaniel, Christie III, whose bladder can't be stayed, and whenever the poor dog has to take a piss, he stands by the door whining something fierce and going into an incredibly pathetic jig. That's what Specs seemed in need of—bladder relief. I watched him for a few seconds, smiling, then reached out, took his inflamed cheeks between my thumbs and forefingers, squeezed till they went white as alabaster, bent to him, planted an enthusiastic kiss on the down above the rim of his glasses, and walked out the door. A month later I ran into the bartender walking on Lexington Avenue. When he asked where I had been, I smiled weakly and said, "I wasn't sure I was welcome." He told me to forget about it, that for years he had wanted to do what I did to about 90 percent of the habitués of Clarke's. The following evening I was back among the snug-shoulders, my smile a good deal more timorous.

On leaving Clarke's I always walked to Fifty-third Street, took the downtown train, got off at Fourth Street in the Village, and for the next couple hours drank beer at Minetta's, the Kettle of Fish, and the San Remo on Macdougal Street. By eleven I was always, night in and night out, at Louis' on Sheridan Square. Louis' was one of those walk-down bars, its floor situated a half-dozen feet below street level. It was compact and cozy, its low artificially cobwebbed ceiling rendering its murky, yellow light mysterious, enchanting with smoke. Because of the smallness of the place, it seemed to be always swarming with people, and I took its atmosphere to be the very epitome of Village life, the vibrant, incessant hum of its conversations seeming to whisper of plays, paintings, and novels just short of being realized.

I wonder now if I ever gave thought to how these things

were to be accomplished drinking beer in Louis'. I don't suppose I did, though I knew better. At USC I had taken a course from Harlan Hatcher, who was on summer sabbatical from the University of Illinois just prior to assuming the presidency of the University of Michigan. He was a little wistful, a little surprised and perhaps dismayed by his rise in the academic hierarchy. He, too, had wanted "to write" when young; and if I took anything from his course, it was an observation he had made on Hemingway in Paris during the twenties. He said that while he and others tried to talk their novels out in sidewalk cafés, Hemingway was locked up in a room getting on with the business of his life, that though he did not know Hemingway, he knew of him, as all the young Americans in Paris did, and that Hemingway proved a constant provocation to them, like a furious clarion that books do not get written on the Montparnasse. I suppose I must have been aware that there were even then, out above me in the Village night, young men and women seeking to commit to paper or to canvas their all-consuming visions of America; occasionally I noticed at the bar a more provoking silhouette, a man whose isolated intensity suggested that he was even then phrasing in his mind darkly beautiful paragraphs. But I did not let these things provoke me, and went blissfully on my way, thinking of Boswell's description of Johnson at work on one of his books. Remembering how the good doctor, having fallen heir to melancholia halfway through the manuscript and unable to write, had sent for the publisher and had dictated the remainder of the work while he lay abed (the beauty of Boswell's humanity was that he never saw the humor of this), I saw myself lolling on a sateen divan, spitting grape seeds like Spencer Tracy's Mr. Hyde, and dictating my immortal words to my Vassar blonde, taking five minutes out now and then for an orgy. In Louis' in those days, one could believe in anything.

The patrons of Louis' did not like each other very much. It is only now that I can see that we represented to one another wasted time and crippling dreams. Because of this we did not contain our tempers or our insults, and after a time I seldom talked with anyone save the bartenders, Mike and Red. Unable to communicate, we stood together at the bar caught up each in his own vision of the future, quite unwilling to respect each other's dreams.

The only man I liked in Louis' I never got to know, the cinema star Steve McQueen. I only spoke to him once or twice. Even then he was quite unapproachable, as if he were already the man he would one day become; and the one time that I definitely remember having words with him, they were about a girl for whom we both had eyes, and the words were childish and petulant, involving as they did a good deal of sizing each other up. But I still have a very clear picture of him as he was then; in a way he seemed to represent all of us, at that time, in that place. Wearing the snug cap affected by sports-car enthusiasts, a cap that seemed to sit precariously atop his thick blond hair, a heavy green wool sweater, and corduroy trousers, he used to stand by the hour hunched over the bar, staring broodingly off into space. He had a casualness about him that suggested the indifferent aristocracy; but on closer inspection, there proved to be a very real hardness about him, the hardness of a gutter fighter, and one suspected that he hadn't been corrupted by any pretentions he had picked up in a Yale "classics" course. There was an incredible hunger about him, as if he stood poised to devour the universe, and though I did not know what his particular dream was, I was sure that of all the habitués of Louis' it was he who would make it. A few years later (and which madhouse was I in then?) I turned on the television and saw him in a cowboy suit pumping furiously away with some kind of sawed-off rifle, and a few years later opened *Life* and found that he was the hottest thing in Hollywood since John Wayne. Studying the photos, I wasn't surprised to notice that he seemed not the least surprised at finding himself a King. In those days we all stood at the bar poised on the threshold of some rhapsodic destiny. Frank Gifford, more than any single person, sustained for me the illusion that fame was possible.

In the year I spent in New York, I became a fan. I became hooked. I didn't intend it that way, or, for that matter, didn't comprehend it when it did happen. But happen it did; it was in those days that Sundays began to take on for me a frantic and nervous exhilaration. I would purchase all the Sunday newspapers, drop those sections I didn't read into the gutter along the way, then take my Sunday breakfast at a diner on Third Avenue. It was not a clean place, but the food was cheap and edible and abundant, mountains of scrambled eggs and thick-cut bacon and home-fried potatoes and great mugs of fresh coffee (the place is gone now, given way to a pastel lemon and orange Hot Shoppe). After breakfast I used to go back to my iron cot at the Y, reread the articles about the Giants over and over again, and plan my strategy. Steve Owen was gone, and the new coach, Jim Lee Howell, wasn't "showing" me very much. About noon I would rise and head for the Polo Grounds.

The crowds at the Polo Grounds were nothing whatever like the crowds one sees in Yankee Stadium today. The sportswriters hadn't as yet convinced the public that something very special was taking place on autumn Sunday afternoons, something that in its execution was at times beautiful, at times almost awesome, at times almost art. The writers were beginning to clamor, but the tone of most sportswriting is a clamor, making it difficult for the fan to isolate the real from the fantastic. Still, these writers are a tough breed to tune out, the public would eventually listen, and in a few seasons the Giants would have moved to the Yankee Stadium, would have changed their jerseys from a crimson to a formal navy blue, would have added to their helmets a snooty *N.Y.* emblem, and would be playing, week in and week out, to sell-out crowds of Chesterfield-coated corporation executives and their elegant-legged, mink-draped wives. The Polo Grounds was never sold out.

Arriving at the field shortly before one, I would buy a bleacher seat for a buck, then for another dollar bribe my way into a seat between the forty-yard lines. With the wind at my back I had to stand at the back of the stadium during the first part of the game until the usher, having decided what seats were going to go unoccupied throughout the afternoon (usually near the end of the first period), steered me to an empty. Waiting, I always stood with a group of men from Brooklyn who also paid the bribe. An Italian bread-truck driver, an Irish patrolman, a fat garage mechanic, two or three burly longshoremen, and some others whose occupations I forget—we were a motley, a memorable picture. Dressed as often as not in skimpy jackets, without gloves, we were never dressed warmly enough. Our noses ran. To keep warm we smoked one cigarette after another, drank much beer, and jogged up and down on the concrete. The Brooklyn guys talked all during the game, as much as Brooklyn guys ever talk, which is to say hardly at all. Brooklyn guys issue statements. There is a unity of tone that forbids disagreement. "Take duh fucking

bum outa deah!" or "Dat guy is a *pro*"—that designation
being the highest accolade they allowed a player for making some superb play. Hollow-chested, their frigid hands
stuffed deep into their pockets, their eyes and noses running, they looked about as fit to judge the relative merits of
athletes as Ronald Firbank. Still, because of the cocksure,
irrefutable tones in which they issued their judgments, I
was certain they knew everything about football, and I enjoyed being with them immensely.

And they liked me. I was so alien to their hard, sophisticated, and wordless enthusiasms that they—oh, grand
irony!—considered *me* a freak! Especially because I was so
partial to Gifford. Whenever, smiling, I joined their con-
clave, sneaking sort of shyly among them, one of them
would always say, "Hey, boys, here's duh Gippeh. How we
gonna make out today, Gippeh?" or "Don't stand next to
me, Gippeh—my fucking back's still achin' from last
week!" Everyone would laugh like a goddam hyena. Me
too. As the season progressed, we found we enjoyed each
other so much that we decided, quite tacitly, to stand the
entire game. Had we moved into the empty seats, we would
have had to split up, one here, two or three there, wherever
the seats were available. So we braved the wind at our
backs, our noses ran, we had large laughs—that laughter
haunts me still—and sometimes, at those moments when
the play on the field seemed astonishingly perfect, we just
fell quiet. That was the most memorable picture of all. We
were Wops and Polacks and Irishmen out of Flatbush,
along with one mad dreamer out of the cold, cow country
up yonder, and though we may not have had the background, or the education, to weep at Prince Hamlet's
death, we had all tried enough times to pass and kick a ball,
we had on our separate rock-strewn sandlots taken enough

lumps and bruises, to know that we were viewing something truly fine, something that only comes with years of toil, something very like art.

They were right about my churlish, extravagant partiality to Gifford; though I suspect they never understood it, it amused them, and they liked me for that. Already that fall I had drawn parallels between Gifford's life and mine, our having been at USC together, our having come East almost simultaneously, and the unquestionable fact that we both desired fame, perhaps he even more than I, for he had already eaten, in a limited way, of that Bitch at school. Throughout that autumn, throughout those long, lovely afternoons, there was only one number for me, 16, and I cheered frantically for it, pounding my Brooklyn buddies on the back, and screaming, "Atta boy, Frank! Atta way, you bastard!" I caught passes with him, and threw blocks with him, and groaningly sucked in my breath as he was being viciously tackled. Watching him rise after such a tackle, I piddled back to the huddle with him, my head cranked back at the recent executor of the tackle, my voice warning, "Next time, you bastard—"

It was very simple really. Where I could not, with syntax, give shape to my fantasies, Gifford could, with his superb timing, his great hands, his uncanny faking, give shape to his. It was something more than this: I cheered for him with such inordinate enthusiasm, my yearning became so involved with his desire to escape life's bleak anonymity, that after a time he became my alter ego, that part of me which had its being in the competitive world of men; I came, as incredible as it seems to me now, to believe that I was, in some magical way, an actual instrument of his success. Each time I heard the roar of the crowd, it roared in my ears as much for me as him; that roar was not only a promise of my fame, it was its unequivocal assurance.

He was hurt a good deal in 1954; but there were days when he was fine, and all that season I tried to get my Brooklyn friends to bestow on him the name of pro. In the very last game I saw at the Polo Grounds—for I was suddenly to be transferred by the railroad to Chicago—they did so. I don't remember the play, but it was one of those incredible catches that have characterized his career; that awesome, forbidding silence had descended immediately on our group. We looked at each other pop-eyed, shaking our heads in wonder. Then we stared at the Italian truck driver, the swarthy little man who was the arbiter of our fuzzy enthusiasms. He was a very theatrical little guy. He didn't say anything for a long time. Then he looked up at me and smiled apologetically, as though he were giving in. "He's a pro," he proclaimed. *"He is a pro."* Then all the rest of them shook their heads knowingly and repeated, *"He is a pro!"* Lunatic tears brimmed my eyes and I smiled a lunatic smile from ear to ear; we all roared at my sentimentality and roughed each other affectionately with our hands, dancing round and round in the cold winds of the Polo Grounds.

———

"I am an American, Chicago born—Chicago, that somber city—and go at things as I have taught myself, free-style . . . first to knock, first admitted. . . ." Such had my buddy Augie—he who had helped me pass the endless hours locked up in my glass cubicle in New York—begun his wild and picturesque tale. And though for me Augie had never vindicated his claims of Chicago's *somberness,* I was not in that city two weeks before I began to believe that he had not, after all, cast out the *word* idly. I got fired from my job. My boss called me on the telephone from New York and told me that the Texan was launched on another economy wave, which involved cutting from the Central's payroll my rather meager salary. I said okay. There was nothing else I could say. On hanging up, I had lighted a cigarette and through a window had watched the wintry night descend on Chicago's Loop. It was, except for the view, an imposing office on the topmost, the executive floor of LaSalle Street Station. With its picture window, its great desk, its wall-to-wall carpeting, I would hate to give it up. I had no money, and the thought of going back to my aunt's davenport and beginning another assault on New York, and with it the continual and humiliating blows to one's esteem (if someone had asked me at that moment why I wanted to work for HKI & W, I would have removed from my pocket a forty-five, had I a forty-five, and put a tidy little hole between his eyes), all but prostrated me. Worse than anything, I had at the lousy hotel where I was staying picked up a division or two of crab lice. Having got some stinging solution from a pharmacist—whispering through a weak smile, "Something for crabs, please?"—I thought I had rid myself of the vermin, but almost simultaneously with the news of my firing the tenacious heathens had regrouped and begun what felt like Armageddon. Rising, I strolled to the door, latched it, returned to my seat, sat, unzipped my fly, and began doing battle with both armies. A forlorn, a lugubrious, a sad, sad picture, young, suave, brilliant Freddy Exley a thousand miles from home, sans job, sans hope, sans energy, sitting high in the carpeted sky, his bulging eyes down close to his vital parts, spearing with his fingernails those filthy, those vile little curs.

A couple years later I would open the newspaper to the

news that Robert R. Young, after eating a breakfast of ham and eggs, had gone upstairs to his study, had put a shotgun into his mouth, and had blown away the back of his head. I would smile. There was in that smile nothing vindictive; I had never looked on Young as a man of flesh and blood. To me he was a jaunty little thing I used to see bouncing across the upper level of the Grand Central surrounded by a platoon of snug-shoulders. I never believed in his reality. I would smile because everyone I knew at the New York Central, Sybil Radcliffe, the man who had just fired me, and others, had believed that Young was a man of precise direction, a man who would with a few unerring strokes, piggyback freight, lightweight trains, coast-to-coast passenger service, yah, yah, yah, rescue an entire industry. And I would smile sadly, a smile very close to tears: Young, with that one beautiful gesture, had come alive for me, had become a man. For suicide is the most eloquent of all wails for direction. Suicide is what Hemingway does when the world gets so out of focus he can no longer commit it to paper. Suicide is what the man does when the pain caused by the cancer in the bowel blurs the landscape to the eye so that all things look the same and even the defined direction of blackness seems welcome. Suicide—well, it was what Young did, and it was the conspicuous admission of his defeat, his inability to bring direction to that industry, a direction he had boasted he could and would bring.

The man who fired me would not even outlive Young. Coming by superliner from the company's annual meeting in Albany, he had dropped his head to the back of the seat in front of his and died of a heart attack, died there among those paragons of industry. I never saw Sybil Radcliffe again, so I don't know how she took the great man's death. The last I heard she was in Florida with an asthmatic husband who sold real estate or used cars. I was glad to hear it. He is a lucky man. She was a brilliant girl, and my bet is that she got the message.

But I am anticipating. I was sitting in the executive suite high up in Chicago's wintry and "somber" sky, feeling something very like despair. I should not have despaired: this was Chicago—the city that gave everything and asked nothing. A knock, tentative, came to the door. Rezipping my fly, I rose, walked across the carpet, and opened it. In through the door walked Ted Zirbes, who introduced himself as the Director of Press Relations for the Rock Island Railroad, come from the ninth floor where his offices were located to say hello and wish me well on my new assignment. I told him there was no longer any assignment. "Don't worry about it," he said. "C'mon down and work for me." "Are you kidding?" I said. He said that he wasn't; at the end of the month I moved in LaSalle Street Station from the twelfth to the ninth floor, where they gave me a desk, a typewriter, an unlimited expense account, and the lordly title of Public Relations Representative–Managing Editor. For days after, I sat at my desk watching Ted with devout concern, waiting for him to smile and tell me the joke was over. But he never did. Almost all of the things that happened to me in Chicago aroused in me this giddy incredulity.

I loved that job more than any I ever had—or ever will have. My main duties were the writing, the editing, the laying out, and the putting to bed of the company's magazine, remarkably, even a little maniacally, called *The Rocket*, a name taken from the road's quality passenger trains. I did a lousy job, knowing next to nothing about industrial writing and editing, and especially about the reading capabilities of the audience I was trying to reach (I was always being criticized for making my prose either too simple or too obscure) and would now, I know, be embarrassed to leaf through those issues I was responsible for. Still, I *was* trying, and in search of stories I went to towns the very names of which can still arouse in me a frenzy, such was the mystery and the promise they seemed to hold out for me. I went to Denver and Colorado Springs in Colorado, in Nebraska to Fairbury and Omaha. I went to Des Moines and Davenport and Ames and Newton and Iowa City in Iowa, to Dallas and Houston and Fort Worth in Texas. I went to Oklahoma City and El Reno in Oklahoma, to Milwaukee and St. Paul in Wisconsin and Minnesota. I went to Peoria and Joliet and Rock Island in Illinois, to Little Rock in Arkansas. All over the vast, endless, and awesome Midwest I went. I always traveled on the road's Rockets.

On boarding I took a seat in the club car, crossed my flanneled legs, cleared my throat, ordered a Budweiser, and got ready to make jokes with the twangy salesmen. While talking with them, I might reach into my coat pocket, remove my leather pocket secretary, and casually proffer my card, saying as I passed it, "Fred Exley! PR! Rock Island!" Because I had a system or "white" pass, one good enough to take me any place on the road, I was deferred to by porters. "Anything else before dinner, Mr. Exley?" "Why, yes, John"—a theatrical pause here—"you might bring these gentlemen"—regally flourishing my hand to take in the entire club car—"another drink before they have their dinners." The salesmen would smile and nod approvingly at each other. "And so young to have such a big job," those smiles seemed to say. By dinner I was alone in the car. At twilight, leaving Rock Island, I looked down and saw the massive, sluggish Mississippi flow by beneath me and, hardly having digested its historical emanations, its wonder, was passed into the corn country where the stalks, outlasting the limits of one's vision, sway in the wind like the timeless moves of the sea. By nine I was in my roomette in bed. I lay long awake between clean sheets, the blinds flung up, watching, even feeling, the vast middle of America flow by and beneath me, seeing off in the distance the lights of the prairie towns, like the blinking of fireflies on a soft summer's night, so quickly did one pass them by. I awoke, perhaps, at Colorado Springs. Disembarking, I took a deep, dizzying breath of the high, shrill air and, turning, saw the town, like a Dutch miniature of a Swiss village. Beyond the town was the mountain, Pike's Peak, snowcapped in July and rising into the incredibly blue heavens—a mountain so pure of definition that it was all I could do to stay my hand from attempting to reach out and touch it. After my day's work I drank martinis in the cocktail lounge of the Broadmoor, waiting for the blonde who never came, and for whom I never gave up waiting, such was my optimism and my contentment. It was a contentment all the more enhanced by the knowledge that when the trip was done, by Friday at the latest, I would be back in Chicago—home to the city I loved.

There I lived in that section called the Near North Side, a paradise for the young men and women—airline hostesses with airline hostesses, rising executives with rising executives, Junior Leaguers with Junior Leaguers, voyeurs with voyeurs—who overflowed its modern town houses and converted Victorian mansions, men and women who reigned, or were, in youth's obliviousness, sure they reigned supreme there. The section had an absurd though touching notion of itself as the Greenwich Village of the

Plains; but the young men I knew there seemed blatantly and refreshingly unburdened with things of the mind, and the fine, corn-bred, yellow-haired girls as succulently wholesome as cream of chicken soup. Never once in the two years I lived there was I distressed by the possibility—as perhaps I was in New York—that there were men and women in the area seeking to commit to paper or to canvas their joy, their grief, their passion. Never once did I detect in a saloon, as I had begun to detect in the Village, the dark, brooding silhouette of a man apart, a man caught up and held in awe by the singularity of his vision.

If the section was not the Village, it was precisely named; the Near North Side was *near* to everything. In the morning we descended into the subways and were in a matter of minutes conveyed to the Loop where, after cursorily putting in our days at the altar of commerce, we fled back to Babylon. The bars—The Singapore, Larry's Lounge, Mister Kelley's, Gus' Pub—along Rush Street (Chicago's "White Way") were within five minutes' walking distance from anyplace in the area; in those saloons those genial young men, corn-bred girls, and I nightly got quite happily, quite absurdly, drunk. In the summer we sat around gallon thermoses of vodka and tonic, as tribesmen around the beneficent fire, taking the sun on the most exhilarating city lake front in the world (I have never seen any other, so I suffer from no competing claims). Behind us rose the dizzying turrets of Chicago's skyline, pale and iridescent façades rising into the azure heavens, buildings all constructed, it seemed, for nothing save the pleasure of our eyes. At evening we wandered from one apartment to another, as from one room in a house to another, as if the entire Near North Side were but a single mansion to which we had a standing invitation. We flirted crudely and blatantly with other men's dates, grabbing them in the kitchen or on a stairway and, kissing them, our tongues exploratory even as our hands caressed a breast or buttock, demanding some promise for the future (engaged in such nefariousness one night, I got knocked cold by a male dancer from a musical comedy's road show who, for the obvious reasons, I had assumed wasn't really interested in the leggy creature he was with; it was a sucker punch, but I was never permitted to forget it, and in its way it was rather amusing: truth-seeking, virile, haughty Freddy Exley laid out cold on the kitchen linoleum, his limbs limp and all askew, laid out by a fag—or what had seemed to be one—his buddies helpfully pouring iced highballs into his reposeful countenance). If we were lucky—or not, as the case might be—we ended in the sack with some long-legged, energetic, none-too-bright airline hostess who afterward wept while we assured her of our undying devotion, even as we plotted how to get rid of the creep.

These were, for me at least, days of lust—days in which, for the first time since my rejection by the girl back east, my moroseness had vanished and I discovered I was not altogether unattractive to women. I sat in those saloons with them, sipping highballs, and through the muted light of the place whispered outrageous falsehoods into their pink ears. My hand dropped into their laps to feel their thighs tighten and reject my fingers with the rigidity of their virtue. Continuing to whisper and sip my drink, I felt the flesh go submissive, and had to restrain myself from laughing. If I took them home—and occasionally after the thighs went loose as sand and the challenge no longer provoked me, I packed them off in cabs—they always fought, pounding, not fiercely, their tense little knuckles against my chest, to which I smilingly said, "Cut the shit." I took them on the floor and on the couch and in the bathtub, took them with their summer dresses up around their ears, took them greedily, perfunctorily, pointlessly, took them while they wept and said *no, no, no.* Occasionally in a baseness of spirit, I acceded to their demands and withdrew the sweets of my sex, which only seemed to make them weep more heartily. Afterward, smoking a cigarette, I kissed without feeling their pink ears, gone white now in the slackening of the blood. I kissed their flushed faces, their perspiration-coated upper lips, their straw-yellow hair, and even their little knuckles, flushed now too from the half-assed insistence on their probity. I never left till they asked when we would meet again. To that I always said, "Soon, kid, soon," patted them sportingly on the back, and departed.

How did I accomplish these seductions? My comely ir-resistibility? My brute strength? My subtle charms? Well, no, not really; I was neither comely, brutal, nor subtle. I knew something of America's vulgar yearnings (whose were more vulgar than mine?), and I played on these un-mercifully. One had to estimate the lass. What precisely was the character of the copulating organ she deemed fit to invade her downy-matted sanctuary? What were her intel-lectual habits? *Movie Screen?* I was Cecil Rhodes, Warner Brothers' Chicago representative currently promoting Burt Lancaster's latest epic. "Burt'll be in town a week from Tuesday." I'd yawn then. "Like to have you meet him if you're free. Nice guy. A little swishy like all of them"—one couldn't grant any of them manhood!—"but what the hell!" *Reader's Digest?* I was Jonathan Surgrit, cancer researcher at the Ogilvy Labs, Inc. "You know—out in Evanston?" I would look intently over the back bar, searching, I guess, for the cancer virus between the Seven Crown and the Calvert bottles. Taking a remorseful, furious drag on my cigarette, I'd crush it to a pulpy, scabrous pile of malignancy in the ashtray, suck in my breath, and proclaim, "That's the last cigarette you'll ever see me smoke!"

I was all these gentlemen and more, though after a time I settled finally on my favorite, the surgeon-in-residence at the House of High Hopes, young Dr. Horatio Penis (spelled alarmingly, pronounced with Gallic gentility). "Doc Päh-*nee*," I always introduced myself. "P-e-n-i-s. Friends call me Hor." Like Horatio I was steadfast, unobtrusive, gentle, humorless, not unintelligent, and I spent my entire evening, as I hope the good Horatio did on his Prince's death, "absenting myself from felicity." I never looked at my date. Sipping pensively on my vodka (I had heard all physicians drank vodka), I would stare morosely off into space, conscious of her eyes upon me. Of what was I thinking? The cataracts I had to remove from Mayor Daley's eyes at eight in the morning? The grapefruit-sized tumor on the philanthropic society matron's coccyx? No. I was thinking of what she was thinking. That I could have saved her favorite aunt, Aunt Maudie up in Sheboygan, who had died under a butcher's knife? Was she answering the telephone in our suburban split-level? "Dr. Päh-nee's residence. Mrs. Päh-nee speaking." Who knows? After a time, a kind of melancholy would descend on me.

"What are you thinking about, Dr.—uh—Hor?"

"It's my hands."

Uncertainly: "Your hands?"

With shattering finality: "My hands."

"What's the matter with your hands?"

I would hold them out to her now, backs upward; there would be the slightest tremor.

"I don't see nothin'. They look *beautiful* to me—just like a surgeon's hands should!" She might take them in her own hands now.

"They're trembling. Can't you see they're trembling?" Now sadly, impatiently: "And, oh, good Christ, I've got an OGL-33 at six in the morning!" I paused a moment. "I suppose I ought to get married. All this goddam running around. I've got human life—do you understand that? *Human life!*—in my hands!"

She would squeeze those noble hands then and look lingeringly into my glazed, troubled eyes, as though to say, "I understand, I'll make it well." Afterward once, lying in pleasurable exhaustion on the beige carpeting, smoking a cigarette and staring off into the dedicated, medicinal corridors of my life, I had one of those corn-bred barbarians, lying all asweat next to me and gripping and ungripping my leg with her luscious blond thighs, purr, "There ain't nothin' wrong with *your* hands, Doc!"

Alone at the distance of time and miles I am wondering if I were as happy then as I believed I was. I know there came a time when I wept, actually wept, bawled like a baby, thinking I did so for the incredible fullness of my days; but I am wondering now if the tears weren't induced by some quite other reasons. I was sitting with the boys in one of the dives along Rush Street, discussing football and the sexual expertise of a certain neighborhood girl, when I noticed a woman who took my breath away seated at the far end of the bar. She was seated with a woman I knew, a woman who, in her own way, was extremely beautiful, too—that is, she was physically beautiful. She was a well-paid copywriter in a large advertising agency and was often, unjustly, accused of being Lesbian. It was her own fault. She was one of those horrifying Betty Friedan types, disliked not for her intelli-

gence (as they all believe they're disliked) but because she
had competed so long among men that she had utterly de-
feminized herself—done so to the point where even sex
was on her conditions, entered into on her suggestion and
carried out with a kind of militarily sad-comic precision, a
couple minutes of this, two more of that, did you ever try
this, Frederick?—utterly devoid of any romanticism. I
liked her in a pitying way, the only way one can like someone who has dehumanized herself. I wanted a girl I could
take on the kitchen table before dinner, inhaling the pungent odors of boiled cabbage; or in the front seat of the car
at the drive-in movie, Cary Grant or no Cary Grant throwing his ninety-foot-high technicolor shadow on her behind; or—well, wherever the spirit moved me. I did not, in
other words, want to make Huxley-like Tuesday afternoon
appointments with my spouse.

And the girl she was with looked like one who would
take it on a chair-lift dreamily ascending Mount Aspen.
She was about thirty. Her features were fine, and her
ebony-black hair, parted in the middle, was pulled taut to
her head, American Indian style, and brought together in a
great firm chignon at the curve of the back of her neck, a
chignon so perfect that I thought it might be fake. In the
muted light her skin seemed of the most incredibly golden
texture, and her pulpous flesh, what I could see of it, looked
the kind that, though infinitely soft, would in passion be as
hard, hot, and animated as a stripper's pelvis. She seemed
to me altogether exquisite, and I paid her the compliment,
from time to time, of staring lengthily and boldly at her, a
boldness she countered by staring right back. I was lucky in
one way. The boys I was with were very aware of her, too
(we were all staring like crazy, and, on the isles of our sep-

arate vanities, were, I suppose, imagining that her stares were returned to us alone), but none of them had apparently ever received one of the copywriter's abrupt invitations and assumed the woman was already spoken for. I didn't enlighten them; there ensued a memorable conversation.

Speaking with a casualness that attempted to imply that his words had no relationship to anyone in the room, somebody said, "You know, if I was a broad, I could see bein' a fucking queer." "How do yuh figure that?" someone else said. "I mean, I can see a couple broads rubbin' their lovely knockers against each other—and soul-kissin' and—well, whatever it is they do to each other." We all laughed—except one of us. "That's the stupidest thing I ever heard of," he said. "What's so stupid about it?" the first said indignantly. "Well, let's put it this way. If you was a normal broad, I suppose that you could imagine that if you were a guy, you could see yourself rollin' around a clover field with Rocky Marciano. But I don't suppose Rocky would dig it too much." We all laughed again. The first man was insistent. *"Naw.* There's somethin' nauseating about a couple hairy-chested, sweaty bastards rollin' around a bed together. But broads are different. I mean—they're delicate and clean and all. I mean, I don't have any trouble visualizin' a couple of well-scrubbed broads . . ." Someone started singing, "The girl that I marry will have to be . . ." Someone else, in obvious agreement with the sarcasm of the singer, said, *"Clean?* Go take a look in the lady's can. You wouldn't—and you're kind of a grubby bastard—even sit down on the goddam toilet seat!" It was a bad day for the advocate of Lesbos. "Delicate, your ass," still another man said. "You know what my Uncle Louis—you know, the one out in Hollywood?—you know what he was tellin' me?" We admitted that we didn't. "He was tellin' me that Rudolph Valentino used to keep a goddam hanky under his goddam armpit and right at the goddam moment he was comin', he'd shove the goddam sweaty thing right in the broad's nostrils!" We didn't quite get the point. Detecting this, the man exclaimed emphatically, "And they loved it!" We had to think about that for a moment. For the first time in the conversation, someone decided to be relevant. He said, "Your Uncle Louis owns a goddam delicatessen, for Christ's sake!"

That is the kind of Chicago conversation I remember, arguments begun on hopelessly puerile foundations and, out of boredom, carried to impossibly ludicrous limits. This one continued until it disintegrated into a hilarious sobriety. We had by then a barful of change with which we were going to call Uncle Louis in Hollywood, to get the word straight from the baloney peddler's mouth. Someone, though, said he wouldn't take Uncle Louis' word for it— poor Uncle Louis!—even if he had been Valentino's goddam hairdresser. "I mean, how does anybody know crap like that?" We got into some name-calling after that, some threats and counter-threats, and then angrily began drifting off one by one. By midnight I, except for the two women at the far end, was the only one left at the bar. After that I breathed easier—decided against any need for making the move. I did not even look down that way again. It worked. A few minutes before closing time, the copywriter came down, tapped me on the shoulder (I acted surprised), fetched me back, and made the introductions.

"You want to go?" I said.

Her sense of the rightness of things was undermined.

"Aren't you going to buy me a drink?" she asked. She smiled pleasantly.

"You coming or not?" I said. My voice was not pleasant. I was twenty-six, and had the power, and believed that I would always have it.

Over the objections of the copywriter, she came. And she turned out to have the most incredibly lovely body I had ever seen; even now I can see every contour of it, the muscular tautness of her thighs, the fullness of her breasts, all covered by a skin more golden than I had even imagined in the flattering light of the bar, a skin which, even as I lay smoking in interim periods—for such was my need I never slept that night—I had to keep my free hand on, on the hard plain of her stomach, on the sloping hill of her thigh, touch her even as she slept next to me, slept till I reawoke her. I had to touch her because the city's bounty to me now seemed worse than incredible, as if the inessentialness that had always characterized the city had come together in the warm exquisiteness of the body beside me. And I had to touch, and touch, and touch again, to assure myself that everything was indeed real.

She asked me to leave about six. With an evasive smile, she explained to me that her boy friend—an "elderly chap" who was "kind" to her—was due by plane into Chicago early that morning. "We'll see each other again," she hastened to assure me, still not looking at me. Pleased as punch—pleased? oh, "cocky" as hell—that I had been so adroit, so gymnastic, I waited, casually leaning against the door and indifferently puffing a cigarette, while she committed to paper numberless phone numbers, her own, her place of employment, and her sister's in Oak Park, where she had been spending a lot of time in the past months. Her

chatter distressed me. The numbers and names were beginning to form around her an existence apart from that incredible body on those silk sheets. She was spending a lot
of time with her sister because her sister's husband,
Ronald, had just died of a heart attack. Her sister had found
him on the davenport. There had been a smile on Ronald's
face. He was probably dreaming of fishing in Canada because he went there every year, the two of them went together. "Ronald liked to fish," she said dolefully. "Oh," I
said. Taking the paper from her and putting it into my
pocket, I kissed her good-bye, patted her suavely on the
backside, and left. "You don't even know my name!" she
hollered after me. "Sure! Sure I do!" I said. "It's on the
paper!" she said, not believing me. She was right not to.

A few minutes later I was on the Elevated weeping, not
weeping but bawling like a baby. I was alone in the car, and
the city, in the first flush of the morning sun, lay spread out
to my left, more like a dream than I had ever imagined it.
Reaching into my pocket, I removed the paper, crumpled it
into a hard little ball, and threw it down to the far end of
the car. What did I need with names and addresses? The
city gave everything to one, and I bawled like a goddam
madman to be so lucky, never for a moment dreaming that
I might be bored. I bawled until I was hysterical, coughing
great globs of phlegm into my hands, and knowing for certain, as Henry James's Marcher knew forever about the
beast that lurked in his soul, that if ever that life was going
to come to me, that life that would be so much more striking than other men's, that it was going to come to me in that
city, Chicago. A few days later I met Bunny Sue.

———

Bunny Sue was nineteen. She had honey-blond, bobbed
hair and candid, near-insolent green eyes. She had a snub,

delightful nose, a cool, regal, and tapering neck, a fine, intelligent mouth that covered teeth so startling they might have been cleansed by sun gods. Without any makeup save lipstick, her complexion was as milk flecked with butter, the odor she cast as wholesome as homemade bread. On my first breathless vision of her, I wanted to bury my teeth, Dracula-like, into her flanks, knowing that she would bleed pure butterscotch. Her walk quite bowled me over. Slightly toed-out, she didn't so much walk as bounce, skip with the imposing, almost forbidding temerity of her youth and her freshness—so god-awfully sure she was that these were the eternal and unvarying constants of her existence. She was the girl next door who only yesterday ran around the yard with pee in her pants. She was Hudson's Rima, Spenser's Una, Humbert Humbert's Dolly. She was the scarcely pubescent girl modeling the Chesterfield coat in *Seventeen*, resting on the haunch of one leg, the toe of the pump of the free leg aimed squarely at the firmament, suggesting that that place was no less than her destination. She was Wordsworth's Lucy, Tristan's Iseult, Poe's Annabel Lee. But, oh, she was so very American. She was the Big Ten coed whose completeness is such that a bead of perspiration at the temple is enough to break the heart. She was the Sweetheart of Sigma Chi—well, no, not precisely; precisely she was the only sophomore in the history of Michigan or Illinois or Indiana to be chosen, above all those other honey-dipped girls, Homecoming Queen. And finally, she was Chicago's impossible, nearly obscene gift to me. She was the girl I had sought to allay my grief at USC and been too leper-like to find, the girl I had sought all my nights in the Village, and the girl for whom I had waited way off there at the Broadmoor in Colorado Springs. Within moments of looking at her, I knew it was she.

It was only many weeks later that I gave thought to the way I had met Bunny Sue. Though I was given her name by a perfect stranger (a boy who was at college with her) in a bar, I had for many weeks just considered it a piece of my continuing, fortuitous, and incredible luck. I remember that the boy had struck me as a rather sophisticated, even effeminate Holden Caulfield. He had a gold cigarette case, a jet-black holder, and though he had talked rather knowledgeably, even rather wittily, about the sexual mores of coeds—"Good Lord, they're scared to death of pregnancy. By the time they get married, half of them will have forgotten in which cavity conception occurs!"—I had taken him to be a blusterous kid, attempting to cover youth's natural inadequacies. I was, in effect, amused; and he was having a good time amusing me. At one point he had dramatically slammed his palm on the bar (it was one of his many mannerisms) and exclaimed, "Dear chap! There is someone you absolutely must meet!" Here he rolled his eyes around teasingly. I suppose my silence told him I was not altogether uninterested; then he launched into a sexless, very limited ("Absolutely ravishing!") description of Bunny Sue, explaining that she was on a certain day, by a certain train, coming from her home upstate to Chicago shopping, that he was supposed to meet her to arrange to have drinks, but that he couldn't meet her, he was going to be "absolutely too busy." He had written all the pertinent details on a paper, and he now shoved the paper into my hand. "You will meet her for me, won't you?" I said that I didn't know and asked for a more precise description. He teasingly rolled his eyes around again. "Ravishing blond hair! Ravishing green eyes!" I said, "I'll meet her!" We both laughed, and rolled our eyes around playfully. I think his description was going to be a good deal more precise, and I wonder now if I didn't interrupt him to prevent just that. Meeting her, I explained what the note he gave me said, invited her to coffee, and, oh, dear lordy, an hour later, having for the day forsaken my job, my repose, my dignity, I found myself at her heels stumbling through Marshall Field's vast department store; I was that afraid I might lose her.

It was one of those sweltering, near-equatorial June mornings. Hardly any shoppers had braved the heat (we had the great store almost to ourselves), and even those paltry few who had ventured out moved in slow motion, as if the heat were corporeal and staying their progress. Bunny's motion was stayed not in the least. She bounced. She wore a blue and white, fine-checked cotton dress; at her neck she had a little white bow; her white pumps shattered the awful stillness of the store, and as she skipped up the empty aisles, the floorwalkers, the salesgirls, and those few slow-moving customers, all looked, then in benumbed admiration looked again. It was rather terrifying. Now those awful eyes would go to me—to see if I warranted such a prize. Some nodded approvingly, others not (the bastards! did they not see I knew I did not warrant it?). Whether they approved or not, the blood remained hot, furious, and constant in my face; and I found myself dropping a few paces behind her, in deference to her shocking comeliness. It was a comeliness I scarcely dared look upon, one that had me peeking at her out of the corner of my eyes. It was a furtiveness of which she was aware, and it aroused in her an imperious though tolerant smile. She bounced, I stumbled behind her, thinking the morning would never end.

"We" tried on pastel cashmeres, Black Watch plaid skirts, blue ballerina slippers, and it all had the quality of a nightmare that takes place under water. I wanted to get away ("I'll wait for you in the coffee shop"); she wanted my opinion. I sat in a leather chair, chain-smoking and staring at the carpet. Disappearing into a closet, she had the dress off, the cashmere on, and in split seconds (just long enough to visualize those butterscotch thighs) she was parading her choices before me. Did I like it? "Fine. Fine," was all I ever said. Running behind her, my ear lobes perspiring, I thundered up to one counter and stood stupid, aghast, mute, as, without batting an eyelash, she purchased seven pair of pale blue panties, a pair for every day of the week, with Monday, Tuesday, etc., embroidered at a place very close to the crotch. "Pretty corny, huh?" she said to nobody in particular; then to the salesgirl, "Is it all right if I wear Tuesday's on Saturday?" Here she turned to me and winked, and a very sick smile quite froze upon my countenance. Both she and the salesgirl laughed, a mysterious woman's laugh. That morning was the first day in my life when I recognized there were times when I needed a drink; I needed one then as badly, I expect, as I ever had or ever would again. By noon, exhausted, my nerves gone, my arms piled high with ornately wrapped cardboard boxes, I stumbled into the scalding street behind her, fell at her heels into a taxicab, and headed for Rush Street.

It seems to be the fashion to take love as it comes, to examine it rather minutely, and to dismiss it rather lightly, perhaps a little sadly, and move on to greater things. But I cannot do that; I know of no greater things. Oh, I wish I could remember that with Bunny I had been a square-jawed, tight-lipped, virile Frederic Henry who loved, lost, and walked back to his hotel in the rain. But I didn't love in that way; and when I lost, I went quite off my head. At Rush Street the bar's light was mute enough, the gin bucks strong enough, but nothing—even the constant chatter with which we sought to assure each other of the high-mindedness of our persons—dimmed the light she cast or stilled the beating of my heart. Maugham tells us how his painter-hero Strickland, like Gauguin, went to Tahiti and knew that he was home, tells how he had lived his life in an agony of exile until he had come to that place, which he had never seen before—*home.* And that is what I felt with Bunny—except that instead of place I had lived my life in the hope of person, and here she was in the flesh, so that I could, as I had done with that other only a few nights before, reach out and touch her. But I did not dare. I did not touch her then because for the first time I was certain that the city—the city I never did quite believe in—would betray me. Not only did I not touch her, but the only times I looked at her were during those not infrequent moments when she chose to marvel at herself (for she did not quite believe in herself either) in the mirror of the back bar, and at those moments my mind went quite beside itself with pious platitudes. I was "Doc Päh-nee" no longer, neither a seeker after truth, nor anyone save Freddy Exley from up in the cow country—PR Man! Rock Island!—and I saw myself tuxed and trembling, standing before the beneficent minister, a radiantly demure Bunny by my side, a white orchid in her prayer book, saying, "I do. I do. 'Deed I do."

At five I had her back at the station, where for the first time that day, and by a truly enormous effort of the will, I looked directly into her green eyes.

"Come tomorrow night," I said.

"I can't," she said. "My parents will think something's—"

"Funny?" I volunteered. "That we're rushing it?"

"Yes," she said. For the first time that day her composure broke, her face flushed over, and she looked away from me. I touched her then, tentatively, on the shoulder. Then she was gone. Having picked up a timetable to see what time her train arrived in her home town, in about two hours' time, I found that I had to get very drunk that night to prevent myself from calling her and proclaiming my love. The next day I was glad that I hadn't; from her I received two letters, one telling me that she had, with her forefinger in the dust of a Milwaukee road's passenger-car window, written the legend *Mrs. F. E. Exley.*

That summer was my season of love, and though I only saw Bunny five or six more times, she was with me all the hot, sweltering days and all the air-conditioned evenings when, having forsaken all others, I sat alone in the bars on Rush Street drinking till long past midnight, trying to allay my riotous exhilaration. At the time I was sharing the penthouse—we called it, with irony, a penthouse because it was on the top floor—apartment of a Victorian mansion on North Dearborn Street. I did not even pay rent. My roommate, a young, money-making attorney, managed the apartments for a dowager in distant Florida; and each weekend, stripping to my undershorts and stepping out onto a sun roof, I set the attorney's typewriter on a ledge fronting Dearborn Street, and wrote Bunny letters of epic proportions, letters for which I had all the week been making notes. With the fake melancholy of youth I wrote, "I am a creature of the gray and the dismal, while you are of light and of radiance," and though it was selfish of me, I told her, I was looking to that radiance to redeem me. I wrote all day long, and this confession, together with the sun's rays, now turning my body brown, ennobled me. I felt something like grace.

My roommate thought I was writing a novel. Often I heard him caution the pigs—suddenly all the boys had become to me no-good vermin—who lay about our apartment Saturdays watching baseball, guzzling beer, farting and scratching, to "keep it down," that I was "working." But this only increased their curiosity. Occasionally one of them would stick his head out the window and shout, "Put a lot of fucking in it, Ex—*'twon't* sell otherwise!" Occasionally one would sneak up behind me, read over my shoulder, and exclaim, "Jesus, Ex, not another one of those morbidly sensitive fuckers! It won't sell, daddy-O! Ho! Ho! Ho!"

But I paid them no mind and went my way, typing in Chicago's sunshine, knowing that it would "sell." Indeed I wrote so many weekends that some wild charlatan of a tour bus driver, pointing upward, began bringing the attention of his complement of sightseers to me. Unquestionably having been told that I was one of the "struggling artists" said to inhabit the area, these people invariably waved frantically at me from behind the glass dome of their bus, so happy were they to share this fragile moment with one who might one day be hailed a genius, so pleased that they could go back to Omaha and tell Cousin Lucy, "We saw one of them writer fellows—in his underwear!" I never waved back. I thought it might crumble their notions of the aloofness of the artists. Instead, to please them, I hung on my face a carefully cultivated, soulful, near-visionary look, one with which, by opening my eyes as wide as I could, in imitation of Bela Lugosi, I looked quite through their greetings. This made them giggle hysterically and pound each other self-consciously on the back, as though they had just interrupted me in an unseemly masturbation. On the bus's shooting out of sight, I always grabbed onto my stomach and roared a fitful, lunatic laughter, once even tipping my chair over and rolling all over the hot-tarred roof.

At day's end, at summer's twilight, when the cool shadows began to bring goose-pimples to my hot flesh, when the couples began pouring from the apartment houses, to walk hand in hand beneath me on Dearborn Street (I envied none of them now!), I proofread the letters with a concentration my job never got. I crossed out that which might be misread, changed that which might be unseemly, added this afterthought by writing up and all around the margin, now turning over the page and filling it with a rampant, scarcely legible script. Invariably—and here my drunken critics were apposite—the letters seemed much too doleful, and I tried to leaven them with postscripts I imagined to be marvelously sophisticated and witty, telling Bunny that when next we met at the station, I'd be the tremulous young man, poised as if for flight, with a white rose in either hand, one for her and one for me, "symbols of our chastity."

Finally came the day when we actually did meet. I was, lest I explode, slightly drunk and had in my arms not two but dozens of white roses, enough, I think, to bury a Chicago hood. I forced her—and she did not protest too vehemently—to walk with me up Michigan Boulevard: though she tried in her walk to retain the bouncy confidence of her youth, there was in it now a becoming timidity. All along the boulevard people stopped and stared at us, especially at me burdened down by a garden of roses— stared as though I were mad. How they despised what they viewed as a blatant, unmanly admission of love! What did I care for them or their pedestrian, tightly lived lives? I wanted to shout, *"Love,* you bastards! What's it all about without this?" I think that Bunny thought I was going to shout: once or twice, giggling apprehensively, her voice gave utterance to the stares of the people, and she said, "You're mad! You're mad!" But then her hand, in thanks, would come out to rest upon my arm. The huge, ocher sun was falling behind the skyline to our left, bathing the seaside of the boulevard in rouge; from the blue water to our right a warm swift wind blew, lifting the roses, one by one, from my arms and sweeping them furiously along the wide walks to the gutter where they lay, a poor gift, humbly offered, to the city that gave one so much.

At the Italian restaurant the minestrone went cold as gelatin, the lettuce in the tossed salad as limp as spinach, and the veal parmigiana, brought in so steaming and succulently soft, became as hard, cold, and withered as dried apples. The Italian waiter, haughty and temperamental, giving us furious looks, carted each uneaten dish back into the kitchen where we heard trays slam, a glass break, and violent, alien, and meaningless curses. All we could do was drink Chianti. We drank glass after glass in silence, fiercely and furtively seeking out each other's hands beneath the checkered table. Finding them, we squeezed till we hurt each other; withdrawing we fell into agonizing lapses of heavy breathing silence, renewing ourselves for another assault on each other's person. It was when I looked up from one of these respites that she said something I did not quite catch. She was weeping, with great beadlike tears running down her honey-flecked cheeks; between excruciating sobs that rived my heart in two, she said, "I'm not a surgeon."

" 'I'm not a' *what?*" I said amazed.

"A surgeon, a surgeon," she said dumbly.

"Of course not," I thought. "I'm the surgeon—Doc Päh-*nee.*"

"I don't understand," she said. "Don't laugh at me." Then she started to weep again. At that moment I *did understand,* and when I did, the room started going round and round. I rose, dropped a twenty-dollar bill on the table, and led her—or did she lead me?—from the room.

We—Bunny, who was *not a virgin,* and I—went then to the darkest bar on Rush Street, went on my fierce insistence: Bunny, bless her heart, had other plans. I did not realize this at first. Setting her on a bar stool before me, I stood at her back, resting my chin on her head, and reaching around her shoulder for my drink. My first impression was that she had told me out of some sentimental remorse for not having waited, but I hadn't got to my second drink when I knew that this flagrant naïveté on my part was not the answer: Bunny was a most insistent seducer. Refusing to let me avoid her eyes, she kept pulling her blond head from under my chin and bringing her green eyes round to mine; her eyes said, "Let's go."

Now I had never doubted that this moment would come; I did, in fact, even know where. There were always in our apartment house one or two vacant apartments for which, due to my roommate's capacity as landlord, I had the keys; and the day before a particularly suitable place had been vacated. As I often did in return for my free rent, I had gone there with the attorney to help him clean the place in anticipation of a future occupant; no sooner had I walked into its single room than my breath quite ran out of me. Whoever had had it, a commercial artist as I recall, had done the entire room in minuscule, multi- and brilliant-colored mosaics, had done the walls of the closet-like kitchenette, had done the petite round bar, had done the great coffee table before the candy-striped divan, and had even built, smack in the middle of the room, a fantastic, oval, and luxuriously mosaic bed. The place was preposterous, and though I had heard of it before (the other tenants called it "Fags' Paradise"), I could not believe it: it was the iridescent, the peacock, the rainbow land! And I never worked so vigorously to get a place clean as I did that one. On finishing, and after my roommate had left, I blue-sheeted the oval bed, put two snifter glasses, a bottle of bourbon, and two of soda behind the bar, reconnected the refrigerator for ice cubes, sat down on a bar stool and practiced saying through pursed, sorrowful lips, "But surely, Bunny, you've got time for one more drink"—now measuring with my thumb and middle finger and smiling—"just one teensie-weensie one?" Then I was ready, or thought I was. What did delay me that night? Her crossing me up by rendering all my elaborate plans unnecessary? Not really.

To begin with, I was foolish enough to believe that the seduction was going to be mine (as if it ever is!). Where I had come from, seducing a "nice" girl was hard work. In the back seat of wintry cars one chewed on lower lips for longer periods of time than starlets cohabit with producers. One moved lower then, leaving a trail of perfumed saliva on ears and necks along the way, coming to plant already swollen lips on wool-sweatered nipples, inhaling there, as though trying to draw juice from earmuffed oranges. One huffed and puffed, struggling out of fur-collared greatcoats, meeting convulsive, furious hands all the way. The back seat of the car now reeked of love's odors, so that the entire car was like a Great Northern

Womb, and if one was not too drunk or hadn't developed "blue balls" (like a fierce hand squeezing the genitalia purple), one went miraculously on, touching a thigh and working up to the hot silken flimsiness of underthings where, more often than not, it ended with the beast—what admirable will power!—clamping her vicelike thighs about one's hand and hysterically screaming, "I'll tell my brother Ed!" Even if one did make it, if the thighs did not break one's furtive hand, the girl felt duty-bound to pass out, so that confronting one in Trigonometry on Monday morning she could give him that sweetly virginal I-don't-remember-nothin' look. There was very little to remember. By the time of contact it was getting light, very cold, with that glacial, white world spread all about one on the lonely road; and one didn't dare look down in fear of seeing a half-dressed, broken-bra'ed, bedraggled, pimply, snot-nosed, shivery-assed creature feigning her conscience-inducing sleep, trying not to moan, as if indeed a scarcely erect, zipper-scraped, partially raw instrument could induce even tremors, not to mention ecstatic moans (in all truth it occurs to me now that if one girl had, on her parents' night at the Avon, taken me into her bedroom, taken off her clothes, and taken me into bed with her, I would have married her, got a job as a brakeman on the New York Central, raised eleven children, and lived happily ever after on pork chops and Genesee 12-Horse Ale).

Did I want to make this kind of an effort? Well, no, not really; but still, I wanted to be the master of it. It was more than that really: I was afraid—scared to death. I had waited too long for her, lived with the dream of her for always, and the thought of actually grasping it struck me, cruelly and ironically, impotent, in words to say, in motions to make, in every possible way.

I drank a lot more for courage, an awful lot more. When I could avoid it no longer, I took her by the arm, and we walked, somnambulant, to the iridescent land on North Dearborn Street. I say *somnambulant,* by which I mean that at least I was; even today I find it incredible to believe that she, Miss America, in the end, as Lolita did to poor, poor Humbert Humbert, seduced—or should I say *tried to seduce?*—me. At the apartment I broke one of the snifter glasses and we shared a drink from the remaining one. We did not finish it. Rising, we walked to the blue oval bed, and I sat down on the edge of it. She stood next to me, her arms lax at her sides like a child bride. When I asked what the matter was, she said, "Aren't you going to undress me?" Undress her? In the end, she undressed me.

———

That is my love story. Or what I thought was love. For in the end I discovered that I did not love Bunny, that indeed I had never loved her. We continued to write each other, continued to sit in Italian restaurants over uneaten pasta, clawing at each other beneath the table—a clawing which cruelly and ironically never failed to arouse my manhood. It was cruel and ironical for by the time of our arrival at the rainbow land I was invariably as manless as I had been on the first occasion: Doc Päh-*nee* turned out to be Doc No-Päh-*nee.* I tried—tried? oh, ferociously! I assumed the positions, my fanny directed at every nook and cranny of that multicolored empire.

We tried. Together we read a book, *The Frigid Male,* by Dr. Lottie de Bauch, A.B., M.A., Ph.D. Lottie was a very modern woman. Upon exhausting the natural stimulants in the early chapters, she had a chapter on fetishism which seemed to offer the most hope. Perhaps I would like Bunny in a mink coat? It didn't sound like a bad idea, but Bunny's parents, though permissive, hadn't apparently considered her ready for mink. We could have rented one, but we decided against that. Some men like to have their women degraded, and Lottie suggested that to oblige a girl paint herself heavily, wear the gaudy dresses, costume jewelry, and long-heeled crimson pumps of the tart and emit from the corner of her mouth, gangster-like, a torrent of four-letter words to indicate that she was of the lower orders. This sounded fairly interesting, too; but the investment would have been heavy in both money and time: all Bunny had in the way of garments was Black Watch plaid kilts that exposed her dimpled, baby-fatted, and butterscotch knees, and I would have had to school her in the vocabulary of degenerates, which would probably have proved embarrassing.

Lottie was very permissive, considering anything short of physical injury to one another as fair play in the pursuit of "the consummate orgasm." We never got to the end of the chapter. We got to the point where I wasn't sure whether Lottie considered physical injury as fair play or no. When she got to the proposition that some men need "to rape" (her quotes) to realize their manhood, I began to grow uneasy. In this latter particular she cited Gable's Rhett Butler planting a ferocious and coma-inducing kiss on a velvet-clad Vivien Leigh in *Gone With the Wind*, recalling for us how Vivien had passed out and Rhett had carried her limp body up the wide staircase of the Old Manse. Here, buried among some very imposing psychological terms, Lottie explained to us what had happened on their arrival at Vivien's boudoir (I never read the book, so I don't know if she knew from that, or if she just called Margaret Mitchell on the telephone and asked her): Rhett had obviously torn her clothes from her, slapping her around a bit in the process, and had then "symbolically deflowered" her, a defloration that apparently some men have to carry out at every copulation.

It was at this point that I laid the volume down. Aside from the expense of replacing the lemon cashmere and the kilts, perhaps even a bra and panties (one knows how insubstantial they are), aside from the unhappy prospect of sending Bunny back to the suburbs with a black eye (Lottie never explained whether one was supposed to pull one's punches, as they do in the cinema, or really work them over: at this point I remember studying Lottie's picture on the dust jacket and how pleased I was to detect that her eyes were scarless), I was afraid what she might propose should this rather interesting measure fail. There were about twenty pages left in the chapter, and I had visions of myself shopping around Chicago for a cat-o'-nine-tails (how would one ask for one of those?) or having to run upstairs to the penthouse to get my attorney-roommate to get me, as it were, "started," a kind of "symbolic jealousy" no doubt.

These things would never have done: Bunny, bless her, really did love me and threw herself at my impotence with a kind of terrifying and speechless abandon, which both frightened me and made me ashamed. I could scarcely look at her. There were times when I wanted to pound my chest and roaringly boast about my past mastery, tell her about the nights I had had, in order to get any sleep, to remove the phone from the hook. But the words would no sooner rise to my tongue than the tone to speak them in would elude me; and not uttering them I would fall into endless states of unspeaking depression, states in which, for the first time, I contemplated visiting a psychiatrist, states in which she clung to my naked body, weeping onto my chest. In all the books I had read, and especially in the American novels—those disgusting corroborations of our fantasies, books which at every turn were hailed as works of "genius"—the heroes were so unimpeachably virile (if they weren't, they were hero-villains) that it not only didn't occur to me at twenty-six, when one ought to be a little wise but almost never is in America, that such failures, though hardly common, and certainly symptomatic of something more markedly wrong, were not altogether unknown. O world, world, world, they were to me! So bad indeed did the stigma seem to me that it all but removed me from the race of men.

Worse than anything, there came a point when Bunny had a kind of terrifyingly loose and constant moistness, the kind of totally loose submission one detects in a woman he has impregnated, the moist eyes, the warm moist hands, the loose moist breasts beneath the cotton blouse, that utter submission and adoration for the mate that the unborn child arouses in a woman. So overwhelming was it in Bunny's case that I began to wonder if, in some miraculous way, she wasn't indeed pregnant. More astounding still, she began to talk a good deal about an immediate marriage. Why I don't know: Lottie had devoted a couple pages to a case history of a frigid male who had laid his wife for forty-odd years in her wedding gown, though she never told us whether the gown was ever replaced or whether the ever-aging bride was superbly gifted with a needle and white thread. In the end Bunny even insisted that I make the trip to the suburbs to face her parents. It was this meeting that ended everything.

The Allorgees lived in a suburb of a suburb, their particular little suburb being Heritage Heights. It was a suburb that had apparently never caught on. The streets were all there, but there was only one house, Allorgees' Acres, a great, white, one-storied, rambling ranch-type place in which everything from garage to game room to hot-water heater was found on the single story that shot out in all sorts of clapboard arms, like the spokes of a painted wagon wheel. "The Heights" was not on any height at all; this was the American Midwest at its most grotesque, treeless and cold-looking as far as the eye could see, so that it only seemed set on high ground. There was only one thing that broke the endless blue monotony of the heavens—a television aerial that rose so high that it dizzied one to look up at it, an aerial which, I was proudly informed, put the Allorgees on certain clear days in contact with all parts of the Republic. It was a touching monument to their isolation. In answer to my question about its astounding height, Chuck (or Poppy)—as the father was interchangeably designated—said only that he liked "good reception."

That was the only thing I remember Chuck, or Poppy, saying for the entire weekend. The rest of his communication with me consisted of an outrageous wink, a wink that distressed me so much that after a time I began to wonder if I ought not to pop Chuckie, or chuck Poppy. I could not fathom that wink at all. At times it seemed friendly enough, one of those so-you're-the-guy-who-stole-my-Princess? things. But at other times there seemed to be something downright lascivious about it, as though he were saying, "You gettin' in, huh? Huh?" Lord, how that wink unnerved me!

Another thing I remember about Chuck was that one

night he asked me out to the garage with him, and I thought, "Oh, Christ, here it comes." But when we got outside all he wanted to show me was a miraculous device for opening and shutting the garage doors. Sitting in the driveway in the front seat of the Cadillac, he had a little electronic device, like a television station-changer, which, aimed gunlike at an electric eye near the doors, moved them up and down—apparently for no other reason than to save him getting in and out of the car. I watched the doors go up and down about twenty times, like a machine gone berserk. Then he let me try it. Very soberly, I aimed at that hideous eye, deftly flicked the button with my forefinger, watched the wide white doors run crazily up and disappear into the garage's ceiling, enthusiastically remarked the wonder of it, and getting out of the car we, Freddy and Poppy, strode back into the house together. The rest of the weekend Poppy sat in the snug little breakfast nook in the kitchen. He was, I gathered, in the "insurance game." A pencil on his ear, the insurance records spread out before him on the table, a can of Pabst Blue Ribbon at his right hand, his ear bent to a portable radio turned to the Cubs' baseball games, he sat in what was apparently his own little world. The Pabst came from a little red electric cooler next to the pink refrigerator; on the top of the cooler someone had stenciled in great ivory letters the legend "POPPY," and the only time I saw Poppy the rest of the weekend was on those not infrequent occasions when I went to the cooler for a beer of my own. At those times I got the distinct impression that he was keeping a count on the number of cans I was consuming, that he literally considered POPPY's cooler Poppy's. Whenever I opened one, frightfully conscious of the noise of the opener against can, I always turned and smiled apologetically and was always met with that unnerving, enigmatical smile. To this day I don't know if he was a dirty old man or a fool.

If there was a certain ambivalence about Poppy, about the mother there was none at all: she was a perfect horror. Bunny had been born to her late, after a number of heart-breaking, unsuccessful pregnancies. She had, in fact, been born at great emotional and physical expense. Because Mums dropped stillbirths from her womb as facilely as certain sturdy-loined creatures drop rosy twins, she had had, during the final months she carried Bunny, to lie abed with her thighs thrust upward, supported by some hammock contraption or other. She related this story to me one early morning in the kitchen, apart from Bunny and Poppy, and as she told it her tone was one of scarcely contained and monumental pride. When she told me this story, and I have no idea why, I couldn't erase from my mind the vision of Bunny's blond head—precisely as it was then, lovely beyond all other honey-dipped heads—popping fully formed out of this woman, cradled in her goddam hammock, and shouting, "Hi, gang!"

Because of the unhappy time she had had in bringing Bunny forth, it was quite natural that she was solicitous of, even obtrusive in the fashioning of, Bunny's destiny—a destiny to which, because Mums was the usual garden-variety middle-class woman, I was certain I did not belong. I was certain that before my visit untold arguments about me had occurred, and that Mums had not yet quite given in. All Mums's friends were attorneys or physicians and referred to in that way, "my friend Lawyer Brown" or "my dear, dear friend Dr. Wright," it never having occurred to her that in the milieu about Heritage Heights the average professional man might be a doltish, incompetent ass. There was a lot of talk about clubs, the country club (I knew that she had had visions of Bunny married to an orthodontist and whacking golf balls at the local one), bridge clubs, and book clubs, the latter, I think, being thrown in to show me she was an intellectual (she "adored" *The Caine Mutiny* and "serious things like that"), trying, as it were, to find properly sober bases with her aspiring son-in-law. In the two days I spent there, she never took her hard, appraising little eyes from me (like all possessive mothers, and without in the least understanding it, she was trying to see herself in bed with me: "Brother," I thought, "if she only knew!"), and though she obviously hated to make any concessions that indicated to me a surrender on her part, she made one or two, inquiring of me in the most blatantly stupid and innocent manner both my salary and my methods for communicating with God, inquired just as the horrible grotesques do in *The Caine Mutiny* and the other books she read. To my salary I suavely added an incredible three hundred dollars a month, to which she nodded soberly and approvingly (though I think she tried to restrain her surprise); as for my pipeline to God, I told her I communicated through the agency of the "high" Episcopal Church, to which she also nodded approvingly. I gave her, in effect, the kind of response her ludicrously asinine questions deserved. Like the average American Mums, there was really no end to the woman's horridness.

From Bunny I had learned that, though Poppy made a good deal of money, he was just this side of bankruptcy, the mother having convinced him that he could make boodles of money by buying, landscaping, and paving the morosely vacant area called Heritage Heights. But the local inhabi-

tants had steadfastly refused to recognize the comeliness of
The Heights, had kept perversely away, and there was no
doubt in my mind that Mums—whether Poppy made
twenty thousand dollars a year or not—had laid the ven-
ture's failure squarely on Chuck's sour business acumen.
Moreover, by that remarkable viciousness of which the
American Mums's mind is capable, it also became apparent
that she had laid her own physical shortcomings as a
woman squarely on the guy's penis. As a result, there were
that weekend all kinds of hushed conversations from which
Poppy was excluded, an exclusion invariably instigated by
Mums, and to which I was now—being of that charmed
circle at whose heart Bunny lay—permitted. These conversations were more often than not concerned with moneys to satisfy Bunny's apparently near-insatiable needs—a
half-dozen more sweaters, a new car in the spring, a rac-
coon coat (at this point Bunny had suggested that if they
were going to go into fur, they might as well get mink, and
to Mums's outrage she had turned to me and winked), *ad
infinitum.* Whether it was for my benefit, an indication of
what I might expect as the supplier of Bunny's material
whims, I don't know; but Mums always, with the briefest
show of irritation, promised that the moneys would be
made available somehow. Then she would put her finger to
her mouth and say, "Shish. Don't tell Poppy—he won't understand," saying it in such a way as to indicate that the
man was all but moronic and would be no more capable of
understanding the noble destiny that between them—it
was presumably between us now—they had projected for
Bunny than he would be of understanding Relativity. At
the time, as I say, I thought I had felt rather sorry for him,
but I can see now that I hadn't. I had despised him for so

docilely permitting his own emasculation; and what I had really wanted—incredibly!—was for him to come charging through the door, Pabst beer can in hand, to punch them both about a bit, and then to kick both their asses right out the door into Mum's dim-witted dream of Heritage Heights!

The weekend proved a dismal enlightenment. At some point in it I fell into an unspeaking depression, and Bunny asked me repeatedly, "What's the matter? What's the matter? Is it something about my parents?" "No! No!" I protested. "It's just that I'm sick—something I ate, I guess." Indeed I was sick, though the poisoning had nothing to do with the Allorgees' rather bland table fare. That weekend I had been browsing through an unread issue of *The New Yorker* and had come across a very funny George Price cartoon showing a whole boodle of his hatchet-faced low-lifes sprawled about the living room before the television set, guzzling beer, and all (grandma, too!) got up in Dodger baseball uniforms. I was chuckling like a madman, but suddenly the chuckle became very like sobs—because I had made an awful, a horrifying transposition. Substituting for the Dodger uniform a New York Giant tuque I had seen pictures of the players wearing while working out in frigid weather, I suddenly saw myself consigned to the breakfast nook with Poppy, our Giant tuques pulled down about our ears, our tongues lapping at the Pabst cans, our ears glued to the radio, now and again raising our eyes to look self-consciously at one another and to make not very funny jokes about the women-folk in the other room, jokes that, sadly, admitted our helplessness before the jewel they carried between their legs. Yes, I saw myself sitting out there in Heritage Heights with Poppy, whose "reception" was so good and who had a marvelous gadget for opening the garage doors, and, oh lord, the thought that this might indeed be my heritage, my fate, struck me all the more impotent, quite unable to even satisfy Bunny, something which I had till that night always taken a kind of melancholy pride in doing—one way or another.

It was Sunday, and after watching Ed Sullivan and *What's My Line?* in the game room with Mums (Poppy was still in the breakfast nook poring over his insurance records and slugging away his Pabst), Bunny and I, having made previous arrangements, met in her room at midnight, a room which lay in one of the clapboard spokes at the opposite side of the house from her parents' room. Through *The Frigid Male* Bunny had made herself charmingly conversant with sex's more devious possibilities; she had high hopes that in that consecrated room, that there among the innocent memorabilia—the one-eyed Teddy bear, the gold-plated piggy-bank, the cheerleader's megaphone—of her infancy and adolescence, that in that lovely place something wonderful might happen. She sat on the bed, legs crossed Indian style, wearing a short blue nightie and looking more stunningly caressable than I had ever seen her. Without speaking, I lay down beside her, motioned for her to turn out the light, and lighted a cigarette. Nothing whatever happened. I lay there for about three hours, conscious of her tensed body beside me in the darkness, thinking how fantastically inventive life was, how terrifying really in that it sometimes does give substance to our airy dreams. And really, what good are dreams if they come true? After a long time, when I sensed that the breathing beside me was labored in sleep, I rose, bent over, kissed her unseen face, and walked out. It was all over then; the terri-

ble thing was that we yet had to go through the formal motions of dissolving it; we had, as humans do, to lay blame,
to kill each other a bit, to pick up the pieces and move on.
Still, our relationship ended more quickly and more satis-
factorily than most.

Back in Chicago, after having seen her in the ghastly
light of her parents, I brought things to a quick conclusion,
though at the time I was so distraught that I didn't realize I
was ending things. For many months after, I actually succeeded in believing that Bunny's decision to leave me was
as arbitrary as the winds. The first thing I did was take out
her letters, which I kept tidily bound in a dresser drawer,
and reread them. They were, as I suspected they would be
in the light of my recent visit, astonishing displays of her
ignorance; they might, I thought, have been written by any
literate seven-year-old, characterized as they were by a
chafing and moronic romanticism. Such information as
that she had written my name in the dust of a train-car
window—which once I had found unbearable in its touching quaintness—now seemed to epitomize her childish
(everything and everybody were either "neat" or "not
neat") and gross intelligence. Moreover, the English Department at her particular Big Ten factory must have been
partial to the dash and the exclamation point; one read letter after letter without encountering a single comma. As for
the period, she substituted for it an exclamation point, such
was the unswerving homage she thought should be given
every bland phrase she uttered. I had, of course, begun
rereading the letters with a sense of giddy misgiving; I
ended with a sense of benumbed horror, a horror which,
upon our next meeting, turned to a strident and vicious
cruelty.

For some weeks I had been disturbed by the sexual expertise with which she strove to please me, thinking that such abandoned mastery might derive from experience. And the next time we met I made her relate that experience. Oh, my God, yes! I made her tell me against her will, assuring her of the largeness of my tolerant heart. "I'll understand," I said quietly. Eyes avoiding hers and smiling painfully to myself, I lay on the candy-striped couch knowing, and not admitting that I knew, that each word she uttered—between each terrible sob (and what pleasure I derived from those sobs!) put her that much further from me. It was not a pretty picture. Miss America, it seems, was a Lolita after all and had been indulging herself, with a remarkable lack of discrimination, since a high school fullback had taken her at a scarcely pubescent fourteen. I heard all the names after that, Tom and Dick and Harry, and all the sordid details, and eyes avoiding hers continued to smile in that painful way. She told me lastly about the effeminate Holden Caulfield who had given me her name. "And how about Mr. *Absolutely?*" I had snapped at her. "Who?" she had sobbed in bewilderment. "Mr. Absolutely," I had bellowed. "The creep who gave me your name!" He had been, it seems, "like a drug." Then she went on to relate the sexual practices to which he had introduced her, relating them in penitent, terribly groping tones, as if she were relating Sins Monumental. The practices were no more than the average indulgent couple has engaged in, or thought of engaging in, at one time or another; and the horror was not in discovering that she looked upon them as degenerate (Christ, she was just a kid!) but that they put dirty pictures in my mind, in discovering that I was not worldly at all but Farmer Freddy Exley from up in the cow country with dreams of pure and virginal worlds populated with glimmering and upright people, in discovering that I was incapable of loving that which was tainted (damn you, Hollywood and Herman Wouk!). When Bunny finally finished, crushed and made ugly by the burden of her forced confession, I assured her, kissing away her tears, that everything was okay, that I understood perfectly. But I must have known then that it could never be okay with her, that in impotency I had assumed what I was and had committed a grievous assault to my own manhood, and that I had, in effect, made it possible, nay, necessary, for her to turn from me.

I only saw her once after that, in a restaurant in the Loop. She would not come to the apartment, which hurt because I had had two weeks to get used to her humanity and knew, surprisingly, that things were going to be all right with me, that though I couldn't seduce a dream, I could a rather ignorant blond doll from Heritage Heights. I begged her to come with me, but she wouldn't, telling me that it was over. I made a lot of agonizing phone calls to her after that, tearfully pleading with her to give me a chance to "make it up," saying things she probably didn't understand like, "Look. You've got to understand. I was just a goddam farmer with a lot of crazy dreams. Look. Give me the chance to put away the dreams!" But with each call her voice grew less distinct and finally drifted into memory. I know now that it was best that way.

I know because I had seen myself consigned to the kitchen with Poppy, our Giant tuques pulled down about our ears, swigging beer from the Pabst cans, and making weak, worried, and self-conscious jokes about the womenfolk in the other room. But having seen this, did I really know that I would have been unhappy, or should I say any less happy, in that life? I did not. I do know that the road I was to take would prove neither particularly pleasant nor edifying nor fruitful. No, all I knew in the end was that walking away had rescued me from the slow, dwindling emasculation undergone by so many of my brethren; and this, ironically, perhaps even a little miraculously, was the truth. For in the same way that a man's defect can be his virtue (as a gross physical ugliness often renders in its bearer a fine, subtle, and true aesthetic), I came to understand that my sexual failure in the end redeemed me, saved me from an almost certain castration. The failure was never to recur, so that I have no way of understanding it save in the light of that place, Chicago, at that time, a time when more than any other I felt at one with my country, and with that American girl, Bunny Sue. Had I gone erect with the awesome passion that I then felt for everything, had my penis mingled with that honey-dripping, corn-bred womb, who knows that I ever could have walked away? And I still do not know what saved me. Oh, I know the Freudian voodoo, the feelings of inadequacy that sometimes come to a man, the latent homosexuality, and so forth, and even the probable causes for such things. But it's all hogwash. In the end a man has to have an explanation he can live with, and I have one of these, one that would only occur to an English teacher, and one whose levity I can live with. I like to think that my penis started withering on its stump when, the day after I met her, I received those two letters from her, that I was saved, as it were, by the *dash*—and the *exclamation point!*

After Bunny, Chicago went cold and horrid for me, and the story of my dizzying descent into bumhood is the usual

bleak fantasy, so I will omit the details. After repeated
warnings about my excessive drinking, I was fired from my
job. Both of my bosses were good, even excellent, men. All
they wanted from me was a sober confrontation, an admission on my part that a problem existed, so that, in trying to
help me, they would not feel obtrusively puritanical,
holier-than-thou. I wasn't man enough to give them that
confrontation, and the day that we made our good-byes,
both of them, while I shook their hands, turned away from
me in sorrow.

For the next few months I drew forty-five dollars a week
in railroad unemployment, and with this, together with
moneys I quite shamelessly bummed from my roommate
and other barroom acquaintances, I was able to stay drunk
continually. I didn't shave, I didn't wash, and I became one
of those stark silhouettes—perhaps the first in the history
of that ingenuous city—against the Near North Side bars.
The strangest thing of all at this time was my search for the
girl with the coal-black hair. The copywriter who had introduced us had gone to New York, or to the Coast, nobody
seemed to know precisely where, and I spent hours trying
to re-create in my mind's eye the note I had crumpled up
and thrown away, trying to visualize a single number, name,
or address that had been written upon it. All I ever came up
with was the given name Ronald—he who had died of a
heart attack with a smile on his face dreaming of fishing in
Canada. Eventually I began taking the Elevated north.
Getting off at stops that seemed familiar, I would walk for
hours nipping on a pint of bourbon, looking for that elusive
apartment. Once or twice I was sure I had found the building, but I was unable to recognize any of the names on the
mailboxes. I did buzz what appeared to be single women,

Margery Winsaw, Edith Starkweather, Beverly Heartstick, *et al.*, divorcees and widows and Lesbians and ugly-buglies. None of them was she.

Ringing bells, I was engaged in the search one night when I felt a tap on my shoulder and turned to find two policemen who had answered a complaint that I was mashing. It was a bad situation. I was drunk, unkempt, unemployed, and sensed immediately that the only explanation that would save me was the truth. So I told them about the girl with the golden skin, and how I had incredibly, stupidly, unforgivably (I screamed in desperation, "I don't even know why!") thrown away her note. Did they believe me? They probably did. There was about my tale that element of madness contained in all truth, but they pretended not to believe me. One cop said, "It was probably just a wet dream." To that they had both laughed like hell. I had, too. At any event, they were good guys—Chicago guys—and they let me go, even driving me in the patrol car to the Elevated. All the way back to the Near North Side, I laughed, thinking the cop's explanation had been as good as any.

I had been in Chicago for almost two years by then, 1955 and 1956, and though I had completely disregarded football my first year in that happy city, during the autumn of 1956, after losing my job, I once again found that it was the only thing that gave me comfort. That fall was, ironically, the season when Gifford was having his greatest year in football, which culminated in his being voted by the other players in the league the Jim Thorpe Trophy—which made him, for that year at least, the greatest football player in the world. Most of my drinking companions were Chicago Bears fans—the most fanatical partisans on earth. Because the Bears were that year, as the Giants were in the

East, headed for their division title, I spent most of the fall unmercifully needling Bear fans about what Gifford and the Giants were going to do to them in the championship game. I stayed in Chicago till December to watch the game on television from Yankee Stadium, the Giants winning 47-7, stayed to watch it and to rub it into the boys. I had no grace in victory, though. Chicago had gone bad for me. In triumph I was quite vicious, and within three hours of the game I was in two drunken fist fights, both of which were nasty and bloody, involving broken noses, split ears, cracked heads, and black eyes, some mine, some the other guys'. It was terrible in a way to leave that wonderful city in that mood. Right after these fights I was to pack a bag and go "on the road" for a few months. By the fall of 1957 I would be home on my mother's davenport, staring at the ceiling and dreaming my dreams, waiting to be carted off to the private hospital the following spring, thence to Avalon Valley the immediately subsequent autumn. I know that I was sick even in Chicago; no one ever loved a city the way I loved that place, and it pains me deeply to have this final memory of it, seeing myself flailing away at drunken, angry faces, striking as if I were hitting out at the city that had so disenchanted me. It pains me because that disenchanted city—the one I knew in the final months—will, for me, never be the city I knew and loved for ever so long.

5

JOURNEY ON A
DAVENPORT

At Christmas, in 1951, I flew from Los Angeles to New York City where I boarded the overnight train to Watertown, intent on spending the holiday at home. The train had no club car, but at one end of a passenger coach, serviced by a stainless-steel and closet-like kitchenette, were two booths, cozy and on either side of the aisle. I found myself drinking beer and eating ham sandwiches in one of these booths with a Marine sergeant returning from Korea, a vernal-cheeked coed with large breasts, coming from some cow-sounding college in Pennsylvania where, she had loftily announced, she was studying veterinary medicine, and a goateed and fraudulent-looking surgeon traveling to Montreal. In keeping with the season our spirits were lyrically jubilant, the surgeon was generous in buying the food and the drinks, and after a time we sang Christmas carols. The sergeant had a resonant, self-conscious baritone; and I, having no voice at all, amiably mouthed silent "silent nights" (as my teachers had made me do in grammar school so I wouldn't undermine the melodious harmony of my classmates who, when singing, had stared with haughty disdain at the cretinous contortions of my lips). At one o'-clock the porter asked us to call it a night. Because every-one was crestfallen, the chivalrous surgeon bribed the Negro with a five-dollar bill, though the latter ordered us to knock off the caroling. For that reason we talked about our families and our homes well into the early morning, drinking the beer the bribe had procured us.

By first light, only I was left awake. As though the fatigue of war had abruptly caught up with and sundered him, the Marine had put his head on his folded hands on the table and was sleeping with such heaviness that his fore-head appeared to have depressed into and become part of his wrists. The coed, her outsized breasts now demure and maiden-like, was snoozing in the shelter of the doc-tor's salt-and-pepper sleeve, the surgeon's cheek, flushed now with boozy contentment, resting familiarly on her soft brown hair. During the night the north country had undergone its worst storm in years, and for the eighty-mile distance from Utica to Watertown, while those inti-mate strangers slept huddled all about me, and while the steam engine heaved and fretted through the brilliant, the near-dazzling whiteness, I looked out the window and watched the cold, the frozen world go by me. In the vague way one is aware of the contours of the back of one's head, I had always been aware that my corner of America was farm country, but only that morning did I re-alize how very northern or "Russian"—almost steppe-like—it really was. After watching the slightly rolling, nearly treeless landscape for a long time, and doubtless abetted by the unconscious knowledge that I was rising on the map, I began to experience the oddly comforting sensation of ascending to the very top of the world, of rising to some place apart from the fitful concerns and harsh sorrows of men, to a glacial and opaline haven where a man, having been hard-used by the world or having used himself hard, might go and ask himself where things had gone wrong.

At the precise moment I disembarked and my foot hit the icy platform, I looked first at my instantaneously white-flecked sleeve, then skyward to see that it had begun snowing again. In what was to be the most memorable holiday of my life, it scarcely stopped snowing the entire week I was home. Snow clogged everything. Its plowed and mountainous banks hid the houses from view. No cars moved, and because the sidewalks would be days in getting cleared, one was forced to walk in the middle of the glistening streets between the snowy mountains on either side, a dreamy white world wherein one ambulated without fear of being flattened by an Oldsmobile. Their faith in the supremacy of the Detroit product lamentably touching, middle-aged men shoveled furiously, attempting to loosen their Fords from Nature's perverseness. As if those automobiles were extensions of themselves without which they could not live, they wielded their shovels with bent-back and vapor-exhaling dedication. The sky cleared, a few cars were loosed and began moving splutteringly through the embanked and narrow aisles, the sky once again clouded over, snow came, and the cars chugged, chugged, and stopped again. With renewed and exasperated vigor (it never occurred to them to walk), the men once again engaged the snow with angry shovels, their rampantly palpitating hearts threatening to burst (I don't know how many we lost to coronaries that year), while in a gang my friends and I moved up the shimmering white corridors, jeering at them. My friends were younger then and did not know that this was this, that that; though some of us might have been acute enough to know that though Detroit owned America, Detroit didn't yet own us; we had the youthful and heartfelt hopes of being "our own men." With youth's arrogant confidence that we were so markedly dissimilar from those shovelers, we walked in that remembered brilliance, shouting, "Shovel, you fucking dummies!" That the shovelers might know our four-letter bravado was not to be trifled with, we then pounded each other on the back and roared with haughty laughter: a strained camaraderie designed to deter any of the braver shovelers from approaching us. Making our way to the next saloon, we drank draft beer in comfortable booths, cribbed and passed off as our own a favorite professor's remark on Plato or Aquinas or Twain, and continued to sneer at "dummies" unable to see the beauty and completeness of a world in which one did nothing but walk about in the snow, drink draft beer in crowded booths, and try to understand a world not governed by automatic transmissions.

Now I see in that laughter a good deal of desperation and sadness. About to leave the haven of our separate universities and be thrown onto the brutal free-spinning of the world, as we walked arm in arm through the snow, we carried with us, if only unconsciously, the knowledge that it would be our last holiday together; and we drank and laughed and sneered with the resolute sadness of men who knew that tomorrow we'd be trying to free our own mortgaged Buicks from our own snow-locked drives. That is what most of us ended doing. I didn't; but I don't question that my friends were right and I wrong, that they were happy and I was not, that theirs was the hard and mine the easy way. What always saddened me on confronting them was the surety that had I been foolish enough to bring up "old times," none would have allowed himself a memory of sticking his finger into the vaporous and flaky air and shouting, "Shovel, you fucking dummies!" A self-destructively romantic man, I accepted our jeering defiance as a pact; forever.

———

The "top of the world" was where I went when I had ceased to function on the road. After fleeing Chicago in early 1957, I had live din many cities, and in the late fall of that year had ended in jail in Miami where I was brought before the splenetic judge and told I was a "fatuous lunatic." Those words stinging me into numbness, I decided it was time to head north. Because my mother had for years been remarried to a man I scarcely knew, I had qualms about doing so. I was aware that her husband owned a business that would put food in my stomach, and that as a wedding present he had bought her an old limestone farmhouse at Pamelia Four Corners (an irritant in the highway some ten miles north of the city) where I could—if I were taken in, and utterly divorced from the comings and goings, the struggles, the victories, the defeats of other men—ask myself where things had gone wrong; but this awareness did not mitigate my fears of being turned away. That my lunacy had been recognized was chastening enough, but the judge's gratuitous "fatuous" carried with it intimations that I was in a blubbering, nose-picking state; and I had visions of arriving at my mother's door, garbed not in the "attractive," melancholic dementia of the poet but in the drooling, masturbatory, moony-eyed condition of the

Mongoloid. That I feared my mother would turn even the latter away indicates the extent paranoia had already dented my psyche.

Offering the excuse that she wasn't good at "things like that," my mother never learned to drive a car. It was not that simple. The melody of her life was as unvarying in its scale as a moon-June rhyme put to music: she believed in wholesome food, clean clothes, and warm beds for her family, and she viewed things like driving automobiles as extraneous, perhaps decadent, as if the artless melody would be burdened down with precious and contrapuntal themes. Such a blunt engagement with life never failed to astonish and charm her family, though there were times when we grew impatient with it: we yearned for her sophistication and longed to make of her a swan-necked lady with lorgnette. Deferring to such yearnings, she once in fact took a driving lesson.

With my father play-acting the amused and tolerant tutor in a world of buffoons and in a jolly, whimsical style preceding her into the front seat of our Model A Ford roadster, she got behind the wheel, on his direction shifted into first gear, accelerated the gas pedal, released the clutch, and froze. Before doing so, and for reasons unfathomable, she had "strangled" the wheel violently to the left, and the Ford went round and round the churchyard in increasingly large circles. Losing his suave tutorial cool and going ramrod straight, my father bellowed at her to relax. Doing so tentatively, my mother's partially lax hands on the wheel caused the weird and ever-enlarging circles. At the same time, the released energy dispersed to her foot and weighted the accelerator, so that with each new and widening circle the car accumulated maddening speeds. At the edge of the yellow field stood my brother and sister and I, not knowing whether to shriek with laughter or terror. There was only one massive, horny-trunked elm in all that great yard; and when it became evident that on the next lap, or certainly the one after, the blameless Ford and the innocent elm would meet, we stood agape and tremulous with anticipation. At the last possible moment, having regained his impressive nonchalance, my father thrust his leg over the shifting gear and trenchantly applied the brake, halting the car only inches from the tree and giving both Mother and himself a thumping forehead crack against the flush and durable windshield of that marathon automobile. In its frustration the Ford rocked thwartedly back and forth. From underneath its biting tires there arose great clouds of August dust. The car shook itself to a stall, the dust settled, and silence descended. Breathless, my brother, my sister, and I ran to them, where we remained speechless, searching for bruises, for dangling limbs, for those obscene gashes ready to yield up their torrents of fatal blood. Unable to gauge the condition or temper of the car's stunned occupants, we were frightened. When finally they disembarked, both were ashen but, except for their already ballooning brows, they appeared to be unhurt. With my brother, who was the eldest, taking the lead, we laughed joyously with relief. Joined quickly in the laughter by my father, who pensively rubbed his brow as he laughed, we watched my mother thunder angrily toward the cottage. She was pained and humiliated at our amused reaction to her already professed insistence that she was not good at "things like that."

In the long winters my brother and I went on windswept Saturdays to the Strand and Olympic and Palace;

and for ten cents, and between viewing Jane Withers in *Little Miss Nobody* and the Three Stooges in *Crisis at the Antarctic* and Johnny mack Brown in *Yellow Stallion Canyon* (Johnny always spurned the pig-tailed lass in calico and rode off into a black-and-white sunset with a bewhiskered and lovable old ragamuffin named Fuzzy, so that even now it is something of a miracle to me that I didn't end in some remote YMCA embracing some other, more comely, Fuzzy)—between viewing what we now know to have been these not so *virginibus puerisque* flickers, we got during the newsreels our first looks at the madmen who govern the great world. We did not laugh at first. Watching the ample-assed and cretinous-looking Hitler review his goose-stepping legions, or the statuesque and farcical posturings of the raving Mussolini, we watched with the morbid fascination of children being exposed for the first time to lunacy. Withering, shrinking down in our seats, and smiling weakly there in the darkness, we felt embarrassment and compassion for what were obviously sick men. Taking our cue from our elders and gurus (Mencken, who hated claptrap because there was so much of it in himself, and others convinced us that these uniformed grotesques were really no more than naughty boys), we did laugh later; we stood and laughed and jeered and clamorously pounded the rickety seats in front of us. Hooting, we had no idea that my brother, who jeered as loudly as anyone, would in no time at all be in a rather ludicrous uniform of his own, with a few million other Americans called upon to pay the heavy toll for having failed to recognize insanity for the pernicious evil it is.

Other wars were imminent. My father had begun to cough. Standing over the toilet bowl, he woke us to that

cough. His hack was like some alarm clock with faulty
gears. He hacked and hacked and hacked. Shivering, we lay
in a state of acute wonder, listening, anticipating that his
chest would explode. He would raspingly clear his throat
and emit the ponderous glob of cohesive sputum. The
hacking would begin again, again the cleared throat, again
the spitting. Into that sputum one awful day would come
the minute crimson clot heralding the start of a war—unlike that which my brother and other men would fight
simultaneously—that could not be won.

My mother's war was perhaps the most sapping of all.
Not only had she to follow my father from hospital to hospital; she had to keep the family together. When, hope exhausted, she finally brought my father home from Ray
Brook at Saranac Lake to die, he was placed in the Jefferson County Sanatorium, a lovely hospital with sweeping,
tree-shaded lawns at the top of Coffeen Street hill in Watertown. Unable to comfort my mother, my brother, at seventeen, was off at the ends of the earth fighting the
"naughty boys"; at an age too "tender" to witness the horror of lingering death, my sister and I were packed off to a
sympathetic and generous aunt in Westchester; and because she had not the means to view such a costly death in
philosophical leisure, my mother took a job in the cafeteria
of the telephone company. She made bean soup and tuna-
fish sandwiches for the clerks and operators of that lunatic
corporation, and each afternoon, after washing the dishes
and diligently preparing the next day's menu, she got on a
bicycle (never having mastered driving), rode it to the
city's outskirts, disembarked, and began the long walk up
Coffeen Street hill to hold my father's hand.

On first hearing of that bicycle in one of my mother's

letters, I was dumb with amazement. Then I began to laugh. Almost as quickly I was embarrassed, overwhelmed with the crushingly self-centered embarrassment of adolescence. My mother was a heavy woman, and the thought of her pedaling about town nettled me immeasurably. Trying to envision it, I hoped that, like a wealthy matron out exercising, she would affect a *beau monde* haughtiness. But I knew she wouldn't. Guileless, she would simply *pump.* Awful possibilities suggested themselves. I especially imagined my high school friends (from whom I was now separated) spotting her and saying, *"Jesus,* ain't that old lady Exley?" Perhaps they would even jeer her. "Hey, Ma! Hey, get a horse! Hey, would cha?" O lord! And though I never saw her ride that bicycle, my vision of her doing so stayed, and will stay, with me all my days. So much did the image of her pedaling haunt me at one period of my life that I became obsessed with the question of how, on reaching the bottom of Coffeen Street hill, she had managed to get both herself and bicycle up to the hospital. The question was with me always; on a hundred different occasions I meant to ask it, but I could never find the casual tone with which to speak the words. I couldn't because her probable answer had somehow taken on a dreadful significance for me. As though I were the Sphinx and she Oedipus, I came to fear that on hearing her answer I would, in mortification, cast myself off the rock and perish. It was only some weeks after returning home that I finally did ask her. Lying eyes ceilingward on the davenport, I tried to bring lightness into my voice. My mother did not understand the question. "I mean," I said, "when Dad was dying up at the San, how did you get the bicycle up the hill? Ride it up? Walk it up? Leave it at the bottom of the hill, or what?" "I walked it up," my mother said dispassionately, the question having no relevance for her.

—

On first arriving from Florida, I brought my mother's face close to mine, slid into a pair of well-worn loafers, some faded dungarees, and a royal-blue, zippered sweatshirt; piled the marble-topped coffee table adjacent to the davenport high with long-neglected volumes; walked into the kitchen and from the pantry closet removed a package of Oreo Creme Sandwiches; returned to the living room and flicked on the television, which after a momentary lull began its incessant and hypnotic drone; invited Christie III, my mother's saucer-eyed, russet-and-white cocker spaniel to share the davenport at my feet; and then lay down until the spring of 1958.

In a land where movement is virtue, where the echo of heels clacking rapidly on pavement is inordinately blest, it is a grand, defiant, and edifying gesture to lie down for six months. Lying with my legs wide apart, I saw what I saw of the world—a sad-eyed, bewildered canine—through the weary V of my feet. With my neck comfortably braced up by luxurious, pliant cushions, I lay with my left hand on my crotch, my fingertips conscious of the inert penis through the coarse denim of the dungarees. A supernumerary check of the member's reality, there was nothing erotic in the gesture. It was a palliative. In it there was something of the parvenu scanning and rescanning his accounts, as though those soothing figures had no reality beyond his sight. Awakening to my body for the first time, I heard the rhythmical, occasionally syncopated, and always audible contortions of my heart, now and then hearing from beneath the monstrously hot layers of flesh the plangent and

ominous rumblings of unimaginable visceral parts. I made
sublime discoveries. I learned, for example, to distinguish
between the odor of a sweat produced in a passion of labor
or love and that of the effluvium from the stationary body,
the latter having a foul, self-conscious stench. After a time
I became acclimated to the stench, to the hotness of my
flesh, to its alien rumblings; and by then I had drifted into
a subliminal world and was insensible to touch or odor or
taste or sound or sight, so that the immediate world—this
penis, this hum from the television, this sentence on the
white page, this scratching of the dog, this taste of chocolate—all existed in a dawnlike realm where I seemed to be
aware of absolutely nothing.

Seemed to be is the secret; for there are only two kinds of
time (time-future being the province of melancholy seers,
jocular quacks, and somber religionists promising king-
doms they haven't the *congé* to promise): there is time being
lived, and that same time as it is relived in the mind five
minutes, five years, five centuries later; and because these
times are never analogous, the historian (browsing amidst
his ponderous tomes and dusty parchments and, by comparison with the shabby rest of us, imagining himself a
creature of consequentially high purpose) lives the biggest
lie of all. Though I believed that during those months I had
reached a plateau whereon I was insensible to everything
and at twilight could never remember anything that had
occurred that same day, by the time in early spring when I
began to hear from my mother's bedroom, above the unsettling whispers, the words *sick* and *psychiatrist* and *hospital*
and knew that my days at the farm were over, I had made
every significant self-discovery I would ever make; so that
if the coming years of hospitalization were necessary to

me—and they were—they were necessary only in that one man might make his peace with a new and different man. All this I see in time-relived; I then believed that nothing whatever was at work, that I was drifting quite aimlessly on a davenport, when in fact that davenport was taking me on an unwavering, rousing, and often melancholy journey.

During those months I discovered that just as my mother hadn't been able to come to an easy intimacy with our Model A Ford roadster, neither did my heart know repose confronted with the new dynamics. Continuously emanating from the television, in both flickering image and somber rhetoric, were invitations to the languid viewer to join some bright-eyed, clean-jawed men in galactic journeys. I especially remember the recurring image seen from the ass end of a space ship as it exploded as stealthily as smoke through the firmament; stars as big as Bijou popcorn glimmered brilliantly and moved ferociously by as the earth receded and receded until, in a matter of moments, it was a dark, pitted lump in aeons of frigid space. My mind wasn't up to it. With the American Indian I suffered the belief that Sweet Earth was born when my eyes first feasted upon it; and as I watched this same earth recede into indefiniteness, my being seemed to extinguish in staccato pops as trees blurred into plains, plains into mountains. In childhood I had never been up to those travelogues opening with the habitual stock shot (invariably disfigured by the akimbo prop of the airplane's wing splitting the screen) of the teeming Technicolored jungles of Borneo or Brazil; as the plane ascended, took on speed, and traversed entire green subcontinents at finger snaps, my mind went blank; and by the time the reassuring tones of Mr. Fitzpatrick had brought me back to earth and were showing me the sacred horned oxen of the River Ganges, I was lost and sat, a sweaty and forlorn child, in the foul-stockinged odor of the dark and cavernous theater. Whenever on the davenport I tried to discover an adventure commensurate with my timid soul and contractile mentality, I was forced into dim history. The most I was capable of was seeing myself as a velveteen-knickered first mate to Bartholomeu Dias as, astrolabe in hand, we floated in the equatorial waters off the Dark Continent, waiting for a breeze that would carry us to the tip of Africa in search of the fabled Indies. Such pioneerings into the unhurried past, though, were as close as I could come to envisioning myself a grim-jawed astronaut seeking commerce with pink, antennaed men whose overdeveloped skulls held the forbidding secrets of the universe.

It wasn't possible for me to adopt the wherewithal by which my mother lived in consort with the modern horror. Each morning on my stepfather's departure for work, she made and received her daily telephone calls; and though at the time I believed I heard not a word of these conversations, I heard every word. Certain businesses in Watertown were now giving Plaid instead of S & H Green Stamps. From an inspection of the Plaid Stamp catalogue, it was believed that the Plaid People offered a greater variety of goods than the Green People, though someone "in the know" claimed that the Green People offered a higher-quality merchandise. The pros and cons of the two stamps were ardently debated; and, like all scrupulous magistrates, the women ominously reserved judgment. A new shopping piazza containing an A & P supermarket, a beauty salon, a Fanny Farmer candy shop, a tonsorial expert, a liquor store, a Marine Midland bank branch, an apothecary, a Grant's department store, a Dairy Treat luncheonette, a Christian

Science reading room, a tailor-dressmaker, a Family Bargain center, and possibly a Chinese restaurant, was scheduled for opening somewhere on the outskirts of the city. The women decided unequivocally and (since it never opened) with unerring correctness that Watertown wasn't ready for more Oriental cuisine, Willie Gee's familiar place downtown lending our fair northern city whatever cosmopolitan touch it needed.

Much telephone talk was devoted to the menstrual cycle, pregnancies, breech positions, tubes blocked and unblocked, and change of life; to cancer of the breast, cervix, rectum, lung, and small intestine; to measles, mumps, whooping cough, and the various childhood diseases; to respiratory infections, fatty livers, goiters, and gout; to arthritis, rheumatism, and bursitis; to hardening of the arteries, diabetes, cataracts, hemorrhoids, dyspepsia, heartburn, and general orneriness; and to obesity, high and low blood pressure, strokes, heart attacks, and coronary occlusions. Following hard on this catalogue of distress came footnotes on the local medical profession. Never did I hear a doctor condemned for anything other than charging one or two dollars above the going price for house calls. By the women, the Watertown doctor was considered "brilliant," "smart as a whip," and, the highest accolade of all, "a nice guy." Occasionally such encomiums were lavished on a man I had heard to be an apathetic, nurse-fondling, heavy-handed old faker; and at the women's touching generosity to him, I smiled ruefully. A man known to the family, or to one of my mother's confidantes, was said to be beating his wife, the result of his drinking. This was doubly dolorous and a spine-chilling indictment of alcohol as the man was said to be a "prince" when abstemious.

Often during these conversations, my mother caught me

in an ironical smile, and invariably at a time deemed inappropriate. One caller had a neighbor who worked the swing shift in a factory. With his wife confined to the bughouse at Ogdensburg, his home was being kept for him by his two comely teenage daughters, aged thirteen and fourteen. Every evening at five minutes to midnight a hot rod loaded with black-jacketed, black-booted goons screeched up to the house and discharged the daughters who fled through the front door, ran up the stairs, disrobed, hopped into bed, and in a feigned sleep closed their eyes in anticipation of their father's homecoming bed check of them at five past midnight. To my mother's dismay, I laughed loudly at this. There was something so Rabelaisian and Elizabethan at the thought of this beleaguered, much-used, and benighted papa looking in on his "innocently sleeping" progeny, no doubt still quivering with the healthy flush of their nightly ardors, Papa dwelling in saintlike unawareness that he was viewing two Ogdensburg inmates in embryo.

It wasn't so much that I chuckled out of perverseness as that I seemed to be listening in on comically alien tribal rites which had nothing whatever to do with me. Like John Jay Chapman, who used to lie at night wondering whatever was the matter with his native Bostonians, I lay on the davenport wondering whatever was the matter with Watertownians that they could find no more dignified way to confront the hydrogen age than fretting about Plaid Stamps or the lustful appetites of neighbors' daughters. In those languidly optimistic days, I still owned the distasteful hauteur of one who believed the world could be shaken until the pieces fell together into the pattern of my own promised land, and had no idea what an exemplary world it would be if, like housewives, everyone sensed his inadequacy for Divine Missions and confined himself to worrying over grocery stamps.

Because he had gone there before me, I elected to follow my father to Hobart. His career at Hobart was sweaty, contentious, controversial, and short-lived (as, in a different way, mine was too), lasting anywhere from a day or so to two weeks. By going arduously through the forlornly disordered pile of his yellowing and deteriorating scrapbooks, I could put together a facsimile of what happened from what I remember to be vaguely though indignantly worded newspaper accounts. But I shan't. In telling the story over the years I have added such a captivating touch here, omitted such a bland one there, that the tale is now so aesthetically the way I prefer it that I'm sure the bare facts would prove inimical to my own version.

In the summer of his seventeenth year, 1924, my father was a lifeguard at the small St. Mary's Street pool on the north, the less fashionable, side of Watertown; and one azure and balmy day he was approached there by two men who invited him, hang the expense, to come to Geneva with them and play football for Hobart. Today, when muscular, two-hundred-and-thirty-pound gladiators quake at the mere mention of Notre Dame, Texas, Alabama, and USC, such a proposition almost smacks of the insultingly laughable, but in those days football was pre-eminently an Eastern disease and Hobart played what was considered a formidable schedule. Although my father was indeed flattered, he suffered the misgivings of being two or three credits short of his diploma and of having been named the previous spring to captain his high school team for the upcoming season, for what, in effect, was to be his senior year.

What sophistry or arm-twisting these men used on my

father is not known, but apparently the recruiting of athletes in those days was not nearly so guileless as one likes to imagine. Whoever they were and whatever their connection with Hobart, they persuaded my father that a diploma was a trifling and dispensable *sine qua non* (and considering for what they wanted him, I expect that it was), not to be given a second thought. Thereupon they escorted him home, helped him pack his bags, stood by as he kissed his bewildered mother, and explained to her that he was off for the greater glories to be claimed on the green fields of academe; and without (one somehow imagines) as yet having let him out of their apprehensive sights, they piled him into their Model T Ford roadster, spirited him south to Geneva, put a uniform on him, and turned him loose among the Hobart mercenaries.

How long my father worked out with "The Statesmen"—the decorous patronymic hung on Hobart athletic teams, and one that by the time of my arrival there had become devilishly apt—I do not know, though I have always told the story in such a way as to indicate it was long enough to have the college's president, the dean of men, the Episcopal chaplain, and the entire coaching staff smacking their lips in anticipation of the imminent autumn. "Yeah," I always (and certainly apocryphally) told my version, "when the roof fell in, Hobart had their whole fucking team built around the old man!"

The "roof" which fell and aborted my father's candidacy for All-American honors was Gary M. Jones, principal of the high school. I never knew Jones. At my unremarked (for me no coaches waited breathlessly) arrival at the school, he was long since retired or dead, but summoning him back produces in me a certain stiff-backed reticence. From what

I remember of his photos this rigid deference to his ghost seems exorbitant, for in appearance Jones was a luminous-domed, roly-poly, jovial-looking soul. As a child, though, I remember grownups speaking of him in the respectful tones of men who in wayward youth had experienced the awfulness of his justice, awful, I gathered, because it was always so uncannily appropriate to the offense committed. Jones was tough and fair and approached as a principal should be approached but almost never is today: with respect, with trepidation, and with guarded affection. Precisely what he said on learning my father was at Hobart—and whether he was more concerned with my father's not having graduated or his being lost to the high school's football team—is also conjecture; but he said it with such stinging animus that the Hobart authorities had little choice but to repack my father's bags, tell him they'd expect him back the following autumn, and send him home where he captained his team to an undefeated season (along the way defeating one opponent 119-0), and where he so added to his growing mystique that, alas, Hobart's bid was no longer tempting enough.

Somewhere among his now-tattered papers are many offers, including two or three telegrams from Lou Little solicitously inquiring after my father's whereabouts. Little was then near the beginning of his career at Georgetown University in Washington, D.C., the wires are dated in the early days of September, 1925, and the controlled indignation of their tone indicates my father had made Little a promise he hadn't kept. Little wanted to know not only why my father hadn't shown up on the Georgetown campus but what the problem was. Was it finances? Was it illness? When I was a boy and on rainy days used to drag my friends up to the attic to spend the long afternoons leafing through the scrapbooks, it was these telegrams that impressed them above anything else, even above the ardent-treacle prose style with which the newsmen of his day had described my father's exploits.

By the time my boyhood friends and I were in our teens, Little had gone on to Columbia, achieved a national eminence, and become to athletically minded boys the symbol of a man who breathed the very fire of immortality into one, a man who, as though with putty, molded All-Americas with little more than his sinuous and invigorating fingers. Hence, although my friends and I were able to laugh skeptically, even jeeringly, at the photos of my father and his teammates in their patchwork-quilted football breeches and spartanly black wool jerseys beneath which it was impossible to detect pads; although we were able to giggle disparagingly at their greasily slapped-down hair parted sinisterly—in the style of the cinema gangsters of the twenties—down the middle of the scalp; although we were joyously and swaggeringly able to "make book" that the teams of our own epoch could have beaten those spindly-looking men by untold touchdowns—"Ten at least!" someone always shouted—still, these telegrams never permitted us to dismiss my father out of hand, and there inevitably came a moment when, unable to sustain such jeering, one of the boys, reverently lowering his voice, would ask the obvious: "How come your old man didn't take the scholarship?" Though the answer was simple, it was not one easily understood by boys, and I always evaded replying or lied by saying that my father had been sick or that he had incurred an injury which prevented his accepting. During his senior year my father had fallen in love with my mother and had determined to marry her at the expense of either education or fame.

Thus it was that the days of my youth flew by like violently clashing confetti, the pale scraps of my life as I imagined I was living it opposed to the vividly multicolored hues of what-might-have-been. My father became an unhappy lineman—he loathed that job to desperation!—for the Niagara Mohawk, struggled to eke out a subsistence for his wife and children, and took his pleasure in the grim Sunday afternoon world of semiprofessional athletes seeking violently to recapture a sense of a talent that may never have existed. Still, I always imagined a world infinitely more glittering, one in which my father had indeed become an All-America and had afterward, partly on the strength of it, risen to the top of some huge industrial complex. In adolescence, in a euphoria of possibilities, I had no difficulty believing that I summered at Cape Cod with splendid, golden maidens; roomed at Exeter with Ronald Farquarson III; or that I would one day go all tan-faced, broad-shouldered, and gleaming-toothed to Yale where I would be hushingly pointed out as "the son of Earl Exley." Thus it was, too, that for many years I imagined my childhood infinitely more execrable than it was. Macaroni and cheese was more common to our table than lobster, and clothes were (if possible) handed down from sister to sister, brother to brother (it was, Dr. Freud, those inherited run-over shoes that drove me mad!); but I doubt we were any less well off than most of the populace in an economically depressed America. Now I can also understand that my father, for all his melancholy aspect, was as happy as any man can be who has performed his most poetic feats before twenty. But I am perhaps being unkind and unfair. There is a possibility that in the end he performed the most poetic feat of all. Though I have elsewhere remarked that the pain became such that he begged for morphine, there is a possibility that he knew for a long time he was about to die—and that he did so well.

My father wrote a letter of appreciation to the people of Watertown from Ray Brook Sanatorium, dated January 6, 1945, and addressed to the editors of the Watertown *Daily Times*. On New Year's Day six nights before, attended by much hoopla, there had been an Earl Exley Night basketball game, the proceeds of which had gone to my mother to help defray medical and other expenses. On the day he wrote the letter my father had seven months to live. Held in sway by worlds that never were, I had not gone to the game, having apprehensively hidden in a movie theater while it was being played. I hadn't gone because rooming at Exeter with Farquarson III on the one hand and accepting charity on the other were too vexatiously incompatible. There was a moment when I might have gone, but on coming home from school one night I found my mother distraught at the news that the fundraising committee was contemplating giving her the money as she needed it— twenty dollars here for groceries, thirty there for the doctors—that they were going to make of it something it didn't have to be—charity with strings, generosity begrudged, kindness disfigured; and though some cooler, more sophisticated head eventually prevailed and persuaded the committee simply to turn the money over to my mother, that they were considering doing otherwise brought home to me the humiliation of charity, and I, who after all summered in quite other, more golden worlds, refused utterly to sit red-facedly in that packed gymnasium and allow people to beam their beneficence down upon me.

Syntactically, the letter is painful. Composed for The Public, the sentence structure is strained to ungrammaticalness, the language is pretentious (he uses "mentor" for "coach," phrases like "For me or any of mine to forget this noble gesture would be a sacrilege in its basest form"), and in no way does it reflect my father's intelligence, humor, or style. He thanks his friends for their generosity, he unconsciously, immodestly, and amusingly accepts their verdict on his athletic greatness, and with that damnable sentimentality peculiar to celebrities, in three paragraphs he says that he was no greater than his teammates, his coaches, the sportswriters, and the fans made him (though we are left with the feeling that he rather doubts they made any significant contributions). The letter would, in fact, be too painful to keep were it not for one unnerving line. With so much going for him, the love of his family, the prayers and kindness of his friends, the best the medical profession can offer, he says not that he will not die but that it seems "next to impossible to die." There is a dreadfulness about that "next to impossible." How my mind reels and shudders at the qualification of that "next to." This man who in his bouncy, pigeon-toed way did not even walk like other men; this man who joyously and for nothing other than the love of contact knocked down men twice his size; this man who in rage could leave a man a mouthful of bloodied teeth; this man who had an affecting need of intimacy with broken humanity, my father at forty has been touched by the inexplicable and horrendous specter of death and knows that life is over.

Though I know very little of him during this time, over

the years I have come across two people, a nurse and an X-ray technician, who did. I didn't, as I yearned to do, earnestly implore, "Did he die well?" There was no need to do so. On learning who I was, both of them voluntarily remarked their proximity to my father at the end, both smiled warmly, both had a brightness come into their eyes, and both wagged their heads in fond reminiscence. That fond head-wagging endures in a way no game by which a community buries a favorite son can ever endure.

—

Though the television droned all day, and though by day's end, to save my head from decapitation, I could not have related to my tormentors a smidgen of anything I had seen, now I remember the shows clearly. I saw the quiz shows in which contestants stood as tremulous as condemned men in outhouse-like glass prisons, the flanks of their skulls encased in great Buck Rogers-like earphones. Watching them strain, look abstracted, purse, wet their lips, and roll their eyes while searching so zealously for an answer, I laughed heartily and knew that the show was either rigged—the contestants were such abominable actors—or—watching them, all phony sighs of relief, give their farcically esoteric answers—that the contestants were mental freaks unworthy of the homage a boy-minded country was paying them. I watched the jolly comedies that induced no laughter save on that Orwellian laugh track. Implying, as in its sinister intimidation it did imply, that there was a green and salutary land just off the wings where pink-cheeked, wittily precious people were grasping things beyond my brutal sense of humor, that laughter soured me utterly. The louder the belly laughs grew, the more puritanically severe became my distaste until I began to feel like an obtuse Presbyterian perusing Rabelais.

I watched—but there is no need to enumerate. Not once during those months did there emanate from the screen a genuine idea or emotion, and I came to understand the medium as subversive. In its deceit, its outright lies, its spinelessness, its weak-mindedness, its pointless violence, in the disgusting personalities it holds up to our youth to emulate, in its endless and groveling deference to our fantasies, television undermines strength of character, saps vigor, and irreparably perverts notions of reality. But it is a tender, loving medium; and when it has done its savage job completely and reduced one to a prattling, salivating infant, like a buxom mother it stands always poised to take one back to the shelter of its brown-nippled bosom. Save for football I no longer watch the tube, and yet my set is always on. In the way one puts a ticking clock in a six-week-old puppy's pillowed box to assure him that Mom is always there, I come in from having one too many beers, flick on the switch, and settle comfortably on the davenport. The drone reassures me that life is there, life is simple, life is unending. Starting up abruptly at 3 A.M., I am at first chagrined and terrified by the darkness; then suddenly I am conscious of the hot hum of the voiceless tube and turn to receive the benediction from the square of brilliant light shining directly upon me from out of the darkness. How I envy those people who live in areas where all-night movies are shown.

To say that I took no pleasure from television is untrue. The endearing world of the soap operas captivated me completely. I don't remember the names of any of them; nor do I remember anything of the plots save that the action moved along with underwater creepiness. I do remember the picture of America they apostrophized was truer than either the tongue-in-cheek writer or the lumbering actors imagined (the latter all walked left-handedly through their parts, letting us know they were between roles in The Legitimate Theater).

The world of the soap opera is the world of the Emancipated American Woman, a creature whose idleness is employed to no other purpose but creating mischief. All these women had harsh crow's-feet about the eyes, a certain fullness of mouth that easily and frequently distended into a childish poutiness, and a bosomless and glacial sexuality which, taken all together, brought to their faces a witchy, self-indulgent suffering that seemed compounded in equal parts of unremitting menstrual periods, chronic constipation, and acute sexual frustration. Though I do not remember the plots, I remember there was a recurring scene in which these females, like the witches about the cauldron in *Macbeth*, gathered together in shiny kitchens with checkered muslin curtains and ovens built into beige bricks; that there, seated over snowy porcelain tables adorned with exquisite china coffee cups and artificial flowers, they planned for, plotted against, and passed judgment upon all the shadowy and insubstantial characters who made their flickering entrances and exits through the kitchen. They produced plans and plots and judgments which the writer, for all his cynicism, his two thousand dollars a week, and the corny lines he gave them to speak, never questioned as being any less than their right to make. If Kit's stepson Larry was so ungratefully and willfully contumacious as to want to buy a hot-dog stand instead of accepting his engineering scholarship to Yale, a means was devised to dissuade him. If Pamela's husband Peter was drinking (and how the women lingered on and gave pregnancy to words like *drinking,* rolling them lovingly around on the palate like hot pecan pie), it was determined, not that Peter might be buckling under too much responsibility but that he did not have enough and that "Pammy ought to have children." Woe unto that philanderer Judson, now having a fling with his new secretary from out of town (as with the Southern mind, all the evil influences in the soap operas came from "out of town"); within days he was certain to meet his horrifying death in the holocaust of his overturned Jaguar.

Wondering constantly how accurate a portrait of America it was, I saw this world as one in which these witches were without motive save that of keeping everyone about them locked and imprisoned within the illiterate and banal orbit of their days, a world to which the passionate and the singular aspiration were forbidden. If these women seemed drawn with an alarming accuracy, in their nonexistent way the men were even more to the target and were not unlike the ball-less men one sees every day on Madison Avenue. All wore button-down shirts and seemed excellent providers, all deferred to the women's judgments and seemed unburdened with anything like thoughts, and all possessed a Gregory-Peckish gentleness best reflected in their adamant refusal ever to raise their voices. Like most men they had somehow got the notion that the voice under control is the voice of civilization. A restraint admirable to the point of being miraculous, it seemed to say, let the Tower of Pisa complete its poised trajectory and fall, let the Taj Mahal ooze into the mire of Agra, let our madhouses overflow and India repopulate until its people elbow each other into the sacred Ganges, but in the interests of sanity and civilization let us still maintain our modulated tones.

It was at this point that I began talking to my set. Like those lonely shut-ins who write chummy notes to the Arthurs Godfrey and Linkletter (whom in my own days on the davenport I regally dubbed Arty the Fartys I and II) and greet them daily with a familiar "Hi, Arthur!," I began remonstrating with the men in the soap operas. If I had learned nothing else in Chicago, I had learned that one assumes impotence only at the risk of impotence; and, *sotto voce,* I spent a lot of time unctuously urging the men to take a stand and tell the witches to blow it out their asses. Indeed, so difficult was it to imagine an enormous penis rising up and bursting forth from behind that curtain of gray flannel, I began to wonder how those apple-cheeked children who contributed so many crow's-feet to the women's eyes were conceived unless by an incubus. Straining mightily, I often did imagine it. At that moment when the heroine's misery was most acute, when her eyes were shockingly luminous little beads of self-pity, when her mouth was distended to the very essence of pouting witchiness, I'd picture John Gentle rising suddenly up out of the perpetual lethargy of his saintlike patience and smacking her right on her nose. I saw him hovering over her, so suddenly and inexplicably leonine that her aspect was one of unadulterated incomprehension, then quickly horrified with the thought of what was taking place. By now I was directing the scene. With a maniacal glee on my face, I watched her retreat in somnambulant, terrified, and scarcely concealed ecstasy to her floral-patterned davenport, saw him violently topple her there, smiled as his tremulously voracious hands cupped her flabby thighs and began to spread them. My cruelty knew no bounds! I ordered my cameras dollied in slowly for a loving close-up, closer, closer, closer. On my face now there was something quite obscene as I envisioned my audience of homemakers beginning to flail their bosoms, pull their hair, and swoon in terror, a whole distaff segment of the American body politic rendered loony by a sexual confrontation and passing out over their ironing boards. The white panties were torn off, my cameras were on it now, closer, closer still, closer until the entire screen was one great, throbbing vulva opening slowly to expose a clitoris as big as a crab apple. By now I was giggling hideously. Was anyone, I wondered, still conscious? For them I had a *coup de grâce*. My pantless actor was standing just off camera. From the glassed-in director's booth I gave the sign, shoving my right arm furiously forward and catching it at the elbow with my left hand. "Bury it!" I shrieked hysterically. He obliged me with a vengeance. No fade-out was necessary, my audience having long since faded out. It was a memorable vision, the thought of them spread askew on their wine-colored carpets; lying across their kitchen tables, their faces sunk up to their ears in cottage-cheese salads; one caught in mid-sentence on the telephone, lying now on the floor, the receiver still in her hand, her mouth yet formed and frozen into the banal piece of witchery she was about to impart to a neighbor.

It was only infrequently that I was able to bring my imagination to such improbable heights. Most of the time I watched the shows in a state very near fainting myself. I shoveled one Oreo Sandwich after another into my mouth, holding onto my tired penis for dear life. During that two-hour daily orgy of soap operas I ate so many cookies that even Christie III, whose tummy had a more natural check on its abuses than mine, would after the first hour or so decline his share and sit watching my nervous eating with something very like incredulity on his sad face.

—

The books on the coffee table were those of Edmund Wilson. Coming inadvertently across an autobiographical sketch of his, I was at first astonished, then pleased, to learn that but a few miles south of me, at Talcottville, the legendary critic inhabited for part of the year a limestone farmhouse of his own, an heirloom from his mother's side of the family. This was a remote and flimsy parallel upon which to build a literary romance, but I had little to cling to in those days; and the knowledge that we were in a way neighbors sent me to all his books, which I read chronologically, beginning with *I Thought of Daisy*. At those few moments—and, as with the telephone conversations, most of the time I thought I wasn't absorbing a word he said—when I seemed to be conscious of his words, I imagined Wilson and I were having a literary duologue. But this was absurd. Owning neither the mental equipment nor the gnostical insights to take issue with him, I was a fuzzy-cheeked, impressionable, and adoring pupil sitting at the feet of a strong-minded and hirsute professor: Wilson spoke and, pursing my lips in a suggestion of wisdom, I nodded a vigorous assent. Oddly, though, in the next few years I discovered I had read him more sedulously and had understood him more precisely than I would have dared claim. Prior to this I hadn't read a great deal; from then on I would read rangingly but sporadically, and time after time, on arriving home and settling comfortably onto the davenport, I would discover that the volume seemingly so randomly plucked from the library shelf, say Chapman's *Emerson and Other Essays*, had been selected directly on the "boss's orders," and that I wouldn't be ten pages into it before I was murmuring, "I know all about this guy."

In the decade since then I have also manifested a singularly pilgrimatic habit. Whenever I depart this glacial haven for Utica, and thence for the rest of the world, I make it a point to take the "high road" out of Lowville, rising up through Turin where they ski and where there are brightly red-trimmed chalets and shiny ski lifts and where everything looks like a children's village enigmatically set out in the cow country, and down into Talcottville, where in passing I am able to get a hurried glimpse of his limestone retreat. The glimpse reassures me. In another, later piece Wilson had expressed his astonishment that he had endured where so many of his contemporaries from the twenties had failed to do so, gone to madness, to alcohol, to causes betrayed, and it gave me a very real warmth to know that a man could live with truth so long and survive. He was, he knew, an anachronism. He did not drive, he could not "abide" the radio, and leafing through the weekly picture magazines, he could not recognize their contents as reflecting a single aspect of the America he knew; so that, in his own word, he felt himself "stranded" from his country. Often, when driving by, I repressed an overpowering urge to slam on the brakes, to disembark, to proceed blithely to the door, to knock boldly, and, on his opening to my knock, to shout, "Eddie, baby! I too am stranded!" Because Wilson elsewhere had said that literary idolaters fell somewhere between blubbering ninnies and acutely frustrated maidens, I never did stop.

One bright day in early September when the grass was new-cut, I stopped at the filling station next door. While the attendant was feeding my car two dollars' worth of

Regular, I nonchalantly inquired whether that wasn't the house of *the* Edmund Wilson. It was indeed. Not only that, but the attendant, an obliging fellow, pointed out the very window behind which Wilson could often be seen praising or damning the literature of the generations. As I looked my heart did a neat and complete flip-flop: unless my imagination was playing tricks, the great man was at the very moment moving behind and away from the window. Wilson was right about literary idolaters. During the nine- or ten-mile drive to Boonville where one again picks up the main route south, like an unrequited lover I was in a state of grieving agitation. At Boonville I stopped at the lime-stone, white-trimmed Hulbert House, certainly one of the most beautiful hotels in America. There I drank three beers, simmered down, and proceeded south out of the cold country, thinking that next time through I would con-jure some marvelously ingenious excuse to approach his door and knock, at least tentatively.

Occasionally I did some "writing" of my own. Rising from the davenport, with Christie III hard on my heels, I ascended the stairs, sat at a round card table in my bed-room, and tried to construct paragraphs about anything save Bunny Sue, who had brought me to that farm to lie on that davenport, feeding cookies to a dog. I tried to write about the way rain falls on a city street, the way a pretty swimming girl moves through the water, the way darkness comes to towns along the Pacific littoral. Sometimes I lin-gered for an hour over a single sentence, marveling at the intricate and various combinations words could take. It was an act of luck and relentless stubbornness if I finished a single paragraph. My stamina was such that most of the time I'd complete no more than three or four sentences run together precisely the way I wanted them, and by then I would be literally too tired to sit up in a chair. Rising, at the same time throwing mental bouquets to those men who had mastered the art, I would take the half-dozen steps to the bed and lie next to Christie III who had lain at the end of the bed watching every move of the pencil. Once I was on the bed, Christie III relaxed and closed his eyes, and I indulged myself either in memories of my father or in what had become for me an alarmingly elaborate fantasy, about neither of which it then occurred to me to write.

The crowd's wedge between my father and me effected its most distressing cleavage when I was a freshman in high school, playing (or not playing) junior varsity basketball. Not a starter, my vanity wouldn't allow me to believe I shouldn't be on the first team. At thirteen I was already having my abilities unfavorably compared with those of my father. Not having the stomach for such witless collations, I had for a long time wanted to quit not only that team but sports entirely. The desire became uppermost, and a matter of grievous expediency, when one night prior to the varsity game the Jayvees were scheduled to play against an old-timers' team led by my father. I got sick. My father sat on the edge of the bed and gently rubbed my head; and though we both knew why I was sick, we avoided saying as much. Gently he asked me to get up, for him; to go through this one game, for him; telling me that if I did this one thing, for him, he'd permit me to quit the team after the game. The gymnasium was packed, and the better part of the evening I sat on the bench stupefied, drifting between nausea and fear of having to go into the game. In an effort to humor the crowd, the coach ordered me in to guard my father in the waning moments of the final quarter. Nearly thirty-nine then, sweating profusely and audibly huffing from years of Camel smoking, from the center of the court and to the jubilant hilarity of the crowd, my father sank three set shots, characterized for me by a deafening *swiiissshhhhh* of ball through net, in the less than two minutes I covered him.

After the game we walked home to Moffett Street across Hamilton Street, which was a lonely street then and settled with very few houses. The cold was fierce, the moon was bright, and the snow uttered melancholy oaths beneath our boots. In penance my father had his gloveless hand resting affectionately on my shoulder. "I'm sorry about tonight," he said. "I was lucky." But we both knew that he hadn't been; and all the way home I had had to repress an urge to weep, to sob uncontrollably, and to shout at him my humiliation and my loathing. "Oh, Jesus, Pop! *Why? Why? Why?*" I have always been sorry I didn't shout that humiliation. Had my father found the words to tell me why he so needed The Crowd, I might have saved my soul and now be a farm-implement salesman living sublimely content in Shaker Heights with my wife Marylou and six spewling brats. Neither of us knew that night that in little over a year my father would be dead from the cancer which was doubtless even then eating away at him. But at that moment, with his ungloved hand exposed to the fierce cold and resting familiarly on my shoulder in apology for the words he could not utter, I was wishing he were dead. Among unnumbered sins, from that damning wish I seek absolution.

The fantasy I nourished had only figuratively to do with gold mines in Eldorado or the seduction of dusky mulattoes in Port Said. While on the road I had worked for a time as a bartender in Colorado and had lent to a white-haired and dignified-looking stranger, with one tale of woe or another, twelve dollars to get home to Cheyenne. On my meager salary, it was a gesture which my boss deemed insane and wouldn't permit me to forget. Motivated by the guilt of his own stonyheartedness, and at every opportunity, he sneeringly referred to me in front of the customers as "Money Bags" and "The Poor Man's Friend, Freddy Exley." Without really believing it, I responded by saying, "Don't worry about it—he'll send it." But as I continued to try to justify myself against my boss's constant baiting, his irrational, near-lunatic wrath, I came after a time to believe that the man really would send it, adamantly and tiresomely repeating, "I know he will. *I know goddam well he will.*" Notwithstanding my self-induced brainwashing, the kindly-looking man never did send the money; I went back on the road, forgot all about him; and it was only on settling onto the davenport for my extended siege that I again began thinking of him, except that now, instead of twelve dollars, a battery of attorneys arrived one day at the farm and told me that the old boy had died up yonder there in Cheyenne. His heart had ceased to pump at the very moment his latest well had gushed forth its four hundred barrels per minute. In gratitude for a kindness once rendered him, he had named me his legatee to the tune of—well, first it was a million, then ten, and then, as the weeks progressed and my needs became more extravagant, a cool billion. Why not two?

The first thing I did was purchase the New York Giants, which cost me a bundle—fifteen million. The price was so unbridledly dear because the owners of the team, the Mara brothers, were doing what they most wanted to do in life; and as one of my more articulate counselors had pointed out, "Yuh can't buy a happy man." To that questionable premise I had taken a long, contemplative drag on my Benson & Hedges; had looked evenly, perhaps a trifle coldly, at the platoon of snug-shouldered legal lights seated anxiously about the mahogany conference table; and with something like ice cubes in my voice had said, "Well, let's put it this way, *counselors*"—I was utterly menacing by then—"you make those *happy Irishmen* an offer they *can't* turn down." A forbidding, awesome hush had descended upon the table. Legal eyeballs had clacked round in their sockets and had terrifyingly confronted one another. "You mean, chief," one bewildered attorney had finally ventured, "that the sky's the limit?" Taking another drag from my Benson & Hedges, I had taken my sweet time exhaling the smoke and had jauntily replied, "You got the point, *bright* boy." That is how I went through my first fifteen million.

Among the Thousand Islands, I then built for the team the most elaborate training camp imaginable. In the same way that Bunny Sue had been my dream of person, the lush green islands, the heart-stopping blue river, had always been my dream of place—the place to which, while "traveling" about America, I had compared all other places and found them wanting. Scattered in an intricately planned pattern about the islands were football fields, conditioning gymnasiums, and posh living quarters for the players and their families, a theater on this island, a golf course on that one. Smack and rather astonished-looking in the middle of one of the larger islands in my pigskin empire was a vast, gabled, candy-striped hotel, the Giant Inn, rooms by reservation well in advance only.

Occupying and making my headquarters in red-leather

booth Number 1 of a heavy-beamed, mahogany-lined bar, I was a kind of intellectually aloof Toots Shor and inaccessible to all but a chosen few: Ernest Hemingway, Marilyn Monroe, Edmund Wilson, Lee Remick, John Cheever, Sophia Loren, Vladimir Nabokov, Ingrid Bergman, Saul Bellow, Elizabeth Taylor, Robert Penn Warren, Mary McCarthy, Norman Mailer, and some select others. Behind a pair of shaded spectacles, dressed in herringbone, vested tweed suits, sipping sour mash on the rocks, browsing through the essays of Chesterton, everyone, even "my" players, pointed me out rather breathlessly. It was a homage to which I occasionally responded. Nodding to my press agents who hovered constantly about the bar that I was at the moment "available," I'd permit either player or guest (one had to give the latter something for his fifty dollars a day) to be escorted to my table for an introduction and on very rare occasions—occasions which they unquestionably cherished throughout their pedestrian lifetimes— I invited them to join me for a single drink, no more, and I had a devastating way of arching my brows into half-moons to herald the end of the conversation. Trying to determine how accessible my table should be to Gifford gave me the devil's own time. Finally deciding that it would be bad for team morale to favor him over the other players, I did concede him a rather cursory nod as he passed to and from the bar and had a grand time imagining him thinking, "I know that smug son of a bitch from someplace."

In the hot afternoons I took my private elevator from the bar to my penthouse suite at the top of the hotel. A wide, carpeted, cool suite done in pastels, its great picture windows opened to view the islands for miles around. Showering, and drawing the beige curtains so that the room was bathed in a burst-of-morning Venetian light, I lay down on the bed and buzzed downstairs to have one of my hand-picked, college-girl lifeguards sent up to me. Sighing contentedly, I lighted a cigarette and hummed. They came meekly, standing timidly in the middle of the carpeted floor, their golden arms hung laxly at their twitching sides. With trembling fingers I slid the straps of their black, Olympic-style swimsuits from their finely tanned shoulders, exposing them to the waist. "Gee, Mr. Exley," they invariably said at this point, "I never thought you'd get around to me." My lips caressed those shoulders then; just before slipping the suits the rest of the way off and lifting them onto the great sateen bed, I suavely paraphrased a little Eliot: "There is always time, my young one—time for you and time for me, and time yet for—"

On awakening I would kick Christie III in the ass, say, "Wake up, yuh good-for-nothin' bum!" We would descend the stairs, flick on the television to the Kiddie Kartoons, lie back down on the couch, and wait for Mom to call us to supper. It would not be to the two-inch-thick cuts of prime rib I favored at the Giant Inn but to ordinary meat loaf.

———

Except about Christie III, whom she thought I pestered too much, I don't once remember having a talk with my mother during those months. It was true that I pestered the dog. Such was my loneliness that after a time I ascribed human characteristics to the mutt. I talked to him constantly ("Let me tell you about the ambiguity of Henry James, Christie"). I taught him to sit up manlike, his spine leaning against the back of the davenport; and with my arm thrown buddy-like over his shoulder, we sat and "watched" the television together. I even made him a little blue sweat-shirt, a replica of my own, and with fastidious care dressed him in it. My mother said, "Oh, *don't!*"; but she laughed. "For Christ's sake, he loves it," I said. Then I picked him up and rolled him roughly around my chest while he feigned growling ferociously and snapped, toothlessly, at my nose. "He's my lover boy. It's all very homosexual! Right, Christie?" My mother laughed, but added, "You shouldn't talk like that." An innocent who had for so many years kept her mind unsullied by evil, she was weighed down by my silent refusal to offer an explanation of what had brought me to that davenport, but not nearly so much as by what that silence told her of the things I had discovered within myself. Looking abruptly up, I would find her studying me, alarmed, at times almost astonished; and then, detecting that I was aware of her, she would timidly turn away and go back to her dusting. Steinbeck never explicitly tells us what happened to Kino, who, having gone out in the world and discovered its evil, and the evil within himself, comes back to the estuary to live among the simple fishermen. But he tells us enough to suggest that Kino lived out his life a man apart from those innocents, a man who aroused in them shudders of distaste for something they understood only instinctively. Looking at my mother, I often sensed in her something like this shuddering repulsion. She was right in feeling this way. Out on the road I had discovered my own putrefaction, had discovered in my heart *murder*, utter, brutal, and conscienceless murder.

———

Fleeing first from Chicago to Los Angeles, I had established residence with a couple drunks I had known at USC, had showered, shaved, rinsed the long months of alcohol from my mouth, and had paid my last—or certainly my last sincere—obeisance to the American Business Community. Thinking that I might outlast what had become for me a dim and cheerless world—I envisioned myself escorting boodles of cinema starlets around the world on promotional tours—surrounded and buffered from that grayness by the beautiful, the talented, and the generous, I wrote letters to the Messrs. Warner, Wald, Disney, and Zanuck, and to MGM, RKO, CBS, NBC, *et al.*, inviting them to consider me for publicity work. For my trouble I was given the courtesy of one odd and unsettling reply.

Answering the telephone in the apartment one forlorn evening, I found at the other end of the wire the Vice President for Public Relations of one of the real behemoths of the entertainment industry. He was, I think, slightly drunk. He told me that some days before he had received my letter, that its "sincerity"—my heart leaped in wild anticipation—had impressed him, and that he had had me on his mind now for some days. What ensued was an hour's conversation in which he did all the talking, I the listening, and in which there was not, as I hoped there would be, a job offer. Not only did he not offer me a job, but he insisted adamantly, peevishly, even desperately, that I stay away from "his" industry. The people one dealt with, he said, were neither beautiful nor talented but rotten, corrupt, self-centered, vicious, and double-dealing. And though I know that I had never for a moment doubted this, the conversation was, notwithstanding, a most unnerving one. The man's voice was dishearteningly weary, as if reflecting the long years of his humiliations and degradations, his paying homage to, and groveling before, these people. Above this and more singular still, there was a false articulateness to what he told me, as if, though drunk, he were giving a memorized speech. It was too orotund and rhetorical; and after listening to him for a while, I began wondering if he didn't make this call often. By the time he hung up I was almost certain that he did; and I conjured this weird picture of him living out his days in that phony, that insubstantial world and, come five o'clock, stuffing letters from "sincere" young men into his pocket and running home to telephone them with his tiredly savage and paternal advice. Though I chuckled with tentative appreciation, I feared for the man. It seemed to me that he was not only under heavy mental duress but that he might one day find one of those young men more ambitious than "sincere," and that it was only a matter of time until his employers were informed of the opinions of the public relations chief. Having nothing better to do, I spent a morning writing him a note in which I thanked him for his kindness and in which, with some nice subtleties, I worked in my apprehensions concerning him. I never sent it. Subtlety is wasted on a drowning man, and I had no way of knowing whether or not I was an isolated case who had caught him at a bad moment. No doubt he is still busily engaged in convincing people of the beauty, the nobility, and the innate rectitude of the Hollywood product. Or he is cringing in a corner and weeping scalding tears in a madhouse.

Whichever he's doing, I took his advice, forgot about pulpous starlets, and a few weeks later I found myself a publicist for the missile systems divison of a large aircraft corporation. Only a few years older than myself, the boss was an obese, doughy, chain-smoking, harassed-acting man who had appeared to staff his department with surly misfits made in his own image and who weren't likely to pine after his job. The striking blond ponytail with the fine behind and thick, lazy legs who had, on slippered feet, led me through a number of barricaded doors for my interview, and who acted as the department's receptionist, was the only eye-pleasing thing in our beaver-boarded, barracks-like offices; and it developed that she *was* a thing. Detecting that she seemed almost upset one day, I solicitously asked what the problem was. "My mother is a whore," she said with calm finality, and that is the only thing she said in the two weeks I was with the company. A top scientist delivered a classified speech to a classified society and then, attempting to blow his own horn, demanded that I make an unclassified news release out of it. He sent my efforts back with the comment, "This is terrible!!!" When I tried to see him to get a more complete idea of what precious machinations were involved in making classified material available to the public, his secretary, a black ponytail with stunning azure eyes, informed me that her boss was a "genius" and never offered explanations other than "This is terrible" or "This is okie-dokie." "I see," I said, and retreated pensively to the publicity department.

Seated engagingly at the desk next to mine, behind pictures of his four-eyed wife and three adorable children, was Harold. Pathetically, Harold imagined himself a bright, ambitious, clean-cut, and rising young executive. Harold sweated and picked his nose. He was neither ambitious nor bright. On the one hand, he was the worst kind of sycophant, a whimpering, womanish, two-faced Stinky Pete whose toadying to the boss bordered on the obscene; on the other hand, he was a man of, at first perplexing, then benumbing, and finally, a horrifyingly vast stupidity—a cretinism that became colossally evident one day when he asked me to read, and comment upon, a script he had prepared for a "pep rally" for the company's sales force, a little get-together to spur those shiny-toothed men into selling bigger and better missiles. Written in the format of a television show, the script, or what I read of it, was predictably inane, innocuous, and infantile. Reading to the point where, to the tune of a Pepsodent commercial, he had inserted a nifty little jingle about missiles—a jingle whose contents escape me but whose substance was not unlike: "That's the way the missile goes/Pop goes the world!"—I had found the words blurring on me, I had lost all intelligibility and had sat pretending to read, from time to time looking up at the creator of this masterpiece, who, while I "read," had hung anxiously by his buttocks from the edge of his chair in gleeful anticipation of my approval, an approval I gave him, chuckling madly and nodding little accolades of approbation in his direction.

"Chuckling madly" is a precise description. Even as I nodded at him it occurred to me that, without feeling any remorse whatever, I could kill him, destroy him, remove him from the race of men. For years I had been aware of the theory, expounded by Orwell and others, that the world was in all probability mad, but I had consoled myself with the notion that such men were dyspeptic malcontents, and it was shocking to discover in that simple-minded jingle and childishly self-congratulatory face that their case against the world was such that the world would be best advised to plead *nolo contendere*. Something happened to me then, something snapped. For days afterward I sat staring at Harold and imagined killing him. The world's insanity, and therefore its tragic evil, seemed to reach a kind of culmination in his sweaty, clean-shaven, and infantile face. I saw myself waiting in ambush for him, and then bashing in his head with a sledge hammer. Here I ran over him—he turned at the last moment and I saw that mindless face show horror—with a tractor trailer. Here—well, I saw myself destroy him in a thousand ways, each more ingenious and cruel than the last, and any of which I should have got away with, my motives being outside those understood by The Law. The circumstance that finally shattered my concentration on him was that the script was used, none who heard it took exception (indeed, all found it amusing), and thus I found myself in need of a machine gun. Doing the obvious thing, I quit, packed a bag, and went back on the road.

I went to Phoenix, where for a time I lived off the largess of a friend I had made in Chicago; to Colorado, where I lent my future benefactor twelve dollars to get home to Cheyenne; back to New York, where I jauntily bummed money from guys from out of the past; southward to Baltimore, where I had two bartender jobs, from both of which I was fired for drinking; and finally to that sunny cesspool Miami, where I worked for two hours as a dishwasher but was too weak from not eating to get the big pans clean, and where I was confronted by that tart-tongued judge and given the choice of coming up with some money or going to the county farm. As I had done so many times over the past months, it was then I telephoned home for help; my mother, correctly surmising that I'd never board the airplane if she sent cash, paid for my plane ticket in Watertown. Not that I minded, but it left me no choice except to go north. On arriving at the farm then, I had little to say to my mother, though I'm certain my silences told her many things she'd rather not have heard. Still, she did not insist on words being uttered; and in a way this insulating herself from life's unpleasanter hues proved kind to me; she let me be, dressing Christie III in sweatshirts, and what I needed for my journey was time.

—

My stepfather proved another matter. Ironically, it was not he who provoked me but I who chose to make his days uncomfortable. It was on my part an unwise, intolerant, and thoroughly wrongheaded decision, and one that unquestionably hastened my journey to the madhouse. After Harold's script had been used and found jolly by the company's executives, the world's lunacy had dispersed itself, like the rays of a full moon, flooding every nook and cranny; and for many months I had lived my life without any proper object against which to spiel my fury. Like a man whose enemies, being omnipresent and inexhaustible at the same time, insidiously and outrageously present him with no defined face to bash, rendering him numb and impotent, I was a paranoiac in a state close to crisis. Though I did not then understand this in any utterable way, in an instinctive and very real way I knew that to survive I needed a target, and needed one badly. I chose my stepfather, though I did not strike in any open or head-on fashion. Oh, no! I was much too clever and self-protective for that.

The nature of my stepfather's business was such that all his life he had done extremely heavy physical work. As a result he had great hands and a thick, massive upper body, a torso that suggested not only strength but the power to destroy. One day—for God only knows what reasons—I began to see that physical presence as the very abstraction of Babbittry, it seemed to me so astonishing that this great power should have been created in the pursuit of money. Other than the obvious Freudian aspects—a mother, a stepfather, a mother's grown son under the same roof—I can see now that my baiting him was motivated by nothing other than the guilt I felt at accepting his bed and board.

Were he any day going to throw me out onto the street and tell me to go to work, I would have the satisfaction, before he did so, of having confronted him for a long time with a face of unwavering and unmitigated scorn. It never for a moment occurred to me—as it never does to people for whom the world has soured, creating in them the perverse capacity to measure everything and everybody in their own rancid image—that my stepfather had no intention of kicking me out. He was a man of dignity, kindness, and constancy; and, simply stated, he believed in his marriage vows and was accepting me as the "worse" opposed to the "better" the minister had spoken of.

His composure in the face of my onslaught was admirable, in its way, inexpressible. For weeks I saw him only at supper; and if I said anything to him at all, I said it with selfish and bitchy aloofness: "How's business?"—pronouncing *business* as though I were saying *turd*. Without giving him a chance to answer, I would issue an absurd little chuckle in response to my own question, as though to say, "But, my dear fellow, you can't really believe that I have the slightest interest in your idiotic business." He bore all this stoically, smiling good-naturedly; and when I detected that I was unable to arouse him, I stopped talking altogether. Our meals became endless, eye-averting repasts of an almost furious silence, punctuated by the obscene clanks of silver against china, the hideous noise of our masticating and swallowing, and my mother's obvious and touching attempts to inject conversation. "My, it's Saturday already—the week's just flown by." No response, either in word or gesture. So distressing did these meals become that I eventually stopped eating with them altogether, fleeing to the upper regions of the house whenever I heard my stepfather's car pull into the drive.

It was at this time that I inserted a truly masterful stroke into my contest with him: I feigned an actual physical fear of him. Prior to entering a room, I would stick my unshaven face around corners, "peeking," and if he were present, I would snap my head fearsomely back, as though his presence represented an unfathomable danger. On one or two occasions I heard him ask my mother, "What the hell was that all about?" And I chuckled gleefully. But there was never any victory in my laughter. When he asked, his voice reflected amused perplexity more than anger. There were times when avoiding a confrontation with him proved impossible; we would meet in the dim-lighted hallway or coming to and from the can. At these times I would fix on my face a look of utter incredulity, as though to say, "Oh, you live here, too?" or, "My, my, this house is just full of odd little surprises." It is no easy admission, but I know precisely what I wanted him to do. I wanted to provoke him into some unpleasantry, infuriate him into striking me or kicking me in the ass. I yearned to run into Mummy's arms and shriek, "You see, Mummy, the brute you're married to?" I desired to have Mummy defend me against him and thereby receive verbal assurance that I was welcome at the farm. But I underestimated my man. For that is what he was, a man, and as such would not be drawn into any such asinine and infantile games as these. What was worse—oh, the sad, incredible insidiousness of sickness—was that I was never unwelcome at the farm.

During the final weeks of autumn it was only during the football games that I permitted myself the company—if company it can be called—of either my mother or stepfather, having by then taken to spending all my waking hours (and daily these had become fewer and fewer) lying in my room, with Christie III at my feet, spinning my fantasy of owning the Giants. In direct proportion to the extent of my isolation, the fantasy grew increasingly elaborate and by now had me administering something called the New York Giant Foundation, curing cancer, a patron to indigent writers and painters (my dreams weren't entirely selfish), my table now occupied by the world's great and near-great, the De Gaulles and Jonas Salks.

On one of these Sunday afternoons my stepfather took his only overt action against me. In deference to my mother, whose eyes over the weeks had gone from astonished alarm to the myopic squint of pain, I would on these Sundays take what had become for me a weekly shower and shave and sit with them through a silent meal of pot roast. Rising from the table and entering the living room well before game time, I would snap on the television and begin pacing up and down my mother's lovely hooked rug. My stepfather, Sunday cigar in mouth, joined me first, taking his easy chair. On finishing the dishes, my mother, followed by Christie III—the latter having gorged himself on the scraps—walked into the room and took her place on the davenport. Christie III sat next to her. Everyone nodded demurely at each other. Everyone was ready for the show that began with the kickoff. While my stepfather smiled and my mother laughed, and poor Christie III, his sad saucer-like brown eyes fearfully following every move I made, licking his chops apprehensively, his neck sunk in his shoulders, huddled in the protective warmth of my mother as if about to get the thrashing of his life, I ran about the room with the desperate, stored-up energy of the endless week—hurling either bloody oaths or heartfelt benedictions at Quarterback Conerly, cursed him or praised him according to the character of his game. On third and long-yardage plays, I dropped to my knees, made the

Catholic sign at forehead and chest, and, depending on the team's success or lack of it, rose and cast holy water on the tube or fell to the floor, pulled my hair, swooned, and hurled unadulterated blasphemies at the gods. Whenever the Giants appeared particularly inept, and I found myself rolling speechless with rage about the heavy wool rug, I would jump suddenly up, dash to the telephone, feign picking up the receiver, and screech, "Get me Yankee Stadium!" The hysteria in my voice suggested no less than that I was about to discharge the entire organization en masse.

During these Sunday afternoons my mother said little save cautioning me to watch my heart; but one afternoon my stepfather, having become aware over the weeks of my inordinate partiality to Gifford, took what I considered his initial gesture against me, what I deemed to be little short of an assault upon my person. In retrospect, I know he said it only in fairness, perhaps only in the hope of engaging me in a conversation, which in all those weeks we had never had. "You know, Fred," he said, "there are other players in the league as good as Gifford." I froze in mid-step and turned to him with menacing slowness. I slammed my hands onto my hips. With a look of utter incredulity on my face, I snarlingly demanded that he repeat his filthy assertion. "I said," he said, smiling weakly, already sensing that his efforts to be engaging were somehow going awry, "that there are other players in the league as good as——" Refusing to permit him to finish, I turned savagely to my mother and fixed on my face a look of crushing hurt, a look with which I meant to say, "You see, Mummy? He's struck! The beast in him has finally revealed itself!" Turning back to him, my voice tremulous with rage, I shouted, "As good as Gifford? As good as Gifford?" Emitting a mocking, scornful laugh, just before fleeing the room, I added, "You, sir, are crazy!"

It was an hour or better before, lying on my bed, I felt my heart quiet to a temperate beat. When it did, I found that replaying the mad scene in my mind's eye I could laugh—which was a beginning. After a long time Christie III mustered the courage to come upstairs and join me. For many moments he sat on the end of the bed, his droopy ears still back in trepidation. When finally I spoke gently to him, he walked cautiously and wide-legged across the softness of the mattress (the way Dana describes "salts" boarding a schooner), bent his head down, and began lapping tentatively at my hot face. Sensing his prudence, I wilted, felt again my terrible rage, and began a laughter close to tears. For some days now I had been hearing the muted whispers below me, and through them the words *sick* and *psychiatrist* and *hospital,* and had been meaning to make a journey into my past in search of my nemesis, who was Bunny Sue, or who I foolishly thought was Bunny Sue. I wanted to make the journey because I was terribly ashamed by what seemed the explicitness of it all. Over and over again I heard myself saying to a psychiatrist, "Look, it's very simple: I was rejected by a girl, Miss America," to which, with a suave smile, he invariably replied, "You look: we've all been rejected by a girl. So what else is new?" As nothing is ever this simple, I should not have feared the journey. Feeling Christie III warm up to the job of lapping my face, I did let my laughter run to tears, thinking that I had instilled fear in the helpless mutt. Picking him gently up, I rolled him round and round on my chest in our game, letting him growl and snap toothlessly at my now wet face. When he was quiet, and asleep in my arms, I went back into the past.

I went back to Chicago and replayed the memory of it;

it was that day I first sensed that I had never loved Bunny Sue—I could not even put her features together—and that my inability to couple had not been with her but with some aspect of America with which I could not have lived successfully. Replaying everything I could remember about Chicago, I understood that had I mingled with that womb I never would have had the strength to walk away. Concluding with the mental rereading of her childish letters, I laughed heartily at the thought of my being saved by the *dash*—and the *exclamation point!* I liked that joke very much. It was the one with which I hoped to break the ice with the psychiatrists. I didn't know then that one doesn't approach these doctors with levity; or that, on discovering this, I would end by telling them hardly anything about myself. But, having discovered the joke, I was now ready to face them; to go to Loony Lodge or wherever it was my mother wanted me to go; ready to do anything to alleviate the awful tensions I had created at that once-quiet farm.

———

During my final weeks at the farm I did an odd thing, scarcely knowing at the time why. Though I now presume I created this room that I might one day come back and put down these words, I was unquestionably distraught at being deemed insane and was avoiding, as long as possible, being locked up. For that is what I did: I created a room. An upstairs room in an early addition to the south side of the house, its ceiling, save for a five-foot strip running down the middle of the room, slopes down at the hazardous angle of the roof; and from where I am now sitting (for I did come back) I can reach up and touch the rouge wallpaper which I myself put on. The room is twenty by twenty. When, not long before I left for the hospital, I began remaking it, it was used for storage. Piled high with trunks, broken baby carriages, and cardboard boxes containing the sad, accumulated refuse of my mother's life, the place was ugly and melancholy, being sprinkled daily with a plaster which made its way through split layers of wallpaper and, falling to the floor in great chunks, detonated, laying a heavy gray fallout over all. Rolling up my sleeves and taking a deep breath, I one day began, to the dismay of my mother (for there was no other place in the house for the refuse), moving the junk out and tearing the wallpaper and plaster from the walls and ceiling. When I had the room stripped bare, my stepfather had little choice but to buy me the plaster, wallpaper, and paint to put it back together again. I expect he didn't mind. After I had spent so many months on the davenport, it must have been a welcome sight to see me doing anything at all; indeed, such was the fury with which I worked—and like most men who don't know why they work at what they do, I worked with a fury that prevented my asking why—that after a time, as if caught up in the vortex of my lunacy, both my mother and stepfather started working with me, helping me. Though I felt them intruders, I daren't say so. When we had finished, I thought it the most beautiful room I had ever seen.

Beneath the grayness of time, the floor turned out to be the original. Made up of wide (one of them measures two feet across), liberally knotted pine boards, the floor was stunning after I had sanded it and applied a clear Tungseal finish. Behind where I am now sitting, at the south end of the room and twisting up between its only two windows (deeply recessed, curtained now, and from which one almost always gets a cooling breeze from the direction of Lake Ontario), runs the upper part of the living room fireplace, its great, ponderous limestones exposed where for hour on endless hour I scraped away buckets of plaster, coughing, gagging, and nearly throwing up as I did so. I furnished the room with a dresser, a single bed, a dry sink, and a schoolmaster's desk, all of an old pine that finished beautifully. My proudest possession was a great, low pine table which I fitted with an old horse-carriage seat and which I intended to use as desk and chair. At a later Christmas when I hadn't any money, I gave the schoolmaster's desk to my infant sons to be used, opening as it does like a trunk, for their toys; and by the time they will be old enough to appreciate the work that went into it, in their innocence they will have wrecked it and it will have long since been consigned to the junk yard. Deciding (and I can hardly blame her) that I was a "traveling man" unmindful of and embarrassed by the permanent character of furniture, my sister took the pine table and carriage seat for her own house; and when I finally came to put down these words, I had to fashion a new desk from an old pine kitchen table. My mother added a rust-colored plaid rug, a ponderous, old-fashioned gray couch, and a television set. Then I added the finishing touches.

In front of me now, flush against my writing table, is a great oak beam unknown to houses being built today, on which sit the forty or so volumes now constituting my library, everything from McKelway's *True Tales from the Annals of Crime and Rascality* to Nietzsche's *The Birth of Tragedy*. Scotch-taped to the wall above the books are two pieces of paper bearing legends. The upper one, the smaller, is a rejection slip from the editors of *The New Yorker* for some brief pieces I sent to their "Talk of the Town" department. Until I recently returned here, I had completely forgotten writing them. The letter is not unkind. It says that, though they cannot use the material, they are no less grateful on that account and hope I continue to think of them in the future (I did—with no better luck). The other piece of paper seems more remote to me; and if I could understand it, I think I could understand the man I was then a good deal better than I do now. Typewritten in capital letters on a piece of eight-by-eleven bond paper (yellowing now and heaving and bubbling under the Scotch tape), it reads: "DO NOT TAKE COUNSEL OF YOUR FEARS." It is not an original saying with me; it is a motto I picked up someplace and that must somehow have seemed to give me comfort for the months of hospitalization that were ahead. At the time, too, I'm sure I had some vague dream of doing something absolutely Wilsonian. Instead of reading systematically through the literature of socialism, as he must have done to make his *To the Finland Station,* I expect I was going to read through the literature of football and write my *To the Yankee Stadium* (though I would have had an extra foot unless I pronounced the latter *stad-yum*). If that, or something equally absurd, were my motive, I never did anything about it. On finishing the room in early spring, I returned to the davenport; and my days at the farm were numbered then.

In those final days I withdrew from my stepfather my arch and unwarranted hostility and began talking with him whenever I could, both during supper and in the living room when the commercials were blaring away. He was a strong man in every way, and a good man, and that strength had not been acquired in pursuit of the dollar but for the reasons most decent men grow strong: by meeting the needs of those people close to them. He had raised one large family of his own, gone now their various ways in the world. He had then married my mother, taking on the responsibility for her family. In his love he had given her this lovely stone farmhouse, a home she might never have otherwise had. It was a home to which her own children, whether hard-used by the world or coming back to display the laurels received from it (and we were not all losers), might return and, if only momentarily, remember that they had been children together when neither success nor failure mattered nearly so much as popcorn and fudge on a Sunday evening.

Over the next few years, as I was in and out of the hospital and was (in secondhand suits from the Salvation Army and the Catholic Charities) making tentative and awkward attempts to use teaching as an entrance back into the world, my stepfather and I spent much time together, and things were never better between us than on autumn Sunday afternoons. Though he always had had a great affection for sports, he had been a neutral observer interested more in the game than in loyalty to a single team. But after a time, hardly noticeable at first, he caught something of my enthusiasm for the beauty and permanent character of staying with someone through victory and defeat and came round to the Giants. When after many years and many autumn Sundays, he died, he did so at that high and exhilarating moment just prior to the kickoff. Seated on the edge of the davenport watching the starting line-ups being introduced, he closed his eyes, slid silently to the floor, and died painlessly of a coronary occlusion.

One day I packed a small bag, and the three of us, along with Christie III, piled into the car and began the journey to the hospital—a journey I thought would take three weeks, at the most three months, and which ended by taking three years. It took so long because there were so many things I didn't then know, didn't even know what Shakespeare knew three hundred years ago: that one cannot "minister to the mind diseased," that "therein the patient cures himself." No, I had no idea that I would have to experience and later articulate a rage against the insensitive quacks; that I would then have to go to Avalon Valley; that I would have to listen for the devil within the Negro; that I would have to feel the strength of Dr. K.; that I would have to hear the sobbing of others to make my own self-pity seem trivial and contemptible in the extreme; that I would have to see Paddy the Duke minister to himself; that I would have to make my peace with this new and different man; and that, walking round and round The New Parrot Restaurant, I would finally have to say, "I want to live." No, that day in the car I was buoyed up with that typically sham American optimism and had blissful dreams of miraculous cures and overnight remedies, believed that in a matter of days I'd be calling home and proclaiming, "Maw! I'm okay, Maw! Bake an apple pie!"

At the swank hospital I kissed my old buddy, Christie III, who made a terrible commotion. I kissed my mother, who looked tired and pained and who wept quietly. Then I shook hands with my stepfather. His strong hand was limp and uncertain, as though he didn't know how we stood, and he turned quickly away from me and descended the concrete steps. I wanted to call to him then, to tell him I was sorry for so many things. I wanted to do this, for I had suddenly seen that the pain I had caused my mother had become his pain, and that that pain bound us together as much as ever filial affection does, that, in a way, he was my father now. But I hadn't the strength to call after him. Instead, I turned and went quickly into the insane asylum.

6

Who? Who? Who
Is Mr. Blue?

In the autumn of 1958, during the final weeks of my initial stay at Avalon Valley, the ones in which I had lived in such an apprehension of the future, and in which I had, save at the AA meetings, lost interest in Paddy the Duke, I had had, one Sunday, a visitor. Thinking it to be a member of my family, I had hung on my face a look of monumental aggrievance and had charged out the door prepared to attack—if only because they were *outside* and I *in*. It was standard operating procedure with patients, and expected, a protest that one was as sane as the Pope and that one's incarceration was all a dreadful joke. In the parking lot I saw only an attractive girl with roan-colored hair, dressed in a camel's-hair coat, leaning against a steel-gray Mercedes 190 SL convertible. If in the dismal world of Avalon Valley she did not look obscenely ostentatious, she looked singular indeed. Scanning the parking lot while mouthing my pleasant salutation—"When the hell yuh gonna get me outa here?"—it suddenly occurred to me, with an alarming and jolting tightening of the body, that *the girl* was my visitor, that I not only knew her but that I had once, in my half-assed and cursory manner, paid her a kind of court. Taking a deep breath, I turned, smiled embarrassedly, and said, "Hello." My voice was somewhat hysterical, still containing that element of histrionic indignation with which I had planned to greet my relatives.

"I hope you don't mind my coming," she said.

It was not an easy meeting. Leaning on the Mercedes next to her, so that she could not, without continually and obviously turning her head, study my ill-kempt appearance, I smoked her Parliaments and answered the questions she forced herself to ask with such rudeness that I was surprised she didn't leave before she did. "How is the food here?" "Swell." We smoked two, three, four of her Parliaments apiece while I mumbled my answers and framed in my mind a perfectly hysterical epistle to my family, demanding to know what right they had telling anyone I was in the loony bin. By the time I had the letter completed, mentally scrawling a violent signature (very formal: *Frederick Earl Exley*) across the entire bottom of the page—oh, my sense of outrage knew no bounds!—she was in the car, the motor was running, it occurred to me she was leaving, and, panicking, I stammered, "Look, come back some time, will yuh? I'm, I'm—it's one of those days, yuh know?" She looked at me quizzically for a moment, as if she perhaps didn't know; then, speaking in a voice that told me nothing, she said, "Maybe—if I can." Watching the Mercedes till it was out of sight, I walked slowly back to the ward and with Snow White watched Ed Sullivan. Snow White had a running dialogue with Ed and all his performers. Ed said, "Good evening, ladies and gentlemen"; Snow White replied, "Fuck you, Ed."

One Sunday went by, then another, and on the third

Sunday she came. She brought me a carton of cigarettes. I thanked her so profusely that she came the following Sunday, and by then I had of course come utterly to rely on her visits—a dependence which, despite my attempts to act detached, she soon came to recognize. More than that, she was aware that in the act of visiting me initially she had instituted that dependence, and because she was a person of character—and I suspect that it was as much for this reason as out of any affection she felt for me—she continued to honor that obligation. She continued, and that fall became for me the one I will remember above all—the autumn I discovered the Hudson Valley.

I drove. With the top down on the Mercedes and the chillness of the season cutting our faces a fierce pink, we shot through the autumn-lemon hills of Putnam County, and across the snakelike mountain roads into that valley. Beyond the river, its waters flat blue and cold now, rose the mountains, rose just as Irving had said they did, now purple, now russet, now shrouded in mist. I especially liked the antiquated towns where the old limestone houses sat flush with the streets beneath the fall trees. Looking at them, one thought of cavernous hearths opening onto great, smoldering logs, of huge copper kettles, of the odor of things baking, of family reunions, of rooted people with a sense of the past, warm, loyal, dignified people who endured in a kind of unending autumn—I could not, and cannot, imagine that valley save in autumn. We—the girl with the roan-colored hair and I—stood at outdoor stands inhaling the pungent odor of burning foliage, feasting on hot dogs piled high with sauerkraut, and watching the cars, whizzing by, tear up the leaves and send them scurrying, like little furry animals in flight, across the bonelike highway.

By two o'clock, and as likely as not before then (such was

my anxiety), we were in one of those country taverns with spotless checkered tablecloths and no customers, as if the owners—an amiable, starchy, and aging Dutch couple—had been granted their existence to serve patrons that very day, that very hour, and then would be no more. We drank coffee, sometimes draft beer, and nibbled on potato chips and old cheese, making small talk about the wonder of our complexions. The moment the game started she fell silent, studying me, I'm certain, with that bemused curiosity with which a woman views a man's enthusiasms, knowing, as she instinctively does, that for the most part a man's preoccupations are trivial, even contemptible things.

"No, no—not now!" I would exclaim, raising my hand with forbidding finality if I even suspected her on the verge of introducing some topic foreign to what was taking place on the television screen. I never looked at her when I did this, to gauge her response. I didn't have to. I knew that she would be smiling, not exactly as if I were mad, simply as though I were a man.

"Oh, Jesus, Frank! Do it, kid! Catch it, baby!" Now would come a breathless silence, followed by an incredulous, "He did it! He caught the goddam thing!" I would turn to her then. "Cha see that? Cha see that, for Christ's sake?"

Though she would smile and say that she had, I knew that she hadn't, finding my show—as she would that of an exhilarated child's—much more interesting.

More often than not we had to speed back to the hospital to get me there on time; even when the Giants played at home, and the television blackout surrounding New York City was in effect, in order to see the game we would drive way north, at times nearly to Albany. It was on one of these trips back, when I was punishing the Mercedes, that she asked me a question which led to my making a strange reply. Only a woman would have been capable of asking it. Another man would have simply thought him my favorite athlete.

"What is this thing with you and Gifford—or whatever his name is?" she asked.

The question took me unawares, and I did not answer her for a long time. I had never before tried to articulate what the thing was, and I was fairly sure that whatever I said would come out badly and be taken all wrong. But I thought I would say something. The heavy hum of the wheels was beneath us, the darkness of the cab enshrouded us, the atmosphere seemed conducive to talk. I told her about my first year in New York, how I had had this awful dream of fame, but that, unlike Gifford—who had possessed the legs and the hands and the agility, the tools of his art—I had come to New York with none of the tools of mine, writing. I told her how I had tried to content myself with reverie, envisioning myself emblazoned across the back of dust jackets. I told her how I had gone each lonely Sunday to the Polo Grounds where Gifford, when I heard the city cheer him, came after a time to represent to me the possible, had sustained for me the illusion that I could escape the bleak anonymity of life. At the time of my "confession" Gifford was reaping the benefits of the Jim Thorpe Trophy, and, I told her, as a kind of ironic comment on the extent of my own failure, it seemed that every time I picked up a magazine in the hospital I was confronted with his picture. There was, I said, a particularly distressing advertisement that continued to appear in the pages of *The New Yorker* and *Sports Illustrated*. A tartan cap tilted rakishly to one side of his head, a football tucked under his arm, a how-the-hell-did-I-get-here? expression on his face (exactly the kind of thing I might once have imagined for myself), he was showing the reader how splendidly handsome and virile he might look were he to wear a V-necked Jantzen pullover. That sweater, I said, seemed to make my state-issue cotton plaid shirt burn hot on my flesh, the hot humiliation of having hoped for too much.

She was silent for a very long time when I had finished. Then she said something which elicited a singular reply from me, a reply that kept us both in silence for the rest of the trip. Whether she ever grasped my meaning, I can't say. I know I never completely did, though I suppose that in the act of revealing so much of myself to her I had begun to have this thing for her.

"I should think you'd despise him," she said. "Oh, maybe not despise him. Envy him to the point of disliking him immensely."

"Despise him?" I said. I'm certain my voice reflected my great incredulity. "But you don't understand at all. Not at all! He may be the only fame I'll ever have!"

———

Within not too many days of this revelation, within a few days of Paddy the Duke's departure, I, too, left the hospital. Had I gone directly to the girl, I think I might have made it on the outside and thereby thwarted Paddy's smug prophecy that I would one day return to Avalon Valley. Shaking hands first with Dr. K., I had the boys crowd round and say the things they say: "Don't let the shits get yuh down!" and "Don't let us see yuh back here, *yuh heah?*" I had laughed, and to the latter had proclaimed, much too vehemently, "Don't worry about that!" and had sensed in the shrill falseness of that protest with what trepidation I was actually going out.

I had a right to my misgivings. Within three hours of leaving the hospital I was standing on the upper level of the Grand Central Terminal, debating whether in fact it might not be the wiser alternative to return to Avalon Valley. For a fleeting moment I thought then of going to her, but I immediately discarded the notion, thinking that at some later, happier moment I might go to her in an aura of more presentable splendor. Presently I also rejected the idea of returning to the nuthouse and found myself on the train moving to the upstate city where the Counselor was then practicing law. All the way there my mouth tasted of old leather, iodine, and blood, the way my mouth tastes when I have made some wrong and seemingly irremediable choice.

———

A thickset, balding, timid little man I had met at the AA meetings had asked me to telephone long distance to his sister in Rochester and ask her if she wouldn't be willing to take him into her house until he was working and could set up for himself. He told me, his voice grave as doom, that his sister was his last chance, that though he had two brothers both had refused to take him. There was no rancor toward the brothers. Each of them, he said, had over the years sponsored untold "new lives" for him and in a way he felt rather relieved that they had finally spurned him, he was so afraid of disappointing them once again. For the first time he overcame his timidity and, popeyed, he looked directly at me.

"Give she and the kids my love," he said, "and impress on her, uh—you know—the urgency—"

"I know," I said.

Then he forced two wadded, filthy, and oily dollar bills into my hand and began anticipating for me all sorts of objections his sister, and especially his brother-in-law, might have to taking him in. I did not want to take the money. But I did. I thought it would give him, at least momentarily, some surcease from the hopelessness of his situation, thinking, as he would, that having been given the money I couldn't "forget" to make the call. Requiring such glib verbosity, such pleading cries to often all-but-deaf ears, I didn't in the least want to make it. But I had no choice whatever. Having once been in Avalon Valley, one never leaves the place and finds oneself, consciously or otherwise, forever obligated to those wretched men weeping their fierce tears in the night. I took the train to New York, fingering the oily bills in my pocket all the way. Getting two dollars' worth of quarters, I put the call through from Grand Central.

It was at the far end of the rush hour, about seven in the evening, but the closed booth was compact and soundless and I heard the ringing as clearly as though I were calling next door. The sister answered. She had a good, pleasant, and either sultry or timid voice; and I conjured an image of an attractive, perhaps sensual woman quite at home in a starched apron in a cheerful kitchen. In the background I heard a dog bark, a little girl shriek ("Dumbhead's after the cat!"), the canned laughter of the inevitable television set, and once—distinctly and from some remote corner of the house—the cascading rush and gurgle of a toilet flushing. Coming down on the train, I had planned my pitch pretty well. Rather than risk her thinking me just another loony, I explained to her that my name was Earl Fredericks, that I was an attorney at law, that I had recently been visiting a client at Avalon Valley, and that there I had met her brother who had asked me to telephone her. Couching my language in what I deemed impressive-sounding legal jargon (gleaned from Avalon Valley's "clubhouse lawyers"), I explained to her the problems connected with her brother's ever getting out without her assistance, throwing in a lot of lunatic phrases like "the state takes the position that" and "the courts hold that your responsibility is negligible," summing up by explaining that *all that was really necessary* was that she affix her signature to the most innocent of papers and feed her brother and give him carfare to look for work.

As I talked, I was very proud of myself. She had not once interrupted for explanations. All she had done was come in with those peremptory *yeses, uh-huh's,* and *I see's,* indicating that she understood and sympathized with me completely. Incredible as it seems to me now, I got the distinct impression that on finishing my heavy monologue she was going to say, ever so gaily, that she'd be pleased to help in whatever way she could.

She fooled me. What I had not been able to isolate in her voice was not sultriness but timidity, a family trait, I had no doubt.

Silent for a long time when I finished, she then excused herself and began calling upstairs to her husband, asking him to pick up the extension. Having anticipated this, I wasn't unduly worried until the husband, instead of picking up the phone immediately, began calling back downstairs and asking what it was about. Twice she called back her brother's name, but she did so with such unsettling timorousness that I could scarcely hear her myself and thought, "Uh-oh, the poor bastard's name must be forbidden in Rochester."

George (for that was the husband's name) obviously

heard her though. *"Who?"* he suddenly shouted into the phone; and when she sheepishly repeated the name into her downstairs extension, he said, *"Oh, Christ!"*—spoken not in a groan that gave me hope, a here-we-go-again thing, but with such absolute loathing that I all but dropped the receiver.

Up to this point, as I say, I had been pleased with the sane and reasonable timbre of my voice; but now, having to begin my tale all anew for George, and a George whose hostility was heated, I began, alarmingly, to disintegrate. My voice grew more quavering, clammy perspiration began running freely down my sides, my hands grew so slippery that it proved a monumental effort to hold the receiver, and I had to keep shifting it from one hand to the other, intermittently drying my free hand on my trousers. The inflexibility of George's eardrums seemed palpable. Like his wife he kept saying *yeah*, though unlike her he spoke not with any comprehension but with the staccato and impatient *yeah-yeah-yeah's* of a man not hearing a word being said. Worse than all this, the television had with each moment seemed to grow louder, mocking. And I began to think that George had purposely turned the volume up, that he used it, this squawking idiot box, to keep himself utterly removed from the pain of life.

"He's a no-good bastard!" George suddenly shouted.

"Pardon?" I said. The blood rushed to my face, and I felt as humiliated as if I were confronting the man in his own living room.

"He's a no-good bastard!" George cried from what passed with him for a heart. He seemed in a perfect paroxysm of rage. *"Never sends the kids so much as a card at Christmas!"*

Frankly, I was by then so totally unmanned by George's inordinate anger that I could scarcely find my voice and kept clearing my throat. When finally I could speak, I said, "Well, he's been *sick*, you know? He told me to send his sister and the kids his love. That's what he said, 'Give them my love.' "

After that I just rambled on, losing all coherence, attempting to appeal to their sense of family, their decency, their humanity. The sister was still on the downstairs extension, and it was she I was trying to reach. Very painful to me as I talked was the memory of that timid, balding, popeyed little man. He was one of those who had made his grim confession at the AA meetings; and I was remembering that above all the others he had moved me with the groping, sheepish, and awful sincerity of his tale—so much so, in fact, that frequently my eyes had sought the floor in refuge from his pain. Above all, I recalled that his tale had been full of the airy and alcoholic dreams of gestures he had wanted to make on the side of life, not the least of which had included great, extravagantly wrapped gifts for these very nephews and nieces.

"Look," I said, "he's probably in his heart given more to your kids than you'll ever know."

"Couldn't have him in the house," George said. He seemed to be talking around a cigar; there was not a shred of equivocality in his voice.

"I know, I know," I said, remembering that the man had anticipated this objection for me. "He said something about a room over the garage!" Then I volunteered, as though it were my idea: "He could stay there!" I was helping out, arranging, solving problems, showing everyone how limpid things were, simple as mud. "He could stay there!"

"No dice," George said. "Couldn't have him around the kids—*and that's all there is to it.*"

The television was still blaring on, louder. The program

was one given over to frolicsome domesticity and starring Lucille Ball. In the hospital I had often watched the show in the company of Snow White and had laughed myself silly, not at Miss Ball but at Snow White's running and one-sided conversation with her, most of which had to do with Snow White's suggestions on how Miss Ball might please him sexually. In the show, Lucy had done wonderfully witty things like look cross-eyed in mockery of the world's ugly. Invariably she had had a scene where, by blacking out her teeth, she had smiled to expose a wide expanse of gums. More often than not she was feigning madness, palsy, or idiocy; and she must have had America rocking in the easy comfort that it was neither so zany, so lunatic, nor so ugly as she. But it did not seem so hilarious to us at Avalon Valley; and only Snow White's unrelenting and wildly droll derision of her had made it bearable. Snow White explained it to me once. Unlike Chaplin, he said, who was always *with* his tramp, or Breughel with his peasant, Miss Ball's farce was conducted on an incredibly cheap level and one never doubted that she was no more with us than was the rest of the world out there.

Thinking of that explanation, I suddenly bellowed into the receiver: "For Christ's sake! What's he gonna do to the fucking kids that the television isn't already doing? Corrupting them! Putting their brains to sleep! Ruining them, brother, ruining them!"

I had to laugh at what George said next. His voice reflected hurt. "What kind of a way is that for a lawyer to talk?"

"Look, I'm sorry," I said, and just as suddenly I *was* sorry. "*Really sorry.* Look," I pleaded, "give the guy a goddam chance. If it doesn't work out, all yuh gotta do is call the authorities and, *bam*, he's back in the goon garage!"

I decided now to play my ace card. "How do you feel about it, Mrs. X?" I said. "He's *your brother.*"

That was my fatal mistake. For George was aware of what he unquestionably deemed his wife's weakness concerning her brother.

"Never mind how she feels about it," he said. *"This is my goddam house, he's not getting in here, and that's all there is to it!"*

The extent of his own anger must have embarrassed him. Suddenly he added, considerably more quietly, and obviously trying to get me to hang up, "This call is costing you money, isn't it, counselor?" He then imitated something like a deferential chuckle, as though telling me that he could appreciate my generosity in making the call but that no useful purpose was being served by continuing it.

The reference to money was the final indignity. For a moment I thought I might disintegrate with humiliation and loathing. I was by then doubled up into a hot, fetus-like ball, with my eyelids down, scorching my eyeballs, the sweaty receiver gripped fiercely between my shoulder and cheek, and my head slumped over and lying heavily against the plastic-covered advertisement on the front interior of the booth. Time was running out and I was trying to think of some monstrously brilliant stroke that might salvage the situation. Then it occurred to me that the sister was weeping, quite terribly; and those tears, dribbling no doubt into her chalk-white Princess telephone, told me as nothing else could that any further appeals were futile and that she had not the tenacity of character to stand up to George and demand that she be permitted to help her brother. I had, I thought, some vague notion of what she was experiencing. A family—*her* family—was breaking up before her eyes, and she was beginning to undergo that terrifying isolation that has become so common to the American. The weeping had gone to sobs, and the sobbing was quite horrible. Certainly she sensed that if she did not help her brother now he would be forever dead to her, and she was, in some dim, excruciatingly painful way, beginning to suffer the vast loneliness of those who do not at any price keep the family together. Because I had botched it so badly by losing my "legal detachment" and getting involved, I felt like bawling, too. I thought I had best hang up before I did so. But I had to leave George with something. It was the voice of the inside calling to those on the outside.

"Money?" I said. *"Costing me money? Why, you stupid cocksucker! I'm talking about a man's life! You know what I mean?"*

George began gasping into the receiver; as though he were suffering an advanced case of emphysema, he seemed to be fighting violently for breath; and—I couldn't help it—I started to laugh. I had finally got to him. Catching his breath, with an effort that was absolutely audible, he screeched at his wife to get off the phone, the implication being that her ears were too delicate for such obscenities. Which made me laugh even louder, more idiotically. What he wanted, of course, was to protect her from the truth about himself, and what he seemed not to understand was that her tears had already signaled that she understood him too well. At least I thought I might apologize to her; but before I could do so I heard the receiver click; she had rung off, and George was making hysterical threats about putting the police on to me.

"May you rot in hell," I said. Then I hung up.

I sat in the booth for a long time, my hand still clutching the receiver in its cradle. The operator rang and asked me to deposit four dollars and change for overtime charges. I told her I wouldn't. I said it in just that matter-of-fact way. *"No. I won't."*

Incredulous as only those automatons can be when The System begins crumbling, she exclaimed, her voice tremulous with indignity, *"But, sir. You made the call!"*

"Yeah, I know," I said. "But I didn't make the connection."

Then again I placed the sweaty receiver in its cradle, rose, slid open the door, stepped out of the booth, and walked across the marble floor to the middle of the concourse, where for a long time I stood studying the Kodak advertisement which spread, as panoramically as a John Ford scene, across the entire east side of the terminal. It was a winter vista, and the snow was more brilliant than real snow, though not nearly so brilliant as the glaring and pearly-white teeth of the models depicting the American family. They were all dressed in iridescently blinding ski togs. The children looked good enough to eat, and the parents looked youthful, alert, charming, and vigorous. Surely this was the coveted America, these perennially rosy cheeks and untroubled azure eyes, these toothy smiles without warmth, eyes without gravity, eyes incapable of even the censorious scowl, eyes, for that matter, incapable of mustering even a look of perplexity. Well, it was *not* the America I coveted. I was well aware of my pretensions to intellectuality and that the hues of my being were preponderantly and inordinately somber—a somberness that was no doubt governed not a little by self-pity. But better that, I thought, better seek and take on the woes of Jesus Christ himself than yearn after this mindless milieu populated with these Technicolored and felicitous goons.

Abruptly, without thinking, I expectorated distastefully

onto the marble floor. All during the phone conversation my mouth had been dry as dust; since hanging up, I had sensed the saliva flooding back into my mouth, and the thick and rich glob of sputum just missed a passing matron dressed in a mink coat, landing just in front of her and causing her to come to a tottering halt. She cast on me a look of outraged severity. The sputum had neither hit nor splashed upon her, I was sure. What did she want from me? "I'm not a gentleman," I said. Still she lingered, looking even more indignant. "What do you want?" I said finally in exasperation. "You bastards have just had a year of my life!" I was becoming very distraught, and apparently she wasn't going to move on. Rolling my eyes into the bridge of my nose, cross-eyed, I singled out the forefinger of my right hand, shoved it up into my right nostril as though seeking a monstrous bugger, fiercely grabbed my genitalia into the cup of my left hand, let out a cowboy-like *Whooopeeee!* and started doing a frantic, devilish jig, all of which sent the startled woman, going *Ooh! Ooh! Ooh!* and looking back over her mink-draped shoulder as she went, scurrying across the concourse.

Regaining my composure, somewhat winded, I went back to studying the advertisement. Thinking again of George and Rochester, I wondered if he didn't work for Kodak. When years before I had been at Hobart, there was a much-repeated legend, perhaps apocryphal, that the founder of Kodak, Eastman, had once offered to give the college—oh, billions, I guess—stipulating only that its name be changed to his own. The college had refused, losing the billions but retaining the name of its founder, Hobart, a bishop or prelate or monsignor or some such thing in the Episcopal hierarchy. I had always liked the story be-

cause it so reflected the integrity men like to remind themselves exists, the kind of tale a fraternity man, having just
come from the sanctum sanctorum of the fraternity house
where he has blackballed a Jew, passes on to a wide-eyed
WASP pledge as an example of the decent and civilizing
traditions he is inheriting. Integrity, it seemed to me, was a
thing invariably removed; and, sadly, I had no doubt whatever that George imagined he knew what it was.

Then I saw him sitting there, drinking his beer and
watching his television, so fat-assed and content. My guess
was that he liked shows in which virtue triumphed, justice
overcame, probity reigned unfettered. As Matt Dillon
gunned down the bearded miscreant, I saw George's breast
swell with the loftiness of right being done; as Perry Mason
exonerated the kindly old widow, surely George oozed fat
tears that lawfulness was part and parcel of his heritage;
perhaps George even came to attention, the muscles in his
backside bristling with haughty pride, as Ed Sullivan lec-
tured him on the virtues of paying daily homage to the
American flag. No, never for a moment did I doubt that
George had very "real" notions of decency and honor and
integrity, nor did I doubt that he believed we of Avalon
Valley were *not good,* as his brother-in-law was a "no-good
bastard," because we could not accommodate ourselves to
Mr. Sullivan's America. I could not loathe George for it, so
bombarded was he by the power cliques that rule America.
But if I could not loathe him, neither could I live with him,
get into bed with him. And I knew then that I never should
have placed the call, that I had attempted much too quickly
to break the American sound barrier.

Standing there, so wrought up, I knew that the only
question was where I might go. For a moment I considered

returning to Avalon Valley or going to the girl. Then I thought of telephoning the Counselor and inviting myself for the weekend. "Stay as long as you like," the Counselor said. Then I was on the train, sitting by the west window and moving rapidly north by the river, the taste of blood in my mouth.

—

For fifteen years I carried a recurring vision of myself. I was somewhere in Africa (Rhodesia?), sitting in a rocking chair on the screened veranda of an imposing, two-storied, clapboard building of brilliant white, an English colonialists' club. My hair was neatly trimmed, my face tanned and clean-shaven. Wearing a Palm Beach suit so snowy it glistened, I also had on a pale-blue shirt, a regimental necktie of maroon and gold, and immaculate white patent-leather Oxfords. In my right hand I held a tall iced drink whose cloudy, perspiring, and thinly cylindrical glass I brought infrequently and abstractedly to my lips, to take there the most absurdly delicate sips. My expression was ironical. In it there was a suggestion of amusement, directed, it seemed, as much against myself as against anything or anyone about me, as though I were taking myself not quite seriously, *cum grano salis*.

Nobody at the club knew who I was. Or where I came from. Or for that matter even the sound of my voice. There was a time when English voices had invited me to sit at bridge or to exchange my name for theirs; but to these discreet overtures I had neither responded nor looked up from my interminably rocking chair. After a time everyone ceased to bother with me and I became a human fixture on the screened veranda, rocking, silent, sipping, enigmatic. In the expansive, cool rooms behind me I heard the bidding of bridge—two hearts, pass, three spades; heard the talk of cricket; heard the khaki-shorted, mustachioed gentry ordering their scotch and sodas. Over the wide lawns, to my left, the young folks, their sturdy legs glistening in the sun, played at tennis and swam in a great blue-green pool, shouting gaily to one another. The timbre of their voices was euphorically English, so soothing and civilized. From in front of me, indeed from all about me—from out there in that vast and harshly beautiful land—came still another sound, one compounded of suffering and rage and humiliation. The latter was, of course, the sound of Black Africa; and my irony, my amusement, my infuriating smugness were caused in no small measure by the knowledge that I was apparently the only one who heard this other sound. It was as if those others were deaf. Or dead. They played at bridge and tennis, they talked cricket and sipped at scotch and sodas; and a young girl, ready to dive, stood poised on a board above the blue pool, her thighs in the sun so lovely that one wanted to transform the vision to find one's head resting in her maidenly lap. Constantly one yearned to dispel the reality in favor of the idyllic. But then that other sound would come, that wail.

For the life of me I could never fathom why I did not get up and walk away before it was too late. The augurs were unmistakable. Occasionally the din grew to an almost clanging howl (I peeped about to see if anyone was hearing: alas!), a great anguished wail signaling the world's modifications, regroupings, new beginnings. Still I remained glued to my chair.

I had a clairvoyant notion of the future's horrors. When they came, brandishing their spears and glimmering knives, their black bodies besmeared with dung and ashes, their pearly teeth exposed in the idiocy of their revengeful smiles, I expected to offer an absurd protest in tones quite as modulated as those behind me. "But look here, chaps," I expect I should have said, "I don't give a ruddy damn about these people—*or you.* I am here neither to Christianize, colonize, nor educate you. Nor do I come bearing Coca-Cola and Campbell's chicken noodle soup. Nor do I seek your bloody vote in the UN General Assembly. You see, I am uninvolved, and my posture in life is one of detachment, irony, and amusement, which may not be a particularly lofty posture but which nevertheless has the redeeming merit of having not the slightest notion of what is good for you." Such protests would, of course, do no good, and I fully expected to have my throat slit by one of the barbarians. I expected, too, that I would still be blabbering away in some such genteel fashion when one of them made his violent incision, reached in, snapped up my kidney or liver, and, popping it between his hideously smiling lips, began blissfully chomping away before my horrified eyes. Why I did not get up and move away proved perplexing in the extreme, though in truth it was not dying with these colonialists that bothered me. There was, in their steadfast inability to see or hear an ingenuousness such as that possessed by children stunned and held in sway by those glittering worlds that never exist save in their charming fancies. It was as simple as this: I was altogether helpless to abandon them.

As sooner or later always happens to one who bears such visions, mine began to take on the hard dimensions of reality in the four months I was the Counselor's guest. During that time he provided me, no questions asked, with his davenport to lie upon, with paperbacks to read, with food, and with liquor. Those months were for me a most pleasant time, and I might have stayed indefinitely had not the behavior of certain visitors to the apartment seemed to me more singular than anything I had witnessed at Avalon Valley—or in my vision. When I began to discern this and, worse, began to sense that apparently no one saw anything in the least erratic in the actions of the apartment's habitués, it was then, whether dressed in a Palm Beach suit or not, I started to see myself as the suave, knowing chap in the rocking chair. Ominous sounds heralding grave changes were dinning all about me, but I seemed altogether too helpless or indifferent to make my concerns known.

But look:

Afternoons one or another of the Counselor's married peers brought his secretary or girl friend to the apartment for sex. The girl was invariably knock-kneed but a young and shy and brave and lovely little thing, and I used to lie on the davenport trying to concentrate on Humbert Humbert's searing avowals of love while overhearing the joyous and erotic laughter from the adjoining suite, used to lie there dying of longing, envy, and boredom. As stolidly as a rhinoceros the sofa perched itself hard by the apartment's door; and whenever a couple would leave, the girl, her cheeks aglow with love, would smile demurely at me and the man, strutting his absurd virility, would wink lewdly. To either farewell I nodded and smiled amiably; in that smile there was a hint of simple-mindedness: I was a most convincing and good-natured cretin. No one seemed to know who I was, or what I was doing there. Nor did I seem to provoke any curiosity in these siesta sex partners.

One of the prettier girls (her legs were straight and there was something like intelligence in the way her eyes were

set in and complemented her fine brow) did speak to me
one day. Winking as lasciviously as ever any of the men
had, she nodded in the direction of *Lolita*, clutched open
and cover face up against my chest, and with a great sigh
remarked to me the book's alarming sexuality. That sigh
was wrought with heavy sensuality, as though merely calling back the huge and lustful appetites of the book's characters all but prostrated her with fatigue. She was the only
one who had so far spoken to me, I liked her intelligent
looks and fine legs, I pitied her the fake sophistication of
her predicament, and I should have accepted her pleas-
antry for what it was. But I was by then drunk on Nabokov's
prose and loathed her facile misreading of the author's in-
tentions.

"Quite the contrary," I said. *"Lolita* is about as sexy as *Little Women."*

My tone was tendentious and abrupt, and though she
came often afterward, she never spoke again. Her *mon-cher*
barrister, a black-tied, horn-rimmed, hairy-nosed, and
towering old fraud (as might be expected, he was, I later
learned, very good at The Law), continued to speak, invariably remarking his wonder that I was still "on *Lolita."*
He'd wag his horn-rimmed head, smile secretively, wink,
and proclaim his astonishment: "Still on *Lolita?"* Then he'd
issue a past master's chuckle by way of letting me know
that he and I were joined in some scatological conspiracy.
It never occurred to him that I might be reading the book
for the fourth or fifth time, and as the days passed I know
he came to regard me as either depraved or the most moronic reader in Christendom. *"Still on* Lolita!" became a recurring din, like a daily summons to waken. In response, I
gave up nodding my moronic assent and to please him

came after a time to feign utter cretinism. He'd shout, and prior to answering I'd knit my brow into a painful knot and fake a tortured reading, zealously and gropingly forming "all them hard words" with my mouth. "It's kinda hard reading," I'd say. "It is, huh?" he'd shout, solicitously steering his paramour toward the boudoir. Eventually they both came to view me with that compassion one reserves for burlapped monks and homely girls. "Really hard reading!" I'd exclaim as the door was closing in preparation to their erotic play. Then I would hear them giggle and had a grand time envisioning them wagging their superior heads in sympathy with my driveling addleheadedness.

With both his money and his time, the Counselor was easy. He had an open face, suggesting timidly gregarious possibilities, as though, were he approached, he would be willing to be drawn into discussions of the relative merits of best-sellers or the batting averages of baseball players. Beneath that blond brush cut, behind those clear blue eyes and even white teeth, though, there resided the intelligence of an authentic cynic. The Counselor possessed this Ishmael-like quality, this thing ungroomable, this cowlick in his psyche; and watching him listen to one tale of woe or another, I was never sure whether he listened in sympathy or with scarcely contained amusement. Watching him listen, I was never at ease. After hearing and seeing them through their troubles during office hours, he had no heart for ridding himself of his clients during nocturnal hours; and all sorts of them, wringing their hands, mad with grief, and outraged at a million injustices, gamboled in and out of the apartment, more often than not chanting hurts that could not be remedied by law, man or God's.

Ham-handed, enormous-muscled, and great-shouldered

Studs—the plural always summoned up for me visions of multiple penises—had sleek black hair, a sleek black mustache, a matching leather jacket, and hip-hugging dungarees that exposed both his bowed legs and his virilia. By profession Studs was a plaintiff. Or the Counselor suspected he was and for that reason refused to take any more of his cases. "What do you mean?" I said. Studs, the Counselor explained, had been in a series of one-car accidents, cars that had missed turns and careened into virginal trees, cars that had hurtled headlong into solid bridge abutments, cars that had somehow and rather miraculously gone out of control, smashed up, and whose passenger roster had invariably been made up of four or five of Studs's black-jacketed and adoring disciples. There was, besides, the Counselor continued, something somewhat peculiar in that only the owner-driver, who couldn't sue himself, who was always heavily insured and who was of course to be sued by the others, and Studs, the ubiquitous passenger, were the only ones left unscathed by these mishaps. Or rather, as the Counselor explained, "The only things Studs hurt were his fists." His motley and unfortunate followers came up with a superb collection of swollen lips, cracked teeth, broken ribs, squashed noses, and hideously outsized purple-yellow shiners. "In fairness to Studs," the Counselor said with mock solemnity, "he might have strained himself when they were pushing the car into the tree." Then I had this vision of this black-jacketed mob selecting some innocent maple, shoving the Chevrolet down some incline and into it, and broke up laughing as I saw the goons solemnly lining up before the bemuscled Studs to have their injuries administered. In both their duncedom and their wickedness there was something touching, and the thought that Studs was beating the rapacious auto insurance companies out of dollars made me admire him immensely.

When I got to know Studs better, I suggested that he invite me on one of his accident parties; but he explained that I had no income to have "loss of" and hence wouldn't be worth much in the eyes of the companies. He laughed as though he were joking, and at the first opportunity I told the Counselor what he had said to me. "That's the worst of it," the Counselor said, and went on to explain that over his accident-prone career Studs had become altogether too conversant with such legal jargon as "loss of income," "pain and suffering," and "contributory negligence," those determining factors in whether or not and how much one collects from the companies. The Counselor suspected it only a matter of time before Studs began bringing him negligence cases before they occurred and seeking his judgment as to whether slipped discs or the absence of upper teeth would be held dearer by a jury. "You, Studs," the Counselor would say, his voice chilling with menace, "are going to find your black Wop of an ass right in Sing Sing and I'll be goddammed if I'll go with you."

Immediately be it said in the Counselor's ethical defense that Studs never admitted a knowledge of what the Counselor was intimating and always in a histrionic way proclaimed his innocence of any such collusion. His bowed legs skimming up and down the carpeted living room, he would feign hurt at the Counselor's implications, almost sagging to the floor under the awful weight of such immoderate and unjust accusations. Like most Italians he was a consummate, if not superb, actor, and at such accusations he was marvelous at blessing himself, raising his hands in

protest to the heavens, or, both hands slammed and forming a rood across his chest, swearing on his mother's grave
or saying, "Couns, as the holy Virgin was the mother of the
infant Jesus—" "Is all that really necessary?" the Counselor
would say.

Studs admired the Counselor greatly. He dwelt in that
dimwitted world of roadhouses, western music, brawling,
Genesee 12-Horse Ale, aborted girls, and B-class movies;
and he derived vast pleasure that a man of the Counselor's
tweedy refinement could speak his language and refer to
him as a black-assed Wop. "The Counselor," he told me in
breathless admiration on our first meeting, "has got a lot of
savvy—I mean, *savvy.*"

Because I was the Counselor's friend, Studs soon developed a crush on me, too, and within the dimensions of his
B-class milieu began to romanticize about me. Detecting
that I seldom left the apartment, that I lay there unshaven
and morose, he at one point got it into his head that I was
"on the lam" from something (as indeed I was) and "holed
up" in the Counselor's apartment until the latter determined it a propitious time to surrender me to the authorities (I'd volunteer to "turn state's evidence"). In whatever
manner, my paranoia presently seeped through to him, and
he became convinced that the forces of authority were
hotly pursuing me. *Anybody you want me to take care of?* became Studs's daily query to me. It was always put with such
snarling sincerity that there were times I wished I could
summon out of my past an image of someone I loathed
enough to have his jaw broken, undoubtedly one of Studs's
specialties. Like most Americans, though, I had led that
numbingly chaste and uncommitted existence in which
one forms neither sympathies nor antipathies of any en-

during consequence. Hence, sighing, I was invariably forced to respond, "No, not today, Studs."

"Well, baby," he'd say, flexing his enormous biceps, "if you ever think of anybody, you just let Studs know."

"A deal," I always responded. The two new friends would beam boundless admiration on one another.

Still another of these "clients" was Oscar. The son of a wealthy New York realtor, he was Ivy League from his molded haircut to his grained, expensive loafers, bespectacled, and so gaunt he listed. Though a "high" Episcopalian, his wife had obtained from him a civil divorce and until the Counselor had rectified the matter had refused to let him see his six remarkably handsome children. Removing a photo of the latter from his wallet, he was utterly mad (which he was, it turned out, anyway) on showing it about the apartment, and there were days when, for approbation, he thrust it at me a half-dozen times. The print was much soiled and tattered from intense and loving care.

On the grim morning I met Oscar, he crept stealthily into the apartment and without acknowledging me slumped furiously down at the end of the davenport, almost atop my malodorous and stockinged feet. Though it was a cool day, he was sweating heavily, and in the forehead harbors of his receding hairline were globs of perspiration as full-bodied and shiny as Vaseline. Where the perspiration had seeped into the hair, there were dark wet splotches, giving his head a sad-comic checkered effect. It was the first time I had seen an Ivy League cut so ill-kempt (one brushes and brushes to achieve this farcical composure and still grief comes!). Sitting there, totally oblivious of me, Oscar once, twice, three times emitted the groan of a man in terrible agony. Hardened to agony, I ignored him.

Then he broke down and began to weep uncontrollably, the racking sobs hideously contorting his spindly frame. As much in annoyance as in sympathy, I rose, walked to the kitchen, poured a stiff drink of whisky, returned, and handed it to him. Ten minutes had elapsed and that proffered drink was the first acknowledgment either of us had made of the other's presence. Sipping, he began to talk, often weeping as he did so. The police, cab drivers, Mafia types, mystery men—men, all sorts of men, were searching for him.

"What for?" I said.

To beat him up, to knock him down, to kick his teeth in, to rip his intestines out. For what else? He sat there sneering at me, his frail and empty hand clutching fiercely at his imagined eviscerated parts. He left me no doubt that he considered me simple-minded.

"I see," I said, nodding knowingly, much as a few months before I had acquiesced to the Negro with the little man inside him.

After that I just kept pouring drinks for Oscar until, in no time at all, he got drunk and passed out. Removing his tweed jacket, his black-rimmed glasses, his Scotch grained loafers, I tenderly (I was as solicitous as a maiden aunt) laid the poor bastard out on the davenport, put a wool blanket over him, and lovingly tucked him in. While doing so I could feel his skeletal ribs through both blanket and shirt, and it occurred to me that Oscar was so distraught he hadn't eaten properly in weeks. For two hours I sat in a chair across from him and took pleasure in his heavy, contented sleep, punctuated only now and again by a startling and heart-breaking groan. When the Counselor came in that night, he looked at Oscar, rolled his eyes up to his brows, wagged his head in feigned and weary exasperation, and proceeded into the kitchen. Following him there and cornering him, I came as close as I would ever come to expressing my concerns about the behavior of the apartment's habitués.

"Of course, you know," I said, "that this Oscar, or whatever the fuck his name is, is sick. I mean, *nuttier than a fruitcake.*"

The Counselor laughed. "He's all right," he said. "Been through hell. He'll pull out of it." Then, by way of an afterthought and as kind of consummate explanation, he said, "We're *all* sick, Freddy."

The Counselor rolled his eyes again, let his tongue sag out over his chin, and put on his most cretinous façade. He, too, was sick, he was saying. He was also testing my nihilism.

I met that test.

"Actually," I offered in mock protest, "I'm sicker than Oscar is, and all I'm *really* worried about is your figuring he needs the davenport more than me."

"No sweat," the Counselor assured me. Still he played the slobbering idiot. Rapping me gingerly on the pate, as though fearful a heavier blow would unleash unimaginable demons, he repeated, "No sweat at all. There *ain't nobody* sicker than you, Freddy."

I smiled my agreement.

Many girls came to the apartment. The Counselor, bless his black and insatiable heart, often had one going out the back door as another came in the front. He was most magnanimous with his castoffs. One arrived one azure and sunny Saturday and departed the following gray and rainy Friday, leaving then only because she was the next day being married. She had pale, heartless eyes; high, prominent, and lovely cheekbones; and the nostrils of her pert nose dilated constantly with an incandescent and disarming contempt for all humanity. At the end of the second day she took me, and for the final five of her prenuptial days we lay naked about the apartment, drinking and making love till we went limp with exhaustion. She did not talk at all, and because I had my own pain I did not attempt to draw her out. At one undetected point the alarmingly hostile dilations of her nostrils abated, and twice each day she made phone calls, to her mother and to her fiancé, calls both to account for her whereabouts (presumably a resort hotel in the Catskills) and to explain that she was thinking things through and that everything was going to be okie-dokie. Often during the calls we engaged, at her perverse insistence, in that cruelly cynical sex (so that her conversations were punctuated with the laborious breathing of love and brought solicitous queries from the other end), afterward slumbering heavily in each other's arms. It was through her I discovered my animal nature. Then it was Friday, and as arbitrarily as she had come she went. Two, three weeks later I saw her on the street with her husband. Oscar, whose wallet always contained, along with that soiled print, plenty of green, had taken to buying me beers during the long afternoons; and walking down the main drag toward a favored saloon, I heard Oscar, his voice tremulous, say, "Isn't that—?" and looked up to see them.

Both were handsome and elegantly dressed; they were laughing and chatting at a furious clip; they were in love. In the moment of our passage I studied them as well as I could. The man was prettily handsome, but not without a rough gaiety that lent him virility; his suit was dark and beautifully cut. But it was she who astonished me. All pink and bounce she was. Her mute apathy had led me to believe that she was moronic or so repressed as to be unredeemable; but now, with her cheeks fierce pink with bliss, dressed in her pink and white checkered dress, bouncing along on her pink pumps, she appeared the unqualified vision of the health-exuding, intelligent, and attractive "young married." Passing me, and with a barely perceptible withdrawal of attention from her husband, she all but shouted, "Hi, Fred!" In her voice was conquest, and that conquest forced the blood to my face. *This,* she seemed to announce, *is ever so much better than that.* At first I was furious, but the ire instantly subsided and, grabbing hold of Oscar's arm, my body broke and bent under the weight of sudden and unrestrained laughter. Why take it out on me? It was that week of degradation that had provided the contrast by which her marriage now seemed so pink, pure, and thrilling to her. After all, unsolicited, that pert and dilating nose had spent a good part of the week buried in my genitals; and she seemed now not able to grasp that her animality had been not a lapse but as much a part of her as the marrow in her bones. Still clutching Oscar, I stopped, pivoted, taking Oscar with me, and, laughing, watched them bounce up the street. "She sure acts different," Oscar said in solemn amazement. "She sure does," I agreed.

The straight-legged girl and her hairy-nosed attorney continued to come to the apartment; he continued to wink lasciviously and remark his wonder that I was still on *Lolita.* Studs came daily and, like a caged animal, skimmed his bowed legs up and down the carpeting, intently seeking the names of people I wanted "done in." Oscar was always there. He liked to mix the drinks and light everyone's cigarette. But as jovial as he tried to be, he could muster no interest in the girls, and those girls who became interested in him were quickly discouraged. At a moment during the course of the evening, he invariably produced from his wallet the soiled print of the six kids and showed it about to the uninterested company, in his drunkenness taking particular care to point out the woman whom he called "wife," who was not his wife and who sat stolidly behind the handsome children. She was a horn-rimmed, stout, pale, severe-looking old cow, but Oscar loved her and one knew that it would be a long time before another woman moved his manhood to desire. Oscar was largehearted and beautiful to be with. Some days he was very good and coherent, but as the days passed he got very bad and seemed to be getting worse. The last I heard of him—some months ago—was that he was confined in a madhouse and expected to be there a long time. I think of Oscar quite a bit; on those infrequent occasions when I wonder about the efficacy of prayer, I think I would like to ask God in His infinite mercy to restore Oscar to life.

—

By the time the man called Mr. Blue arrived at the apartment I had come to expect anything and hence did not know that in the end he would be the cause of my getting off the davenport and moving on yet again. Mr. Blue claimed to be fifty, but I suspect he was closer to sixty, perhaps older. He stood five feet, three in his shiny black shoes, elevated and made of alligator. He had thin, snow-white hair splotched with an aging, uncomfortable yellow, and crinkly, sad, great-sized eyes of so penetrating a blue that when he looked directly at me I found myself fingering my face for food particles or nose phlegm: his eyes seemed a constant reproach that one did not live up to his expectations. Around his knifelike mouth were many deep wrinkles, giving his face a feline quality; when he talked I stared at his lips apprehensively, as though I expected vibrissa to sprout there. Tiny and slender, Mr. Blue weighed no more than a hundred and fifteen. Still, his strength and agility were incredible. From a stand-still position he could do either a front or back flip, in machine-gun-like succession twenty hand springs without even winding himself; and on anyone's suggestion he would drop proudly to the floor and oblige the apartment's stunned occupants with a hundred push-ups. It was wondrous to watch the old codger go at these feats.

There was a period of three weeks when Mr. Blue came daily to the apartment and passed the afternoon hours with me. During these visits we talked about professional football, about which Mr. Blue knew nothing, and about the two things which interested Mr. Blue most: aluminum siding, which he sold, and cunnilingus, on which he suspected I was an authority.

In the aluminum siding racket Mr. Blue was a "closer." He traveled about with two or three fuzzy-cheeked, comely, spirited Ivy League types who were "canvassers" and whose job it was to get Mr. Blue into a house so that he could get the buyer's signature on a contract, thus "closing" the sale. Mr. Blue would park his powder-blue Cadillac in a neighborhood ripe for sales; the canvassers, leaving Mr. Blue in the car with a copy of *True Detective,* would fan out in various directions, ringing doorbells. If a canvasser got into a house, he was at some point in his pitch to explain to the housewife that her luck was indeed running hot as a "factory representative" from "Alcoa" was in town that day, that the man was distressed, oh, heartsick, at the absence of aluminum in her neighborhood, and that if, as a sales inducement to her neighbors, she would apply siding to her house, the canvasser was certain the "Alcoa" man would do the job for nothing—well, practically nothing. If the gullible *Hausfrau* agreed to hear more, Mr. Blue was hastily lured from reading "The Rape of the Vassar Girls" and all five feet, three of him, carrying a great portfolio case loaded with siding samples, color samples, and contracts, attempted an entrance spectacular enough to cow the housewife before the talks even began.

Mr. Blue sighed. The canvassers had no class or style today. They did not even know how to make an introduction properly; nowadays most of them expected Mr. Blue to carry his own portfolio case, which was, it seems, undignified for the "factory representative." When Mr. Blue had started in the business as a canvasser years before, they had used a chauffeur-driven black Cadillac "about a goddam mile long." Their favorite driver had been a very dignified "nigger" named Seedy who stood six feet, six and who had a "jawful" of marvelous gold teeth. The Cadillac had pulled up in front of the customer's domicile, Seedy had jumped out, opened the back door to discharge the great man, grabbed the portfolio case and the roll of carpeting, and had begun running up the sidewalk toward the house. "And he *ran* his black ass off," Mr. Blue said.

Here Mr. Blue paused, wondering whether what he had to say would find sympathy with me. He took a chance. "Not like these independent black bastards today," he said. He gave his words the semihumorous and cowardly twist men do when they aren't sure they can enlist one on the side of their melancholy ignorance. I'm certain my rum expression showed neither sympathy nor disapproval. This bewildered Mr. Blue into a qualification, a grudging one to be sure. "What a guy Seedy was!"

"I'm sure," I said.

On gaining admittance to the house, the first thing Seedy did was open the red carpet and begin rolling it down the middle of the living room for the closer (i.e., the "Massa") to make his grandiose entrance on.

"A carpet?" I shrieked in delight. "Didn't that offend the customer? I mean, mightn't she think your factory man thought he was too good to walk on her carpet? Or something?"

No. No. No. Mr. Blue was impatient with my levity. In those happy days all the closers had been "psychologists"; if they sensed they were causing offense, they simply explained they knew how hard the woman toiled and hadn't wanted to dirty up her home. "Yeah," Mr. Blue said. "There was one closer, Sally DiMidio, if you got him into a house, you automatically had five hundred bucks. Three hundred for Sally, a hundred and a half for me, and half a yard for Seedy."

Mr. Blue was still concerned about my lack of response to his racial sympathies. "Oh, don't worry about that," he assured me. "We took real good care of Seedy. That black bastard always had a roll as big as his dong, and every high-yellow broad in Jersey City laid down her golden ass for him!" Mr. Blue shook his head nostalgically and sighed. Heavily. When Mr. Blue sighed, it was immeasurably sad, like high winds blowing through leafless autumn trees. When Mr. Blue sighed, he had an unnerving habit of obliquely studying one to see if one sensed the depth of his sadness. When Mr. Blue sighed, I always pursed my lips in the most commiserating way and did my best, to little avail, to form great-sized tears in my eyes.

Was Mr. Blue full of shit? Somehow I couldn't be sure, but his tales, under the harsh weight of reflection, seemed glaringly preposterous. Whenever, for example, I envisioned the timid housewife, expecting the Brooks Brothers type "Alcoa" man and opening her door to the six-feet-six Seedy, smiling a roomy smile to expose his great glittering teeth, the only vision I got was of her swooning dead away. So whenever Mr. Blue told me these stories—and Mr. Blue told me these stories all the time—I found that I had to repress a terrible urge to interrupt him, employing the dramatic pauses and gravity of Mr. Blue himself, and say, "Mr. Blue, you know something? ... *You're full of shit!*"

Talking shop was with Mr. Blue a one-man oratorio. He did the recitative, performed the aria, acted a plaintiff chorus. His voice rose and fluttered with excitement. He chanted explanations. Reverently, he emoted with the nostalgia of poetry. The young men of today, he wailed, wouldn't deign to use some of the methods he had employed for gaining admittance to a house. Mr. Blue had rung doorbells and immediately had backed off the porch and walked to the middle of the yard. When the owner had answered the bell's jangling summons, he had found an exasperated Mr. Blue, hands jammed furiously down on his hips, rocking impatiently on the balls of his feet, standing in the middle of the lawn and staring in mock-horrified disgust at the man's house. "What is it?" the man would ask. "Yes?" Pivoting slowly, ever so dramatically, Mr. Blue would suddenly start screaming at the man. Save that no words came.

In imitation Mr. Blue made his mouth go for me,

mouthing his voiceless anger, disgust, disappointment. He
did it superbly. His great blue eyes widened in rage, his
rubbery mouth opened and closed with desperate sincerity, even his aging, hairy ears seemed in fury to distend
perceptibly from the sides of his snowy head. Still—*no
words came.* He was like that superb double-talker who appeared in the cinema comedies of the thirties and forties;
no matter how often one heard him, one always strained,
sweated, tilted one's head, and gasped painfully attempting
to decipher the indecipherable. Standing but a few feet
from my prone figure on the davenport, Mr. Blue had me
convinced that an impenetrable curtain had suddenly and
insidiously descended over my ears. Laughing wildly, I
paid Mr. Blue the homage his artistry deserved.

Cupping his hand over his ear and actually listing
toward me, Mr. Blue now became the distraught customer.
"Huh?" "What's that?" "How's that you say?"—as he was
being drawn slowly, presumably unconsciously, down his
steps and across his lawn to the magnetic and fatal Mr.
Blue. When Mr. Blue had the man next to him, it was, one
guessed, *all but over.* Placing his arm about the man's waist,
and theatrically flourishing his arm in the direction of the
man's house, Mr. Blue, using his voice for the first time,
wanted to know of the man whether he wasn't ashamed of
having a house in such sorry repair, whether he didn't think
his home a blight and an eyesore on the entire neighborhood. Mr. Blue's tone was now one of earnest solicitation.
He liked the man. He wanted to help him.

Mr. Blue stared at me. Was he getting through to me?
Apparently not. Asking me to rise from the davenport so
that he might demonstrate, he pulled me into snug contact
with his thin and muscular torso. While he talked sooth-

ingly to me, as father to son, his hand alternated between clutching me vice-like and opening to pat me tenderly on the layer of fat above my waistline. Again sweeping his free arm in the direction of what was supposed to be my shack but which was only the apartment's bare beige walls, he earnestly, and with just a touch of melancholy, asked whether I wasn't embarrassed by what I beheld. When I made no answer, still not grasping my role, Mr. Blue demanded, "What would you say?"—meaning, I guess, if I were the luckless homeowner in the wiry little grasp of Mr. Blue's fanaticism. Smiling sheepishly, I stutteringly agreed that my house was indeed a cyclopean atrocity. "Naturally that's what you'd say," Mr. Blue said, releasing me from his fierce grip and allowing his chest to expand with the pride of his craft.

As he always did, Mr. Blue now jammed his hands down into the pockets of his suit coat and strutted, peacock proud and pensive, about the living room, giving his time-worn and hard-won lore time to seep through to me. Smiling, I imagined that now Seedy and Sally DiMidio would slither up to the curb in the mile-long Cadillac, disembark, and the three of them, with the six-foot-six, dear-toothed, jet-black, and carpet-bearing Seedy leading the way, would descend on the house for the slaughter.

Seldom during those three weeks did I ever cease laughing—drifting between outright roaring and an exhausted giggling—with Mr. Blue. And though I was enjoying his visits immensely, I had no idea exactly who Mr. Blue was and what he wanted of me. Whenever I questioned him about his relationship with the Counselor, he became moody and silent, for which reason I suspected that he had retained the Counselor in a criminal matter, probably, I surmised, something to do with his rather shady vocation, perhaps an illegal contract? One of the things that led to this suspicion was that of all the characters who crept in and out of the apartment, it was Mr. Blue with whom the Counselor was least friendly. To be sure, passing from the front door to the bedroom, the Counselor came after a time to acknowledge Mr. Blue by mock-ordering, after the manner of a Marine sergeant, "Give us fifty, Mr. Blue"; but as often as not, laughing, he passed on before the mildly red-faced and popeyed Mr. Blue had reached his twentieth push-up, a slight which never deterred Mr. Blue's finishing the push-ups for my admiration. And so, though I did not for some time learn Mr. Blue's mysterious relationship with the Counselor, he one day told me what he had in mind for me: he was, he said, in the manner of one making a marriage proposal which he knows will be disesteemed, seeking a new canvasser, one with *class*, and he had, after giving it no little thought, decided that that canvasser and I were one.

By that time I had again fallen prone to the dreamer's abysmal ways and again for days at a time lay unshaven on the davenport. Thick scales of ugly dandruff clung to my scalp, coffee stains as big as silver dollars patterned my fragrant ivory sweatshirt, and sitting all about me on the floor, like a scale model of some ominous and ghastly city of the future, were Budweiser beer cans, empty and half-empty, through whose can-opener apertures I had stuffed my scarcely smoked cigarettes. That behind this grimy front Mr. Blue could envision an I'm-working-my-way-through-college type moved me to near-hysteria and I ended, to Mr. Blue's chagrin, by rolling all about the floor, toppling the "towers" of my nightmare city and spilling the contents of stale beer and irriguous cigarette butts onto the carpeting.

But Mr. Blue was a tough closer and hence proved an oppressively pertinacious suitor. He had some deranged notion of the typical housewife slinking about all day in a reeky housecoat, chain-smoking, scratching her "hairy ass," and undesistingly yearning for oral stimulation of her labia. "That's all they think about!" Mr. Blue said. "It's a *thing* with them!" Moreover, he had come to believe that there was about me an aura of abandonment (an Ivy League one?) which intimated I had spent a good part of my near-thirty years with my cheeks flanked by luxurious and crushing thighs. Contrary protests did no good. The more stridently I objected, the more Mr. Blue smiled knowingly, letting me know that it was perfectly okay with him if I were blighted, so much the better as "broads can spot lappers" and doors would open for me *like so*, and here Mr. Blue snapped his fingers so startlingly that goose-pimples played a tune on my spine. Often I became angry. "Jesus, Mr. Blue! Would you get that notion about me out of your head!" But my ire, of course, only reinforced what he already "knew," and ultimately, exhausted, nearly tearful and laughing simultaneously, I shouted petulantly, "I give in! goddammit, I give up!"

Ordering me to rise and seal the partnership with a solemn handshake, Mr. Blue then celebrated the ritual with two front flips and a fantastically frantic little fandango, danced on his lunatic, elevated, alligator shoes. Further directing me to shower and shave, Mr. Blue gave me the money to get my seersucker jacket from the cleaner's and took me downtown to visit "his" barber.

In the four days I canvassed for Mr. Blue, I got him into

one house, that of a young woman who was in fact deaf. Though she had smooth, well-made legs, melon-like, in-mate's dreams of breasts, and a charmingly languorous glow (about none of which was she overly conscious), as Mr. Blue had so sibyllinely claimed she would be, she was dressed in a sleazy housecoat and was voraciously wolfing the evil weed. Unable to understand me, she asked me into her kitchen, sat me at an indigo-enameled table, and gave me a pad and pencil with which to express my wants. After I did so, she gave me a piece of cinnamon toast and a glass of milk; and while I ate and drank these, she told me about her deafness. While explaining it, she sometimes talked, which she did perfectly well; at other times, she usurped the pad and wrote things down, as though, unable to hear herself, she at times doubted my capacity to do so. She said her deafness was at first thought to have been caused by a childhood illness; but as the specialists could find no phys-ical damage to the ear, they were now suggesting the cause was psychosomatic. She smiled a self-disparaging smile and good-naturedly asked if I thought she was nuts. Taking my maxim from the Counselor, I wrote on the pad: "We're all a little of that." Talking, we both laughed a lot, and as easily as the intimacy of those melon-like breasts displayed above the V of her housecoat allowed. Despite the easiness, it was obvious that the deafness was *the event* of her life, the happening which had lifted her from the deathlike drudgery of housework, and as she talked of it her eyes as-sumed the lambency of passion.

Telling her tale took some time; and because I so ad-mirably forbore, she felt the least she could do in return was listen to Mr. Blue's sales arguments. Though I was cer-tain she wasn't going to buy any siding, I thought it would give him respite from the sappy sadism of his *True Detective* and a chance to stretch his legs. I thought, too, that in his penetrating blue eyes I might for a moment appear a more adroit partner than I was. As she was only doing it as a favor to me, I shouldn't have wasted Mr. Blue's time; his confrontation with her was to turn into a nasty business anyway, and I mention it now by way of suggesting that in the four days I worked for Mr. Blue I didn't get him into any other house. I wasn't a good canvasser.

Over the days passed in the apartment Mr. Blue had hortatively acted out the techniques for getting into a house; and though I had attentively, not to say *raptly*, watched these memorable performances, all Mr. Blue's methods seemed to me too canny and frenzied. Within me I retained an ingenuous purity of heart that didn't allow me to believe that Madison Avenue had so dunned the American buyer that to sell him necessitates pounding him on the top of his beleaguered dome, sticking thumbs into his eyeballs, and kicking him in the groin. Moreover, my hair was still black, my figure svelte (well, almost svelte), my eyes didn't yet reflect the soul's discontent, and as Mr. Blue had so often implied, I believed a demure, college-boy approach would serve me best. I rang the doorbell, nervously hummed, tapped my foot, and cleared my throat while waiting; heard eager footfalls; amiably watched doors open on abruptly hostile and suspicious eyes; smiled my good-guy, strictly aboveboard smile; and brimmingly announced, "I'm selling aluminum siding!" *"Donwanannny,"* the customer said. "Okay," I said, and walked jauntily off the porch. To the next house I traversed wide lawns fraught with familiar though forbidding obstacles: accursed canines and their shoe-fouling droppings, overturned tricycles, catchers' mitts, unseen croquet wickets, and lawn sprayers forming whiplike, penetrating, and devilishly unpredictable patterns. At the next house I said, "I'm selling aluminum siding!" *"Donwananny,"* the customer said. "Okay," I said, and walked somewhat less spiritedly off the porch.

By the start of the fourth day both Mr. Blue and I knew that as a door-to-door man I was ruinously lackadaisical, a problem of Sisyphean knottiness; but as we were having such an exhilarating time, we avoided saying as much. Daily we knocked off at one o'clock, went to a saloon for what was supposed to be a hurriedly gulped cheeseburger, and remained there the rest of the afternoon, drinking. Moose's or O'Reilly's or Big John's, these were neighborhood bars consisting of imitation paneling, gallon jars of emetic, red-dyed pickled sausages, and quaint sayings and tenth-rate prizefighters Scotch-taped to the mirror of the back bar: "YOU DON'T HAVE TO BE CRAZY TO WORK HERE, BUT IT HELPS" and "Good luck to Big John, a real swell guy, from his old pal, Slugger," whose glossy print indicated he had taken more slugs than given. Invariably from some nook in the room a life-sized, cardboard, and Technicolored waitress named Mabel winked forever lasciviously and invited one to shout, "Hey, Mabel," and demand a bottle of Black Label. From me, whenever possible, Mabel got ink-serrated upper teeth; a Mischa Auer mustache; and, enclosed in a hastily penned cartoonist's balloon, a gratuitous piece of graffito: "Norman Mailer is a straight lay," "Naughty Hester Prynne fornicated," or simply, "Support Smut!"

Whenever we entered Moose's or O'Reilly's or Big John's, said proprietor, along with his beer-abstracted clientele of pallid, swing-shift factory workers, sallow-faced, obese whores, purblind welfare recipients, and toothless, wheezing old men, was distracted momentarily from the television to stare at us with that distaste the inhabitant of cockneydom reserves for the peerage. If he meant to intimidate us, he didn't know Mr. Blue. The proprietor, for his rude stare, got from him an enthusiastic, up-from-the-belly belch; a theatrical, hip-wriggling stretch; an oh-me-oh-my yawn; an unctuous, affectionate scratching of his balls; and a "You got any food in this dump?" Not even Big John ever challenged such brashness.

Mr. Blue professed neither to drink nor to smoke, but he did both. He didn't drink a great deal. Each day he said he'd have one I. W. Harper on the rocks to toast what was certain to be his most remunerative collaboration to date; but he always ended by having six or seven, by which time he was tipsy, garrulous, and profane, and attempting to regale the bar's patrons by doing handsprings or front- and back-flips up and down the aisle of the barroom. Watching a nectareously obsequious or cretinously eye-rolling announcer on the television, the patrons were not regaled; they didn't even look at Mr. Blue. In the dreary cosmos of those saloons it was as though there were operating a tacit though inviolable interdiction that prevented the patrons viewing anything genuinely remarkable—for that matter, anything alive. Druggedly watching the television and dopily chuckling on cue, they waited clockwork-wise for the swing shift, dreamed of being wealthy satyrs, fingered the quarters the state had given them, and wheezingly gummed their cigars. Knowing what effort Mr. Blue was expending to please them, I used to indulge a rage at their heavy-skulled indifference. Whenever Mr. Blue was engaged in his gymnastics, I quelled an urge to shout, "Hey, you guys—*look at this! Look at Mr. Blue!*" I quelled the urge because I hadn't faith in my ability to resurrect the dead.

Unlike the cigarette panderers who reluctantly allow that smoking *may be hazardous* to one's health, Mr. Blue didn't equivocate. *"Cigarettes,"* he said, *"will kill you fucking dead."* By the second drink, though, he'd have lighted one, and from that point on he chain-smoked and coughed. Caressing the illusion that an addiction must cost cash, he never bought any cigarettes; and for that reason I developed the habit, whenever I went to the cigarette machine, of buying two packs of Chesterfields, opening them both, and sliding them between us on the bar so Mr. Blue could permit himself the luxury of believing he was only occasionally filching one from me.

With the enthusiasm of a too-long-dormant guru, there always came a time during these afternoons when Mr. Blue felt the need to instruct me in still another method for getting into a house, and each method proved more beguilingly ludicrous than the last. Now that I was in the racket, though, I couldn't laugh and had to sit, a dutiful student, on the edge of my barstool, my hands folded primly on my lap, nodding very solemnly. Most of the time Mr. Blue reverted to his oratorio, calling up some crackpot dream of sales that he foisted off on me as historically authentic. Once, for example, he had been "way the hell up and gone" on some country road and had come across an isolated farmhouse. "A real dump," Mr. Blue assured me. Having gone without a sale for weeks, and broke, Mr. Blue had decided, "What the fuck." A tall, wiry farmer had answered the door. Mr. Blue "did" him for me. Hypnotically bulging his eyes, working his Adam's apple, tortuously compressing his lips, letting his arms go lax at his sides, and thrusting his bony wrists far below his shirt cuffs, Mr. Blue became an American Gothic. Humorless, stoic, crab-featured, prairie dust on his shoulders, cow dung on his gaiters, he allowed in an imitatively toneless drawl that he did indeed want something. "I want some of them redwood storm windows," he said. Mr. Blue, who sold aluminum storm windows, became Mr. Blue again, tacky, coy, cunning, persuasive. "You don't want those," he lied to the farmer. "They cost a hundred and twenty dollars apiece. Now, aluminum—" Abruptly all Adam's apple and horny hands and toneless drawl, Mr. Blue was the farmer again, interrupting. "I didn't ask how much they cost. I said I wanted some of them redwood storm windows." Striking a dumfounded stance for my present edification, Mr. Blue rolled his eyes with that mock wildness by which one conveys to a third party he's aware he's dealing with a blubbering lunatic. Shrugging, Mr. Blue decided to challenge the "old fart." "Just how the hell yuh gonna pay for *some of them* redwood storm windows?" he asked. In his voice there was a subdued irony; but, always the salesman, he put the question pleasingly enough. "Cash, son," the farmer replied. *"The way I pay for everything I buy."* Thereupon the farmer removed from his pocket, if Mr. Blue's globed hands can be credited, a roll of bills as big as a grapefruit. Breathlessly—oh, swooningly—grabbing the tape measure he carried in his inside jacket pocket, Mr. Blue now ran from window to window of the bar, showing me with what antic dexterity, with what accelerated and unspeakable passion he had run about the house measuring and counting the farmer's windows. One, his silently upthrust forefinger counted for me, two, three, then five, now ten, now the backs of both his hands flashed twice in rapid succession. *"Twenty?"* I cried in gleeful admiration. Still silent, Mr. Blue shook his head dramatically and emphatically *no*, and with equal gravity held up yet another finger. *"Twenty-one?"* I shouted. With a curt nod Mr. Blue gave me a precise *yes. Even so.* That I might savor the extent of his triumph, he now walked silently and slowly back to the bar and stood haughtily beside me, his chest expanded with cosmological serenity. "Twenty-one goddam windows in that dump," he said finally, shaking his yellowing head in heavy and exaggerated disbelief. Having driven furiously back to the city, he had bought the windows for eight dollars apiece, had charged the farmer the quoted price of a hundred and twenty dollars, had been paid in hundred-dollar bills, and had netted twenty-three hundred and fifty-two dollars. "More than the whole fucking house was worth!" Majestic with self-approval, Mr. Blue added, "That was the winter I spent in the Yucatán."

"The Yucatán?" I cried; but before I could say, "Aw, now listen here, Mr. Blue, you come off that nonsense, will yuh?" he was off and running.

Unnecessarily explaining, "It's a peninsula in Mexico," he said, "Broke one minute, in *Ol' Mayheeco* the next. That's the way it is in this business. Usually I spent my winters in Acapulco, but this time I wanted to go someplace they never heard of aluminum siding." He sighed. "Trouble was," he said, "those fucking Indians in the Yucatán never heard of nothin' but donkey shit and beans." He smiled ruefully, heavy with life's melancholy. But in the soothing memory of that sale, real or imagined, he couldn't sustain his gloom and presently was embarked on a series of drunken handsprings down the middle of the barroom. Completing the arc of the fifth one, Mr. Blue lost control of his legs, and the long, effeminate heel of his alligator shoe caught the corner of a table, toppling a glass of beer from it onto the lap of a pursy, perennially weeping whore. Not only volunteering to have the dress cleaned, Mr. Blue ended by giving the woman fifteen dollars for a new one. Rendered munificent by the memory of that long-ago coup, Mr. Blue then bought drinks for the bar. "On me, fellows!" he shouted. "On me! Drink hearty! God bless you! Cheers!" But no one turned round to thank him, or even took his eyes from the television. "Oh, Jesus, Freddy," he said fondly, *"those* were the days."

"I'll bet," I said. And I was quite unable to be derisive, and against my better judgment found myself caught up in Mr. Blue's faulty but enthusiastic reminiscences.

The farmer, Mr. Blue said, was what is known in the trade as a *gopher.*

"A gopher?"

"Yeah! *Go fer* anything," Mr. Blue bellowed, and thereupon, with hyperbolic tenderness, he laid his yellowing head against my breast and, spaniel-like, coquettishly rolled his big blue eyes up to look into mine. "Cut the shit, will yuh, Mr. Blue?" I said. Owning the charm of legendary charlatans, Mr. Blue had an intuitive sense that though I didn't believe a word he said, I much preferred listening to him to listening to Mr. Bert Parks.

—

I am now faced with the uncomfortable chore of recording something of Mr. Blue's sexual fixation, about which I perhaps know a good deal less than I imagine. I was almost certain that though he longed to kiss the female pudendum, he had never done so. In retrospect I recall his conversations as little more than formal, Oriental bridges joining islands lush with *that,* the inevitable subject. Obsessed with the vision of his hoary, aging head dipped down between golden thighs, and the disturbing notion of translating that thought into action, Mr. Blue had become maniacally purposeful, his eyes so narrowly focused as to be crossed. Like a *jeune homme féroce* of the arts caught up by and spouting some *soi-disant* aesthetic salvation in a Parisian bistro, he was pushy, distasteful, immoderate, and megalomaniac; and like the latter he seemed to believe that once articulated his vision would open doors to paradisial princedoms. What continually preyed on me, what quite wearied my feeble brain with perplexity, was what exactly Mr. Blue hoped to gain by kissing a cunt.

That I might not panic and flee in terror, Mr. Blue led me gingerly into his madness, though he did so with a certain disarming vulgarity. The first day I talked with him he interrupted a conversation I imagined to be proceeding at a genial and exemplary clip and shouted, "They tell me if you get by the smell, you got it licked!" "Pardon?" I said, taken aback by a curious irrationality in his voice. "You heard me," he said saucily; then he smiled challengingly at me, as though to remind me that I shouldn't take him for a fool and that he knew all about guys like me. I laughed uneasily. What else could I then do but admit that if one got by the smell, one did indeed have it licked?

It was when I detected that Mr. Blue wanted a good deal more than a yes-man and was passionately seeking technical expertise that I grew nervous. Within two days he had interrupted an involved explanation I was making of the New York Giants' umbrella defense to shout, "How do you get by the smell?" "Pardon?" I said (with Mr. Blue I said "pardon" quite a bit). "You heard me," he said. "How do you get by the smell?" With strident purposefulness he narrowed his blue eyes on me. "How the hell would I know?" I said. "Hold your breath, I guess." I giggled self-consciously. Such levity appeared to displease Mr. Blue, and when it did so, I grew somewhat impatient. "Well, for Christ's sake," I said. "It doesn't have to smell, you know." Then I essayed a detailed, admirably wrought, and charming little talk on the art of douching, and the powders, lotions, perfumes, and so forth that were available to render *la petite pussé* as aromatic and palatable as a toasted marshmallow. Despite the "artistry" of my monologue, Mr. Blue pretended he would have none of it; and all the time I talked he paced the floor, his hands jammed deep down into his jacket pockets, fiercely sucking in his feline cheeks and then blowing out—*ppttoooooeeeee,* as though, toasted marshmallow or no, even the thought of such "perversities" (as though I were suggesting them!) was more than he could endure and forcing him to emit a furious spit: *ppttoooooeeeee.* Whenever he did that, I'd giggle like a damn fool; and to show me that his displeasure was less than intransigent, Mr. Blue would giggle, too, tentatively. Then he'd compound my bewilderment by staring at me as if I were the ultimate heresiarch.

Whenever Mr. Blue and I spoke of cunnilingus, and within three days I was aware that Mr. Blue wanted to speak of little else, we found ourselves giggling with a peculiar, naughty-boy relief. By chance I once found myself at a summer camp next to that of a lovely girl of seventeen who, having just graduated from high school, was preparing to enter the university in the fall. Though I had never before met her, I knew her parents. They were a very even, almost sane, couple who went to church Sundays, who thought Richard Nixon an admirable man, and who would have had one sign a promissory note against a five-dollar loan. Nothing was wrong with them save that they were damnably hung up on all sorts of banalities, orthodoxies, and affectations they imagined had something to do with life; and thus one day on the diving float in front of their camp I was astonished, as even recalling it today I still am astonished, to find myself teaching the daughter to measure off a chunk of her arm and enunciate *fungoo*. Explaining that she had seen the fellows on the high school football team do it, she asked me what it meant, I told her, and she tried it herself a number of times—*fun-goo, FUN-goo, fun-GOO*—becoming moderately adept at it. Before I fully realized what was happening, at her own insistence, though abetted by my coaching, she was mouthing all sorts of obscenities—mouthing them between waving gaily to her Mom who sat some distance off on a lawn chair knitting a red wool sweater to keep her baby warm at the university.

Never was there any thought of sex between the girl and myself; and I slowly, rather amazedly, came to understand that the girl had been drowning in an unhealthy finickiness of atmosphere and that what she was so touchingly striving to do was pulverize the mystery from the forbidden words: *fuck* and *suck* and *cunt* and *prick* and *cocksucker*. Wanting no longer to be repulsively enthralled or struck tongue-tied in the face of the moronic graffiti scribbled on bridge abutments and toilet walls, she desperately yearned to come to an intimacy with forbidden things and thereby negotiate terms with a whole segment of life which had only recently begun opening to her. Not only did she want to learn to measure off her arm (she never got the hang of that, a man's gesture apparently) and bellow *fungoo*, but she insisted that I coach her in offhandedly dropping expressions like "Up yours" and "Suck a big dick." Nor did I have any compunctions about such coaching or fear lest she corrupt her freshman dormitory when she arrived all fresh-faced and filthy-tongued at the college, knowing that once she could casually and carelessly throw away such ribaldries, for her they would never hold trepidation again, would cease to mean anything.

Thus it was, too, that when I thought she had handled an "Up yours" with a particularly easy sophistication, I became very schoolmarmish and complimented her. What joy my praises gave her! To them she'd bound up on the raft, stretch out her arms as though in free flight, and in her bikini do wild, sharp-stepping jigs about the edge of the rocking float, all the time exclaiming, "No kidding? Did I really do good?" Then she'd wave gaily to Mom, who would wave gaily back and continue stabbing her needles into the embryo sweater. When, with an emphatic *really*, I'd assure her that she was becoming an authentic debauchee, she'd lower herself slowly back to the canvas of the float, lie face down next to me, fall silent, and become excessively self-absorbed. Then quite suddenly she'd begin giggling with that peculiar relief, the relief at inimical things being rendered familiar.

And though Mr. Blue giggled, he proved, unlike the girl, a hard, intractable pupil. He had made of cunnilingus a shibboleth of Chinese Wall proportions, and his giggling appeared to me little more than an attempt to raze that wall with switches. Despite his absorption with the idea, within him he harbored some fixed and enduring hostility to acting upon it, and for that reason he was quite helpless to unclutter his mind of the fascination it held for him. When he was embarked on the subject, I often shouted, "Peace—oh, Mr. Blue, give me peace!" Never did it occur to him that such activity was a way of giving a woman pleasure or of paying adoring homage to the very special sweets of her gender; instead, Mr. Blue was hypnotized by the ambivalent notion that such oral endearments would either defile him utterly or unlock the gates to Rosicrucian insights. Just how nutty Mr. Blue was on the subject didn't become totally apparent to me until the fourth and last day I worked for him, when I took him to see the deaf woman.

At an oppressively fastidious dinner I once said, "Pass the fucking butter," putting the emphasis on the obscenity so that my host wouldn't be rattled by doubts and would thereby be unmistakably offered the alternative of knocking me down or, subject to his sense of the decencies, at least exiling me from his table. What distressed and finally enraged me about Mr. Blue's approach to the woman was that she apparently had no such alternative. No sooner did Mr. Blue convince himself of the genuineness of her deafness than he began—the grand legs, the appetizing breasts, and the soiled peignoir must so have conspired to complete his fantasy of the archetypical housewife that the temptation proved irresistible—mouthing aloud all sorts of scabrous suggestions related to his fixation.

Like Seedy, my predecessor from the long-ago, carrying the great portfolio case, I had led Mr. Blue up the sidewalk, with the aid of the pad had made the introductions, and we were now seated about the indigo table with the portfolio case open displaying colored aluminum samples mounted in the interior of its topside. A paragraph at a time, Mr. Blue dictated his closing arguments to me, and after writing them down I passed them on to the woman to read. Like Khrushchev dictating to his translator, Mr. Blue sat there unswervable, somewhat magnificent. As he dictated, the unhearing woman, impressed with having the "Alcoa man" in her house, smiled respectfully and diffidently at him; and as I (and as Khrushchev's translator was once or twice said to have done) edited his nonsensical spiel onto the pad, she turned and smiled considerably more easily at me. All this time, and while she was reading what I had written, Mr. Blue let loose, enunciating very distinctly, a torrent of four-letter words. Twice I turned to him and said, "Shut your fucking mouth," but he only winked, implying that I must of course be joking. Not only hadn't the woman the alternative of slapping Mr. Blue's face; she had waxed so enthusiastic over the color samples that I thought we might actually be making a sale and that, acting as he was, Mr. Blue was going to scuttle that sale. When she was reading perhaps the dozenth paragraph I'd prepared, and Mr. Blue was glibly mouthing his latrine chatter, the ordeal reached an unexpected and jarring climax. Detecting that the woman's cheeks had risen to a high and incendiary red, I recalled the doctors' pathological prognoses and, my body going instantaneously rigid as a pipe, I thought, "My God, she's hearing us!" Was it possible? And immediately I thought, "Yes—it is possible!" Behind a "deaf" middle-class housewife one might drop cherry bombs or smash inflated paper sacks to no avail, but what if one crept up stealthily and over her right shoulder whispered, "How'd you like a prick stuck right in your left eyeball?" But of course she was hearing him! Jumping abruptly and wildly up, I slammed the portfolio case shut, snapped its fasteners, picked it up, and dashed into the dining room headed for the front door. Just before going through it, I heard Mr. Blue's voice: "Hey, what the—" Then I was going down the steps, hurrying across the lawn toward the Cadillac.

Excessively silent, perplexed and brooding, for perhaps half an hour Mr. Blue wove the Cadillac round and round among the blocks in the neighborhood before, my anger finally abating, I turned on him, intent on saying dreadful things. *"The Yucatán, huh!"* I was going to say. "Why, you've never been out of this crumby city. Not only that, you're crazy to boot! A proper loony! If you're going to eat a snatch, eat one! But for lord's sake, shut your bloody yap about it! You're turning me into a spluttering idiot! *An eeeed-yuuhhht!"* It was going to be a superb piece of venom, it was! As though it were all in some way his fault, I was even plotting ways to tell the Counselor off. Before he got a chance to roll his eyes about, dribble his tongue over his chin, rap me tentatively on the skull, and calmly say, "Straight-shooter, it is, I think, about time you went away again," it would be necessary to disarm the Counselor. Creeping up behind him, I'd just start screaming, "I'm the one who's supposed to be nuts!" Perhaps here I'd pound myself dramatically on the chest. "I'm the one who's been locked up! But everyone who comes to this fruity apartment is nuttier than I am! Absolute, unequivocal lunatics!" "By God," I thought, "all those madmen will get a real dressing down; sheer murder, they'll see a real paranoiac in action! Ha!"

Ha indeed; for when I turned and looked at Mr. Blue, I found that I couldn't even begin on him. Sheepish and saddened by my fury, he hadn't said a word in the half-hour we had driven around and had sat there hunched over the Cadillac's wheel, just a runt whose legs barely reached the brake pedal, an earthenware dwarf. He was dirty, hot-browed and weary, old—*old*. About him there had always been this lapse of personal care intimating slummy origins: if his shoes were shined, his collar was dirty; if he wore a spanking-new tie, his soiled, three-day socks cascaded over his shoe tops. As a "factory representative" he had never been able, so to speak, to put it all together at one time and make himself convincing. On this day the brow and the face were sweaty with fatigue, the fingernails and hands smudged with dirt, the shirt and collar wrinkled and stained, the pants oil-flecked and unpressed, the shoes turned-over and scuffed, the nostrils and ears gardens for unseemly hairs—everything was wrong. Moreover, studying him I was suddenly sure that it wasn't so much a princely neglect of person as a thing ingrained. He exuded tenement beginnings, an aura of dark and oppressive places, rat-filled infancy, Saturday-night baths, underwear fouled with three days' sweat and intimate body dirts; and I knew, too, that that *ppttoooooeeeee* wasn't so much a hyperbolically farcical gesture as an unavoidable one. Rising up from such dreary places, it was little wonder he couldn't accept the labia as a proper altar at which to place one's murmuring devotions. And, as I have suggested, worse for me than anything was how old he suddenly seemed, perhaps even seventy! For all his youth-seeking exercises, his arms looked infinitely frail, the ancient muscles falling prunishly away from the humerus. The femurs of his stubby legs showed so fleshlessly prominent and sticklike through his unpressed trousers that I wondered if the flesh of that other, that "poignant bone," hadn't shriveled, too, wondered if his oral fixation wasn't sublimation for the irremediable impotence of age. I almost asked, "Can you still get it up, Mr. Blue?" But I didn't. Then I almost demanded, "How old are you *really*, Mr. Blue?" But in the same way I was unable to sustain a need to vent spleen, watching him hunched up over the wheel of the Cadillac that was too big for him, so unkempt and so giving off his harsh beginnings, I couldn't say anything finally.

Nor did it make any difference. One o'clock, it was time to go to Moose's or O'Reilly's or Big John's for "lunch." Doubtless motivated by the tacit knowledge that our partnership was dissolved, we remained in the bar for seven hours that day and got very drunk. Despairing that I'd ever get him into any houses, Mr. Blue had increasingly given his tales over to dreams of sales; and that final day proved the one he related the barmy nonsense about the farmer's storm windows and gave the whore fifteen dollars for her dress. Since he spent perhaps fifty dollars that day, I must say that Mr. Blue was a prince when parting with dough. When by eight o'clock I had drunk myself sober, I found that I still had four, ice-melted highballs in front of me, and that Mr. Blue was passed out with his head face down in the sour booze of a table behind me. Knowing that I'd somehow have to get him home, I told the bartender to take away the drinks, ordered a cup of coffee, and removed the Cadillac's keys from Mr. Blue's clasped hand laid out before his head on the table.

—

When I met Mr. Blue's common-law spouse, the *U.S.S. Deborah,* I understood the ultimate reason why he approached cunnilingus with such single-minded and fastidious wariness. In high school we had had a math teacher, a great wide, jolly soul under whose thunderous stride the creaky halls had trembled ominously and who, by one of those brilliantly cruel strokes to which adolescents are given, had been dubbed (to endure forever, luckless lady!) the *U.S.S. Clarabelle.* No sooner had I cast a blurry eye on Deborah than I made a mental note, should I ever by chance find myself chatting with one of her pupils (for Deborah was a teacher, too), to test the nickname on him—"*Oh, so you have the* U.S.S. Deborah?"—that I might determine how the naughty humor of my ingenuous generation held up with present-day sophisticates.

Bit by bit Mr. Blue had revealed his domestic situation to me. For two years he had been "shacked up" with a schoolteacher. Occupying adjoining apartments, they had begun by sharing their meals, he had gradually found his way into her bed, his clothes had found their way into her closet, his razor into her medicine cabinet; and though, for the sake of Deborah's reputation, he still paid the rent on his own apartment, they were for all practical purposes "hitched." "A great girl," Mr. Blue had said. "A little on the tall side."

Deborah, a girls' gymnasium teacher, was indeed "a little on the tall side": six feet, one. With a Sapphic coiffure approaching a brush cut, shoulders that wouldn't have gone unremarked in the Giants' shower room, from earth to sky she was caparisoned in dirty tennis sneakers, navy-blue gymnasium trousers striped down the sides with white, a maroon sweatshirt bearing, of all things, the legend *Property of USC* in gilt lettering, a corded whistle hanging about her formidably bemuscled neck, and a black baseball cap mounted with the New York Yankees' emblem, *NY.* As other women exude the musky, arousing aromas of lilac powders and lavender perfumes, Deborah gave off an aura of rubbing alcohol, athlete's-foot powder, and sweaty athletic supporters; nor should I have been surprised to discover that she was the Olympic champion hammer thrower from the Soviet Union, now defected to the West. Even above the astonishment her over-all presence inspired—

and at first look I had christened her the *U.S.S. Deborah*—one thing glared out at one: her imposingly blocklike jaw was as blue as an adman's dream. In the hour I passed in the apartment, and whenever I could do so with impunity, I gave that jaw a most scrupulous going over; and though, amazingly, nothing like a beard revealed itself, her jaw was, notwithstanding, a brilliant and utterly disarming blue. So blue was it that I continually conjured an image of Deborah facing the television camera, her gymnasium-trousered right leg propped up on a locker-room bench, her forearms resting comfy on the thigh of that upraised leg. A voice off camera earnestly inquired, "Deborah, what does it *really* take to make a good defensive tackle in the National Football League?" Deborah smiled modestly, a hole opened in that striking blue jaw, and she mumbled, "Speed. Tenacity. Timing. An ability to get the job done!" Presently she was holding up to the camera a can of Alpo (no, that's dog food, isn't it?), she was holding up to the camera a can of Jet-Shave and inviting the incredulous viewer to share an analogy between flattening Jimmy Brown and disposing of his morning chin hairs. Deborah had a big blue jaw.

When Mr. Blue and I had first entered the apartment and had gone into the kitchen, where Deborah was washing dishes and angrily clanging knives and forks into the silverware cup of the strainer, and I had got my first open-mouthed look at her, I believed I was in for a gay evening, thinking that here was a girl who had unquestionably cultivated a sense of humor about herself. On the sidewalk in front of the apartment house, a bewildered (I had difficulty in convincing him that he was home, and that I had driven him there), word-slurring Mr. Blue had led me to expect as much, insisting that I come up for a drink, a laugh, and an introduction to the little woman, rather ominously implying that unless I did so he wouldn't give me cab fare back to the Counselor's apartment, at the opposite side of the city. Meeting the little woman was not what Mr. Blue had in mind. Gaiety was not one of Deborah's more evident hues, and what Mr. Blue wanted, I now know, was for me to provide him immunity from a good physical thrashing.

No sooner did Deborah look at him than she shrieked, "You've been drinking!" Alas, this was true: Mr. Blue was wet- and red-eyed, staggering and belching drunk. Yet, as most wives are willing to do, I thought Deborah might have given him a chance to protest his innocence. Mr. Blue attempted as much. Staggering toward her at the sink— apologetically muttering, "Ah hon, ah hon, ah hon"—as he went, he tried to put his arms about her thirty-two-inch waist, and affectionately rest the cup of his right ear on the nipple of her massive left breast (he didn't even have to bend down!), right at the lower curl of the *C* of *USC*. But he never completely made it. Heatedly casting him off when his ear was within an inch or so of the teat, she cried, "And you've been smoking, too!" For the first time she wheeled and sniffed accusingly in my direction. I started to quake. Though it was spineless of me, I wasn't about to be disputatious with the *U.S.S. Deborah* and found myself self-righteously nodding my head in vigorous assent to her steamy indignation. "Drunker than a coot and smoking like a fiend," that nodding agreed. Compounding my treachery, I sighed dramatically, shrugged my shoulders, and, palms upward, threw my hands out from my sides, as though to add, "I've done all I can for the little bugger, but he utterly refuses to help himself!" "Your supper's been in the icebox for hours," Deborah sneered. "Get in the living room, *you little weasel,* and I'll bring it to you."

Moaning "ah hon" and something about being embarrassed in front of "mah guest," neither of which amounted to a glimmer of real protest, Mr. Blue resignedly turned and, head weighed down with heavy and burning humiliation, staggered through the door into the living room. Still quaking, I fled right at his elevated heels.

Mr. Blue and I sat on the davenport, and Deborah sat in an easy chair facing us, her blue-trousered legs crossed, displaying through the pants the long, bulging thigh of her topside or right leg. On her lap she held an open book, *From Here to Eternity,* which she feigned reading, occasionally looking up to allow the hole in her blue jaw to open and whistlingly sneer something in Mr. Blue's direction. On a snowy china plate on the coffee table before Mr. Blue sat his supper, at which he nibbled grudgingly, almost painfully; and on the table before me sat a bourbon and water whose single ice cube had long since melted and which, between bright smiles, I brought to my lips for minuscule sips, biding my time until I could get the "little weasel" aside and extract the promised cab fare from him. Having offered me some supper, which with the most brimming thanks I had declined, Deborah had informed me that though Mr. Blue and she didn't drink, *she* wasn't so boorish as not to be aware of her guests' needs and kept liquor in *her* apartment for them. Looking with homicidal intent at Mr. Blue, she had added, "Locked up!" Beginning her explanation with *"Mr. Blue—Ha! Ha! Ha! Ha! Ha!—*and I don't drink," she had ended it by drifting into a rowdy and demented hysteria which made me wonder if she weren't a bit tetched, and which made me quake all the more. But I kept gritting my teeth and maintained my cheery, near-Mongoloid smile; Mr. Blue continued his painful nibbling; the hole kept forming itself and sneering, *"Not so much salt*—it's bad for your kidneys"; and Mr. Blue kept offering something like a protest: *"Ah hon."*

My sanguinity was not altogether rigged. In front of Mr. Blue sat a twelve-ounce glass of what I had taken to be orange juice but which Mr. Blue had informed me—by prodding my elbow, distastefully wrinkling his nose, and drunkenly whispering—was *carrot juice,* a slander that didn't go unremarked by Deborah, and which elicited from her a battery of triumphant *Ha's!* Apparently a "health" dinner, the rest of the meal consisted of a dozen hard-boiled eggs, a half-dozen celery sticks about a foot long, a couple pounds of sliced raw tomatoes, a half raw cabbage diced into almost edible squares, and a mountain of something I couldn't distinguish but which may have been cold pickled cauliflower. Smiling amiably, I was thinking I might have accepted something to eat.

Another reason for my jolliness was a fantasy I had been indulging inspired by the *U.S.S. Deborah's* library, the volumes of which filled a small, white-enameled bookcase directly facing me, set to the left of and against the wall behind Deborah's easy chair. Though Deborah was of an indeterminate age between thirty and forty, I wasn't surprised to see that she had kept her college texts, *Adolescent Psychology, Living Religions of the World, Philosophy of Education,* and the inevitable Margaret Mead, those symbols that she had suffered exposure to loftier things and by such exposure had become a sanctimonious and blubbering ninny. What did surprise me was the dozen or so novels, ranging in time from *Moby Dick* daringly down to the fairly recent

All the King's Men, books which indubitably represented the "required reading" for a course in "The American Novel."

Other than the text and the novels a good part of Deborah's library consisted of books designed to titillate the sweat glands, books on mountain climbing, speed walking, water treading, muscle toning, gum massaging, and dumbbell lifting. By far the larger part of it, though, was given over to volumes Deborah had undoubtedly accumulated since her virginal and unmourned departure from the university (had it really been my alma mater?), *Successful Love, Love in Marriage, Pride of Orgasm, Blissful Bunkmates, Sunniness in the Boudoir,* that kind of thing, volumes which in the jarringly aseptic prose of the Ph.D.'s are given over to naughty erotic nuances and which, still seeing no way of getting an egg-munching Mr. Blue aside, led me easily into still further fantasy, this time envisioning the *U.S.S. Deborah* and Mr. Blue abed together.

His runty, agingly muscular and naked body curled up fetus-like to one side of the bed, Mr. Blue was lying elfin-like with his snowy head resting atop his pillowed hands, his eyelids blistered fiercely to his eyeballs in a frenziedly feigned sleep. Next to him, propped stolidly against both the bed's pillows, sat the imposing, block-jawed Deborah loudly reading aloud. From the waist upward she still wore her *Property of USC* sweatshirt, and from the waist downward, under the commonsensical plain white linen sheets, she was naked, too, the muscles and glands tingling, poised, anticipatory. Knowing that Mr. Blue was not asleep, she read, as I say, loudly. "To make oral contact with the female clitoris—" Here I paused. Why, I wondered, did they always say *female* clitoris? What was the *male* clitoris? "To make oral contact with the female clitoris one should gently insert his thumb and index finger—" *Finger*, I thought, would never do; there was something egregiously sordid about the thought of fingers, something that in such a tome would smack of the untidily human. Throughout all of this, incidentally, my brimming smile, turned back and forth between a chomping Mr. Blue and a sneering Deborah, never left my face, an equable façade that might have been housing angelic visions. "—one should gently insert the thumb and index member—" but wasn't *gently* rather too suggestive?—"of either hand (depending on whether one is right- or left-handed) into the vaginal area and, much as a gynecologist uses his surgical tongs to distend the labia in a pelvic examination—" At this point in my fantasy I saw Mr. Blue's body tense, his eyelids became glued even more fiercely to his eyeballs, and I laughed with sibilant heartiness as he issued a half-dozen histrionic snores charged with the whistling tremors of deep sleep, his body shuddering with intimations of inviolable and innocent dreams.

"Ask Freddy!" Mr. Blue was suddenly and irascibly demanding of Deborah. "Ask Freddy!" Whatever prompted the argument I was meant to settle had pushed Mr. Blue round the bend. He was on his feet, his body stricken with rage, his nose thrust out with the defiance of a boar's snout. In the face of Deborah's stolid sneer, such defiance seemed to warrant medals. Whatever had caused it, Deborah had this time pushed Mr. Blue too far. Choking back angry tears, Mr. Blue again demanded, "Ask Freddy!"

"Ask me what?" I said good-naturedly, having by now risen completely from my reverie.

"She says I never exercise any more!" Mr. Blue's face was

livid with the pain of false accusations. "Tell her! Tell her, Freddy!"

"Well," I hemmed, still possessed of an aversion for disputing with Deborah. "He exercises quite a bit. Front flips, back flips, hand-springs, push-ups, that kind of thing." Deborah's fiery eyes were flashing hate in my direction. "Between drinks, of course," I hastily added, and chuckled amiably at my own cowardice.

My treachery proved more at the moment than an enraged Mr. Blue could endure; and before either Deborah or I could prevent him, and intent on showing us both, he had placed his hands on the narrow wooden spine atop the davenport's back and with a barely perceptible effort had pulled himself up on it, amazingly ending in a beautiful, perfectly back-arched handstand, his white hands pinched a fierce red by the sharp wooden edges of the one-inch spine. Standing thus, he turned his upside-down head— furred tongue, nostril hairs, and inverted eyebags—in Deborah's direction and, adopting her sneering tone, challenged her. "You never could do this!" Thereupon, slow hand over slow hand, and with his back always perfectly arched, he began a splendid handwalk down the davenport's painful spine. He almost made it, too. He had got almost to the end of the davenport, his breathing excessively labored, when he stalled, tottered very slightly, then fell.

Falling very rapidly and straight down, *whissshhh* and *carruuummp,* he broke his nose on the davenport's spine; no sooner had he come to a face-up rest on the floor than the nose, already distended to cover a great area of his face, loosed a torrent of blood. Seeing it, Mr. Blue also loosed an effeminate, spine-chilling shriek. Guffawing and sneering her venom, Deborah cracked her thigh and walked round back of the davenport to where I already stood over him. Looking wildly up at us, Mr. Blue moaned, and then wept, not so much in pain, I thought, as at the humiliation of his aborted feat. Attempting to bring his right hand up to wipe away the blood and embarrassing tears, he got it only part way, gave it up, let it fall back to the carpet, and then closed his eyes, or rather his eyes closed. He had passed out cold. Disgustedly reaching down and placing her hands in Mr. Blue's armpits, Deborah raised him up to where she could prop him against her lowered thighs, got a firm grip on him, picked him up, threw him over her shoulder, carried him into the bedroom, and flung him on the bed. After that Deborah and I stood over him, while I wrung my hands and like a quack medico murmured clinical notions. Finally I offered what I thought an inspired remedy. "You think we ought to wash the blood off?" Deborah guffawed again. "To hell with his blood, *the little weasel!*" she cried, and thundered, floor creaking, out of the room.

Having washed him thoroughly with hot soapy towels, foolishly stuck three Band-Aids on his nose, stripped him, and tucked him in, I was putting his mussed and bloody clothes on hangers and hanging them in the closet when Deborah, having re-entered the room unseen, demanded to know what I was doing. Believing she had been for some time behind me and had seen me take from Mr. Blue's trousers the five-dollar bill for the cab, I smiled sheepishly and said, "It's just a loan till tomorrow—one Mr. Blue promised me for a taxi." With something quite else on her mind, she had no idea what I was talking about. *"Get him out of here,"* she said. "You *certainly* don't think he's going to stay here, do you?" I was standing there, open-mouthed with bewilderment, holding Mr. Blue's jacket on a hanger.

Quickly surveying the closet's contents, I confirmed a sudden doubt. Mr. Blue had—thank God!—told me the truth: his clothes were hanging there among Deborah's. "Aw, be reasonable," I said. "Your personal life's your own business. You don't think I'd say anything about—about all—" Here I nonchalantly wafted my arm over the closet's contents. Deborah was standing right beside me now, her jaw thrust furiously at me. "I don't care what that bastard told you! He doesn't stay here!" Snatching Mr. Blue's jacket from my hand, she threw it crazily to the floor. Thereupon she removed, item by item, all his clothes from the closet, flung them on top of the jacket, and started jumping insanely up and down on that mountain of Mr. Blue's wardrobe. When she finished, she was sweating profusely, her hands were settled in a posture of defiance on her hips, and her jaw was thrust even closer to me, as though to say, "How'd you like a little of the same?" Unable to resist it, and smiling as I did so, I threw my best punch. A sucker punch, it caught her flush on that monument of a blue jaw; and with nary a muffled syllable she went ever so slowly down and lay flat out, spread-eagled on the mattress of the bloodied clothing.

By the time I had reached the street, hailed a cab, and settled comfortably into the back seat, I found that I was whistling. In my sporadic and undistinguished pugilistic career over the years, the *U.S.S. Deborah* was my first kayo. And I was inordinately, whistlingly proud.

—

Mr. Blue's mysterious relationship with the Counselor turned out to be more mysterious than I had imagined: it was nonexistent. Though I was sure Mr. Blue wouldn't come for me the next day, I was equally certain, knowing what an appreciative audience I was, that after he'd found a new canvasser and got his business humming, he'd stop by to entertain me, perhaps even thank me for decking Deborah. But when a week had come and gone, and he still had neither appeared nor telephoned, I began to grow morose. For me Mr. Blue had become the real and vivid world, and the other habitués of the apartment merely penumbral, incorporeal dross. Worse, without his riotous stimulation, lying on the davenport, I began to detect that I was becoming perilously logy, not only incapable of a *jeu d'esprit* but in conversations unable to form syntactical or meaningful sentences. Rolling from my right to my left side in search of comfort, my bones crepitated like sticks under heavy boots. What little stimulation I had in those two weeks was provided by some cotton-mouthed, pause-punctuated, long-distance conversations to Scarsdale in which the girl with the roan-colored hair and I weighed the pros and cons of our possible marriage, rather timidly and anxiously finding in favor of the pros.

When at the end of two weeks Mr. Blue still hadn't appeared, and I thought that he'd surely be showing up to discuss his legal business with the Counselor, I one night asked the latter where "his" buddy was. "What do you mean *my* buddy?" the Counselor said. "I never saw the crazy man in my life till I saw him talking with you."

At first I thought he was joshing, but after repeated questioning it developed that he wasn't in the least, and this revelation led me to an attempted reconstruction of my first meeting with Mr. Blue. No matter my attempts to place him with Oscar or someone who could have brought him to the apartment, I couldn't erase the truth that one day I had wakened to find him standing over the davenport and we had begun talking. This in turn led me to the rather startling conclusion that Mr. Blue had simply wandered from the street into the apartment and into my life. Why this singular fact should have nonplused me so, I can't say; but it did upset me terribly; and in direct proportion to my dismay I found myself admiring the Counselor's character. So much more adaptive he was than I, so amenably courageous in leaving his door ajar for any who would enter, so chameleon in his ability to strike just the proper postures for the hand-wringing, grief-stricken lunatics who sought haven there; whereas I, no doubt already somewhat institutionalized, was fearful of life and wanted my universe regimented and at moral attention, my meals scheduled, my ball-points all in one jar, my acquaintances at my fingertips, and my door bolted against the grief-bearing intrusions of the world. "You're some sack of shit, aren't you?" I said affectionately. "Now, *what* do you mean by that?" the Counselor said. "Well," I said, "you might begin by telling me just who in the hell Mr. Blue *is?*" After pondering the question lengthily and with mock gravity, the Counselor said, "Well, straight-shooter, I don't honestly know. But it's a good question. It has a ringing but obvious alliteration. 'Who, who, *whooooo* is Mr. Blue?'" I laughed appreciatively, and the next day I phoned the party in Scarsdale and told her to expect me within a matter of days, not knowing when I talked with her that I'd see Mr. Blue again.

In a saloon I frequented with Oscar I had struck an acquaintance with a transplanted newsman from London, and it was while with him that I again saw Mr. Blue. A handsome, late-thirtyish, and much-decorated British Commando of World War II, the Englishman had after a hoodooed romance in London elected to "come give America a see" and had since his arrival here drifted from town to city, from copy desk to general assignment, "seeing" America through a jaundiced but forgiving eye. An able writer, in his clipped English he told me a wry tale about his longevity span on American newspapers. Sooner or later he found himself writing the paper's editorials, "all very solemn and indignant and bloody highfalutin," he remarked, and as long as he wrote these imprisoning the laughing man within him, he stayed on the job. When the day came (and like a bloody bowel movement, he said, it always came) that he discovered himself writing in incendiary tones about the need for a traffic light at the "corner of Myrtle Avenue and Shoshoni" (he reverenced and collected our Indian names) "Boulevard" and laughing aloud—roaring really, helpless to stay the tears streaming down his cheeks, all eyes in the city room cast apprehensively, somewhat amazedly, on him—he resigned in the interest of his "bloody sanity" and moved on to Wichita Falls—yearning, one gathered, so steadfastly for Fleet Street and room-temperature beer that one was always repressing an urge to ask why he didn't go home.

On hearing that I was going to Scarsdale to marry, he said, "I'll drive you," explaining he'd heard the Westchester countryside was reminiscent of England and that he longed to see it. And on a suffocating day in late spring, with the wistful Londoner driving his Thunderbird, undoubtedly ruing the wheel's being on the "wrong" side and buoyed up in the anticipated comfort of vistas of green places and hedgerows, we were driving through a suburb leading out of the city when my eye fell on Mr. Blue.

Portfolio case in hand, a sale in the offing, he was anxiously traversing a wide lawn toward a *fin de siècle* Victorian house, a three-story clapboard colossus of such proportions that a siding contract for it would have been a windfall of epic proportions. "Stop the car!" I said to the startled Englishman. "Stop the car!" Sticking my head out the window even as the Thunderbird was spluttering to the curb, I called, "Hey, Mr. Blue! Mr. Blue! It's me! Freddy!"

Under the furious momentum of his stride Mr. Blue halted waveringly, set the portfolio case down, straightened up to his full five feet, three, saluted me in the military manner, and with genuine affection called back, "Freddy!" He did not say any more, and I understood that with that massive house looming in the background he had precious little time for me and small talk. Still, I was immensely fond of the pussy-bedazzled old bastard, biases, bullshit, and all, and I yearned to think of something that would stay him from his frenzied course for just a moment more. Probably no little in envy of the all-afternoon "lunches," I didn't at all like the looks of his obese, luxuriant-haired, and silk-suited canvasser and deeply resented his making Mr. Blue, the "factory representative," carry his own portfolio case. He was not at all the Ivy League canvasser of Mr. Blue's dreams. Having reached the house first, he now stood at the bottom of the steps with his hands on his womanish hips and stared moodily at me by way of letting me know I was interrupting enterprises of great pith and moment. "Fuck you, fat boy," I mumbled under my breath. Then, scarcely thinking about it, I shouted, "Give us fifty, Mr. Blue!" To the astonishment of both the canvasser and my British chauffeur, down went Mr. Blue, and up and down, and down and up, and up and down. By the time he had reached his fifteenth, perhaps twentieth push-up, the Londoner was mumbling an intrigued "Why, the bloody, dirty old man is mad!" and the canvasser, numb with fury, was standing over

Mr. Blue angrily beseeching him not to ruin the sale with such maniacal shenanigans. Laughing, I said, "Drive on." Suddenly the thought of remembering Mr. Blue going so laboriously yet somehow so effortlessly up and down, and down and up, appealed overwhelmingly to the anecdotal within me.

Helpless to stay it, I let my easy laughter fill the car for the better part of the next fifty miles. When finally, seemingly too exhausted to laugh a moment more, I fell quiet, my friend, asking the primal newsman's question, said, "Who in the bloody world is Mr. Blue?" That started it all over again. Beginning to laugh even before my reply came, I said, "Oh, yes! Oh, yes! That's it! Who, who, *whoooo* in the bloody world is Mr. Blue?" and ended, to the beguiled and somewhat uneasy chuckling of the Englishman, by roaring all the way to Scarsdale, much too preoccupied to discover if that nostalgic Limey ever that day found the comfort of familiar scenes.

The next I heard of Mr. Blue, some months later, was that he was dead. Standing at the Commodore Hotel's commuter bar which opens onto the lower concourse of Grand Central, I had been in the city being interviewed for a job I hadn't wanted and had glibly refused (before, I might add, it was even offered) and was devotedly sipping a beer, fingering the two dollars or so of silver in my pocket (the extent of my fortune), and fabricating for my wife a tale of a horrendous personality clash between the interviewer and myself, when someone very close to me guardedly spoke my name and I looked up to see the gray-flanneled, horn-rimmed attorney who had registered such surprise at my endless lip-reading of *Lolita*. He told me that he had been in New York trying a case, but because I was indifferent to him I elected to believe he was in town filing a brief, probably, I surmised, somewhere as pedestrian as at probate court. For drinking funds to stimulate the fantasy and add just the proper details to the story of my ghastly interview, I immediately hit him for twenty dollars. I thought of asking him for ten, but, bad luck for him, I was indifferent enough to him to make it twenty. Hurt that he didn't wince as he gave me the money, I thought I'd better offer him some notions of my plans for repaying him. The following weekend I was to get a fifteen-hundred-dollar check from the Columbia Broadcasting System. Since seeing him last, I explained, I had been studying direction under Lee Strasberg at the Actors Studio and in coaching would-be actors had so impressed him with my own thespian ability ("Golly," I injected, "something I never dreamed I possessed!") that he had recommended me for a cameo role in an upcoming *Playhouse 90* and—God's-in-his-heaven-all's-right-with-the-world—I had got the goddam male lead!

"Actually," I said, "I just this moment left rehearsal and am fagged—*but fagged.*" As I thought he would be, he was impressed. Coming up on his tiptoes and listing toward me in anticipation, he demanded all the details.

"It's tremendous," I said, pronouncing it *treee*-MEN-dous and stalling for time. "A real message play. Tennessee Williams' first original for TV!" Hadn't he heard about it? Now that I mentioned it he thought he had read something that morning in the *Times* (oh, how bullshit begets bullshit!), but tell him more. Well, I played this Chicago-born surgeon, Horatio Päh-*nee*, married to an exquisite, aristocratic Southern belle, Miss Melissa Jennie Coker, from Charleston, South Carolina, and as the play opens I am living in an ocean-front mansion on Charleston's Battery with her and my three sons, Legare, Manigault, and Ravenal, and am one of the two Northerners accepted in the community, the other being Paul Muni, who plays a four-star general, retired, and an ex-President of the United States, "sort of," I offered, "a rough-hewn Ike, you might say," and chuckled. "You have to get the background to get the full impact of what follows," I said and went on to explain that as the curtain rises I am president of the Charleston Historical Society, on the board of the Confederate League of Respiratory Surgeons, a generous contributor to the Union for the Eternal Maintenance of the First Cannonball Fired on Fort Sumter, sergeant-at-arms for the St. Cecelia Ball, and musical minister to the Society for the Preservation of Carolina Spirituals. "Enter Fate, with a capital *F*," I said, jamming my middle finger up into the smoky though virginal air. My brother, played by Mickey Rooney, who is a base and vindictive little garage mechanic in Chicago and who has always envied me my hard-won esteem, shows up in Charleston one sunny day and lightheartedly offers me documented and indisputable proof that I'm a "fucking nigger." I let that sink in. "Oh, it's *treee*-MEN-dous," I repeated. "As pretty and sweet a thing as Williams has ever done. It's all about the consequences of this discovery. A lot like *Hamlet* after the prince discovers that Claudius has all along been fornicating with his Mom and has done in his Pop." Sighing, I told him I shouldn't say more for fear of spoiling the drama for him. Enough to say, I said, that the consequences are not happy: all the better people get smashed one night down at the Carolina Yacht Club and come and burn down my waterfront mansion; Legare, Manigault, and Ravenal are taken from me and spirited off to their uncle, a mystical and besotted mining engineer in

Cambodia; my mother-in-law locks herself in a steamer trunk in the attic and passes her days gnawing on chestnuts and acorns; and the last we hear of my wife, Miss Melissa Jennie Coker, she has taken to running naked up and down the concrete sea wall that runs along the Battery and protects the mansions from the arbitrary whims of the sea.

Thinking that ought to hold him till he dialed in *Playhouse 90* the following Thursday and found no Manigault, no Melissa, no Tennessee, no me, I changed the subject and began to query him about some of the madmen who had frequented the apartment. We discussed this one, having a laugh, and that one, having two laughs, and when I asked about Mr. Blue, my informant went preternaturally grave. "Mr. Blue," he said, "is dead." Not only was he dead, but because the attorney's uncle had been the investigating officer I was able to get many of the details.

The calamity had occurred just prior to Christmas. Because the *U.S.S. Deborah,* a champion of robustness, had apostasized smoking, Mr. Blue, a nonsmoker, had acquired the habit of doing his chain-smoking in the can, his muscular buttocks settled anxiously on the throne, fiendishly wolfing in the smoke, flicking his ashes into the sink, afterward washing them down with tap water and flushing his butts whirlingly down the toilet bowl. From a storage-rental warehouse Deborah had removed her plastic Yule tree and orange crates stuffed with her silver icicles, her canned snow, her tissue-wrapped green, yellow, red, and blue ornament balls, her *papier-mâché* Magi, her delicate and gossamer-winged seraphs, her cardboard representation of the Nativity, her life-sized and jolly imitation Santa Claus, and her God only knows what other execrable prettyisms and, pressed for space, had these ghoulisms crammed cheek to jowl in the bathroom against the starry-eyed and anticipated ritual of Christmas Eve. Shortly after one of his smoking respites, Mr. Blue was curled up on the davenport reading ("The Surly Sodomite of Santa Rosa"?) when he smelled smoke and almost immediately thereafter caught the unmistakable crepitation of a fire in the making. Calling to the *U.S.S. Deborah*, who was in the kitchen, to grab a pail of water, Mr. Blue charged to the bathroom and flung open the door precisely at the instant a jumbo-sized can of mentholated shave cream detonated, a lethal and ragged piece of it careening with furious impact into his Adam's apple, severing his carotid artery and causing him to topple headlong into the holocaust. By dousing both the flames and Mr. Blue's inert body, an hysterical though resolute Deborah managed to quell the fire, by which time neighbors had summoned policemen and Mr. Blue had, in the eeriest scene ever witnessed by the uncle-policeman of the attorney, all but given up the ghost. He lay, according to the lawyer, face up in the burnt-odored bathroom amidst the ruined rubble of those blackened, soaked, and ersatz Yule trappings, the piece of shaving can still wedged fiercely into his Adam's apple, the hideous contractions still pumping a venous blood that already covered him from neck to waistline. The explosion had hurled shaving cream every which way, and that which had landed on Mr. Blue had freakishly formed a nearly perfect beard. So that with his naturally snow-topped dome, his beard of riotous and fluffy mentholated green, his shirt front so vividly cerise, and surrounded by the scorched Magi and seraphs, he looked a kind of pygmy *Sant Nikolaas* in his death throes.

Weirder than anything to the uncle-policeman, and which, till it was later explained, he had chalked up to the momentary dementia of excessive grief, was the behavior of Deborah. Apparently she had all along known that Mr. Blue's claim to chronic cacation was a hoax and that his frequent trips to the can were for cigarettes. While the police had tried to minister to Mr. Blue, all the *U.S.S. Deborah* had done, to the bewilderment and embarrassment of the curious neighbors, was thunder up and down the living room self-righteously proclaiming, "I knew cigarettes would kill him. . . . I knew cigarettes would kill him. . . ."

I didn't want to hear any more, told the guy I didn't need the twenty after all, walked across the barroom into the terminal, and started looking for a train to Scarsdale.

Mr. Blue's way of death was fitting. He had been utterly corrupted by America, and I find it proper that his carotid artery should have been severed by flak from a jumbo-sized can of mentholated shave cream. Like James Joyce, who tried to bend and subjugate the ironmongery of the cosmos with words (wasn't it The Word Joyce was after?), Mr. Blue tried to undo the empyrean mysteries with Seedy and his red carpet, with his elevated alligator shoes, with the ardent push-ups he seemed so sure would make him outlast time's ravages, with his touching search for some golden pussy that would yield to his lips the elixir of eternal life. And like Joyce's Leopold Bloom, like Quixote, Mr. Blue had become the perennial mock-epic hero of his country, the salesman, the boomer who believed that at the end of his American sojourn of demeaning doorbell-ringing, of faking and fawning, he would come to the Ultimate Sale, conquer, and soar.

And though Mr. Blue's way of death was fitting, I never tell anybody the way it really happened; any more than in a hundred places in these pages I have told what "really" happened. I can't tell the mode of Mr. Blue's death because in actuality it was so right as to force the reader's credibility to the breaking point. Attempting to make Mr. Blue's death more believable, I considered a number of possibilities. I thought of giving him the courage to go finally down between the *U.S.S. Deborah*'s legs and have her, in the moment of ecstasy, press those gymnast's thighs about his head and thereupon extinguish the life from the luckless Mr. Blue. Standing on the lawn of some forlorn abode and mouthing his voiceless anger, Mr. Blue might have carried some typically bombarded American consumer round the bend and at point-blank got both barrels of a shotgun, scattering not aluminum siding but bloody bits of Mr. Blue all over the "dump." Anxious about his impotence in this land of sexual gargantuans, he could have sent to a degenerate mail-order house for a faradic device which attached to the genitals helps stimulate with electrical charges a more rapturous sexual act, only to have the device miscue and electrocute him, frying off his balls in the process. On my thirtieth birthday I learned that a quite respectable couple I knew vaguely had died in such a fashion, and at an age when I shouldn't have been, I was shocked and grieved at soul. At odd moments over the next few years I reconstructed what I knew of them in the light of their death, like a would-be writer built their story from its end backward; and lying face up on a beach in Florida, my eyes opened to a universe of yellow blinding brightness, it one day occurred to me that, though had I lived to acquire the wisdom of Solomon I never would have ended their life in such a way, it really couldn't have ended any other way. As for Mr. Blue's death, there were any number of possibilities, none less credible than the severed carotid, and all more believable than the knowledge I carry in my heart.

Yet the endings, both the "real" and the imagined ones, I now know lack something for me, somehow don't surfeit the romantic man, the hopeful creature, within me. With a stranger, two at the most, I am sitting at some distant saloon at two in the morning and, the bar empty now, we are sipping beer and recalling the childhood idol dead at nineteen at Anzio, the pulchritudinous creature who took our virginity, or that melancholy, self-deprecating teacher who gave so much more than all the others. And when I tell the story of Mr. Blue, and if I have good listeners I invariably do tell the story of Mr. Blue, surprisingly I have yet another ending. He died, I always say, doing a flip. He was at that point of the flip, his back arched, his face to the sky, at that point of his trajectory when he was closest to heaven, when for just an instant one was certain he was going to *soar* out and escape the meanness of his life, it was precisely at that moment, I say, that his heart gave out. And I always leave it to the listener to judge whether, so close to the sky and under the furious momentum of his flip, he continued toward heaven or simply thundered ignominiously back to earth.

And then I light a cigarette and take another sip of two-in-the-morning beer, and because I am embarrassed by my sentimentality and the paltry poet within me, I always add, "Whether he ever got around to kissing a snatch, I can't say. But if he did," I end the story of Mr. Blue, "I like to think it was some other than the *U.S.S. Deborah*'s."

7

Lament for a
Conspiracy

Patience, the girl with the roan-colored hair, and I lived in the heart of Scarsdale at the General MacArthur Towers on Escutcheon Court. The Court—which was not a *court* but a very short street—was on either side, and behind rows of pretty shade trees, lined with storied, gabled, vine-covered apartment houses of brick and stone. And though in all the time I lived there I knew no one but the building's maintenance man, an unintelligible though generous Greek with whom, in his cryptlike office in the basement, I occasionally used to drink a bottle of Metaxa brandy, I came to suspect that I was the only person in the Court who hadn't dreams of moving a "little farther out," to a place of long, cool lawns and picture windows, to a place which would give to the recipient of the news, "I live in Scarsdale," some image less fraudulent than the Court's.

For me, our apartment was perfect. It was only two rooms, with a spacious, chandeliered, and mirrored hallway; but Patience, whose taste in clothes and food and furniture seemed to me flawless, had appointed it wonderfully well in Sheraton. Moreover, my bookcase overflowed. Books lined the mantelpiece, books made their way into the recesses of the windows, and books strewn by me on the floor were eventually picked up by Patience and stacked in neat little piles in the hallway. In the corner of the living room, surrounded by a multitude of lamps, as though I believed the lurid glare would stay me from indulging in muddy thinking, was my writing table varnished to a brilliant, gleaming surface. Next to it stood a new metal typewriter stand atop which sat an equally new Smith-Corona, its white keys sparkling in the vivid light. My pencils were honed as fine as needles. There were reams of both bond white and yellow second-sheet paper. I had a hard-cover edition of Fowler's usage dictionary, one of Roget's *Thesaurus,* and one of Webster's *New Collegiate Dictionary.* To gauge the dictionary's breadth when buying it, I had looked up *thurible,* an Oriental-looking container in which one burns incense, and *gorp,* a freakishly obese person who eats constantly because he achieves a kind of erotic splendor when sitting on the throne. The former was listed, the latter not, and because the latter never is listed, because I don't to this day know where I ever heard the word, and because it didn't seem likely I'd be called upon to use it, I bought the dictionary anyway—it was cheap. And finally, because Patience was out during the day preserving sacred institutions (or whatever it is that Bryn Mawr girls do), I had the apartment all to myself. Thus it was that I had all the time in the world, and tremulous with apprehension, I had little choice but to sit at that brightly lighted table and try.

Like Beerbohm's Felix Argallo, my thematic concern was to be *pity,* "profound and austerely tender pity."

Though the novel's population of prepossessing, yeoman-like, and enlightened public relations men, currish, porcine-featured, and saber-rattling clients, and dazzling, nymphomaniacal secretaries had been done untold times and was not in the least conducive to such thematic notions, I didn't know it and, like Argallo, couldn't in any event write about anything that *didn't* sadden me. Hence I assumed I would rise above my material and that my warmhearted reader would be given glimpses into the soul of a genuinely magnanimous if slightly bellicose writer. I was to forgive the tyrannical client his boorishness, the juicy nymphomaniac her exorbitant need of dongs. And as, disguised in blond hair, blue eyes, and horn-rims, I was to be the gallant public relations man who finds at the climactic moment for integrity, there would be no need to forgive me. I was certain, though, that in writing of myself I could find much to pity, and that there wouldn't be a single episode relating to myself that didn't sadden me. It was to be a very sad book.

From one of the many tomes I had read on the "art of fiction," I had got the idea that, like Athena, the goddess of wisdom who sprouted full-breasted from the head of a man, the majestic sweep of my novel would roar out once I could "see" my first sentence—roar out like Niagara through the head of a pin. I wrote, "I live in Scarsdale," added a period—. —and for the next few weeks sat staring moodily at these words. They made me sad. At the end of nine months, after unnumbered rewritings, giving the sentence striking contours and florishing curlicues, I had made it read, "Alone, I live in Scarsdale, Westchester County, New York, twenty to twenty-five minutes from the Grand Central on the New York Central Railroad commuter trains." And though the book was by then ready to pour out, as I hadn't written a single other word, I was still sad.

Such an exiguous output forced me, during those months, into a Machiavellian parrying with an unwitting Patience, making me tell her that I'd prefer she didn't read the manuscript until it was completed, that by reading it in fits and starts she'd be oblivious to the "sweep of its pitiful grandeur." "It won't be long," I'd assure her brightly, and Patience, a very patient girl, would smile blessedly in the suspicion (unceasingly encouraged by me) of being mated with a genius, perhaps envisioning herself on the dust jacket with me. To one side of my sparkling writing table I kept a stack of manuscript envelopes stuffed with blank paper and labeled with perspicacious chapter headings— "The Morose Merchants," "The Sad Sirens," "The Pitiful Prattle"—which on her Bryn Mawr oath Patience had promised she wouldn't "read" while I was out of the apartment; and whenever she came in at night she'd find me— having just risen from, and slid Nero Wolfe beneath, the davenport—yawning and stretching over the typewriter on which, word for word, I'd just copied two pages of *A la Recherche du Temps Perdu,* in translation, of course. While the steaks simmered below the stove's pink top, and the peas simmered above it, I'd allow Patience to massage my weary shoulders, squeeze and pop pimples on my back, and query me on the progress of my masterpiece. "Fatiguing," I'd say morosely, "fatiguing as hell. But it won't be long. Scratch lower, will yuh, under the right shoulder blade?" *Le roi le veut.*

To say that I didn't write during this period is not pre-cisely true. Her lovely, shoulder-length roan hair in an up-sweep, bespectacling herself in severe-looking horn-rims of window glass, using a minimum of makeup, dressed in tailored, two-hundred-dollar dresses and expensive low-heeled pumps charged to her parents, Patience looked both less feminine and somewhat older than she was; and being both a bright and smartly turned-out young lady, she had managed to get a job working for judges interviewing potential divorcees, of whom in Westchester there were no few. For one judge it was her duty to try to re-establish harmony in the marriage and, if this was impossible, she was to make recommendations concerning the custody of the children to the family-court judge. I taught her how to prepare these reports. When I took the girl in hand, she had a bittersweet habit of reticently sneaking the most outrageous facts into the body of the report, thereby making them appear more egregiously horrid than in fact they were. If by his own admission the husband and father of four had been recently arrested at the urinals beneath Grand Central for reaching over and grabbing a chesty and beribboned army colonel by the penis, in her charitableness Patience suffered a compulsion to ramble on for two pages describing the man's commendable educational background, his undisputed ability as a provider for his family, his deaconship in the Episcopal Church, his unquenchable love for his wife and kids, his lavish grief at the whole sordid business, and—*boom*—here he was grabbing alien cocks. With Patience it was both an admirably feminine diffidence and a true bounteousness of spirit.

"Believe me, Patience," said I, "you're doing these people a grave disservice by evading the problem and indulging their egos with all that sham nobility of theirs. That's all this divorce shit is about, egos being stomped on and in turn demanding satisfaction. Like a bunch of emotional Frenchmen insulting each other and sending for their seconds. So he grabbed a colonel by the balls—so what? That old fraud of a colonel probably loved it!" Patience laughed uneasily, unsure of herself. "Seriously, though," I said. "Just write the reports sans editorials, including, if you think it pertinent, that the guy went to Harvard and blew the Hasty Puddings and that he keeps his kids in velveteen knickers and banana splits. When you get that done, at the very end, and in a paragraph or two, make a sincere appraisal of the situation along with your equally sincere recommendations. There's no one," I said, and I was not being facetious, "to whom I'd rather trust my marriage. Do it my way, and you'll see."

Patience still wasn't convinced, but I was determined to have my way in this and persuaded her to let me work up the next dozen or so reports ("cases," they were called), minus the summarizing recommendations. Patience wouldn't let me write the latter since I invariably suggested divorce (left to me, I'd have had the whole of Westchester divorced) and that the "issue" be placed in the "loving" care of an institution, anyplace save with their wretched, grief-indulging parents. Within two months both judges had complimented her on being the best counselor they'd ever had, using such laudations as "relevant, intelligent, and possessed of a hardness tempered by compassion." In the highest accolade, a judge called her "a real professional," and for that Patience gave me a kiss.

That Patience and I were saving others' marriages while ours was squirming on such wobbly pins provided me over the years with a certain rum irony. We worked on these cases week nights; when Patience was home weekends, I had my most trying time. On Saturdays and Sundays I was compelled to sit for four and five hours a day at my type-writer, over and over again typing "Now is the time for all good men to come . . ." This debilitating lunacy was finally alleviated when, mutually agreeing that we were both "working" too hard, we started spending our weekends in north Westchester with Patience's sister Prudence, her husband, and their three small children, two girls and a boy who were all indiscriminately referred to by their father as "Sam," for which reason I never did learn their names.

———

Before me now—as though in my relationships I hadn't al-ready paid the price of a little peace—I see Christopher ("Call me *Bumpy*") Plumpton, who was married to Pa-tience's sister Prudence and who was therefore my brother-in-law. Give or take a year, Bumpy was my age, twenty-nine, and there the resemblance ended. Having been bright (or rich) enough to be admitted to Dartmouth, Hamilton, Wisconsin, and Colorado College, Colorado Springs, after five years and still without enough credits to enter his junior year, Bumpy had decided that he and higher education should never have married; and with the bitterness resulting from an unsavory divorce, Bumpy for-ever after coddled an unhealthy and surly yen to appear the most uncouth nincompoop in Christendom. Whenever Bumpy told me where he was from, he invariably identified a different place as home: Palm Beach, Scottsdale, Southampton, Shaker Heights, Beverly Hills, Greenwich, Bucks County, Winnetka—"wherever," as Fitzgerald said, "the rich are rich together"; and though I had thought he was joshing me, or that he was one of those people who de-spise being labeled by place, I later learned from Patience that as a child, and a very wealthy child, he had on demand been passed from one covetous and ingratiating relative to another. In his infancy his parents had been killed when a cable on a mountain sightseeing coach in the Pyrénées Orientales snapped and hurled them into the abyss (another telling had it in the crash of a hydroplane his father was "testing" over the Azores); but his grandparents on either side of the family were "in" oil, public utilities, automobile and plumbing supplies, a printing company, and I don't remember what else; and for these grandparents, or their representatives, during the week Bumpy did something in the mysterious world of finance in downtown Manhattan. Because his sixteen-room house was on Todd Road in Goldens Bridge, some thirty miles north of Scarsdale, I one day asked him if he wasn't rather far out to commute. "Naw," Bumpy explained, "I'm a Tee-to-Tee man." "A what?" "Ten to two, Tuesday to Thursday!" Bumpy roared approval at his own bad joke, exposing as he did so his yellowing, food-clogged teeth. There was little about himself that Bumpy didn't approve, a fact perhaps best evidenced in his love for his stomach. For a young man Bumpy had girth, a waistline over the fifty-inch mark. Like an old, canny, and deceptively jovial tycoon, he hickishly wore his belt way below the tummy that he carried thrust defiantly and affectionately forward. Chomping on a Corona, he was always unconsciously patting and pinching and caressing that belly, doing so with something like reverence. He looked about to smile and reveal to a friend that he had just lost all the friend's dough in a gold mine that bore no gold.

Prudence and the children occupied fifteen rooms of the house, and for himself Bumpy kept one spacious room in the basement ("my bachelor's digs"), to which no one save the kids were admitted, and before entering even they had to knock and give "the password," which changed from week to week. Opening the door to the timid rap of his seven-year-old daughter, a real beauty, as indeed all the children were, Bumpy would with mock and intemperate gruffness demand, *"What you want, Sam?"* "Can I come in, *Bwana?"* The kids called him *Bwana.* "What's the password?" Bumpy would ask suspiciously, in the manner of one who knows he's dealing with an impostor. *"San Pietro in Vaticano,"* the daughter would whisper, giggling with the relief of having managed the Italian pronunciation. Severely admonishing her not to say anything to *"that broad* upstairs," Bumpy would then proceed to make her a grilled-cheese sandwich. Most of this nonsense took place on Sunday mornings before the saloons opened (the only time during the weekend that Bumpy or I saw much of the children or our wives); and thus Bumpy, perhaps attempting to leaven the spice of the intrigue with a little "religious training," made up passwords related to Christianity. One Sunday the password was Christ's admonition to "Go … and give to the poor … and come and follow me."

Like Bumpy himself, his bachelor's haven was a mishmash. In his half-sized modern blue refrigerator he kept only cans of Budweiser beer and the bread, cheese, and butter with which he made the innumerable grilled-cheese sandwiches that were his sole weekend diet. Atop the equally modern blue electric stove there was always an unwashed and blackened iron frying pan with a blackened, burnt, and crust-curled sandwich in it; and on the desk, table, bookcase, and unmade daybed were half-eaten grilled-cheese sandwiches spread with a hot mustard now sickeningly staled to a dung brown, tooth-serrated, brick-hard ruins sitting amidst uncountable empty and half-empty beer cans. A collector of hats, boots, and guns, Bumpy had velvet berets, plastic sun helmets, country gentlemen's tweed caps, Australian Army field hats, white-hunter hats with leopard-patterned bands, infantrymen's combat helmets, ten-gallon cream-colored Stetsons, pyrogravure cowboy boots, glossy black riding boots, motorcycle boots with silver buckles, well-shined paratrooper boots, expensive ski boots, steel-toed workmen's shoes, twelve-gauge shotguns, thirty-aught-thirties, twenty-twos, M-1's, a fifty-caliber Thompson submachine gun, and innumerable pistols lying haphazardly about the furniture and the floor.

By far the most striking aspect of the room, though, was the walls, no part of which could be seen. Covering them completely were New York State road signs, "SNOW ROUTE: DETOUR," "STATE POLICE BARRACKS AHEAD"; the inevitable "playmates" of the month from *Playboy* magazine depicting an edible-assed Miss June, or whoever, whom Bumpy had admirably defiled and humanized by drawing pus-running pustules on their sleek behinds or thickets of unseemly coarse hair between their breasts; the original artwork of dozens of bland or unfunny cartoons Bumpy had admired over the years; large poster reproductions of Stalin, Churchill, Lenin, Roosevelt, Truman, Napoleon, Hitler, Disraeli, Trotsky, Commodore Vanderbilt, Eisenhower, and Carry Nation striking the eeriest and most absurd attitudes (Stalin, for example, in a picture I had never seen, appeared to be rather pensively scratching his nuts); and interspersed randomly throughout all this, action shots from various poster advertisements for Technicolored and black-and-white movie epics wherein mayhem, sex, blood, torture, sadism, and skulduggery had reigned supreme—the bachelor's pad of a man who had been debauched irreparably by Hollywood, best-sellers, and the advertising racket.

Most memorable to me were the action shots from the movie *Julius Caesar,* starring Marlon Brando, James Mason, and John Gielgud, and beneath which Bumpy had Scotch-taped cards bearing excerpts from Shakespeare's text corresponding with the action of the scene, more often than not incorrectly. Exasperated by one such error, on the first day I met Bumpy and had, sans password, been invited into his sanctum and given a Budweiser, I finally said, "Bumpy, see that picture of James Mason? Well, underneath it you've got *'Et tu, Brute?'* " "So?" Bumpy said. "Well," I explained, "Mason played Brutus, *not Caesar.* That caption belongs back there under the one of Louis Calhern with his toga all bloodied and his right arm extended, pointing. *Obviously* at Brutus." "Aw, what's the diff?" Bumpy said, stuffing half a grilled-cheese into his mouth and, after a barely perceptible mastication, beginning to wash it down with a long swallow of beer. Then he looked petulantly at me, as though I were an old spoilsport; then he belched. Embarrassed that my tone had seemed so pedantic, and anxious to rectify it, I said, "Did you ever hear where Brutus put his sword in Caesar?" "No, where?" Bumpy said, coming attentively up on the edge of his chair. "Right in the balls," I said. "In the balls!" Bumpy cried, jumping to his feet. "In the balls! *Oooooohhhhh!*" With that eerie cry of anguish Bumpy grabbed himself by his own balls and did an agonized dance of feigned pain about the middle of the room, his stomach joggling up and down like jelly. "In the balls, huh? Where'd ya ever hear that?" "Read it in Plutarch," I said.

"Plutarch, huh?" he said. "Sounds like a *real horny* book. Have to get ol' Bumpy a copy of that!" Pleased that "ol' Bumpy" was no longer upset, I said, "Did you ever hear how Trotsky's assassination was done?" "Trotsky? Which one's he?" Christ, I thought, he doesn't know *who* he's got on his walls. "That one over there standing at a lectern, making the typically raving speech of a political animal and apparently picking his nose." Still on his feet and beginning to leer rapaciously in anticipation, Bumpy decided to guess. "They shoved a Coke bottle up his ol' bazooka and broke it off?" *"No,"* I moaned, laughing despite myself. "The story is that the assassin hit him repeatedly on top of the head with a tack hammer." "Gol dang," Bumpy said admiringly. "You must be some reader, knowing all that stuff!"

When Patience and I returned to Goldens Bridge the following weekend, Bumpy couldn't wait to get me into the cellar to show me the changes he'd made in the walls. Over Trotsky's head he had placed a cartoonist's version of a thumb and forefinger gripping a huge tack placed for driving into the top of poor Trotsky's dome. Beneath a bloodied bandage the thumb was blue and swollen from the repeated misses of the unseen and incompetent carpenter, and above the head a gigantic hammer was bearing irrevocably down with such merciless force that Bumpy seemed intent with this one awful blow to drive the tack all the way down into the raving Trotsky's intestines. Laughing appreciatively, I said, "A tack hammer, Bumpy—*not a tack!*" "Aw, what's the diff," Bumpy said, giving me that pouty look. What he had done with Plutarch was rather more fetching. Refusing to accept the fact that Louis Calhern had played Caesar, he had a picture of a togaed James Mason lying on his side with a dozen bloodless cartoonist's swords sticking out of him, some appearing to have no more than broken the skin. Though obviously in his death throes, the old scalawag still had a pinch of life in him, one eye was open, and in what presumably was a rather irritated afterthought, Bumpy had the man who bestrode "the narrow world like a colossus" saying, "Hey, Brutus, ol' buddy, didya have to get me in the balls?"

Though I wasn't to reciprocate it for years, or even understand that I cared to reciprocate it, Bumpy fell passionately in love with me the first day of our meeting, the day which was to set the Sybaritic tone for so many future weekends. On Saturday, after the horny jokes Bumpy had "stored up" for me during the week, two cans of Budweiser, and a grilled-cheese sandwich, Bumpy would suddenly look at his watch and exclaim, "Gol dang, it's getting late! Let's go for a drive!" Rakishly attired in his leopard-banded, white-hunter's hat; his silver-buckled, motorcyclist's boots; a pair of well-faded, rear-accenting Levi's; and a khaki hunter's parka on the breast of which were slots for shotgun shells, Bumpy, belly out, would purposefully lead me to the garage where, ignoring three shiny new cars, we'd climb into a hard-used Ford Ranch Wagon. In the back of this wagon were loaded rifles of various calibers, the omniscient remains of sandwiches, and a couple dozen cardboard quart containers for bulk ice cream, empty now and floating as lightly as feathers as the wagon thundered and joggled over the sinuous, narrow Westchester highways. Stopping at the Rendezvous Restaurant a half-mile down on Route 22, Bumpy, The White Hunter in Suburbia, would disembark and strut in. Presently returning with two ice-cream containers full of draft beer, he'd hand me one, pile in, and off we'd go, invariably discovering at the first curve we negotiated that the beer's froth had spilled onto our laps.

Retrospectively, I see Bumpy and me on those weekend afternoons and early evenings as stopping over at every bar, saloon, and restaurant in north Westchester, from Pound Ridge on the east to Armonk on the south, from Yorktown Heights on the west to Brewster on the north, bars in which Bumpy was loathed, patronized, and feared; held in amusement, contempt, and awe; but never—no, never—really liked. Constantly he punctuated this shuttling between bars with an abrupt screeching of brakes. Furiously wheeling the wagon to one side of the highway, Bumpy would reach in the back and grab one of the rifles, jump out, take split-second aim, and shoot squirrels, rabbits, crows, and— to my dismay and repeated warnings that we'd end in jail— stray cats, which he despised. In his youthful, less moderate days he had killed them by injecting pure iodine into them with a hypodermic needle (before dying, Bumpy told me with considerable amusement, the cats had endured excruciating pain and had gone into flip-flopping fits) or by tightly joining their tails together with wire and dropping them over a clothesline where they'd clawed each other to death. Suffering himself few restraints and fewer social niceties, and perhaps thinking that, being married to Prudence's sister, I nourished notions of what was expected of a host, on the first day Bumpy took me on a rapid tour of the nearest village of any size, Katonah. Explaining that spelled backward it was named after an Indian, Chief Hanotak (Was Bumpy kidding me? another Mr. Blue?), he showed me the New York Central station where he got his train to Manhattan, Weinstein's Drugstore where he got the glycerin suppositories for his chronic constipation, a haberdashery where they had "terrific" belts for his proud girth, the public library where he got nothing at all, and, set high on a green sloping hill, a school which was merely a red-brick school, though it did have, and I don't know why, a quaint white wooden belfry topping it. Among all these "sights," Bumpy repeatedly pointed out property he owned and which, now The Texas Cattleman, he invariably designated as "one of mah spreads," one of which was a dilapidated corner grocery with rain-faded candy-bar and rusted Coke signs tacked to its unpainted façade, and from which, according to Prudence (and she'd have known!), Bumpy never collected any rent.

The tour took no more than twenty minutes, and, having finished our containers of draft, we were driving out a tortuous road headed for the nearest saloon when Bumpy pointed at a nondescript piece of land carpeted with anemones and conifers and matter-of-factly said, "That's where Scott Fitzgerald's wife Minerva got burned up in the nuthouse fire." "Zelda!" I cried, and "Where?" I cried, and "Stop the car!" I cried. Impatient to move on even before the motor had begun to idle, Bumpy said, "What ya lookin' for? There's nothin' here now." "A road," I said, upset and terribly abstracted. "There must be a road!" "There ain't nothin'," Bumpy assured me with finality. "Nothin'." Without being in the least conscious of it, the words rose up within me; and somnambulantly, as though in a crushing, heavy-aired dream, I quoted, aloud: "I left my capacity for hoping on the little roads that led to Zelda's sanitarium." That is the moment I score as the one Bumpy fell irremediably in love with me. A mental brute, Bumpy wouldn't have been capable of articulating what so moved him about the line; but move him it did, and from that day forward, like a child forever demanding the repetition of a favored fairy tale, Bumpy would say pleadingly, "Tell me that line about Minerva." *"Zelda,"* I'd exasperatingly correct him. "C'mon, Bumpy, you know that line. You've already had me repeating it till I'm going barmy." "Naw, I don't—*honest,"* Bumpy would assure me. "I don't remember it. Besides, *tell me the way you say it!"* So I'd repeat it, afterward studying him to see if his gray, agate-like eyes had misted over as usual. Abruptly trying with brashness to cover what he, this Boom-Boom Bwana, must have deemed his lapse of manliness, he'd bellow, "Gol dang! You sure know everything, don't ya? Gol dang!" Watching him so worry and wag his weak head with wonder, I never bothered to tell Bumpy that Fitzgerald's line was hardly an esoteric one.

Bumpy's courtship of me began in earnest the following week when I received from New York a post card and a package that were to set both the precedent and the tone for Bumpy's weekly wooing of me. "Ex!!!" the card read. "Am sending book the swishy clerk told me was horny as Hades! Skimmed thru it and found guy diving in bush on page 113! Have marked same! Wow! Hope you like it! See you Saturday?" He had signed the card, as I later discovered he answered the phones at both his office and his home, "Bumpy here!!!!" The package contained the latest best-seller. Patience was pleased. She said, "I guess you've really got yourself an admirer." "It appears that way," I said, giving her the best-seller to read. "Well, well," she said. "Thank you, Bumpy." She laughed. Many weeks later, in a pensive mood, she said, "I'm glad about Bumpy, *really* glad." She was glad, too. "Why are you glad, Patience?" "Oh, I don't know," she said. "His parents died when he was only two or three and he's always been such a fat lonely boy—

and, I might add, one with a decidedly cruel streak. You might do him some good. I think he wet the bed till he was a sophomore in college." "That would have been about his tenth year in college, wouldn't it?" I said, and Patience laughed appreciatively. We were eating one of her exquisitely prepared dinners of lamb chops cut from the loin, baked potatoes topped with sour cream, asparagus, and an Italian salad. When we had finished the apple Huguenot and were sipping our coffee and lighting cigarettes, I said, "How did Bumpy's parents die—in a plane crash or what?" "Plane crash, heck," Patience said. "Don't listen to any of those stories. It's an absolute *thing* with Bumpy. They died right over here on Greenwich Avenue in Greenwich. Bumpy's father swerved the car to miss a cat and ran into a street lamp. There wasn't a mark on either of them—oh, a couple bumps on the head—but they were both sure as heck dead." "A cat?" I said. "A cat, huh? Then Bumpy's father wasn't a test pilot?" *"Test pilot,"* Patience cried. "Lord, that's a good one! From what I've heard all he was a drunk with enough money to bully anyone, including Bumpy's mother, whom he is said to have treated like dirt, once knocking a couple of her teeth out right at the bar of the Pickwick Arms Hotel in Greenwich. They say that a little bit of a man, a stranger, once beat him half to death in the very same bar and that the patrons rose en masse and applauded." Patience paused for a breath, trying to determine whether her tone should be harsh or sympathetic. "He loved cats, though," she said. "And he sure as heck proved the maxim about being destroyed by what one loves."

Every Wednesday or Thursday I received the post card and the package containing the latest masterpiece of

Ayn Rand, Sloan Wilson, Grace Metalious, the Irvings—
Wallace and Stone—and what must have been the works
of every writer in the Grove Press stable. No matter how
much I protested his generosity to Bumpy, or told him if
he had to send something I'd much prefer mysteries,
he wouldn't hear of it, explaining that, "Wanting to be
a writer and all, you should read good stuff—maybe you'll
learn somethin'! If only how to dive in the bush! Har!
Har! Har!"

Weekends in the bars Bumpy introduced me to bartenders and acquaintances with the pride of a lecherous
octogenarian presenting a young and ravishing bride. He'd
beam salaciously. "This here's my brother-in-law. He's a
writer! There ain't nothin' he don't know!" Soon I understood that, though I wasn't expected to volunteer *mots*, with
the wisdom of eternal woman I was expected to arbitrate
barroom disputes and have at my fingertips such esoteric
information as what Yankee pitcher's World Series no-
hitter had been undermined by the Dodgers' Cookie
Lavagetto, the populations of pre- and post-World War II
Warsaw, and the number of islands comprising the Republic of Indonesia. During a lull in the conversation, Bumpy
once called me into the floodlighted downstage area. "Tell
these swine that line about Minerva," he said. "Now, listen
here, Bumpy," I said; but before I could prevent him, he was
priming the audience for the showstopper, explaining how
Minerva was in the "bughouse" and how Scott Fitzgerald,
"you know, the writer," wrote this "gol dang great line" in a
letter. "Now, tell them," he ordered. My face red, my eyes
cast downward, I obediently mumbled the words for fear of
being taken for a damp-souled, unaccommodating chap.
"That ain't the way he usually says it!" Bumpy excoriated

me to my audience. In the station wagon going to the next bar, I said, "Bumpy, you've got to stop this nonsense about my being a writer and making me repeat that Fitzgerald line. In the first place, I've never had anything published. In the second place, it's embarrassing as hell. I mean, I suppose every one of those guys has heard that line before." I wanted to add, "Everyone's not as finger-lickin' uncouth as you." "You're absolutely right," Bumpy agreed, but his agreement had nothing to do with anything I'd just said. "Lines like that are just wasted on swine like those guys. They're not like us—*sensitive and all.*"

For the most part Bumpy demanded nothing of me save that like a young bride I sit at the bar, obediently sip my drink, look pleasingly discerning and attractive, and exude intimations of possessing recondite sexual expertise. Fortunately for me, Bumpy had no capacity for not upstaging all the bit players, including myself, with whom he came in contact. Ludicrously attired in a straw boater, a red suede vest making his stomach look like a rubescent mosquito's ripe for bursting, his faded and frayed Levi's, and a pair of glossy paratrooper boots, on entering a place he would make a direct, nearly maniacal line for the biggest assemblage of talkers at the bar, an assemblage that on spotting him seemed to shrivel visibly, to grow troubled and wan, to exude an unmistakable aura of sniffing recoil. To all of which reaction I invariably smiled. Young advertising men and bond salesmen, they were in their twenties and thirties, some in their forties; they wore Paul Stuart or J. Press jackets and bow ties; they puffed suavely at cigars or pipes; they sipped their scotch with a kind of Old World *sang-froid*; they saw themselves as the kind of tweedy squires to whom the advertisements of *The New Yorker* and *Esquire* are directed—ironically, they saw themselves as having the kind of money Bumpy had, not realizing that that kind of money gave Bumpy immunity from having to dress like them. Bumpy approached them forthrightly. With a furious flick of his fingers, he undid their bow ties. He gave them unsignaled, "playful" punches on their arms. He cuffed them "affectionately" on the back of the head. To those sitting on barstools facing him, their legs propped up and slightly spread, he reached up near the groin and ferociously gave them "chummy" little pinches on the inner thigh that drained the blood from their faces. Ordering drinks from the bartender, Bumpy bellowed, "Give us a drink here, you ape!" and thereupon disdainfully threw a fifty-dollar bill on the bar. Without the least heed to what their previous conversation might have been, Bumpy immediately began telling the dreadful jokes he had "stored up" for me during the week.

"There was this farmer, see, whose wife couldn't pop her nuts! Har! Har! Har!" Frothing at the mouth, his forehead glistening with sweat, tears of laughter streaming down his feverish cheeks, he disintegrated into a state of sickening and hysterical ribaldry, his obscene clucking denigrating his words into meaninglessness. Watching him, most of the men became salaciously hysterical themselves, as though caught up in a tornado of monstrous smut. Some few of the men sat defensively, like shrilly priggish women, forcing sickly smiles, and priming themselves to be ready to ward off Bumpy's unexpected punches, cuffs, and pinches, which continued to come even as he told his stories. These were the men I watched, the ones who gave my afternoons a kind of perverse pleasure. It was obvious they wanted to knock Bumpy down, but they never did. Why I don't know—one good blow to the belly would have been all that was required. Certainly part of their restraint was due to their nauseating deference to Bumpy's money, part to the reputation with which Bumpy had surrounded himself, that of a "tiger." Beneath his wooden jollity, Bumpy was consuming himself with hate; and for one so seemingly self-conscious, so oppressively inward, so apparently aware of nothing outside his own filthy tongue, Bumpy had an acute, nearly pathological insight into the temperature of all those about him. Just before the temperature reached the boiling point, Bumpy struck. Just at the moment one of the more courageous of their number was about to call him or challenge him for one of his vicious pinches, unexpectedly, violently, fist doubled, the weight of his obese body entirely committed to the blow, Bumpy struck the man in the face. Standing over the prone and bleeding figure, Bumpy would focus on him with his finger and say, "Next time, you pisspot, I'll shoot you fucking dead." Belly out, he'd make a hard-charging, theatrical exit. He hated all of them, but not nearly as much as he yearned to be hated by them. Within twenty minutes of one of these episodes, he would have hit the brakes, pulled to the side of the highway, and grabbed his thirty-aught-thirty. Under the impact of that weapon's shell, a cat so disintegrates that state police can't find the evidence to convict one. Watching him smile to himself after this, I could see that he reserved for himself some irony I couldn't comprehend. It was at these times, watching him so full of hate and smiling that sneering, inner-directed smile, that he looked absolutely brilliant, a creature of world-shaking capacities. It was at these times that I knew Bumpy had a good deal more intelligence than one supposed.

—

What Patience and Prudence did in the sumptuously furnished fifteen other rooms while Bumpy and I were embarked on our Saturnalian outings is easy to imagine: Prudence talked and Patience listened. Older than Patience by a year, Prudence was a three-child version of my wife, hippy, hard-used, and looking ten years older. The same lovely roan hair, Prudence's was always dim and lank with poor care; where Patience's mouth was full, inviting, and quick to smile, Prudence's had defined itself into a perpetually severe and unappetizing slash; where my wife's eyes were limpid green, calm, and friendly, Prudence's had become crow's-footed, directed inward, and charged with bile. Though she hadn't had a child in four years, Sams' ages being seven, six, and four, she always seemed puffy and brimming with the fluids of a pregnant woman, a flatulence that had me always accusing her to Patience of being a "closet" drinker. "If I ever saw one!" I'd emphasize. So often and so vehemently did Patience deny this that she grew weary of doing so and one day, with no little exasperation, said, "I don't give a damn if she drinks a gallon a day, do you?" Embarrassed by my obvious stridence in behalf of false accusations, I said, "No, I suppose not. But she's so suffocatingly high and mighty, I'd like to boot her in the ass!"

My affection was reciprocated. Dear Prudence loathed me with something like genius. Except for the slight influence she always had had and still had on Patience, I didn't much care. Bumpy's basement daybed was more utilitarian than decorative, there was something gravely wrong with his marriage to Prudence, and she was blindly spitting the hurt of that wrong in all directions. Twice on coming un-

expectedly into a room I overheard Prudence admonito-
rily advising Patience that once I got my life "straightened
out," some moneys due her from an estate would be forth-
coming. It was in this way I first learned that because of me
Patience was being denied access to her own money, presumably quite a bit. Everything that Prudence said to me
was filled with the venom of her own disappointments.
With Bumpy she had staked her happiness on trappings;
now that she had the three cars, the fifteen rooms, the mink,
the nurse, the maid, the cook, she knew they weren't
enough; and yet, such is the dangerous vindictiveness of
unhappy mentalities, she loathed anyone for being presumptuous enough to dare hope for anything other than
the grief she had given herself. With a hate out of all proportion to the subject at hand, she one Sunday morning
identified Thoreau as the most "despicable, loathsome,
self-centered, and phony man I ever heard of."

Unlike Bumpy and Patience, Prudence saw through my
literary pretensions. Each weekend she asked, "How's the
book coming?" in a tone of such contemptuous mockery
that I suspected she had sneaked into our apartment and
found the labeled envelopes stuffed with the blank pages;
immediately following this savage query with one about
my "job prospects." "Patience and I," she said, as Patience
sat shaking her head that it wasn't true, "have had a long
talk and have decided it'd be better if you had something to occupy your mind during the day. You could *write*
evenings and weekends." "What I'd suggest, dear sister-in-
law," I said, "is that you occupy your *own* mind with your
own marriage." "Now, now," Patience said, clucking repro-
vingly at me. "That's telling her!" Bumpy said to me. Looking hatefully at Prudence, he added, "And knock off that

stuff about Thoreau! Talk about somethin' somebody understands!" "What's *that?*" Prudence asked, and there is no need to indicate how she added, "Grilled-cheese sandwiches and beer?" "Up your ass!" Bumpy said, to which the oldest daughter, the stunning and innocent Sam, broke into tears and ran from the room. Once when I was in the next room, I heard Prudence say, *"Surely* he can get a job on a newspaper in the city," the smug tone of her voice indicating that, unlike Bumpy who was up to such high and enduring stuff "downtown," any stumblebum could do *that.* Laughing, and unable to let the moment go by, I charged into the room, suavely announced, "Tomorrow, my dear Prudence, I'm going down to the *New York Times* and offer myself as editor of their book section," and smiled with the self-relish of a man who was certain his background as managing editor of *The Rocket,* as dipsomaniac, and as lunatic who had undergone both insulin- and electroshock treatments eminently qualified him for the job. Prudence outdid herself: her eyes corruscated with flaming, unadulterated venom. Driving home that night, I said, "I guess we'll have to stop going there." "Don't pay any attention to her," Patience said, adding, "Frankly, I think Bumpy'd die if you ever stopped going up there. I'm not in the least kidding when I say you're probably the only friend he ever had. And, let's face it, Prudence doesn't have anyone to talk with save me." As things turned out, we were to stop going there anyway. In a contest between Nature and science, Nature had won and Patience had become, alas, pregnant. As an indirect result of this pregnancy, I'd soon be back at Avalon Valley; and though we were to see a good deal of them after my sons were born, on those occasions both Prudence and Bumpy would leave me to my own devices to the point of outright ignoring me; and this, as the reader will see, proved to be fine with me. Oddly, though, and after so many years, I heard from Bumpy only recently.

Beginning his letter, "Ah, to be in Paris, now that spring is here!!!" Bumpy went on to explain that, as he quite often had to get into Africa on business, he was now calling "good, gay, faggy old Paree" home and was, in fact, writing his note from a sidewalk café he frequented in the Saint Germain des Prés. Apparently a lovely spring day, Bumpy wrote, "The birds is singing, the bees is buzzing, the cats is mewing. Though one cat sure ain't," he added ominously. On the route from his apartment to the café a "black bastard" had made the fatal mistake of attempting to steal across Bumpy's path, Bumpy had given him in the "arse" the full kicking force of his cyclist's boot, and in the gutter he had left the "sneaky mudder fudder for dead!" Bumpy's comment on the episode was: "Har! Har! Har!" Never having been good at languages and "all that horseshit," he was yet to acquire a speaking knowledge of French and thus hadn't made any friends, finding Paris lonely, hostile, and inhabited by a "bunch of chiseling, anti-good-ol'-Americee, and muff-diving greaseballs! Utter swine," he emphasized. Heavier than ever, he had been warned by his doctor that his blood pressure was such that he'd never reach forty. Having been ordered to diet and exercise, Bumpy took long walks on weekends, browsing through the bookstalls on the Left Bank and to no avail asking after a book by "M. Frederick Exley." "Did that horny book of yours ever come out?" he asked. "How about sending me a copy? I'll bet it's *hornier than horny, you scurvy old cross-eyed degenerate you!*" Bumpy told me that of course I had heard (and of course I hadn't) about Prudence divorcing him;

and whether it was true or not, I was most gratified to hear that "I just got plumb up to here one day, grabbed my toothbrush, and moved out on that la-di-da Vassarite bitch!" Prudence was now remarried to a Pratt & Whitney engineer and with the children was living in a house fronting Lake Worth on Singer Island ("a swell fucking place to raise kids!") at Riviera Beach, Florida; and Bumpy "gol dang sure" missed the three Sams and bet me that, as they had grown so big, I wouldn't even recognize "the cute little snot-noses." The last time he visited them in Florida he had taken them to a drive-in movie ("we had a fucking brawl") and afterward, because it was still early and a lovely, tropical evening, he and the Sams had sat on the dock in front of the house ("a real dump compared to what ol' Bumpy gave them!") eating popcorn and throwing pebbles into the lake. The location reminded him of a hotel on the west coast of Africa where he often stopped when he was there on business; and now he couldn't go to that hotel without remembering that "gol dang night with the three Sams and feeling all kind of sad and sick inside." Speaking of Africa, he said that the one time he had got to the Congo he had hired a couple "spear-thrower guides" who recalled the incident and after much travail had found the place where his parents had been "slaughtered in the uprising of '33," and parenthetically he added, "I must have told you before, didn't I, how Mom and Dad were killed in the bush uprising of '33?" Finally attempting to get at his reason for writing, he said that he wanted to make amends for his never having visited me when I was back at Avalon Valley, explaining that it was Prudence who had forbidden him to come, telling me that she had in fact called my doctor ("a Doctor K., wasn't it?") and told him that Bumpy and I acted

as unhappy catalysts on one another and that under no circumstances should the doctor allow Bumpy to take me
from the hospital grounds. "Now that I think about it,"
Bumpy added morosely, "I don't suppose the doctor knew
who the fuck she was or what she was trying to say." After
my sons were born and Patience and I had once again gone
to Bumpy's weekends, he couldn't ask me to come along on
his "drives" with him as Prudence had threatened to divorce him if he did so. He wanted me to know after all
these years that his having to ignore me hurt him deeply
and that he took full responsibility for doing so. He should
have taken a stand right there, he said, and an unfortunate
marriage would have terminated that much sooner. "I'm
sorry," he wrote. "You were the only *real* friend I ever had."
Getting dramatically maudlin in the way of B-class gang-
ster movies, he added, "and, like the swine I am, I double-
crossed you!" Then he became nostalgic. "Gol dang,
though, we sure had a brawl, didn't we? Mucking those
tweedy bastards about, shooting the fucking cats, and all?"
Summing up, Bumpy said he was over there trying to save
the family's oil interests in Africa, but that what with one
different "nigger nation emerging every third day and na-
tionalizing the refineries," he hadn't much hope of succeeding and ended his letter thus: "I left my capacity for
hoping on the jet planes that led to the little emerging
nations." Signing it "Bumpy here!!!" he added this postscript: "Write me a nice long letter, you old muff-diver, and
tell me some of those screwy things you know—about
Plutarch and all."

From his opening and inadvertent paraphrase of Brown-
ing to his concluding travesty of Fitzgerald, I had
thought—almost able to hear him boast of his felinicidal

mania, watching him so trouble himself with notions of sinister "niggers" and "emerging nations," thinking of him sitting so fat-bellied and so bebooted at a café table in, of all places, the Saint Germain des Prés and while writing his letter perhaps being taken for a famous author, envisioning him charging up to startled Parisian book panderers and demanding the horny works of "M. Frederick Exley," trying at once to envision all these singular and wonderful twists of life—from beginning to end I thought I had read the letter in a state of wild hilarity. But an odd thing happened. When I went back to reread it, attempting gluttonously to re-experience that gaiety at Bumpy's expense, I found that I could barely discern the words from where the dampness had run the ink, found that after so many years, and as Felix Krull had done for his father, I had finally reciprocated Bumpy's love by paying him "the abundant tribute of my tears."

—

By the time I finished my first sentence and believed myself ready to undertake my epic tale of "pity," in Patience's fourth or fifth month of pregnancy, I began experiencing sudden and excruciating pains in my chest and decided that in my father's image I was dying of lung cancer. Hence I took to a drinking which even by my standards was torrential, characterized, as it was, by an unutterable hopelessness. It is obvious to me now (and of course no psychiatrist enlightened me) that as I watched Patience's body blossom forth, as almost day to day I witnessed the growth of what was to be a responsibility I neither wanted nor could accept, in all its perverse wonder my mind succeeded in bringing me totally and intransigently back to myself, even at the debilitating expense of living intimately, like a doomed and illicit lover unable to help himself, with the thought of my own death. Not that death itself engrossed me. Owning dim memories of that to which my father had been reduced (a man, I knew, more suited by temperament to pain than I), I was sure I couldn't see the disease through to the end; and during the next few weeks all my waking hours were given over to mapping strategies for aborting the malaise's hideous course. Late mornings at Sam's Bar on Gedney Way in White Plains, I ordered the first of my twenty to twenty-five daily Vodka Presbyterians, struck up conversations with strangers, and with only a rudimentary discretion worked the conversation round to suicide. I asked timid clerks and burly beer-truck drivers whether an overdose of sleeping pills caused painful hemorrhaging, what they thought of the theory that a man leaping from the Empire State Building would lapse into merciful unconsciousness before splattering the pavement, if there were any possibility that a twenty-two pistol (I had one of Bumpy's in mind) placed properly against the temple could fail to do the job. Like me, these strangers were daylight drinkers eluding their own phantasma; and yet I found it oddly edifying that none of them found the subject bedeviling; none exclaimed, "Let's leave off this morbidity!" Such was the clinical and speculative enthusiasm for the subject—"Now, if I was gonna knock myself off . . ."—that I came to see suicide occupying a greater piece of the American consciousness than I had theretofore imagined. And this gave me comfort. Thinking that so many men were ready to make jubilant jumps into oblivion, or to put tidy little holes in their heads, with me, I was unable to view my own self-destruction as anything but a trifling and dreary item.

At Sam's they served sandwiches jammed with a thinly sliced, mouth-melting roast beef; and during the course of the day I consumed three or four of these, with lettuce, salt and pepper, and mayonnaise. Having set cancer's "sudden loss of weight" symptom, which I knew to be a relatively late one, as my clarion to tell Nature to go screw and put the pistol to my sideburns, I ate hoping to defer that clarion as long as possible. Hence I became the first man in clinical history to put on twenty pounds while "wasting away" of cancer. Cozy with vodka and held in thrall by the ways and means of suicide, I went for hours without pain. But the moment I became happily conscious of its absence, it struck. Furiously, mercilessly, it struck, causing me to grab breathlessly at my chest and, for a distracting pang, to hurl myself into the bar's blunt edge, against which I pressed the humerus of my arm with all the weight and strength in my body. So real was the pain that I strangled for breath, tears of anguish formed in my eyes, and invariably I cursed the arbitrariness of Thanatos, whispering, "I'll fix you—you obscene, unspeakable shit!"

Following a day when the pain had been particularly acute, and wanting her relaxed when I told her, I sat a pregnant Patience in a chair; and with what in my drunkenness I thought a certain manly aplomb, I related to her the results of my imagined X-rays and the fictional prognosis of the invented lung surgeon. Twenty-five hundred dollars, I matter-of-factly explained, was needed for immediate lung surgery. Poor Patience, I never loved her as I loved her enduring the pain I gave her at that moment, never felt gratitude like the gratitude I felt at her generous reaction. Of course I could have the money! To whom should she make the check? Oh, God! Who was the doctor? She had to speak to him right away! For when was the surgery scheduled? Where? That I so underestimated her intelligence is the most eloquent statement of how aberrant I had become. Calmly (though somewhat sepulchrally) explaining that my survival chances were the statistical one in twenty, I told Patience I had decided to undergo the ordeal alone, that one had hope (not much, my doleful eyes seemed to imply), and that if things worked out swimmingly, I'd return to her and the yet-unborn child. "You can't go through pregnancy and my dying at the same time," I magnanimously suggested. Having made plans to steal Bumpy's pistol, I was going to take the money and flee to Manitou Springs, Colorado. On my bartender's day off, I had used to drive there, sit shirt-sleeved on a concrete-and-wooden bench before a tidy green triangular park, and stare at snowcapped Pike's Peak rising into the heady blue of a Colorado sky, wondering even then if my life were over and bolting up frequently to walk across the bonelike street to a rustic bar where I drank enough bourbon to dream myself back into life. That was the way, and where, I had decided to spend my final days; and I wanted to have enough money to do so in style, even planning to leave the matronly motel keeper a few extra dollars to clean my brains from her aqua walls. Unfortunately, with an unidentified surgeon operating on a nonexistent lung lesion in a fantasized amphitheater, it abruptly developed that the fees might be hard to come by, that they might, in fact, be impossible. "You could get the money from Bumpy!" I cried. Patience began to weep, terribly, her pregnant body racked with sobs, her nostrils dilating with moisture. "Of course I could," she said. "Or from Prudence. Or from any number of people. But you've got to let us help you!" What saved me at this point of the drunken nightmare I don't know—Patience's tears, the subconscious thought of what it was she carried in her, vague memories of the man I might have been. Whatever it was, I never mentioned my "illness" again; and though I did nothing to make it easier for Patience, drinking day and night, I left her alone to come to whatever peace her resources could bring her.

Each morning, with the stealth of a second-story man, I rifled Patience's pocketbook for twenty dollars, or forged her name to a personal check, and went to Sam's, where, stolidly cursing Patience for her hardheartedness, I no longer bothered to eat roast-beef sandwiches, drank vodka, stopped talking with strangers, and endured a pain which I am unable to describe. After two weeks of unremitting drinking, I awoke at midnight of one room-swimming evening to find that the goblins and the gremlins, the beetles and the bats, had descended en masse and were tearing great chunks of flesh from my body. While Patience (a long way from Bryn Mawr now!) sat rigidly horrified in a chair, I dementedly climbed the walls, tore Venetian blinds from the windows, knocked books from the shelves, and battered furniture to pieces; did this until, exhausted and in a paroxysm of sobbing, I flung myself atop the bed, where for an hour or two, perhaps three, I slept a fitful, haunted sleep. Waking in need of another drink, I poured a triple, then another, and with the third came that short-lived, boozy, fuck-it-all contentment of the drunk. Bumpy, accompanied by two policemen, came the next day and took me away. Even after the Avalon Valley doctors had taken multiple X-rays and assured me my lungs were clear, the pain lingered for weeks into that spring, as if my subconscious were determined to protect me from the thought of Patience or child.

———

If Dr. K. was dismayed that in only a year's time I had fulfilled Paddy the Duke's prophecy and returned to Avalon Valley, he never said so. He said, "What do you want to do?" He meant *do* with that foul malaise, my life. "Oh, don't you know?" I said in the most sneeringly self-deprecatory way. "Don't you know? I want a destiny that's grand enough for me! Like Michelangelo's God reaching out to Adam, I want nothing less than to reach across the ages and stick my dirty fingers into posterity! Want? Why, there's nothing I don't want! I want *this*, and I want *that*, and I want—well, *everything!*" Taut with self-loathing, I added, "And, incidentally, that's my theme song, you know?" Then I broke into song. "Aye, yi, yii, *yiii* . . . fair sen-yor-eeee-*tah!*"

Dr. K. didn't laugh. Instead, he put me to work. Suspecting that patients were welshing on their jobs, which he felt to be therapeutically vital, he had me make a chart of all of those in our building, together with their hospital occupations. My job was to pick names randomly from the chart and by telephone check on whether they were showing up for work. Though it wasn't exactly sticking my begrimed fingers into posterity, I enjoyed the sense of power it gave me and I was impressing myself deep into the consciousness of my fellow inmates. Not realizing I was only cursorily spot-checking them, mornings a half-dozen of them would come bearing gifts, packets of cigarettes, Oh Henry! candy bars, Mom's chocolate-chip cookies, and wanting to know if I couldn't overlook their not going to work that day. As often as not I accepted the bribe. If the man appeared neat and clean-shaven and I thought he was going to shoot pool or meet a girl in the dugouts of the baseball field for a little hanky-panky (occasionally, I understood, a lot of hanky-panky), I said okay. I hated to take the gifts. Until the last days of her pregnancy Patience came visiting days with cartons of cigarettes and twenty-dollar bills; my mother, sisters, and long-forgotten maiden aunts sent jolly notes of encouragement stuffed with much-used bills; and though he didn't come to visit me, Bumpy eased his conscience by sending me twenty-five-dollar money orders. Hence there were days when I strolled about the grounds dressed in hospital corduroy and my wallet swollen with sixty or seventy bucks. I took the bribes because I didn't want it out that a patient's goofing off was a matter of indifference to me. If the gift-bearer appeared ill-kempt or depressed, and I suspected he was going to sit all day staring at the floor and picking his nose, I said, "No dice, buddy." Then I essayed a lecture to the effect that if he couldn't function in the protected world of the hospital, he'd never make it on the outside. Though those who knew me on the outside would have laughed heartily at me garbed in a mantle of self-righteousness, I thought I wore it gracefully and was proud. Not once in the long months of my final stay in an insane asylum did Dr. K. shame me by mentioning the "carcinosis" which had brought me there.

A private room was a highly coveted possession at Avalon Valley, and Dr. K. got me one of these in a building at the south end of the grounds where I was permitted to write on completing my morning's checking. Not that Dr. K. necessarily believed I was a writer. Still, he seemed to understand that trying to break and adjust people to what may be an inhuman society is an unwarranted undertaking and that rebellion, in whatever form, is not always an unhealthy enterprise. And so, having my first "immortal" sentence, I began to write, though I fortunately abandoned my tale of "pity" peopled with suave advertising men and crusty clients. For the first time Paddy the Duke's smug admonition that I had best ask myself what I was doing at Avalon Valley had begun to haunt me, and taking a deep breath, I started fearfully into the past in search of answers. In many ways that book was this book, which I wasn't then ready to write. Without a thought of organization I wrote vignettes and thirty-page paragraphs about anything and everything I could remember. There are times now when, in nostalgia, I tell myself I'll never again put down the things I did then, but I know I'm only confusing quantity with quality. If nothing else, I wrote a great deal during those months, writing rapidly, furiously, exultantly, heart-sinkingly, and a manuscript of whatever merit began, page upon page, filling up the suitcase at the foot of my iron cot. When I became tired in the late afternoon, I joined Snow White and Bronislaw (the former had stayed in, the latter had also gone out and been sent back) in a booth at the community store, bought them coffee and pie à la mode, and read to them my day's torrential output. From Bronislaw I got for my efforts, all during the readings, shrieks of delight and exclamations like, "Oh, ain't he a fucking bunny!" From Snow White I always got a moody silence during the readings, followed on completing them by either a "pretty fucking good," at which I beamed with unabashed pleasure, or a "pretty fucking bad," at which I felt downcast. I always tried to get Snow White to elaborate the latter criticism. But he steadfastly and mutely refused, shaking his head an exasperated *no*. He was still weary, as weary as I had ever seen him: slouched exhaustedly down in the straight-backed wooden booth, eyes closed, there were times when he was too weary to chew his tobacco and the cud lay for hours, a soggy jawbreaker, between teeth and cheek. Still, I had large love for him and great respect for his intelligence. Whenever he reacted negatively, I always wrote *"pretty fucking bad"* across the day's work and fastened the pages together with a paper clip before consigning them to the suitcase. At some future date, I told myself, I'd have to rework or discard those pages. I hadn't the time then. The past was rushing over me too rapidly. In this way the winter passed; and when one new-green and brilliant spring day I was summoned to the office and told I was the father of twin boys, and though for the benefit of all those present I expressed wonder and joy, I was pleased to see the news affected me not a bit.

On being released from the hospital (I had "beat" them again; even the doctors assumed my sons would instill in me a high and tenacious sense of duty), and on the assumption that Patience, though a durable girl, could not care for three infants simultaneously, by mutual agreement with Prudence our sons were sent to her house and custody until my sense of fatherhood rose to the surface. Until it was too late to do anything about it, it never rose. I was on a writing kick and was by then unable to stay the rush of words. I wrote in joy and in anguish, wrote giggling like a madman and with the tears streaming down my face, wrote at times so exhilarated that I daren't move for fear of discovering I was incapable of what I seemed to be getting down on paper. I wrote and wrote and wrote, filling up one manila envelope, and then another, and still another, until those envelopes of manuscript, set one atop another, began to look like a scale model for a madman's cantilevered sky-scraper and the thought of an editor's ever reading through it aroused in me a desire to make a stop. But I could not stop. There was, that summer and fall, something absolutely abandoned about my output, days when I must have slapped down ten, twelve, fifteen thousand words. Patience continued to go out during the day to save humanity. Coming home evenings, she smiled at my exhilaration, fixed me one of her exquisitely sumptuous meals, and listened to me rage and watched me pound my chest. In my new-found sense of accomplishment, I was a veritable chanticleer.

All this was a good deal harder on Patience than she ever said. Though pleased that my book was going well (or perhaps she hated it—who knows?), she lived her week in an agony of apartness, coming miraculously together on Fridays when we drove north to Goldens Bridge to see the boys. Churlishly, I went, too. My reasons for going were perfectly self-centered, having nothing to do with any desire to see my sons. Now that the book was proceeding with such satanic glibness, my main motive—as it is with every psychopath—was to protect myself until it was finished; and in order to do this I had to suggest to Prudence that I wasn't altogether a monster so as not to get thrown out onto the street, bag, baggage, and manuscript. Having had a lot of practice, I played the game very well and was of good cheer no matter what, smiling amiably in the face of both Prudence's reproachful glances and her not infrequent inquiries about my job prospects. Taking my sons onto my lap, I kissed them unceasingly; to the matronly cooing of Patience and Prudence ("Isn't that adorable?" that cooing seemed to say), I tickled and made over them endlessly. I kissed them and caressed them and squeezed them—and, alas, never once did their warmth permeate me. For all I felt, they might have been yarn-haired rag dolls. It was as if I had been pathetically burned and in the process all the nerve ends in my body had been destroyed. And in a way I suppose they had. I had been consumed by the flames of my own reprehensible desire and was living in the terrifying memory of the flames, spending all my waking hours recalling the horror and the dismay, the laughter and the bitterness, of that holocaust I called my life. Not that I mean to imply that a single sentence I had by then put down possessed any merit. This made no difference at all. Even were that manila tower one great edifice of bland clichés and paltry insights, I had no power to restrain myself from adding another, and still another, floor. Bland or not, it was the only vision I had, I was consumed by it, and I was going for the sky. My sons were dead to me.

When fall came, I had still another reason for going to Prudence's. In Poughkeepsie I had discovered Fitzgerald's saloon where, employing an electronic gadget, they were able to pick up a Schenectady channel and get the Giants' home games, thereby eluding the blackout in the New York area. Each Sunday about noon I dutifully kissed Patience and my sons, smiled apologetically at Prudence, looked anxiously about for Bumpy, who was never there and who seemed to be avoiding me (though I didn't then know why), got into the car (which I wouldn't have had access to had I remained in Scarsdale), and began the drive north through my lovely autumn valley. Over the years professional football had become extremely popular, a number of fans from the city had discovered Fitzgerald's, and the place was always crowded, the cheering high and exhilarating. Surprisingly, though, I myself seldom cheered now. I was still, for I had the power and, no matter how adroitly Gifford handled himself, silently I said to myself, speaking in the direction of the tube, "Have your day, friend. In a matter of months, I'll be more famous than you." Nor was this all that difficult to believe. Gifford's play throughout that season had been characterized—to me, at least—by an embarrassing and painful sluggishness. His timing was bad, nearly wrongheaded. He was dropping passes he once would have caught with ease. He was missing blocks. And against the St. Louis Cardinals he had taken a hand-off from Conerly and had run into the line of scrimmage only to discover—with what must have been a thorny humiliation—that he not only didn't have the ball but that it had even then been scooped from the turf by a Cardinal defender who was effortlessly making his way to the goal for the winning touchdown. Because of such play there were rumors, some of which saw print, that he had lost both interest in and heart for the game. And though I never believed it, these suspicions were not unjustified. Having his own television and radio shows, his own newspaper column in the *Journal-American,* his photo in nearly every publication one put one's hand to, like Joe DiMaggio or Helen Hayes or Robert Moses, he had wedged a place in the city's mentality: he had become *unavoidable.* As a result, I had for some time suspected that the demands required to keep that wedge firmly entrenched in the city's skull were costing him dearly by way of conditioning and that the distractions of High Place were literally taking his eye from the ball. Moreover, he was thirty (was it possible?), if not old, aging for a running halfback. Thus it was that where other men saw in his game a lack of interest, I saw only a touching and worried bewilderment. Neither his legs nor his hands—nor, one suspects, even his heart—were doing what they once had done. And if he understood what was wrong, he seemed to be not accepting: youth was passing. Worse than anything, I had for a long time suspected, known really, in the way these things are sometimes known, that the lethargy which had been dominating his play was going to cost him more than the embarrassment of a dropped pass. It was eventually going to cost him physical injury.

Of course I never finished the book. When the writing was going well, I had lived in a perverse rapture from which it sometimes took hours to unwind. As a result, Patience had reluctantly been giving me three or four dollars daily with which, after a day at the writing table, I could drive to White Plains, go to Sam's, drink beer, and wait for the dreadful exhilaration to subside. As long as the book went well, all was splendid. But then the bad time set in, the time when, unable to avoid it any longer (how many words had I then? five hundred thousand?), I had to tackle that mountain of manuscript and tie together all the "pain" and the "joy" and the "anguish" I had so facilely slapped on paper. And to my horror (for I had read the books which by now all but crowded us out of the apartment) I discovered I knew nothing whatever about the grueling, mundane business of making form out of fragments. Like a man with a handful of exquisite, or what in my vanity I was sure were exquisite, diamonds, I hadn't the slightest notion of how to set them. More vexing still, whenever I went back to those books to see how other and better men (I went to E. M. Forster and Flaubert and Scott Fitzgerald) had worked it out, I discovered I couldn't concentrate for ten seconds at a time. Whether this was from being still absorbed in my own work or from having exhausted myself in getting it all down, I don't know, but my powers of concentration had ceased to exist. Thus it was that almost overnight I went from uncontrollable rapture to black despair; and Patience, detecting this and knowing what it forbode, cut off my beer money and I now lay on the davenport, stared at the ceiling, and waited to be miraculously graced with a sense of shape, occasionally filching from Patience's purse enough money to go to Sam's and get drunk. Unhappily, I filched too much one night, got drunk on vodka, came home, and with bleary eyes read through the entire manuscript. I am sure now that I remember that manuscript more kindly than it deserves. Some of it seemed relevant, some quite good, some of it may even have been—I was about to say art, and that would never do. What there was in places was a rhetorical though high-blown eloquence. Having put it down with furious rapidity, I detected places where in a whirlwind of creation I had achieved a certain grace, that eloquence which, according to Mann out of Cicero, resides in the *motus animi continuus* of composition. Twelve hours reading it, from first to last I read in pain and embarrassment. On finishing, with great and solemn ceremony I gathered it into my arms, walked out the door and down into the basement, where I flung it, with the rest of the garbage, into the blast incinerator. Then I went back to the apartment, lay down on the bed next to Patience, and wept stormily. It was a year of the hardest work I had ever done, a year which for output, if nothing else, I knew I would never again equal. I burned it because on every page I had discovered I loathed the America I knew. A long time before in that private hospital I had learned that hate can redeem as well as love, but I was yet to articulate this truth and hence did not know that in writing a book hate is as valid a departure point as love.

The book's going bad and the puerile and sacrificial burning of it proved my undoing. Not only did I again begin drinking to excess, but save for those Sunday afternoons at Fitzgerald's I had nothing now to sustain me, and lying on the davenport and staring at the ceiling was only able to bring into my ken the most limited of fantasies, say, that of being gainfully employed at a factory, and only this by dint of exorbitant mental strain and for but a few seconds at a time. After lying thus for two weeks, I knew that the men in the white jackets were once again imminent; but try as I would I could not summon the strength to get up, pack a bag, and go away from that place—where the typewriter keys were now gathering dust—before they came after me. Moreover, no longer having my dream to buffer me from the warmth of others, I did the worst thing I could have done: I fell quite hopelessly in love with my sons.

It happened quite simply. One day at Prudence's I found myself alone on the sun porch with them. They were in their play pen, and hardly conscious of it I was staring at them in the most exasperated way (since burning the manuscript, I no longer found it necessary to play the game even at Prudence's), when to my astonishment (for my sons had grown to the point of assuming personalities) I noticed that they were staring back at me with an equal, if not more formidable, exasperation. Though countless times I had been told that they had been manufactured in my image— "Oooooh, don't they look like their daddy!"—I had never particularly noticed it, or if I had, I had ignored the resemblance. Looking at them now, I might, I thought, be looking into a cracked, double-image educing mirror. Both owned the slightly affected, contemplative turn of the head, the same snub noses, the same pouting impatience. Abruptly I started to laugh, loudly and raucously. For many days I had been dreaming of fleeing, imagining how Patience would have me brought back, would forgive me, and would let me lie on the davenport for a few more months. In my heart I knew she wouldn't. She had too much character and financial independence for that. But it was pleasant to imagine her doing so. I was laughing because by one of those quick leaps of the mind I now saw myself, having been found and brought before a judge on a nonsupport charge, beaming innocently at him and saying, "They ain't my sons, your honor," while my sons, their diapers down around their knees, kept yapping, "He ain't our old man, neither!"—after which the incredulous judge, looking from me to them, from them to me, finally said to the bailiff, "Lock these crazy bastards up!" As I laughed, nearly hysterical now, the boys suddenly caught up the feeling of it and laughed, too; so that we laughed together, gleefully and uncontrollably, as though they, too, were conscious of the joke. Rising, I walked to the play pen, took them up into my arms, and we had for the first time, and after so many months, made contact.

That contact proved distressfully unsettling. During the week I now lay on the davenport as moon-struck as any teenager, thinking of them constantly and yearning for some great miracle or tragedy which would spur me from my slumber and get me up and out of there. Once out, I knew (as did Patience, though she never said so; indeed, by then we had stopped making contact altogether) that my sons could come and stay with their mother where they belonged, a place to which they could not come as long as there was a possibility of my once again climbing the walls. To the point of prayer I yearned for something to happen, longed so desperately that after a time I came to live with a terrible sense of foreboding, knowing finally that something was going to happen.

In those weeks Gifford and the Giants were all that sustained me, and I lived only from Sunday afternoon to Sunday afternoon. And though I did not know that the tragedy would be Gifford's injury and that I would in effect be deprived of my last prop, watching his painfully troubled play I had begun to think that it would be. It was at this moment that J., a friend since boyhood and an attorney in Watertown, telephoned me from out of the northern mists of my childhood and volunteered to treat me to a football game. It wasn't specifically mentioned that he would be host and I guest, but it was understood in a tacit way. What friends I still had—and J. was one of the two, the other being the Counselor—had for a long time accepted the fact that the price of my friendship was both emotionally and financially dear. When I telephoned J. collect, out of embarrassment I was no longer able to offer him the explanations which had been lies in any event: money for books, for job-hunting expenses, for Christmas presents. The lies had pained him as much as me, and because they weren't in the least necessary I had acquired the disarmingly blunt habit of shouting into the receiver, "Hello, J.? Fred! Send me twenty-five, will yuh?" And he had sent it. The main thing was not to mention what we both knew: that the money was going for liquor. It was J. who understood—and it troubled him deeply, I think—that my dependence was hurting him scarcely a bit while it was destroying me. He was, he knew, a party to a murder. But being a friend of my Youth he could no more deny me than he could deny nourishment to his body.

———

When we were adolescents (I stayed that way much longer than he), J. and I had formed, without ever bothering to give utterance to our motives, a conspiracy against exclusiveness, one that stayed with us—no doubt an attempt to stay youth itself—well into adulthood. We conspired against doors marked *Private* and *No Admittance* and *Sold Out* and *Restricted Area,* and though I can't speak for J., I think I understood my own motives. With an instinctive cynicism I knew that behind those doors there would be nothing particularly glittering or brilliant or profound, and that if one didn't make "getting in" a contest of the wills, having once gained the other side of the door, one would sense no achievement whatever. Over the years the conspiracy had required ingenuity and dishonesty, cunning and wit, self-effacement and brashness on our part; but we had got into ball games and plays, parties and conventions—all sorts of conclaves which had proclaimed their exclusiveness for so long that did one not know better one might assume that those on the other side of the door were creatures apart, somehow more blest than other men. For this reason I shouldn't have been surprised when, driving down the parkway on Saturday afternoon, and having just asked him in what section of the stadium our tickets were, J. responded that he had no tickets. I shouldn't have been surprised; but I was, terribly so, and that surprise ran quickly to anger and despondency. "Jesus Christ, J.," I moaned, "the game's been sold out for weeks. How the hell—" But J. interrupted me with a chuckle of surprise at what he deemed my new-found sense of propriety. He asked rhetorically,

"Haven't we always got in?" Then he laughed again, trying to enlist me in the spirit of the thing. But the spirit eluded me, and I became tense and depressed. The game was going to require *that* wit and *that* cunning, neither of which I now possessed. I had been wasting away amidst the musty dust of books, seeking to put the past down on paper, and for month on month had lived my life scarcely ever venturing from either the safety of the hospital or the haven of the apartment. Having by now taken to closing the blinds in the apartment, I was living a life in which even the sunshine reached me obliquely, through the windows of the car or not at all. Not only was I incapable of entering the taxing game to which J. now bid me; as the car approached the city, I was made terribly nervous by the increasing traffic, which now whizzed by on either side and had me looking apprehensively right and left over my shoulders, frantically, as though my head sat on a turnstile. By the time we reached Manhattan, I was in such need of a drink—and, more important than a drink, of familiar surroundings—that I almost shrieked, "Park the car on Third Avenue and we'll go to Clarke's!"

We got the tickets from the Giants' quarterback Charley Conerly. We did not get them easily or for some time, until after I had been spurred into the game by J. It was nothing he said to me. It was something his eyes told me. In the process they unfortunately told me a good deal more, something I almost wasn't up to hearing. On arriving at Clarke's and detecting my nervous state—that at least momentarily I wasn't up to helping him—J. gave me five dollars to drink beer, removed his bulging pocket secretary from his inside jacket pocket, and asked the bartender for two dollars' worth of dimes. Looking at the swollen secre-

tary made me smile. Containing the names of people who
knew the brother-in-law of one of the players, or who had
been in the service with one of the coaches, or who were
said to be boozing companions of the ticket manager, or
who were simply people whose station was so exalted that
they, or it was said that they, could get in any place, any
time, the wallet held names and telephone numbers J. had
accumulated over the past months, the equipment, as it
were, of our conspiracy. I knew the odds all too well. Half
of these people wouldn't even know what J. was talking
about; and the other half, the vain ones, rather than admit
their influence to be no greater than the next man's, would
suggest the wildest alternatives, everything from going to
Times Square and looking for a fat man in a black silk suit
with a white carnation in his lapel to calling a mysterious,
unlisted phone number in Las Vegas. Some one or two
would offer valid advice, hold out definite hope of tickets,
and it was for these one or two that one's ear, like a radar,
had to be finely attuned. Though I smiled, I felt altogether
incapable of these shenanigans; and for the next hour,
while on the telephone J. cajoled and threatened, flattered
and beseeched, contrived and made jokes, I stood at the bar
drinking, conscious that the surroundings were not after all
familiar, and that I did not feel easy in Clarke's.

In the years since I had last been there the price of beer
had risen from fifteen to a preposterous fifty cents a glass,
and like most drinkers I felt a heavy distress at being in a
bar where with five dollars I did not have enough to get a
glow on. "Who the hell are these people kidding?" I sneeringly asked myself. That sneer encompassed my entire surroundings. The decor of the room, which I had once
thought so very English, now seemed merely dingy. In the

back a great, barnlike dining room had been added; and with a different kind of luck, I thought, the customers would have scurried to some other place in search of the intimacy that had been sacrificed to the expansion. Feeling cold and hostile, I was standing there wondering why Clarke's, having almost totally changed the face it presented to the public, should be lucky enough to survive, when I noticed the bartender, he noticed me, and in a vague way I thought I understood. The bartender was my chum from the long ago—he who had been caught in the middle the night the blonde's date, whacking away at the bar with his effeminate hand, had demanded my expulsion from the human race. Recognizing each other simultaneously, we did not speak; but our heads nodded in recognition of each other. In its way that nodding was a thousand times more eloquent than anything we might have said. "You look older," his nod seemed to say. "You do, too," said mine. "And how did those years go?" his head asked; to which mine replied, "Look at me—you can see." "Yeah, I can see." It was this nodding, this tacit conversation, that made me see why Clarke's had lasted. Clarke's was a place of youth where we were no longer youths, a place of high optimism where we knew better. And save for one or two perennial adolescents the people who came there now were not those we had brushed shoulders with and hence did not know what the place had been. But the bartender and I knew. And so knowing, we had an amiable warmth pass between us. Ordering a shot, I drank it off; then I ordered another. He did not take the money for this second one; and when I drank it abruptly off, he refilled the glass. Again he didn't take the money, and his nod seemed to say, "It's that bad, huh?" In acknowledgment, I nodded that it was.

All this time J. had been drifting between the phone booth and the bar, filling me in on his progress. So caught up in my own "conversation," I had nodded only cursorily and didn't really think of him again until, detecting that I was about out of money, I asked for more. He met the request with such a look of surprise that my eyes fled immediately to the clock. To my surprise, I discovered I had gone through the five dollars in an hour's time. Attempting to keep condescension from his voice, the tone of adult speaking to child, and introducing that element of false joviality with which people often approach drunks, J. reminded me that the night was young and that we had hours to do the town. This was news of which I was aware and which I met by putting on my face the base, pouting, and churlish grimace of the alcoholic denied. Seeing this, J. suddenly became silent, cutting himself off in mid-lecture, and laid ten dollars on the bar. His eyes were squinted in an agony of apprehension, an unequivocal disappointment no longer muddied by false hopes for me. It was the simple, unadulterated disappointment that signaled the end of the game for me, that told me the final whistle had blown and I wasn't going to get the ball again. What I saw in his eyes struck me mute, crushed me, terrified me! Oh, I had borne the grievous eyes of family and acquaintances, of Patience and Prudence; but the friend of one's Youth—he may be the only friend one ever has—never sees one's defeat. Or almost never; and if he does, one can be certain it is too late for him. Having seen my abasement, that I groveled and had ceased to struggle, unwittingly J. had hurt me terribly. My first impulse—as it always is with the alcoholic—was to hurt him back. Seeking room enough for my grief, I wanted to flee out into the night, leaving the ten dollars on the bar—imagining that J. would spend his entire weekend worrying about me. But I rejected that, thinking of still a hundred other ways to hurt him, rejecting them all in turn as lacking subtlety. By that time, unfortunately, I had already put a considerable dent in the ten dollars. Finally, by luck, through the deep, devious waters of the drunk's mind, there arose the obvious question: why hurt him at all? He was right—God, yes, he was right! Accepting this, I, too, got some dimes, slid them into my pocket, and walked to the other phone booth, in the dining room.

Tentatively, shyly, I began dialing. Whereas I might have just emerged from a Trappist monastery, this game seemed a dreadfully secular business. I called people I hadn't talked with in years; though they offered no comfort in the way of tickets, they seemed rather pleased to hear from me. One of them jocularly said, "How much yuh need?" Another said, "Why, Exley, you dip-shitty old bastard—*I thought you'd be dead.*" He then invited me up to his Riverside Drive apartment to get drunk with him; but in the background his wife groaned loudly and achingly and distinctly said, *"Oh, no— not that crazy bastard!"* That he might join me for a drink, he then tried to find out where I was. But I refused to tell him and said good-bye by saying, "Tell that witch you're married to that she ought to douche out her rancid soul." With each call I became more obnoxiously persuasive, and through sheer balls I finally got through to Charley Conerly at his hotel. Feeling unable to handle it, I got J. and had him talk to Conerly. The conversation was a long one, and other than Conerly's agreeing to leave two tickets for us at Booth 21 of the stadium and the fact of our (for I had my head stuck inside the booth) being as giddy as two teenagers in contact with a cinema star, I remember only that

Conerly had the gift of granting one ease. When he began the conversation, J.'s voice had been hurried and nervous, the way one's voice is with the famous. But by the end of the conversation J.'s voice had become modulated and easy. Whatever it was he said to J., Conerly succeeded in putting him at his ease, a gift not all of the famous are said to have. Describing to him the change in his voice as the conversation had proceeded, I later asked J. what Conerly had said to him. J. couldn't remember anything specific, saying only, "He was a good guy—*you could tell that.*"

Even after we had checked into the One Fifth Avenue Hotel, and while J. was preparing to go on the town and I was lying atop the bed, we kept shaking our heads in farcical wonder, as though saying, *"Imagine? Tickets from Conerly!"* It was our way of agreeing that in the conspiracy we had had for so many years this was our grandest success to date, something to really make the boys back home sit up and take notice. Though genuine—where Holden Caulfield might want to call up old Tom Hardy, and S. N. Behrman, Max Beerbohm, there was no one I'd have rather talked with than Conerly—my enthusiasm was colored by an ulterior motive, that of being pleasant till J. was safely out of the room. With the peculiar canniness of the alcoholic, I had figured out a way to drink all I pleased, and drink it out of the pained view of my friend. Worse yet, having been the one who was responsible for getting the tickets, and with the drunk's really monstrous perspective on the nature of things (it wasn't enough that J. was paying for the tickets and the hotel), I honestly felt I had a right to do what I was about to do. Beginning by telling J., amidst some histrionic yawns and superb sighs, that I was really too, too exhausted to go on the town, I now lay on the bed feigning a heavy slumber and squinting at J. through the curtain of my eyelashes. Though J. was disappointed and asked me a dozen times if I wouldn't change my mind, I think he took my abstinence as a hopeful omen and in his voice there was no real insistence. Spruced up and standing by the door, he asked me once again if I wouldn't reconsider, to which I really outdid myself. Fixing on him the most doleful eyes, and in martyr-like, near *sotto voce* tones, I said, "No, really. You go ahead and have yourself a good time." The door was no sooner closed than I was up, showered, shaved, dressed, and in a matter of minutes sitting at the hotel bar drinking a Vodka Presbyterian and as happy as a fat man in a delicatessen, looking lustfully at all the bottles on the back bar. I could drink as much as I could hold. All I had to do was sign the bar tab with J.'s signature and room number.

———

To those who understand the slightness of an American's traditions, the place of sports in his life, and New York City's need to make do with what it has (the stadium, for instance, is a nearly impossible place to watch football), the Yankee Stadium can be a heart-stopping, an awesomely imposing place, and never more so than on a temperate and brilliant afternoon in late November. The vivid reds and oranges, the plaids and tans, the golds and greens of autumn clothing flicker incessantly across the way where the stadium, rising as sheer as a cliff, is one quivering mass of color out of which there comes continually, like music from a monstrous kaleidoscope, the unending roar of the crowd. And where I have been in Los Angeles' vast Coliseum and Chicago's monumental Soldiers' Field and able to imagine it, I am yet unable to imagine a young man coming for the first time out of those dugouts at that moment just prior to kickoff when the stadium is all but bursting its great steel beams with people. I am incapable of imagining stepping out and craning my head upward at the roaring cliff of color, wondering whether it be all a dream which might at any moment come tumbling down, waking me to life's hard fact of famelessness. The stadium stays. The game proceeds. Autumnal mists set in. At half time the stadium's floodlights are turned on; so that the colors, with each change of light, change, too—become muted, become brighter again, like a leaf going from vivid green to lemon yellow to wine red to rust brown, reminding one that time is passing, that time indeed is running out. It was that kind of a day, that kind of an hour, when the Giants, losing 17-10 with two minutes remaining, came hurriedly to the line of scrimmage, eighty yards from a touchdown and a possible tie. Gifford, whom I was of course watching, had neither thrown off his sluggishness nor played particularly well. Nevertheless, I knew that Quarterback George Shaw, who was substituting for an ailing Conerly, would make the play to him. I knew he would because men under pressure believe in miracles and see what they want to see. Shaw would not, of course, pass to the Gifford who was even now flanked wide to the left side of the field but to some memory of the ball player he once had been.

J. thought otherwise, predicting that Shaw would pass to another.

"Don't be absurd," I snapped, and J. looked at me with great surprise, causing me to flush with embarrassment. Though I'm sure he didn't understand the reason, I could see by his expression that he had gauged my temper correctly. J. saw that I was afraid.

For a few delirious moments Gifford made me forget my

fear and the crowd eat crow for their rumors of his lost heart. In the same way that Shaw perhaps threw to some memory of him, he became that memory. Running one of his favorite patterns, he caught his first pass by moving straight up the left side of the field, beautifully faking one defender to the outside. Abruptly cutting in front of another, he had, when he caught the ball, eluded both defenders and to the deafening roar of the crowd was at mid-field when he was finally tackled. Pummeling and pounding J. on the back, I shouted, "Oh, Jesus, Frank! Atta way! Atta way, kid!" The next play was an all-or-nothing post pattern, i.e., the receiver runs full speed for the goal posts, and the quarterback drops straight back into the pocket and heaves for those posts. Running swiftly and looking back for the ball, having lost the goal posts from his distracted vision and fearful of running into them, Bob Schnelker dropped a lovely, a high, thrilling, perfectly trajected pass. There was scarcely a moan. So sure was the crowd now that it was going to be their day, they seemed happily undaunted. Nor was I any longer upset. Now the Giants were at the line of scrimmage again, and again Gifford was flanked wide left. Running what seemed the precise pattern he had run before, and to another thundering roar of the crowd, he made the catch at about the Philadelphia thirty and was moving laterally across the field toward us, trying even as he ran to find a way by Philadelphia's two deep men, now converging on him, and into the end zone. The crowd was wild. The crowd was maniacal. The crowd was his. J. was the one who noticed Chuck Bednarik, Philadelphia's—there are no adjectives to properly describe him—linebacker. "Watch out for Bednarik," he said. Hearing J., I turned to see Bednarik coming from behind

Gifford out of his linebacking zone, pounding the turf furiously, like some fierce animal gone berserk. I watched Bednarik all the way, thinking that at any second Gifford would turn back and see him, whispering, "Watch it, Frank. Watch it, Frank." Then, quite suddenly, I knew it was going to happen; and accepting, with the fatalistic horror of a man anchored by fear to a curb and watching a tractor trailer bear down on a blind man, I stood breathlessly and waited. Gifford never saw him, and Bednarik did his job well. Dropping his shoulder ever so slightly, so that it would meet Gifford in the region of the neck and chest, he ran into him without breaking his furious stride, *thwaaah-hhp*, taking Gifford's legs out from under him, sending the ball careening wildly into the air, and bringing him to the soft green turf with a sickening thud. In a way it was beautiful to behold. For what seemed an eternity both Gifford and the ball had seemed to float, weightless, above the field, as if they were performing for the crowd on the trampoline. About five minutes later, after unsuccessfully trying to revive him, they lifted him onto a stretcher, looking, from where we sat high up in the mezzanine, like a small, broken, blue-and-silver mannikin, and carried him out of the stadium.

———

In a fist fight that night I got badly beaten up. I could have avoided the fight, but the day's events, coupled with the long years of my defeat, made me seek out a less subtle defeat. On arriving downtown, J. and I passed the time over a scarcely eaten meal of lasagna and sausage, drinking Chianti, and waiting for the morning newspapers. Though J. had business in Watertown in the morning, he lingered with me; and after a time—such was the blandness of our forced conversation—I began to suspect he was playing nursemaid to me, as though he were sure that once out of his protective view I would embark on something disastrous. By acting much too falsely cheerful I didn't allay his suspicions. On the back pages of the *News* and *Mirror* the headlines proclaimed, "GIFFORD OUT FOR SEASON," and the articles on the inside said he would be hospitalized for two weeks with a severe concussion. Both stories implied his career was at an end. None of this was news to me: I had already guessed as much. What I hadn't guessed at was the odd bellicosity Gifford would display at retiring. At a press conference the following spring he would tell the assembled reporters, speaking rather too pugnaciously, and prefacing his singular remark with that saw about football's having been good to him, that his decision to retire was in no way predicated on the concussion. No one who saw that tackle could have doubted that it was the precise reason for his quitting; or that, in some ways, it was inexorable. It was the rather brutal homage the league was paying him for catching one too many passes, for winning one too many games, for frustrating and disheartening the opponent one too many times; and I had no doubt that had it not been Bednarik, the next play, or the next game, or the next season, it would have been some other, perhaps more leonine, Bednarik. On reading his exasperating remark, I immediately rose, went out and bought a copy of every New York newspaper, returned, and read their accounts with equal diligence. Searching for the slightest nuance, I wanted to see if any of the reporters had greeted his remark with, if not outright laughter, a splattering of levity. Because none had, I assumed Gifford's posture at the conference had been one of muscle-flexing aggressiveness. The reporters had faced him, or apparently they had, with a straight-faced and obliging solemnity. I understood perfectly. With a magnanimous gravity not unlike that of the reporters, people were at this time meeting my protestations that I could quit drinking any time I chose. Thus it was that at the end, or at what Gifford and I must have believed would be the end for him, it gave me some consolation that we were both addicted to something—he to football and I to liquor—capable of destroying us, if not actually, in humiliation and loss of pride. For the first time since the beginning, when so many autumns before we had had the common ground of large hopes, we were, in our separate ways, coming round to the most terrible knowledge of all: we were dying. And that was the inescapable truth. Though I was some time in articulating it, in that limp and broken body against the green turf of the stadium, I had had a glimpse of my own mortality. As much as anything else, that fist fight was a futile rage against the inevitability of that mortality.

After reading the papers J. and I went for a walk and ended standing on a corner of Times Square. We talked about nothing in particular until J., getting anxious about the time and the long drive ahead of him, became abruptly solicitous of me and asked whether I had the money for the train trip to Scarsdale. When I spoke, I looked directly at him. "I've got to have more money than that," I said. With no sense of authority, he replied, "Go home, Ex. For Christ's sake, *go home.*" To that I essayed a fitful and nauseating little jig. Resignedly removing his wallet from his pocket, J. took from it a ten-dollar bill and laid it in my eagerly outstretched hand. Turning quickly, and without saying good-bye, he walked away. Furious and pained, I stood for a moment watching the garish, meaningless lights of the square, listening to the shamed, embarrassed throbbings of my heart. When finally I turned back, wanting to call to him and shout my apologies, he was gone, lost among the strangers on the street.

—

Fifteen minutes later I was standing in the middle of Sheridan Square in the Village, staring up at a towering new apartment house of brick and stone. I walked to the curb and stared at the place where it had been. Now I walked backward to the middle of the square again, looked up, then to my right and to my left—seeking my bearings, making sure that I was indeed at Sheridan Square. I was. *Louis' was not there.* Trying to recapture a feeling of the future, and thinking that in that place, at least momentarily, I would be able to bear myself back into a time when there had been hope, I had come back to Louis' to drink draft beer. After J. had left without saying good-bye, in panic I had fled back to the past only to discover that even the building where Louis' had been was gone, and that another, a gaudy, whory-looking monstrosity stood in its stead. The past was not there.

After several frantic inquiries in the neighborhood, I got the address of the new Louis' and went there. But it wasn't the same, depressing me even more than Clarke's had the day before. Where the old place, as one descended the steps, had seemed to rise up at one, a subterranean and enchanted place, a place of infinite promise, the new Louis' on Eighth Street was a long, narrow, characterless bar at street level. After drinking a beer or two, I had decided to go uptown and drink at one of the hotel bars near Grand Central when, looking up into the mirror, which was crossed with a wooden X, I saw on one side of the X my doleful, puffy face, and on the other, a young girl, sipping beer and weeping silently. Great, globule-like tears streaked effortlessly down her thin though pretty face. She was about nineteen. Her hair, which was brown and flecked with natural streaks of gold, and which must once have been lovely, was now lank with poor care; and when I turned, I saw that her arms were sticklike, as though they would break to the touch, and that her hands, which were beautiful in form, and delicate, were smudged with dirt. Conscious of the dirt, in an almost compulsive way she covered first her right hand with her left, and then her left with her right, as if she wanted to be a beatnik and then again did not, as if she did not have the gumption to play the role she had assumed for herself. Her breasts were much too big for the slenderness of her frame, and I was sure that in a very short time she had lost a great deal of weight.

Two hours later she told me why. By this time I had gone through most of the ten dollars J. had given me, buying us both beers. In an effort to see her laugh I had been making "funnies." When I finally succeeded, she took her laughter as an indication of our lifelong palship and to my dismay began telling her story. I say *dismay* because the story was like a million others in the Village, and she understood it no better than most. At the end of her sophomore year in an esteemed women's college, she had persuaded her father to let her come for the summer to Washington Square and take some art courses, art being her interest. (She never for a moment understood that she came for the express purpose of being fucked.) She had been lonely for some days; but at the first party to which she was invited, she had met a big, brusque, sandaled, red-bearded poet who, within the first three hours of their meeting, had convinced her that her father was beyond absolution because he sold refrigerators, had read her poetry she didn't comprehend, had got her sauced, had slapped her face, and had, or so she claimed, deflowered her, leaving her exhausted to fall asleep in her virginal blood. When she awoke, though, she was "in love, terribly so"; and during the past summer she and Big Red had been "deliriously happy." (She meant that for the first time she was getting it on a bed on her back, trying to reach the ceiling with her ecstatically kicking legs.) As fall approached and it became time to return to school, she panicked and telephoned the refrigerator salesman. By cajolery and weeping, by threats against her own person, and finally by threatening to withdraw her filial affection from him, she persuaded Pop to let her remain and enroll in art school in Manhattan. This was a piece of jolly news which Big Red met by disappearing. At first she was bewildered, then heart-broken; and when, after he hadn't shown up for a number of days, and by a minimum of checking—for Big Red was luridly indiscreet—she made inquiries, she discovered that the poet was quite contentedly married to a bleached blonde and the father of three freckled and red-headed sons, all of whom, to the greater glory of poetry no doubt, were carried on the city's relief rolls. On the night I talked with her, she had long since dropped out of her art courses; and for the past two months she had been going to three movies a day, weeping whether the picture was happy or sad, and living off popcorn and orange soda.

What the hell could I say? I understood Big Red, but not her—or rather, I understood her all too well. When she recovered, she would go home, marry a Yale man, and her life would be one long tale of self-deceit. I wanted to tell her to go home, to slap her face, to shake the shit out of her and insist that she go home. Instead, by way of an object lesson, I told her about my own early days in the Village and how all these years I had carried with me this memory of place only to discover that very day that that was what the Village was—a memory, a dream, a myth. Go home, I said, and forget it. "It doesn't exist."

By three o'clock we had left Louis' and were walking south on Macdougal Street to her apartment, which she had told me was just south of Bleecker. Though it gives me no particular pride, as I walked I was debating whether to give her a fuck. The streets were deserted, but the moon was good and everything was clear. I to the inside, she to the curb, we were walking in silence. Suddenly understanding that, in the same way I understood her too well, she understood me not at all, in embarrassment I had stopped talking altogether. Presently two men came walking up the street toward us. Both were well-dressed, one a Negro, the other not. With their heads down, they walked rapidly, and talked, both at the same time and with that peculiar intensity which suggests the great world's heartaches are all but put to rest. I heard the names Aymé and Kerouac and Edmund Wilson and Ginsberg and Pope and had to laugh, wondering by what juxtaposition of logic these names could so rapidly succeed one another in a conversation. On top of us they still had not seen us, and the white man bumped joltingly into the girl, scarcely nodded his head in apology or even interrupted his monologue, and proceeded blithely on his way. Then I did a foolish and impulsive thing, hardly knowing at the time why. I now know that

I felt this girl, even if I didn't like her, had been hard used enough—in the way my wife and sons had—by people like themselves, like Big Red, like me, people who brushed others into the gutter with no more thought than if they were dung. They reminded me of me, and I despised them for that. Turning, and with the girl tugging at my arm and beseeching me not to bother, I called, "Hey, creep!" When they did not hear that, I made it, "Hey, nigger lover!" They heard that, freezing in midstep, two silhouettes of rage against the Village night. And I laughed. And the fight was on.

We had words in which I insisted on an apology to the young lady, and in turn the white man insisted I reciprocate by withdrawing that vile appellation. But I couldn't. In his voice was the hysterically cultivated outrage of the white liberal; and I loathed his patronizing what he unquestionably deemed my brutal and irremediable ignorance—I who understood, or thought I did, more about the Negro and dignity and second-class citizenship than he would ever understand. Smiling to indicate my agreement to the childish bargain, I listened to his rather sullen apology to the girl, drew in a deep breath, and in the most despicable tone I could muster, said, "Now get your faggoty ass out of here!"

It was a statement to which each reacted according to his character. The girl fled, running like hell, so that for a long time after I could hear in the clear November air the slap, slap of her sandals along Macdougal Street. Having removed his spectacles and trembling with rage, the white man was now being constrained by the Negro's hand held laxly before his waist, the way a policeman constrains a child at a parade. When I looked into the Negro's eyes, I saw that he was asking *why?* He had heard the terrifying, the unfathomable loathing in my voice; and as intelligent Negroes understand, he had sensed that that loathing had nothing to do with him or his people, that it rose up from deep disappointments within myself—from my own defeats and degradations and humiliations. "Why?" his eyes asked me; and because I knew the answer all too well, I said to the white man, "C'mon, nigger fucker!"

He came at me very fast, running so rapidly and so furiously that I panicked. I was standing at the corner of a side street, Minetta Lane, and immediately started a wild backtracking into the lane, trying to think of a way to protect myself. In high school I had broken my arm and for many months had borne it in a thick cast, often thinking at the time what an exemplary weapon it would make. That is what I thought of now. Retreating as far as I could without tumbling backward, I abruptly stopped, set my legs wide apart, doubled my right arm at the elbow, and with all the strength in my body threw the arm even as he came rushing headlong on, catching him with my upper forearm flush in the nose. It was perfect. I felt so many things go in his face that I almost became sick. But still he fought. He hit me three or four times, hard, on the cheek and on the ear and on top of the head, by which time his blood was flowing profusely down the front of his white raincoat. Noticing it, he stopped as suddenly as if we had been rehearsing a movie scene. Bewildered and horrified, he felt his face with his hands. Then he sat down on the sidewalk, leaned against the side of Minetta's Restaurant, and began to whimper, still bewilderedly holding his face.

The Negro was not so easy. He had seen his friend in agony and had forgotten about reasons *why.* Standing toe to toe, we threw unexpert, pathetically angry blows at each other's eyes and ears and mouth and chest and stomach; threw them, our arms flailing the Village night like furious billy clubs, until the entire upper part of my body was numb with rage; threw them until I could no longer lift them and stood, helpless, taking his weary, scarcely felt blows. And though they say one loses his head in a fight, mine was clear; and I was trying to answer the question that he, who even now struck me in the face, had posed to me: why? I fought for a reason I would discover the ensuing spring—because I had had that day an awful glimpse of my own mortality. I fought because I had gone back to both Clarke's and Louis'—had gone back to the past and had found that the past did not exist. And I fought because in J.'s eyes I had seen the truth of what I had become and knew that he would never again invite me to conspire against exclusiveness. Yes, it was a lament, this fight, a lament for a conspiracy—for both my conspiracy with J. and that other conspiracy against anonymity begun so many seasons before and ended that very day; so that even as I took this black man's blows I could see that broken, blue-and-silver figure, stretcher-borne. And I fought for still a final reason, perhaps the most important reason of all. I fought—

Now the white man was rising, ready to do battle again. Fearing that together they might literally kill me, I slid out from under one of the Negro's now open-handed swats, fled into Macdougal Street, turned north, and started to run. I ran until the sweat, having already rendered my jacket heavy as wet rags, formed pools in the sockets of my eyes and I could not see, sweat that there mingled with the tears and blood to run down my hot, steaming cheeks; ran until I thought my head would explode and my chest consume itself in flames; ran until my legs became wobbly, then mush, and I could run no more. When I finally stopped, I was on Seventh Avenue, many blocks north. Seeing they were not behind me, I staggered into the entrance of a closed drugstore and lay face down on the filthy concrete, the sweat streaming down my neck and dropping in great drops onto the pavement, lay with my head resting heavily on my crossed arms. In a moment I would fall asleep. But before I did, all the dread and the dismay and the foreboding I had been experiencing disappeared, were abruptly gone, and I felt quiet. They disappeared because, as I say, I understood the last and most important reason why I fought. The knowledge caused me to weep very quietly, numbly, caused me to weep because in my heart I knew I had always understood this last and most distressing reason, which rendered the grief I had caused myself and others all for naught. I fought because I understood, and could not bear to understand, that it was my destiny—unlike that of my father, whose fate it was to hear the roar of the crowd—to sit in the stands with most men and acclaim others. It was my fate, my destiny, my end, to be a fan.

8

A Dream of
Sanguinary Ends

A week after I was at the Yankee Stadium, when my face had healed to the point of being recognizable, I got up from the davenport, packed a satchel, and made my second journey to Florida. It was a trip for which I felt exiguous warmth; and one to which, materially or emotionally, I could bring equally little viaticum. Having discovered within me a love for my sons, I had found myself (can one love the children and not the mother?) looking at my wife in a way I had never before looked at her. Though I may not have sought her in the rock-ribbed way women prefer to be sought, before I left I yearned to make her an appreciative gesture for the clothes on my back, for the food in my belly, for the comfort of my bed, for the bright white paper and the sparkling-keyed typewriter, for the uncomplaining months when she must have hoped the book would be spawned if only because it might free me from myself. I wanted to thank her for my sons.

Had I been able to give Patience that book, I know that I could have balmed myself with the notion—as "real" writers do when, dedicating the work, they write, *This book is for Margie Bean, in memory of endearments deep and true*—that I had in a way met the price. It wasn't so much that Patience had volunteered everything material to our relationship as that I had been unable to give to wife or sons the emotional nourishment they coveted. The malaise of writing—and it is of no consequence whether the writer is talented or otherwise—is that after a time a man writing arrives at a point outside human relationships, becomes, as it were, ahuman. During those months spent at the luridly lighted writing table, I had, paraphrasing Yeats, fed the heart on fantasies; and the heart, quite simply, had grown brutal from the fare. To thank Patience I composed a pastiche—

> You gave me bread, you gave me meat,
> You gave me lots of real swell stuff to eat;
> The trouble was, I'm sure you'll agree,
> *Le Poussin en Surprise* never sat well with me

—but for the obvious reason I never made her a present of it. While during the day she was with such feverish compassion refereeing the nearly mortal conflicts of her marital combatants (in the last report I prepared, the husband accused the wife of getting pie-eyed and punching his Mom in the nose while his son and daughter, aged seven and six respectively, stood by ecstatically applauding the action), I wanted to cook up a sumptuous repast of roast loin of pork, wild rice wrapped in banana leaves, and pencil-thin asparagus, capped off with a bottle of La Tâche 1947. After purchasing the wine, I passed an afternoon judging its "bouquet" and "body" and in an excessively fastidious script copying out a grocery list for Mr. Gristede. By 4 P.M., cheeseburgers "with," French fries, and cole slaw were sounding every bit as delectable. But before I could get around to preparing these I fell asleep on the davenport, the empty bottle of La Tâche 1947 still on the coffee table beside me. Such were the heart's calluses that out of my gratitude to Patience I could not in the end put together the movements necessary to walk to the sink, to buss her on the cheek, and to volunteer to dry the supper dishes. Our relationship had become an unending and distant Viennese waltz. To yank her abruptly to me and drift off into a plaintive, hot-panted fox trot would have disarmed her. My battered face proved the ultimate barrier between us.

Improvisedly casting her face into a mask of amiable diffidence, she'd look at me, then look hurriedly away, leaving me no doubt that the swollen blue bruises told her of the violence yet within me and how far she still was from having her sons with her. One welcome morning I looked into the bathroom mirror and said, "Is it you, Exley?" "Such as I am," the mirror suavely replied. I planted an affectionate, lingering kiss there, lightheartedly announced to Patience that I was going back on the road, "Colorado or someplace," and Patience's response made me rue that I hadn't found it in me to complete some gesture of thanks. For the trip she wanted to buy me a badly needed raincoat; and I instantly understood that she had sympathetic visions of my standing on some lonely crossroads in the rain, waiting for the ride to wherever it was I thought I was going. Not waiting for the coat (which undoubtedly would have been a London Fog from Lord & Taylor), I packed my bag in a fury of encroaching tears. A few hours later, drunk, I was on a Greyhound going to Miami Beach to see the Counselor.

During that torporific endless ride I wrote Patience a

letter I never mailed. On reading it in the glaring sun of Florida, I found it maudlin and senseless. It was, besides, painfully pretentious; and I quote now from what I remember of it, embarrassed for the ninny who wrote it. Whether I had talent, I told her, was beside the point. Unfortunately I had developed a characteristic of talented people—the need to stand up to the practical and incredulous world, that world which assails one with its laughing and disbelieving eyes, that world which stands so vigilantly prepared to stigmatize one for his harmless, inflated dreams as mad. "Whether or not I am a writer," I wrote, "I have—and this is both my curse and my virtue—cultivated the instinct of one, an aversion for the herd, without, in my unhappy case, the ability to harness and articulate that aversion." I told her how once in Chicago, through the window of a streetcar, I had on North Clark Street seen a young man passed out on the sidewalk and snoozing in the bright sunshine. He was atrociously dressed, his face haggard and bewhiskered, and people walked over and around him as though he did not exist, as perhaps for them he did not. At the moment my streetcar pulled directly beside him, it stopped abruptly, I looked down into his reposing face, and there I saw my own face with such devastating and chilling clarity that for the rest of the day I had suffered an exaggerated thirst accompanied by vertigo. "For my heart," I wrote, "will always be with the drunk, the poet, the prophet, the criminal, the painter, the lunatic, with all whose aims are insulated from the humdrum business of life. A raincoat? That a raincoat could solve my problems! Would it have come from Lord & Taylor? I say this truly, Patience: never again in my life will I feel easy in anything but the cheapest corduroy, the corduroy that calls up the odors and the tastes, the laughter and the tears of Avalon Valley. Could I have accepted your belief that I was wasting my life, could I have promoted ideas without substance, products without value, cigarettes that kill, could I have sat all shiny-faced and regimental necktie in the carpeted skies of Manhattan and joshed myself that I was engaged in things consequential, then we might have laughed and loved and joined the Westchester Country Club and lived forever. I couldn't do it." To this letter I never mailed I affixed this postscript: "With me you were very patient, Patience. And good, too. In that goodness I was aware of the dignity you were affording my shabby humanity; indeed, dwelling in it I at times felt something like grace. Not that it matters, but I tried to think of a way to repay your generosity; and such payment invariably settled on the truth that you'd be better rid of me. Be happy and tell my sons that I was a drunk, a dreamer, a weakling, and a madman, anything but that I did not love them."

—

In the company of a golden-thighed, pneumatic, and heart-stoppingly glowing dancer in one of the chorus lines along the beach, the Counselor was on an extended leave from The Law. When from Scarsdale I untruthfully wired him that I had been "streeted" from the apartment and asked if I might come down, there was little he could say but come ahead. His permitting me to come was an error. With luxurious living I was swollen at the joints, like Proust I had begun to claim the privileges of the valetudinarian, I was morose mentally; and it was no time before that moroseness, in a rather rum way, seeped into the atmosphere. The Counselor tried to get me swimming and taking the sun, but I couldn't bear to sit among the aging, flaccid bodies on the beach because already my body was beginning to resemble those of the elders. I wanted to drink, and being both my friend and an accommodating fellow, the Counselor eventually allowed that he would drink with me. By this time the Counselor had been some weeks away from his practice, he was without funds, and our booze and our beds depended entirely on the handsome salary of the dancer who, prior to my arrival, had got some idea about the Counselor's setting up practice in Florida and keeping house with her. What the girl hadn't bargained for was me. During the months I had permitted Patience to assume the man's role of supporting me, I had unmanned myself: I had become infantile. My sleek cheeks had grown flatulent, my girth fatty, my thin hand plumper than that of a thriving child's; so that the dancer, suddenly and miraculously, had not only a common-law husband but a fat, cuddly, and altogether helpless infant, the latter of which, alas, she wanted no part. She was a lovely, garrulous, exciting, and excitable girl; could make a most savory meat loaf; and about the sexual habits of famous entertainers had all sorts of tales she managed to convey in such vivid detail that it never occurred to us to ask where she had gathered such information. Having spent her dewy-eyed years being mauled by drunks in two-bit nightclubs, she yearned for muslin curtains and the smell of things baking; but for the life of her she couldn't conceive how my pursy, davenport-prone body fitted into such home-cooked visions. The Counselor tried to explain it to her.

"Freddy is our son," he'd offer in mock protest to her demands that I get my fat ass off the davenport and out looking for work. "Our baby," he'd protest, sticking out his tongue and elfishly rolling his eyes around in their sockets.

"Isn't he an adorable little fatty-watty?" Then the Counselor and I would giggle and pour ourselves another drink from the bottle purchased with the money earned by those thrilling legs. "Our baby," the Counselor would repeat for emphasis, and again those eyes would go flitting about their sockets. He'd sigh and wag his head with weary and resigned exasperation; heavy with responsibility he was. Only he, that mock head-wagging seemed to say, understood the burdens of raising children.

I never ceased to marvel at the Counselor's relationship with women. Though he had reverence for them, he never had any understanding of the homey things that hypnotize them and wasn't truly happy unless he and the girl were running helter-skelter on the edge of the abyss: the Counselor wanted them to gather some glimpse of what hell permanent relationships can be. Two nights before Christmas the dancer tumbled into the abyss. Beginning with some harsh and ferruginous clanging of pans in the kitchen, to which the Counselor snapped, "Quiet, hon, you'll wake the baby," the scene ballooned to encompass a flashing butcher knife, a broken kitchen window, the wail of a police siren. Having fled the hysteria, the Counselor and I stood among some moonlit orange trees in the back yard, dramatically wringing our hands and looking at each other with feigned and horrified dismay, as though quite unable to imagine what had sent the poor girl round the bend. "And after all we've done for her," the Counselor said. That night she moved out and into an apartment with some fellow chorines. By Christmas Day the Counselor and I were without money, beer, cigarettes, or food and were forced to dine off some cookies, wrapped in brilliant gold and silver paper, with which our late hostess, in one of her jollier moods had thoughtfully decorated the Christmas tree. Attempting to ease our financial predicament, we had the night before telephoned the two Watertownians we knew in the Miami area, high school classmates who had fled both the cold and the responsibility of families. Offering to help, the first was extremely solicitous, his voice nearly breaking in sympathy with our plight. He was beautiful. Fearing that he might not find our apartment, he ordered the Counselor and me to stand in front of a drugstore he knew on Collins Avenue. Before telephoning him again, we waited three hours. Without any explanation his "wife" said he'd simply changed his mind about helping us, at the moment was taking a bath in preparation for midnight Mass, and couldn't be disturbed.

The other man we knew, a would-be musical comedy star who was always bouncing breathlessly in and out of the apartment announcing that he was flying to the Coast on Monday for a screen test or becoming a newscaster on TV for five hundred a week the first of the month, was living with and off of a wealthy refugee from Castro's Cuba named Chiquita. Deciding to circumvent our friend, who was generally so busy studying himself in the mirror he never listened to one anyway, we went directly to Chiquita for the dough. She said it wasn't nice to ask for money on Christmas Eve. At three in the morning, three nights later, we heard a guttural, falsetto baritone singing, *"If I loved you, Tiiimmme and again I would try to say . . ."* Opening the front door, we found our friend and Chiquita heavy-laden with three cases of beer, Ritz crackers, potato chips, cheese dip, and cigarettes. The Counselor and I ate, drank, and smoked voraciously while, to the approving and adoring nods of Chiquita, our friend sang the entire scores of *Carousel,*

Oklahoma! and *Show Boat*. He was beautiful, too. By telephoning acquaintances about the country and prevaricating outrageously about misfortunes that had befallen us, we managed to get by wire enough money to live comfortably a few more weeks. Then we exhausted our acquaintances and went home.

Because he had been so long away from his practice, and it seemed to make little difference where he set up shop, the Counselor made the gravest error of his career and decided to hang his shingle in Watertown. Neither of us understood that for us home had become a place we envisioned in much too nostalgic a way. Tail tucked in, I came back to the farm, refinished and sold a few antiques, and still without a job in August, and even after the humiliating interview with the superintendent, I signed a contract to teach at Glacial Falls. Which is what I was doing when at the New Parrot Restaurant I had what, at the time, I took to be a heart attack.

———

It would be nice if I could say that on walking out of the receiving room of the hospital that Sunday I foreswore drinking, returned to Glacial Falls, made the students worship me for my sense of dedication, and became a different man. I didn't. Each weekend I continued to journey to Watertown where, to my consternation and dismay, I found that no matter with what unctuousness I forced myself to cheer I had no interest in the game, which meant in effect no real interest in anything. As a result I took, furtively sticking my tongue out at the superintendent, to drinking during the week (which I had promised him I wouldn't do, a promise he had no right to extract from me), twelve, fourteen, twenty glasses of beer a night. Fearing another nutritive failure, I followed this beer by gorging myself on thick cuts of prime rib or pork chops, on Italian bread larded heavily with butter, on spaghetti, linguini, or ravioli. Crowning these caloric orgies with two or three black coffees containing Tia Maria, a syrupy, cocoa-based cordial, I was home in bed within moments after eating. I took twelve hours of sluggish, dreamless sleep. Rising more lethargically than ever, and furiously gargling some mouthwash, I now faced the children without even the grace of complete sobriety. In a condition of alcoholic asperity I passed the days in the classroom, in the faculty and department meetings, and at the Italian saloon where I could invariably be found at the bar within ten minutes of school's closing; passed the days impatiently waiting for June, when, as prescribed by school policy, I could affix passing grades to the students' reports and get the hell out. Not being in the least needed, I sensed in cashing my pay checks the exhilaration which must accompany highway robbery. Physically I became as protean as a chameleon, able to discern the almost daily expansion of my waistline, the way my neck was increasingly sagging over the folds of my collar. After that unremitting spring of beer, pasta, Tia Maria, and futility, I found my body thirty pounds overweight, my cerebrum as dopey as a eunuch's dong.

To sustain a modicum of stability over the spring I went back to Hawthorne, and especially to *The Scarlet Letter.* My previous readings of Hawthorne had been hostile and sneering; and since so many better qualified to judge him than I esteemed him a writer of the very highest order, I went to him with the uneasiness of one prepared to make cloying amends. His obdurate and unrelieved probing of the evil in men, particularly his so shackling the characters of his somber world with scarcely bearable yokes of guilt, had aroused in me an understandable distress. In the modern and enlightened sunshine of Freud, in this Anacreontic milieu where we were all going to be absolved of guilt and its ensuing remorse, Hawthorne had seemed to me irrelevant and spurious. Reading Hawthorne anew was revealing. Having prostrated myself before the Freudians and found no relief there was only one of the reasons. It seemed to me I had lived long enough in the world to see that sin and remorse are as much a parcel, and a necessary parcel, of men as love and forgiveness are; moreover, not only are there certain things from which, this side of heaven, men should not be absolved (does one ever forgive the German his final solution to the Jewish "problem"?), but employing all the psychological ploys available there are acts from which men never completely absolve themselves. Reading him in the light of this belief, I soon developed a crush on Hawthorne. I forced unanalogous parallels between his life and mine. Because these pages had begun to form themselves in my mind, the parallel I most cherished was his Custom House description of the languor which prevented him, while working surrounded by men whose existence was bounded by the succulence of past and anticipated meals, from sitting down to write *The Scarlet Letter.* "Teaching" children granted immunity from failure, attending meetings chaired by a man who believed what O. Henry was up to was writing, in the teachers' room overhearing my colleagues discuss the previous night's episode of *Ben Casey,* their notion of high and enduring drama (oh, Dr. Casey, talk about the brain's malignancies!); these things, I told myself, were producing in me a similarly impotent languor. When the summer holiday finally came, I returned to the farm, waddled my pasta-bloated body about the wide yard, looked up at the unvarying blue of the sky, and re-experienced that top-of-the-world feeling. Then I entered the house and slowly ascended the stairs to this room. Which I created, and which I love.

In the afternoons I lay face up on a water mattress and watched the compact white clouds run down the sky, or face down looked into the blue-green water—chlorinated and temulent to the smell—of the mail-order, children's swimming pool on which I floated. Seated in a canvas lawn chair beside me, my mother, whose face was lined with age, read to me what *McCall's* and *Woman's Day* and *The Ladies' Home Journal* had to say about fatness. Christie III sat beside her chair, watching every move I made. It was a watching which began the day I arrived and never ceased, as though, since I had left him on the day I entered the hospital, he anticipated that at any moment I would leave him again. He was old, and around his pink and brown lips a number of white hairs had sprouted. Lettuce and green beans and asparagus, my mother read to me, had been designated "fat blasters." It had now been determined that persons have distinct metabolic patterns and can diet forever without losing weight unless, in the one known way to break the pattern and establish new dietary habits, they fast for two days. At that suggestion my mother had looked hopefully at me. Baked beans have five hundred calories per cup. "Can you imagine?" Raising my head from the mattress, I had obliged my mother by looking incredulous. What it all amounted to was that my mother saw me old whereas she imagined me still young, and, worse, uncomely, whereas against the evidence of her eyes she wanted to find me attractive. Because I hadn't the courage to tell her what it was

I was doing, I gave her a lie to live with, telling her that in the fall I was to teach at a high school downstate. Perhaps, though, I needn't have lied. At five, morning after morning, she had heard me in the kitchen drinking coffee, had been conscious of me all the forenoons and all the evenings filling up page upon page of blank paper; and if, surmising the fury with which I worked, she sensed that I was putting down a testament, or even if she knew this and that I had no job downstate, she never said so: she held her peace. Once she asked what I was doing upstairs. When I saturninely replied that I was "making some notes," she said, "Oh," and we went back to the subject of my health. Mixing the dietary with the simplistic mysticism of Dr. Norman Vincent Peale, she told me that it was his belief that if a man saw himself in one way, trim or triumphant or jolly, long enough and hard enough, he became that vision of himself. "Norman Vincent Peale," I said, "ought to be locked up." My mother was obstinate. "I know it's true," she said. So for a long time I lay on the water mattress, smelling the chlorine and slowly—as slowly as ever the clouds ran down the sky—drifted round and round in the children's pool, thinking that perhaps it was so. But now that I no longer saw myself emblazoned on book jackets, now that I could no longer sustain my fantasy of my football empire among the islands, I could see myself hardly affirmatively at all. What I did see was a kind of poor man's Augie seated hot afternoons at the outdoor café overlooking Rome's Borghese Gardens and putting down words, in the hope not so much that they would be read or that they contained poignant or disturbing meanings as that, written more in negative apprehension, once dead I would be dumb forever—which, as Augie said, "is no reason to decline to

speak and stir or to be what you are." There was not much
I had to be affirmative about. Having rejected grandiose
ambitions at thirty-three, I saw myself very narrowly as a
man with one suit of clothes, two thousand dollars' life insurance ("planting" dough), and four hundred bucks in my
pocket, as one who had to go away from this place, this
room, and find a way to live in the world. The thought of
leaving disturbed me greatly.

Within a year and a half of our homecoming from
Florida, the Counselor had been disbarred for forging a
five-hundred-dollar check which had been made payable
both to him as attorney-of-record and to the client. Having
business out of town and shy of cash, the Counselor and I
had driven about one rain-swept afternoon seeking the
client to get his endorsement. Unable to locate him, we had
arrived at the bank only moments before its customary 3
P.M. closing; and in order that the Counselor not be held up
at the cashier's window with explanations of why he was
signing the client's name, without any misgivings I signed
it. That we had so lightheartedly conspired on a "felony"
indicates not only how far we had drifted from home but
how little we comprehended the solemnity with which the
Counselor's colleagues wished to be taken. By the time the
Counselor returned from his trip (when, as there had never
been any doubt he would do, he promptly paid the client),
the forgery had come to light and disbarment proceedings
were already under way. Even then the Counselor compounded his predicament by not taking the proceedings
straight-facedly enough. Imagining that he, like me, had
with some of his colleagues engaged in adolescent-circle
jerks; that he had known others when their countenances
were being assailed by pubescent acne ("whore boils," we

had called it); and that still others were known to him before they knew of underarm niceties and went a week at a
time without underwear changes—imagining these things,
I found it easy to comprehend the Counselor's inability to
accept their self-righteous little foot-stompings as celestial
epiphanies. Unable to accept his attitude as a proper one,
the executive committee of the local bar referred the matter to the Appellate Division, and after a most vigorous
prosecution, the Counselor found himself without a license.

Believing the Counselor the most honest man I'd ever
known, and made heavy with the knowledge that the
money I had accepted from him over the years would have
more than tripled the amount in question, I took the disbarment harder than the Counselor did and on the streets
of home collared every attorney I knew to tell him as
much. One with whom both the Counselor and I had
grown up, a handsome, brilliant, self-assertive man, said,
"Look, Ex, these goofy bastards wanted the Counselor to
grovel about their unwashed behinds, and he didn't do it.
And that's *his tough luck.*" It was this man's way to make such
curt statements and then walk abruptly away, leaving one
to ponder his succinctness for subtle ironies and recondite
meanings. On this day, though, he stopped after two hurried steps, turned, and said, "Pity these guys, Ex. Believe
me, they didn't even know what they were doing and were
more frightened of the whole business than the Counselor.
I doubt there was one guy involved who thought that the
Counselor would get any more than a sixty-day suspen-
sion." "They *thought* wrong," I said. We laughed. "Had the
Counselor been an out-of-town boy practicing here," he
said, "he would have got off with a slap on the wrist. Be-

lieve me, subconsciously or otherwise, and aside from the issues, those Appellate justices must have believed that being one of our own the Counselor was some intractable prick so that we couldn't handle it, chastisement and all, right here at home where it damn well should have been handled." And here, thinking of something, he laughed heartily. "The worst of it is," he said, "instead of being embarrassed, these goofy bastards have found out how easy a disbarment is and half the names on the bar association are popping up before the grievance committee. They've gone power-loony!" He laughed again, placed his forefinger against his temple and made a bang, bang.

That any more could be said on the matter was unlikely, and my persistence in bringing it up was pure churlishness. The last time I did so I was seated in a booth drinking beer with a lawyer whom my mother as a teen-ager had wheeled in his carriage. I was raving loudly, and the lawyer, suddenly interrupting, told me to shut up about it. *"Why shut up?"* I said, surprised at his abruptness. "Because," he said, "the statute of limitations on the felonious forgery *you committed is a long way from expiring."* Dumfounded, I said, "You don't think they'd be foolish enough to bring my part in this before a grand jury?" "Why not?" he said. "Well," I snapped, "for the *obvious* reason that I gained nothing from the check's being cashed. Nor for that matter did the Counselor. Never once during all of this was there a suggestion on anybody's part that the Counselor was attempting to divert funds to his own use. It was all rather like bringing a *Hausfrau* before a grand jury for endorsing her husband's pay check." "You still committed forgery," the lawyer assured me blandly. Very steadily I stared at him for many moments, then I said, "Why, you fucking chicken-shit son of a bitch: I suppose you're embarrassed even sitting with me!" Then I rose and, flatulent with rage, fled out of the barroom. I did so because it had suddenly occurred to me that my home town would have disbarred me from something if it could, preferably the human race.

———

One mid-August day at the farm the wind came out of the north, and such is the character of the country here that in on the wind came both the chill and the odor of autumn. When these harbingers of fall signaled my imminent departure, I became very distraught because I knew that where other men look home with longing and affection, I would look home with loathing and rage, and that that loathing would bind me to home as fiercely as ever love does. More sobering, on leaving I would be once more "on the move," be a part of the bewildering and stultifying movement that America has become; and the curse of movement is that during it one is never doing one's own work but that of the world. I yearned for something essentially Miltonian or Emersonian, and something so apparently little understood today that it makes me feel antiquated and musty to mention it: *I wanted to await my call.* To where that call would summon me I didn't know, but I thought that in a certain pretty milieu, under the right stars or in some clapboarded, sunny, forever verdant New England hamlet, I might yet discover myself a teacher. Unexpectedly, and at what luckily was my last possible decision-making moment, I was offered a contract to teach at one of the resort towns that lies along the St. Lawrence and whose economy is greatly bolstered by the summer people who come to gaze at the wonder of our islands. I accepted gratefully, feeling that given a year's time I might come to a kind of peace with home. Were I forced finally to flee, I didn't want the memory of that disbarment tying me so despondently to place.

The principal was in his third and final year. He wasn't—I didn't know the reason, nor did I bother to ask—to be given another contract or tenure and would not be there come another autumn. Whatever the school's grading policy, under the circumstances he hadn't the authority to enforce it, and I set a standard that though rigid seemed fair. During the year the principal and I met a dozen or so times in the corridors, two solitary figures smiling discreetly and nodding abstractedly at one another. Once I caught him picking his nose, he caught me twice, and this put me one gaucherie up on him. By the sophomores I was asked to be class adviser, an invitation which gave me an unwarrantable pride: tenure teachers shunned such activities. As adviser, my overruling task was supervising the class's attempts to raise money which, on the students' arrival as seniors, would be used—oh, joy!—for a trip to New York City. The outing, I gathered, was to be a kind of initiation into the bewilderment of adulthood; and I had visions of leading my charges through a sunlit Sheridan Square and of pointing at the grotesque apartment house. Prefacing my remark with a sigh, I imagined saying, "There used to be a little bar there—*a long time ago.*" We crossed the Rubicon with a "slave" dance. In a first-period assembly, members of the class were sold at auction, after which they were used by the buyer to carry his books to and from class, that kind of thing. Pretty girls, football players, and the class dunderheads, in that order, brought in the most money. Between the auction and the evening dance we earned a hundred and fifty dollars, an amount my "sponsor" teacher informed me was surprisingly high for such a function. I beamed modestly.

Everyone in the village remarked the fall as the warmest in memory. Promptly on the school's dismissal bell I left the building and walked north along the town's tree-shaded main street to the river. Buying the New York newspapers at a drugstore, I went to a river-front saloon, where, sitting "over the water" at the far end of the bar, I sipped Schaeffer beer while reading the book reviews and football news, occasionally lifting my eyes from the tiring newsprint to look through the wide picture windows and watch the St. Lawrence flow by. Across the way, I saw the hues of the islands go from green to yellow to brown to almost black, the waters from deep blue to slate gray. When by the last days in November the river had gone to the latter color, such was the unseasonal warmth of the weather that one could still see a frequent boat under sail, its flying jib and spanker hard, taut, and lovely to the wind, its bow cutting effortlessly through the slate waters and throwing up a furious white spray that spat itself to pieces. At six I walked to my apartment, where, against a thousand resolutions to begin cultivating a more delicate palate, I invariably dined on broiled Delmonico steak and butter-pecan ice cream, sometimes just topping the meat with the cream. A pleasant bachelor's apartment, its living room had once been an upstairs sun porch. On three sides its walls were made up entirely of muslin-curtained windows which brought to the room a continuously felicitous light. Tastefully furnished, it had beige carpeting; weighty, comfortable leather chairs; and the inevitable television set, to whose flickering image and drone I used—as other people use music—to fall asleep. To the room I added a Degas print framed in gold leaf and depicting a middle-aged beatnik and his long-suffering, "milk-imbibing" spouse (Patience and me?); a half-dozen prints of Paris street scenes rendered by a sentimental Scandinavian; a clear-finished pine bookcase I had made from an old china cabinet; and my cynosure and source of pride: a much-knotted pine coffee table made from an ancient ironing board. One night I picked up the telephone, dialed information, and asked the girl if there were a phone listed for F. E. Exley. The girl told me there was, gave me the number, and I felt fine. At thirty-three, it was the first telephone listed in my own name. Serenely content, I believed my dream of coming to terms with home was being realized.

In late September Frank Gifford once again began to engage me. Having dropped his pugnacity by admitting that "it"—on his back on a stretcher—"had been a hard way to go out," he had the year before come out of retirement; after a year's layoff spent nursing his concussion, he had had a better year than anyone had a right to expect, a season which had encouraged him to play still another. When it came time for him to leave finally, if not to the adulatory roar of the crowd, I was sure he wanted to walk out of the stadium with his legs under him and his wits functioning. In the same way that I yearned to be able to go from this place without rage, he wanted to go out without the bitter memory of that Bednarik tackle. He was thirty-three now; at times his speed and his timing seemed unreservedly gone; and watching him I began to wonder if it weren't his destiny to go out on his back, more remembered for having been the victim of that Tartarian tackle than for anything else. Because he was so ungraciously trying to negate time's passing, I couldn't feel all that distressed for him. What did distress and send me back to him with a passion was the glibness with which fans dismissed him. As the season got into its third and fourth weeks, from down the bar I heard strangers in what came to be a continual conversation about the Giants, and whenever Gifford's name came up, I immediately heard, spoken with disarming and chilling certainty, "He's had it!" Had I known any of the men and had they not been such rugged-looking bastards, fishing guides and farmers and construction workers, I would have turned to them and snapped, "Aw, for Christ's sake, *let him be.* He wants to go out like a man!" I'm sorry now I hadn't the guts to say as much.

The following Sunday, weaving full speed down the middle of the field, Gifford reached back between the two defenders flanking him, even as he was losing his balance took a Tittle pass over his left shoulder, toppled furiously over in a forward somersault, and ended flat on his back in the end zone, the ball still clutched precariously to his stomach. It was an artful, an astounding, a humbling catch; and I can't say whether it or the studied avoidance of his name at the bar the next week pleased me more. Hunched up on the edge of one of the apartment's leather chairs, I watched him intently from that week on. The story became somewhat absurd. Week after week he made one after another catch more incredible than its predecessor; and in the final week of the season he made that one-handed catch against the Pittsburgh Steelers which gave the Giants their divisional title and sent them into the NFL championship game. I laughed with glee. Oh, how I laughed and jumped up and down, exclaiming, "Oh, good, Frank! Good! Very good indeed! I mean, swell! *Really swell!*" One had to hand it to the guy, his gift for living out his dreams. As much as for any other reason, I was jubilant because of the irony. By that time my own naïve dream of coming to terms with home had already gone sour.

What people I had contact with in the area were fringe people, and there was one couple whose situation (the man older and married, the girl young and attractive) was such an agony to themselves that it often resulted in name-calling and face-swatting. I'd like to say that when such a scene took place in my apartment one night, I jumped to the girl's defense. But I had seen the show before and knew that, by way of making it up, they might be in the bedroom fornicating within five minutes. What upset me was that the fencing and face-slapping were taking place over my ironing-board coffee table, and it suddenly occurred to me that if that table should get broken, then somehow the entire order I had given my life would be shattered with it. Jumping up, chest out, I broached the battle, took an indiscriminate though fierce punch, and ended with a whopping shiner which brought about a temporary truce. By the time that black eye got to the school board, it had been incurred in a barroom brawl in the water-front saloon I frequented, and in its imaginativeness the accompanying cause of the fight was quite praiseworthy: I had been—lord forbid!—fighting for the favors of the girls' physical education teacher. Within two weeks, for what it was worth, and that I might attend if I chose and attempt to protect myself, I was told by the nose-picking principal that certain parents were gathering at the next board meeting to discuss the feasibility of keeping me in their community. Though I didn't attend, I learned that one of the key complainants was the mother of a girl I was failing. That was the first indication I had that my students, or their parents, weren't adjusting to my academic demands as readily as I had supposed. The reason I didn't attend the meeting or attempt to protect myself was that I no longer cared.

Teaching was not my call. Accepting as a dictum of classical tragedy that the spectator must experience the sorrow of both the hero's ruin and his inevitable death, I had never felt comfortable in offering the flawless and self-righteous Brutus as the protagonist of *Julius Caesar,* because, oddly, I was invariably more moved by Cassius' death, over the years in gleaning from the text this suddenly revealed clue, this "brilliant" deduction, this "startlingly penetrating" insight, I had developed the perhaps gimcrack theory of Cassius as co-protagonist, a complement to Brutus, passionate where Brutus is passionless, fierce where equable, brilliant where dull, complex where simple, devious where direct, sensible where unfeeling. Having completed a rapid reading of the play, having attempted merely to dazzle the kids with the Bard's poetry, with ever so much scholarly caution and hemming and hawing, I was one day starting back through the text elaborating this theory when a point eluded me, I looked up and off into the class, and my eyes came to rest on a girl who was smiling and weeping simultaneously. A stunningly salubrious and tall maiden with glittering teeth, brilliant blue eyes, and a wondrous complexion, the smile was with her a perennial characteristic—though it was not in the least insinuative or licentious. If a teacher is in the least a man, he soon comes to imagine that his female trusts spend half their nocturnal hours masturbating to his summarily called-up and glamorized image; her smile had never seemed of that kind. An abstract of guileless amiability, as though her heart were large and airy and glad, hers, rather, had always seemed the smile of an innocent as yet unprepared to determine what should penetrate that heart. A poor student, her countenance exuded remarkable intelligence; both her modish dress and fine carriage intimated "background"; when she finally surmised what I demanded by way of examination answers, I had thought her grades would improve. Above the smile on this day, above the lovely Grecian nose and vigorous-colored cheeks, were two great limpid pools of astonishingly blue tears. My first impression was that it was her time of the month, my first impulse to hurry her discreetly to the girls' room. With an alarming suddenness, though, and accompanied immediately by an almost feverish remorse, the blood rushed to my face, I turned away from her, and my eyes fled back to the text: *she was frightened to death of me.*

Terribly vexed and distraught, I was furious with myself for not before having seen that that smile was not in the least a harbinger of friendliness. That distended mouth was as cold and practiced as one on a marble frieze, one of those grand and touchingly brave little smiles with which women confront the impregnable. Understanding it now for what it was, and imagining how she must be envisioning herself failing and being left behind by her classmates, surmising that she was standing apart from and seeing herself as a despicable dunce, I abruptly claimed a headache. Rising, I went out of the room and walked to the guidance office where, for the first time since I began teaching, I checked an IQ. So awful in its mathematical finality, and as I had known it would be, the girl's was dismal. To the ignored *tut-tut's* of the guidance instructor, I lighted a cigarette, took a drag that must have billowed to my toenails, and asked for the "folders" of a number of pupils about whom I had been concerned, going solemnly through them and despairingly eying all those tragic 83's and 85's and 88's. When I had finished my cigarette, and had gravely closed the last of the folders, I was left with the inescapable conclusion that my obligation to the girl and these latter was every bit as holy as it was to the others; and though it made me melancholy, I knew then that I'd never be a teacher. I had neither the patience nor the wit nor the wherewithal to give students less than I knew; worse, whatever intelligence I possessed was of that savagely unsympathetic kind which didn't allow me to understand the student's difficulty in grasping: sadly, I lacked the intelligence to simplify, and with an utterly monolithic and formidable pedantry I thought nothing of demanding that my students feed me back my own quackery. For the girl I felt something like love and wanted to explain that what I had to give had little to do with life, tell her that it would be no time at all before she'd be carrying some goon, lying between those long and luxuriant thighs, into blissful regions; indeed, tell her that if I were younger and she willing, I'd carry her off to some split-level and that there we'd produce a whole race of gargantuan, white-toothed, and shiny-cheeked truck drivers. Thinking thusly, I laughed rather sadly; for that really wasn't—was it?—quite the point. Seeing no sensible reason to save a job I neither wanted nor could properly do, I didn't attempt to protect myself at the board meeting. Determining then to pass everyone who was making, or who appeared to be making, an effort, I ended by being guilty of that which I had so vigorously condemned at Glacial Falls. Hence, too, and as it had been at Glacial Falls, time once again became merely something to be got through.

On returning to the farm for yet another summer, I discovered that Christie III was dying of some unidentifiable and painful respiratory ailment (emphysema?), having already suffered a half-dozen attacks resembling strokes. Occurring in the gray hours of the morning, just before the summer sun jumps the horizon and explodes in brilliance, these attacks are heralded by a violent coughing. During the attack itself Christie's howl is so terrifyingly human that one early morning on hearing it I was quite lifted from my bed—my naked body seemed to jump free of the sheeted mattress, the hair on my neck coarsened, and chillingly frigid goose-pimples arose all over my skin. Furiously pulling on my undershorts and jamming my feet into my sneakers, I went out of the room and three steps at a time down the stairs. On reaching the living room I found that my mother and stepfather were already standing over Christie's stricken and prostrate body. My mother no sooner began to wail (it was absolutely Biblical!) than Christie III abruptly rose to her grief. Standing uncertainly a moment, he then walked erratically, pathetically round and round the hooked rug, his hind legs falling gelatinously away beneath him. Then as suddenly he stopped, sat down, licked his chops, and stared bewilderedly at our half-naked humanity towering above him. For the life of him he couldn't fathom our concern or why we stood at that ungodly hour in that room washed in its deathly morning glow. In unison we ordered him to walk again; and when he did so, we laughed with relief, seeing that he had recovered the use of his legs. According to that *soi-disant* veterinarian who, in order that he might treat it, can't even name the disease, Christie III's death is imminent: he has a week, a month, six months.

If it comes at all, Emerson has cautioned that one's call might not come for years. If it doesn't, he remarks it as only a reflection of the universe's faith in one's abstinence, nothing to move the heart to fret. And if, moreover, one is unable to do the world's work, sell its murderous missiles or cigarettes, as a poised, mute, and motionless man, one need not propagate the world's lies. Thinking I'd like to allow what time I could to whatever gods bestow these gifts, and what with Christie III's coughing a constant clarion of death's imminence, on hot summer days, attempting to get back into some kind of shape, I have been walking ten, twelve, twenty miles a day, waddling my fat ass up and down Route 37. Jammed into its Chevrolet, "America at Play" has roared by me at eighty per and has reacted to this solitary, pudgy, and morose wayfarer in the most peculiar way. Tousle-headed, freckle-kissed little boys have pressed their faces to the cars' windows, looked cross-eyed, and stuck out their tongues at me, their tongues pressed against the windows and steaming them, the tongues appearing like minute human hearts framed and engulfed by life's mysteries. College boys have made *fungoo* signs, laughingly screamed obscenities, and hurled beer cans at me. Even pruny, respectable-looking older couples, grams and gramps, have shrieked and hooted and given me the old razzamatazz. Thinking that the age had become so clockwork that a lone walker could arouse such mischievous incredulity, I was at first bewildered and stunned; but as the insults continued, I grew aggravated and made obscene gestures in return, giving grams and gramps an up-yours finger.

One evening scanning the Watertown *Daily Times* I discovered it wasn't my walking that awakened such nutty aggressions. Our farm lies hard by Camp Drum, a military reservation to which the State Guards of Massachusetts,

New Jersey, and New York come summers to play soldier, and to which there have drifted the past weeks a number of people who call themselves "Walkers for Peace." In protest to the militaristic posture of America, they have been picketing the camp; and the *Times*'s story had to do with their being mucked about by the state police for loitering or disturbing the peace or making themselves a public nuisance. Studying the accompanying art, I realized what was wrong with my walking. A bewitched, rum-looking, and unkempt bunch, the "walkers" wore dirty tennis sneakers and outsized, loony-looking sun helmets and bore protest signs of sticks and cardboard. Directed at peanut-brittle salesmen, bricklayers, Harvard divinity students, and professional athletes who had joined the Guard to evade the draft, and who would have been hard-pressed to find the safeties on their rifles, the signs were touchingly and quixotically misdirected: "THOU SHALL NOT KILL." The getups looked not unlike the singular, sweaty outfit in which I waddle and trot up and down the highway, even to my walking stick, which might easily be taken for a sign's handle. *"Ah,"* I thought, *"so that's it!"* The fierce hoots and jeers were emanating from local cars, and their occupants were taking me for a "Walker for Peace." Attempting to laugh, I found that the spittle tasted of blood in my mouth. What if I were a "Walker for Peace"? Did that give these goons a right to curse and hurl things at me? Of what were they so afraid? Quickly working myself into a rage thinking of it, I contemplated making my own sign and pilgrimage to the camp. But presently reason set in, and I saw that in a pique of passion I was only once more allowing myself to be drawn into the world's work, knowing that settling down on the piles-inducing dampness of Piccadilly with

Bertrand Russell was not my call. Hence I kept walking, the obscenities kept coming, and during the past days I have found that in sleep I have become the victim of a recurring nightmare. And unlike Goodman Brown, who didn't know whether his darksome diorama was real or spectral, though I know mine is but a sanguinary dream, still I can't repress the queasiness it instills in me.

A half-dozen college boys in a white topless convertible go by me, hurling their beer cans and anathemas. Piddling along with my eyes cast downward on the cindered shoulder, an almost rapturous fury and humiliation scorching the nape of my neck, I ignore them. Having passed me "face on," they are now behind me; as there is an abrupt absence of thunder, of momentum in the air, I become suddenly and heart-poundingly aware that, to repair a flat tire or due to some mechanical failure, they have pulled from the highway. Turning, I see them standing outside the car. Somberly, disbelievingly, they stare at the vehicle's motionlessness, now and again looking diffidently in my direction, wondering what I am to do. With all my strength I try to do the "adult" thing and go about my business; but it is always precisely at this moment that a quick and heavy blackness scuttles the dream (as fleeting as the shuttering of a lens this blackness is); and when again the vision comes, instead of walking on I find that I am running fatefully in their direction. So furiously do I come that on reaching them I see by the shyness of their smiles, and by their all but imperceptible gestures of retreat, they are afraid. Gibbering erratically, I am able to catch only isolated fragments of my own hectic spiel. Easy to understand is "Am I an American?" demanded spittingly of them, as the justifiably outraged and egg-bespattered Henry Wallace once demanded of the American body politic. Considerably more enigmatic, and shouted at them over and over again, is the declarative "John Keats was dead at twenty-six!" Because even during my acutest paranoia, my delusions never permitted me to draw artistic analogies between Keats and myself, I put aside that possible interpretation, and by discarding something else, and yet weighing another possibility, I finally settled on a meaning that made sense to me. John Jay Chapman once said of William James that he seemed always to be stepping out of a sadness to meet one; as, a little startled, most of us seem always to be stepping out of our predominant hues, whether of gaiety or equanimity or frolicsomeness or gravity, to meet another; and the nightmarish thing about all these young men is that they seem devoid of emotional heritage. Like cinema starlets who have only recently been manufactured, they are precisely like one another: all are six feet, two; all have fine, golden complexions; all have that admired short hair molded formally to their pates; and all are dressed in button-down shirts topped by V-necked cashmere sweaters, below which they sport iridescent Bermudas displaying youthful, well-made legs. Looking at them, I see they are the generation to whom President Johnson has promised his Great Society; the generation which will never know the debilitating shame of poverty, the anguish of defeat, the fateful irony of the unexpected disease; the generation which will visit the barren moon and find it, because they have been conditioned to find it, more lovely than that river which, though so close to it, they cannot even see; the generation which will all retire to the great American Southwest, where under dry, brilliant, and perpetual suns they will all live to be a hundred and fifty, watching reruns of Ed Sullivan on a colored screen twenty feet high. What I am now certain I am beseeching them to consider is that of itself longevity is utterly without redeeming qualities, that one has to live the contributive, the passionate, life and that this can as well be done in twenty-six (hence Keats) as in a hundred and twenty-six years, done in no longer than the time it takes a man to determine whether the answer is *yea* or *nay*. Furiously taking one of them by the elbows, I make my gravest miscalculation, demanding to know of him whether he isn't ashamed. As unnerved and abashed as any Huxleyan character confronted with historical, forgotten emotions, I can see that the idea of remorse has no place in his dialectic. Arousing in him bewilderment and fear of things unknown, he pushes me violently from him. When he does so, I strike him in the face. Because it is only a dream, and as such no succedaneum for life, I fight very well; considering that they have all jumped in now and I am being beaten bloody and senseless by a phalanx of cashmere clubs, I hold my legs much longer than I should, hold them until I am suddenly engulfed by this new, this incomprehensible America. The dream is weird and unsettling and infinitely sad, and not in the least sad because I am being beaten. It is grievous because for the past few days I have tried with such excruciating diligence to alter the course of it; and with the dying Christie III lying in my arms have lain entire afternoons imagining how tonight, this very night, I will find the strength to turn and walk on about my business. But then evening comes, and sleep, and then the dream, and then that shuttering of heavy blackness. And when again the vision comes, I find that, ready to do battle, I am running: obsessively, *running*.

A Note on the Type

The principal text of this Modern Library edition
was set in a digitized version of Janson,
a typeface that dates from about 1690 and was cut by Nicholas Kis,
a Hungarian working in Amsterdam. The original matrices have
survived and are held by the Stempel foundry in Germany.
Hermann Zapf redesigned some of the weights and sizes for Stempel,
basing his revisions on the original design.